Shadowplay

'Have you been indulging yourself in wanton desires again?' asked Nicholas.

Christabel nodded.

'Many times?' her husband asked.

Christabel felt an overwhelming urge to tell Nicholas about her strange time with the aristocratic and beautiful Daniel Ranelagh, but she kept quiet.

'Many times?' her husband repeated, his fingers closing around her left buttock.

'Twice,' she croaked, trying to wriggle away from his rude caresses. 'Once in bed, last night, and once while I was out walking this morning.'

Christabel didn't know whether to sob with relief or shame. She knew her husband would know the full extent of her weakness and use that knowledge. She also knew how he might use *her*, when the initial sexual punishment was over.

'Are you ready, Christabel?' he asked. The words were menacing, but the tone was loving.

Shadowplay
Portia Da Costa

BLACK LACE

Black Lace books contain sexual fantasies.
In real life, always practise safe sex.

First published in 1999 by
Black Lace
Thames Wharf Studios
Rainville Road
London W6 9HA

This edition published 2002

Copyright © Portia Da Costa 1999

The right of Portia Da Costa to be identified as the Author of
the Work has been asserted in accordance with the Copyright, Designs
and Patents Act 1988.

Printed and bound by Mackays of Chatham PLC

ISBN 0 352 33313 8

Contents

Dedicated to Pam and Dot and Paula,
good friends in a time of trial.

Chapter One
Chiaroscuro

She had known she was going to sleep with him the moment she saw him. It was inevitable. But what she hadn't known was quite how soon it would happen.

He was just another handsome face in a hotel cocktail bar. The sort of place she wasn't supposed to have been in. Not any more. She had promised Nicholas she wouldn't do it again, after the last time, and she'd been making a moderately good fist of keeping her word, until boredom had begun to breed defiance.

Since when had either of them kept promises, anyway? she'd thought. Their recent record was patchy at best and, for her part, at least, the guilt itself was an irresistible turn-on. It always had been. Her body was throbbing as she bore down on her prey.

'This is a fabulous place you've got here,' the young man said. His name was Brad, and he'd agreed without hesitation to pose for her, easily accepting the tired old line about him being photogenic – either at face value or for its underlying meaning. Which was that she'd made up her mind to fuck him.

'Yes, it is, isn't it?' Christabel Sutherland replied, making a minute adjustment to her viewfinder, and hiding her smile behind unnecessary technical fiddling.

1

She couldn't even remember if she'd put film in the camera. 'My husband found it for me . . . He likes me to keep busy. Hobbies and things, you know. When I said I was interested in photography, he bought me my own studio.'

Brad's young eyes widened, and he flicked back his thick shiny hair. A nervous gesture. 'I . . . I didn't realise you were married. You don't wear a ring.' He seemed about to get up from the platform she'd arranged him on. He was sweating too, she noticed, dark circles forming in the armpits of his silk shirt. Christabel sniffed the air. Ah, the pheromones of desire, they were delicious!

'Don't worry,' she said, straightening up and looking at him, her eyes level. 'As I said, he likes me to keep busy.' Make of that what you will, young man, she thought. It doesn't matter that it isn't quite the truth.

Brad relaxed, the situation obviously to his liking. Exactly what he'd hoped for, probably. A bored, beautiful thirty-something on the lookout for a bit of extra-curricular activity. A bored, beautiful, *rich* thirty-something, which was bound to make the dish on offer all the sweeter.

'Open your legs a little wider.' Christabel abandoned the camera and moved closer, maintaining a façade of the same artistic finickiness that photographers had exhibited with her, in her own modelling days. Truth be known, she really would have liked to have photographed him, but she had other, more pressing requirements at that moment. Maybe some other time? she thought, already losing interest.

'I want to see tension in the cloth, just there . . .' She nodded to his groin, which was already displayed lewdly by the pose. The excitement beneath the designer denim was quite distinct. 'Stretch your tendons. Push up. That's it!' His heels were together, his hips were lifting. She slid her hand beneath his thigh, urging him to rise and make the position even more gruelling. She'd held far more difficult poses herself, in her day, and thought nothing of it.

Brad's erection was prodigious now, fighting valiantly against the washed-out blue cloth. She wondered if he was wearing briefs of any kind, then decided not. There was already a faint hint of moisture close to his fly buttons – a helplessly seeping tribute to her beauty.

'This is a bit difficult to hold ... God, my legs are killing me,' he gasped. 'And my arms, too ... Are you going to take a shot soon, or what?'

'All in good time,' murmured Christabel, encouraging him to elevate his hips still further. She could feel him shaking, and not just with the strain. Kneeling down now, she pressed a single finger of her free hand to the spreading stain that marred his groin.

Brad hissed between his teeth and began to drop out of the pose.

'No! Hold the position!' commanded Christabel, feeling her own sex dampen at the shock in her victim's eyes. She swirled her finger a few times around the tip of his prick, beneath the denim, then abandoned his sex in favour of her own. Reaching down and through the slit in her suede skirt, she waggled the same finger that had touched Brad in through the tangle of sopping lace that was her knickers. Her quim was a humid, swollen furnace, and her clitoris was rearing proud of the protection of her labia, demanding attention.

'Oh, God,' she gasped, pressing heavily with the tip of her exploring finger. 'Oh, God,' she groaned, jerking her hips forward in a mockery of her watcher's predicament. She wanted to come, come now and come violently, but she also wanted to save it for a while. Her pelvis waved as she fought the conflicting urges, the greediness. Her fingertip slipped, there was so much juice flowing around it. With a soft, rough cry, she flipped up her skirt, wrenched aside her panties, and crushed her dripping crotch down on to Brad's thigh.

'Jesus!' he yelped as they collapsed in a heap. Christabel wondered dimly if she might have done him some kind of injury, but she didn't really care. All she wanted was the sensation of rough denim abrading her sensitive membranes, and the pressure of hard musculature squashed against her quim. This was the next best thing to having herself filled to bursting with his flesh.

'Oh, shit, I think I'm going to come,' he said, almost ruining her precious dark moment.

'Don't!' Christabel was grateful, in a way, for being balked before she too could climax. Letting her weight fall on him, she grabbed his hair and, without thinking, slapped his face.

The impact of skin on skin cracked loudly and Christabel's mind suddenly focused like a lens. It was almost as if she'd slapped herself, not him. Between her legs, her sense of readiness flared up, too, and she filed the response away for further analysis.

For a few seconds, Brad's eyes were wide with outrage and thwarted lust – then they warmed again. And Christabel warmed to him, too. He knew. He understood the same cause and effect that she'd just experienced. His long lashes flickered down and he muttered something incoherent – but she could see his square jaw flex and tighten. He was trying to control himself – and play the game by a set of rules she'd barely voiced.

Looping her fingers tighter in his hair, knowing it would hurt, she lowered her mouth towards his and began to kiss him. She synchronised the teasing, nibbling assault with delicate, very tentative movements of her pelvis. Slight jerks. An infinitesimal circling. Nothing large-scale or too arousing. She wanted to remain simmering on the plateau, her craving attenuated. Her thought processes were muddied by desire yet, through the puzzlement, new illuminations came. Denial and pain were brother and sister, working in concert, upping the ante . . . Why only now, after all this time, and after all the men she'd been with, was she

4

understanding this? She'd always preferred a swifter gratification.

Brad remained taut beneath her, as if strung out on the pain in his scalp and his prohibited excitement. Christabel could no longer see his groin, or directly feel his erection, but she knew that he'd be getting bigger and harder. She pictured his penis, like a photograph in her mind.

Strong, clean and solid, she saw it rising from between the flies of his jeans. She didn't want him naked; she wanted him exposed. She wanted the portions of his body that he might uncover every day – at the gym or on the beach – closely, almost prudishly covered, and his penis, the taboo totem, untrammelled and free. Bare, to do with exactly as she pleased.

Holding still, she felt the elastic of her panties slide into the niche between her labia and she had a notion that she might not fuck this gorgeous giant after all. It might be nice to just leave him engorged and aching, while she brought herself off. It had happened before, and more often recently. She would find that when she had unwrapped her sexual sweetie, it offered up no true spice to her starving erotic senses. Nothing more, really, than a basic, sustaining, bread-and-butter fucking; and certainly no more stirring than the good sex she enjoyed with her husband Nicholas. The real piquancy in such situations had been to masturbate madly, actually thinking of her betrayed spouse as she did so. She was thinking of him now, she realised, despite the attractions of young, fit Brad.

'I need to see your prick,' she said without preamble, letting loose the boy's hair and cuffing the side of his face to knock him away from her. Feeling the elastic that divided her crotch rock and saw, she rose a little way, then squatted over him, her haunches still spread. When he lifted his hands, to attend to his buttons, she dashed those away, too.

'I'll do it,' she said, reaching for him.

The desired flesh sprang up the instant it was released. He was gratifyingly thick, and his glans was red and glossy.

Oh, yes . . .

Shall I ride him? thought Christabel, still loving the intruding elastic's friction. She waggled her hips and experienced a tiny, fleeting spasm. As her pubis quickened she heard a faint, fugitive sound. Probably nothing, really, but a distraction nevertheless.

'Keep still,' she told Brad as she rose fully to her feet and let her twisted knickers tickle her clitoris.

There *was* a sound. It hadn't been her imagination. The noise could have been coming up from the street outside, but a premonition seemed to reach inside Christabel and clasp her innards like a fist. Acknowledging it, she knew exactly what she should do to save herself . . .

But she didn't do it. Feeling a surge of excitement even more powerful than the one of a few moments ago, she stayed right where she was, staring down at Brad. Nothing would sway her from her purpose now, not even the thing she most feared. Which was, she realised, what she also most longed for.

'Hands by your sides, Brad . . .' she murmured. 'I need to pose you, just exactly so.' With deft, quick actions, she rolled up his shirt and pulled down his jeans.

Belly, prick, upper thighs: all bared. The rest concealed. Yet the composition was incomplete; she needed to go further. Taking her black silk wrap from where she had thrown it on arrival, she covered up the young and handsome face.

Perfection. A rampant, anonymous penis. A sexual object without a needy personality, a grasping ego, or even a voice. Just a thing, really, but a pretty thing. She could grab it and play with it; or she could reject it and take her own pleasure, enhanced by her deviant dreams.

In sudden shock, she imagined – wished! – that she

could tie up the blinded Brad, completely immobilise him, then stop up his ears and his mouth too. But the sounds she'd been hearing for the last few moments were much closer now. There was no time for protracted ceremonial; she had to take her chances, and forget the weirdness of her fantasies.

'Keep still,' she commanded, her voice low as she flipped up her skirt, ripped impatiently at the crotch of her knickers and exposed her genitals like a yin to his yang.

Crouching over him, she felt the spirit of a predator surge through her, as stimulating – no, perhaps *more* stimulating than the sight of a naked rosy prick. She was a black widow ready to strike, the female of some killer species, engorged and fully prepared to annihilate her prey in the service of her own pleasure. With a throaty gasp, she slithered downward and engulfed him.

'Oh, God!'

'Do not speak!' she hissed, not spider now, but snake. Undulating within, she climaxed immediately, strongly and without subtlety. Wanting more, she bounced up and down upon him, crushing him. She didn't know if he was even enjoying himself, and she cared even less.

As the sensations ebbed, she gingered them up by imagining her husband. He was staring at her opened legs and her wayward mind suddenly put a thin black switch in his hand. Her vulva convulsed as he seemed to raise it and murmur, 'My dear . . .'

'Nicholas . . . Oh, Nicholas,' she grunted in time to her own inner throbbing, only peripherally aware that the man beneath her was now climaxing too. 'Nicholas! You bastard!' she cried, grinding, grinding, grinding . . .

'My dear, I'm touched,' murmured a familiar voice just behind her.

Oh, God!

Part of her had longed to hear that voice, but part of

7

her feared it above all others. She felt faint, and filled with a sinking, melting weakness.

'Uh? What?' queried the struggling Brad beneath her, and Christabel felt only irritation that he had intruded into her special, terrifying moment. She was about to rise and shake him out of her body, to turn and confront, when strong hands grabbed her underneath her armpits.

'Get her off him,' instructed her husband coolly, and Christabel didn't need to be able to see to know who was holding her. She simply went limp and let herself be prised, crotch still on view, off the squirming male beneath her. On her feet, she watched as Brad ripped away the shawl, his eyes widening in horror. All fumbles, he attempted to shove his shrunken penis back into the safety of his jeans, but his pathetic efforts only diminished him further. Christabel felt pleasure in the fact that her own sex was still uncovered. The hands that had clasped her arms now held up her skirt, and her shredded panties were a frame for her glistening pubis.

Transfixed by her own plight, Christabel turned and looked into the impassive grey eyes of her husband, Nicholas, searching for – but, as ever, not finding – any trace of his emotions. As she observed him, he took out his wallet, extracted a thick sheaf of notes and held them out towards the thunderstruck Brad. A lesser man would have thrown the cash, but Nicholas's manners were faultless. Was he even angry, she wondered, beneath his stillness?

'Please leave,' her husband said softly, and Brad did so, snatching together his belongings – and the money – and sprinting from the room.

Which left Christabel with Nicholas. And with Jamie, his personal assistant, who was still calmly holding up her skirt. The younger man was just an inch or two behind her, obedient and strong and smelling so appetising that Christabel's breasts tightened and her freshly pleasured vulva reawakened.

How can I be like this? she thought. Only a few moments ago, she had been the one wielding dominion and now she had control neither over her mind, nor her body. She was in a dire situation. A woman taken in adultery, betraying her righteous husband, yet still she desired another. One she had always considered off limits.

But why? Was Jamie Nicholas's in every way? Were they hot for each other? It would account for a great deal, Christabel realised, struck by possibilities in spite of everything.

Nicholas had always kept a distance between himself and her. A detachment perceptible even when they were having sex together, and the very reason, she supposed, why she sought out other men. Why she had needed validation. The word 'had' stuck in her mind – she had no true idea what she wanted now. At this moment.

'So you didn't keep your promise,' observed her husband pleasantly, walking away and dropping into the only good chair her sparse studio boasted. She knew that both men had noted her momentary unsteadiness, but they seemed unmoved by it. Without being told, Jamie turned her to face him, taking her hand and positioning it to replace his in the task of holding her skirt aloft. As he stood to one side, he nodded once in acknowledgement of her, but nothing more, his handsome features remaining graven and inscrutable. In the teeth of her perilous situation, Christabel wanted to laugh. Jamie had clearly been taking lessons from her husband.

'Well?' prompted Nicholas, the very lightness of his tone making her sex flutter. She felt a little of her lubrication overflow her, and imagined it trickling down her thigh in plain sight. He thinks of me as a whore, Christabel reflected, the welling of her shame making her all the more excited. Knowing it was insane, she lifted her chin boldly.

'He was nothing. A nobody. I didn't class him as a real fuck,' she said, holding her back straight and tilting her pelvis slightly – almost displaying her own wetness. 'So, strictly speaking, I wasn't really being unfaithful.' She sensed rather than saw Jamie suppress a smirk.

'A promise is a promise.' Her husband reached into the inner pocket of his jacket and took out a platinum cigar case and lighter. Flicking open the case, he plucked out a slim cheroot, and put it to his lips, lighting up efficiently. He wasn't a regular smoker, but indulged in the occasional mild act of foolhardiness after sex.

'But I was thinking of you,' she pointed out, trying not to grimace. Her sex was swelling now, and the congestion between her legs made it difficult to concentrate. The urge to squat and jiggle her crotch was becoming progressively less and less resistible, and matters were worsened by a growing need to pee.

'Ah, but in what context?' her husband probed, taking a long, elegant drag on the cheroot. Christabel took the opportunity to shift her thighs as he was momentarily distracted.

'Please don't move, my dear,' he continued, proving that his attention had not wavered. 'Jamie, why don't you remove the remnants of my wife's knickers? Then we can see her more clearly . . . Take off her skirt too. I think I'd prefer her to be naked below the waist.'

Is this happening? Or am I dreaming? I'm being stripped and ordered about in presence of my husband's employee, his minion. This can't be real or I wouldn't be accepting it.

As Jamie moved to obey, Christabel thought of all the men she'd had, and the times she'd kissed and sucked them, and been kissed and sucked. None of it had been like this. Almost everything that had happened to her until now suddenly seemed boring. It had all been so

10

straightforward, she wondered why she'd ever bothered.

Discharging her husband's instructions, Jamie was the perfect servant, his actions smooth and effortless. But, even so, Christabel was forced to bite her lips. Jamie didn't touch her flesh even once as he removed her skirt, but his very scrupulousness was somehow a caress. And she could have sworn she felt his breath upon her clitoris as he bent down to slide off her panties.

'Shoes now, Jamie,' continued Nicholas, still relaxed, smoking slowly, his eyes upon her.

Her crotch bloated and liquid, her breasts aching, Christabel felt her head begin to swim and grow quite light. It was as if she were levitating out of her own body and crossing the room to join Nicholas in his observations. Across from her stood a beautiful woman with red-gold, shoulder-length hair, and a slender yet full-breasted figure. She was not old, but no longer a girl, and she was naked but for a thin, tan-coloured silk top and a heavy gold necklace around her throat. The eye of a photographer acknowledged a stunning erotic image.

It was extremely unpleasant being manoeuvred into the shoes, however. They weren't hers; she'd never even seen them before and couldn't understand where they'd come from. High, arched and shiny, the black stilettos made her feel vulnerable and precarious, and she had to lean heavily on Jamie as he fitted them on her feet. To have to concentrate on standing straight, and on containing her water at the same time, was becoming more and more a trial.

Which Nicholas knew, of course, and so did the cursed Jamie.

'If you were thinking of me, why could you not wait for it to *be* me?' Her husband returned to his theme as he stubbed out his cheroot in an abandoned wineglass.

Because you're not always around, she wanted to say.

11

Because I get excited when you're not with me as well as when you are – and something hungry in me wants to 'have' instead of 'wait'. It's the same ravenous thing that wants me to reach down and rub my clitoris right now.

'Oh! Oh, no!' she groaned, feeling the little organ jerk as if it were a living creature responding to its own name. Her hips quivered with the unremitting effort of keeping her still.

'I don't understand . . .' Nicholas's voice was still calm and even, yet it seemed to strum across the membranes of her sex. Each word had pressure. 'You say "no" . . . You can't wait . . . Yet you offer no explanation as to why. I want to understand you, Christabel. You must tell me why you find it so difficult to keep your beautiful legs closed . . . Why you must constantly seek out hard, new flesh to fill you.' Thud, thud, thud. Each syllable torturing her. She had to gyrate. She couldn't help herself. It brought no comfort, only a slight tightening of Nicholas's long, beautiful mouth. 'You want sex now, don't you, my dear?' he observed silkily, looking away from her for a moment, towards the mess in the wineglass. Was he, too, so turned on that he craved another smoke?

Christabel could not speak. She dare not. She daren't even breathe. Her vulva felt as if it were swollen to bursting with her fluids and, though she wanted to be stoic, to resist him because he had never once truly given himself to her in their entire two years of marriage, she would have sold her soul for the opportunity to touch herself. Her fingers trembled where they hung limply at her sides.

'Christabel?'

He wants me to say 'yes'. He wants me to grovel, because I've betrayed him.

Yet somehow she couldn't answer. Wouldn't answer. Gnawing her lips again, she was forced to clench her fists as hot pulsations gripped the pit of her belly. Every last droplet of wine or water that she had drunk during the evening felt as if it were gathered in a ponderous mass against the root of her clitoris. She was about to come, purely from the obscene discomfort of needing to urinate. Already a few drops of her liquid were beginning to ooze from her.

'I don't have time for this,' said her husband, rising abruptly and striding across the studio, towards the exit, without looking back.

'You'd better bring her off, Jamie,' he called out as he disappeared into the shadows.

Chapter Two
Colours

'*B*astard! High-handed bastard!' cursed Christabel, slamming a suitcase down on the bed.

Her nerves were snapping. She had heard nothing from Nicholas since the other night, when he'd left her to Jamie's tender mercies. Not a word, not a phone call, no indication whatsoever of his whereabouts. And now this!

What right did he have to expect her to fester away in the wilds of the countryside? Distanced from even the most rudimentary form of culture or social life?

What right indeed, except that of a man she'd repeatedly betrayed?

All of a sudden, Christabel's anger dissolved. Was it really such an outrage that Nicholas wanted to remove her from metropolitan temptation? If the shoe had been on the other foot, she might have wanted to do the same. Might have wanted to shame him for the way he'd subjugated her.

Back in the studio, she had hardly needed Jamie's hand to achieve her orgasm. Nicholas's pure, pristine voice had tipped her over. Her sex had convulsed at Jamie's first touch, launching into a long sequence of hard, almost painful spasms. She'd wet herself help-

14

lessly and, but for Jamie, she might have fallen. As it was, she'd slid to the floor – her descent made gentle by his sure, unobtrusive support – then lain for what seemed like an age, her body a slippery throbbing mess.

She couldn't put the scene behind her. It had been so mortifying, and so shaming, yet all through it she had felt more alive, and more real, than she ever had before in her life. Somehow, for the duration of her ordeal, she had possessed a whole new set of senses, and the resulting input had been like seeing a rainbow after a lifetime of monochrome. A sparse palette that she'd returned to for the last few days. Perhaps now though, after Nicholas's call, things might change.

In the country, there might be undiscovered colours . . .

Nicholas had rung her from his headquarters in the City. 'We need to get away from London for a while. I've arranged to lease a house and we can take possession of it today. Pack some clothes, enough for a longish stay. Jamie's organising the car.'

She had protested, of course, even though both then, and now, something weak in her had thrilled at being ordered about. Anything was better, it seemed, than being kept at a distance.

'You'll be out of harm's way for a while, my dear,' he had countered, in face of her objections. 'You can pack your cameras. I'm sure the scenery will inspire you to greatness. There might even be a nature book in it.'

With no option but to comply, she had begun selecting clothes and toiletries for this journey to God alone knew where. A veteran of two wealthy husbands, and the concomitant smooth-running households, Christabel left the details of mundane domesticity to her housekeeper. And to Jamie. Let him cancel the milk and the flowers and all her appointments. He was good at cleaning up after her, she'd recently discovered, discreetly arranging for a domestic agency to come in and bring order to her studio, with no questions asked. The

15

least he could do now was call there and collect her cameras and other equipment. She rang him and gave him instructions in a flat neutral voice, trying not to picture herself as the sad, grunting, wet-thighed mess she must have appeared to him, the last time he'd seen her.

A thought occurred to her as she was stuffing handfuls of silk and lace panties into one of her cases. If Jamie was organising cars and suchlike, would he also be going to the country with them? It sometimes seemed that Nicholas could barely function without him. And if they were lovers, as Christabel half suspected . . .

She frowned, momentarily distracted by stockings. Would she need them in the back of beyond? Nicholas's tone had suggested a simple, rural retreat, not the county set social scene. Would it be boring? What the hell had she let herself in for?

You need this, though, she told herself, already feeling the fatal twinges of concupiscence. All she'd done was handle a few pairs of knickers, and already she was imagining herself taking them off for some man. Well, for Nicholas . . . He was the one she really wanted, she supposed. It was only the constant itch in her loins that drove her to seek substitutes.

Perhaps I should masturbate more? she considered, moving to her overstocked wardrobe. Self-pleasure was a lot more reliable than some of the men she had found herself in bed with lately and, what was more, Nicholas approved of it. He'd even suggested it to her as an outlet, on one of the few occasions they'd actually discussed the foibles of her libido. The next day, she'd found a beautifully gift-wrapped vibrator waiting on her pillow when she'd come to her bedroom in the afternoon to change. She'd not got as far as using it yet, but she often wondered how Nicholas had obtained such an item at short notice. Perhaps he'd already had it? Her husband had so many hidden depths, one could have lost the Titanic down there . . . But it was more likely that he'd sent Jamie out to purchase it. She couldn't imagine Nicholas shopping in the sex boutiques of Soho.

On impulse, she opened her bedside drawer and took out the unmarked white box that contained the vibrator, around which she had retied its luxurious pink satin ribbon. I might need you, my little electronic friend, she thought, hefting the box and noticing that a couple of packages of batteries had been thoughtfully slipped into the drawer, too. When had Nicholas secreted them there? They hadn't been in the drawer the other day, when she'd been looking for a lost earring.

You have the means in your hands to satisfy yourself untiringly, she thought, box in one hand and batteries in the other. Letting her gaze flash between them, she groaned. Deep in her belly, she felt her wayward flesh grow heavier.

Either Nicholas or Jamie would be here at any moment. There was no time. What was more, it would be an encouragement of appetites she ought to be learning how to temper. Flinging the vibrator and the batteries on to the bed, she pressed the heel of her hand to her mons veneris, but the hungry beast that lived behind it wouldn't be pacified. She parted her thighs and, standing awkwardly, thought of Nicholas.

His changeable grey eyes held both condemnation and challenge. Satisfaction wouldn't take long, with his battery-driven gift, but, even if he did catch her, surely he'd prefer her to be using it, rather than one of the many Brads in the world?

Why didn't I put a skirt on today? she thought, wriggling on the bed, and trying to prise off her leggings and her panties. Lust having addled her brain, it seemed, she was trying to remove them whilst still wearing her high-heeled ankle boots; but, if she began again, the whole process would take far too long. Instead, she pushed the entire thickness of panties and leggings down as far as her knees, where their elasticity combined and gripped her legs together.

This is stupid, thought Christabel, struggling with the box, and then the vibrator. The device was thick – alarmingly so – and she was going to have to open her labia with her fingers in order to wedge it between them. She rocked on the bed, flexing her knees against the stretchiness of her leggings. The whole situation was ludicrous, yet its very vulgarity made her more determined than ever. She spun the vibrator's bevelled control wheel and the chunky tube oscillated loudly. Between her legs, her clitoris erected, eager for thrills.

Why had Nicholas chosen such a strangely lifelike sex toy? she wondered. Made of some kind of dense, rubberised plastic, the device was well made, weighty and substantial: an exaggerated parody of a real penis. Her clitoris pulsed again, and she felt as intrigued as she was hot and wet and ready.

Spinning the dial back to zero, she shuffled her bottom along the bed and tried as best she could to make space between her squashed-together thighs. With a finger and thumb, she worked through her pubic hair, then parted her labia. Her heart racing, she pushed the bulbous head of the vibrator into the niche that she'd made, then applied its plastic surface to her clitoris.

Oh! Even the simple contact of the cool alien substance had an impact on her. She bucked up against the intruder, pressing down strongly as she did so. It occurred to her that she might bruise herself somehow, but then dismissed the fact. Men were often much rougher in their dealings and usually she found that quite delightful. Making a throaty sound, she spun the bevel again.

'Oh, God!'

The vibrations were far more powerful than she'd expected, and her entangled thighs began to jerk against her leggings. Part of her wanted to take away the relentless stimulation, knowing it would bring her to climax in seconds; another part of her was already a hopeless addict. The deep, grabbing throbs forced a grotesque profanity from her lips but, even so, she rode the crest of them, white-knuckled. From an echoing distance, she heard her boot-heel rip the counterpane.

After her fourth climax, she gasped, 'Enough already!' She didn't care now if Nicholas or Jamie found her, but what was worrying was the prospect of having a seizure! Her clothes were soaked with sweat, as was the counterpane with her trickling sexual juices. 'Little friend, I've underestimated you,' she murmured to the vibrator as she withdrew it from the swamp of her sated sex.

The bed was a war zone when she sat up, and the white raw-linen coverlet had been ripped in several places by the metal heel-tips of her boots. There was no time to replace it, or even remake the bed to hide the damage, so she resigned herself to yet more pinched-mouthed looks from the cleaning woman.

But never mind the cleaner; what would Nicholas think? Surely he'd see the mess when he came to collect his clothes? Would he remark on it? She couldn't imagine a man as erotically perceptive as her husband not making the obvious deduction. The musky smell alone was an instant giveaway.

Still weak-kneed, Christabel struggled ungracefully back into her clothing; then, whisking up the odoriferous vibrator from the bed, she took it through to the bathroom, to rinse herself from its heated surface.

When that task was done, the sight of fluffy towels and her marble bidet was irresistible. She had to take time out and cleanse her body, whatever the consequences.

Once she was clean again, Christabel applied perfume to her pulse points and to her inner thighs, then gathered a few more cosmetics and the newly cleaned vibrator, and returned naked to her bedroom to finish her packing.

Nicholas was waiting for her.

'Not ready yet, I see,' he said, turning from an open bag to face her. At some time during her ablutions, he had come noiselessly into the bedroom and begun his own preparations. He had on a pair of chinos – not his usual style, yet they looked good on him – but he hadn't yet put on a shirt or buckled his belt. The sight of his still-bare feet, as he walked to his cupboard and took out some underwear, set a renegade desire for him clamouring in Christabel's belly.

'I was just having a wash,' she said, feeling off-balance. When Nicholas's glance flicked to the vibrator, still in her hand, she started blushing.

'Amongst other things . . .' His voice was even, the words not a question.

'I found it while I was packing . . . I've never tried it. I . . . I thought I would.' Good God, I'm stammering like a teenager, she thought, feeling scarlet embarrassment coursing into her throat, her chest, her breasts. Between her legs, all her work with soap was instantly undone.

'How was it?' He sounded more interested now, Christabel thought, even though he continued to pack his bag without debate or hesitation.

'I would have thought you'd have Jamie do that for you?' she said, feeling the need to distract him. Crossing to her own bag, she pushed the vibrator in amongst her clothing.

'The vibrator,' Nicholas persisted, smiling now, 'how was it for you?' The smile widened, making his usually serious face look much younger. He was almost fifty, eighteen years older than Christabel; but, still eyeing her closely, he looked like an inquisitive, sexy boy. The impression was further enforced by his freshly show-ered hair. Being tousled and wet hid the random strands of grey.

I want you, thought Christabel, finding her husband infinitely seductive. She suddenly couldn't imagine why she'd ever pursued other men. Nicholas was fabulous;

any normal woman would have been more than satisfied with him. When he quirked his eyebrows at her, the little gesture made her sex ache. She wanted to fall down on her knees before him, get his cock out of his chinos and suck him. He had a large penis, thick, but elegant; and it fitted her beautifully. She had never desired him more than at this moment.

'Did you enjoy my gift?' he said, with a subtle emphasis that she couldn't ignore. He was not a short-tempered man – in fact, she had never once seen him angry – but there were certain times when she knew it was foolhardy to attempt to evade him.

'Yes. Yes, I did.' Her clitoris throbbed in a physical memory.

'Did you insert it?' He was facing her now, his arms lightly crossed in front of him, his packing abandoned.

'No . . . I just touched myself with it.'

'In what way?' His head was slightly tipped on one side, and humour – and what she hoped was arousal – had darkened his eyes.

'I turned it on and held it against my clitoris until I had an orgasm.' She hoped that frankness would pique his interest. He hadn't slept with her since the incident at her studio, and was offering no explanation or account of himself now. Had he stayed at his club, she wondered, or had he found solace and bed elsewhere? Perhaps with Jamie?

'Just one?' He was really smiling; a proper grin.

'I . . . No. I had several.'

'And yet you still didn't put the vibrator inside you . . . I find that surprising, knowing you.' He laughed softly. 'Didn't your cunt feel lonely without the company?'

Christabel wanted to screech at him, but she knew she had no real defence. What he had said, in a certain sense, was perfectly true.

'Do you think it's too big for you, perhaps?' he went on, almost conversationally. 'I would've thought you'd enjoy being stretched ... I should imagine your young friend of the other night stretched you. He looked well built. Well hung. The way you like them.'

Christabel shifted her feet on the carpet. Her vagina felt needy again – she could have done with a big man inside her right at that moment. A huge, humungous man.

'Brad was no bigger than you are,' she said, appalled at herself. 'Not as big, to be honest.'

Nicholas's eyes twinkled. 'So you *did* think of me while you were fucking him?'

'Of course!'

'Of course.' Nicholas's face grew more languid even as she watched him. Had she got through to him? she wondered. Could he be induced to take her quickly, here on the bed, before they left for the country? She was naked, after all, and wet, and completely ready for him.

As if he'd heard her silent entreaties, Nicholas glanced towards the rumpled bedcover. 'Lie down, my dear, will you?' he said, as calmly as he would ask for the marmalade at breakfast time.

Her heart in her throat, Christabel climbed on to the bed as alluringly as she could. Would he be annoyed if she let her thighs slip ever so slightly apart? Clasped her hands behind her head, so her bare breasts rose? She made to move into position, but he spoke again, his voice neutral and carefully controlled.

'Not like that, please. Lie sideways on. Bottom on the edge of the bed.'

Becoming more and more agitated, Christabel shuffled around, then waited for further instructions. Her legs were dangling and she felt ungainly and lumpish. Nicholas moved towards her and, touching her for the first time in what seemed like weeks, he hooked his hands under her knees. 'Lift up,' he said. 'Hold yourself wide. I want to see everything ...' He laughed again,

22

sounding young. Devilish. 'I want to see how big *you* are.'

Again, she obeyed, beginning to sweat. The awkward curled-up pose was uncomfortable, but it was more than that. Her entire genital area felt swollen, engorged, precarious. As she eased her legs wider, she heard an obscene liquid noise from her sex.

'So wet,' murmured Nicholas, moving closer. Without warning, he pushed his finger into her.

'Agh! Oh, God!' grunted Christabel, her sex welcoming him in an instant, wrenching orgasm. She bucked on the bed, her nails digging into her own flesh as she fought to hold her position through waves of pleasure.

'Stay still, my dear,' hissed Nicholas, his finger like a rod inside her. 'Try to control yourself. Don't give in so easily.'

'I can't fucking well stop myself!' It came out as a strangled, guttural sob, as if distorted by her helpless inner flexion.

Nicholas leant close, half lying on the bed. 'Filthy wet whore,' he purred into her ear, the words almost loving as he began to pump his finger in and out of her. 'Dirty bitch. Always on heat. Always ready to be stuffed with some man's huge cock . . .' Pump. Pump. Pump. Christabel could hear her own juices squelching with each rhythmic intrusion. Her husband was abusing her to some perfect unheard beat.

Then, just as shockingly as it had begun, the digital trespass was over. Christabel whined and lifted her body higher to try and retrieve the finger. She wasn't finished, wasn't sated, not by a mile.

'Nicholas! Please!' she implored him, opening herself yet wider, trying to entice him.

'Oh, no no no!' said her husband, pulling away, still laughing at her.

Christabel opened her scrunched-up eyes, and saw that Nicholas's face was alight with mirth. She had never seen him so blatantly pleased with himself.

23

'You bastard! You sadist!' she cried, starting to spring up.

Nicholas caught her immediately, pressing her back against the bed again, his face scant inches from her own. He was still grinning and she could smell peppermint, cool and sexy on his breath.

'Oh, no, my sweet, I'm not a sadist.' He was so close now that she thought he was going to kiss her. But he didn't. His lips moved the air against her face, but didn't touch it. 'At least, not today . . .' He drew back, his expression indulgent. 'I gave you a climax, didn't I? I made you come . . . Even with this puny narrow finger?' He waggled his forefinger – which smelt strongly of her – in front of her nose. 'Be honest with me, Christabel . . . That isn't cruelty, is it?'

'But I want more,' she pleaded, still moving yet hating herself for it.

'You sound like a spoilt child, Christabel,' he said, moving her back into her previous position, and folding her own fingers around the back of her knees, to hold her. 'A little girl whining for her lollipop. Perhaps if you grew up, instead of behaving like a horny teenager, life might be a little easier for you.'

Her pulse tripping, Christabel looked into her husband's eyes, but discovered a surprising lack of anger there. He still seemed amused, and that left her at a loss.

'Poor baby. Never mind,' Nicholas said, wiping away a tear from the corner of her eye, then sucking the tiny amount of moisture from his finger, 'Daddy will make it better.' He touched the same finger to the opening of her vagina, and she rippled. 'I'll make sure that you don't have to suffer that nasty empty feeling . . . Just lie still, my sweet. Hold the position. I won't be a minute.'

Oh, yes, for sure. He'd taken away the nasty empty feeling, thought Christabel, walking uncomfortably down the steps towards the car. Only he'd replaced it with something ten times as plaguing.

24

Every step she took was a jolt, and she kept finding herself trying to walk on tip-toe. Which didn't help at all. There was no way to ignore what he'd done to her.

What the hell is he doing? she'd thought whilst waiting to discover her husband's intentions. The only clue had been the heavy clicks of an attaché case being opened. Then, just as she'd begun to move, to relieve the strain in her limbs and torso, he'd come over to her, and she'd heard the faint jingle of something metal.

'Close your eyes, my sweet,' he'd murmured, as she strained to see what he was doing. 'Just relax . . .' She almost leapt from the bed as he slathered something cold and slippery into her heat.

'What the hell are you doing, Nicholas?'

'Hush, my dear,' he murmured, and she heard the jingling sound again, then felt what could only be straps sliding over the insides of her thighs. 'Now open wide.' She knew he did not mean her mouth.

Straining her legs as far apart as was comfortable, Christabel held her breath. There was a moment's pause, then something thick, rubbery, yet solid was butting steadily against the mouth of her sex.

'Nicholas! Please! What are you doing?' she wailed, opening her eyes and looking down between her legs.

With an intent, concentrated look upon his face, her husband was pressing a short but extremely broad black latex dildo into her body. The flanged base of the device was attached to a network of slim leather buckled straps.

The slow invasion was both grotesque and sublime. Christabel mewled and struggled but her body expanded obligingly. The dildo was modelled on a thick but stubby cock and, even though it was short, it seemed to stuff her entire body cavity. She almost imagined she could feel it at the back of her throat.

'Nicholas . . . Oh, please . . . I can't take it!' she cried, watching him fit the straps into place and fasten them.

'Of course you can, Christabel,' he murmured, admiring his handiwork, then tightening one of the fastenings another notch. Her lower body was now encased in a delicate cage of chains and leather; the monster was held secure, but her every part remained accessible. 'This is exactly what you wanted, isn't it?' He stroked his hand lovingly along her thigh, towards the fat black thing he'd filled her with. 'A solid cock that will always be there when you need it.' To her horror, he then produced a tiny padlock and key, slid it through two metal rings at her waist, and secured the whole contraption irrevocably in place. He twirled the key once between his fingers, then stowed it in his pocket. 'And that, my dear, is how you'll travel to Collingwood.'

Collingwood? Where the hell is that? she thought now. I'll be lucky if I get to the end of the street!

It had been horribly difficult to dress. Physically violated and mentally confused, she'd felt the bulbous object rock with every movement. Why had she allowed Nicholas to do such a thing to her? To dominate her so easily? Yet again. She only knew that there was a dark Christabel inside her that adored what was happening to her – and adored her husband for bringing about the process.

'Oof!'

The step from their frontage on to the pavement produced a jerk inside her that felt like a man thrusting. She couldn't imagine how she was going to climb into the limousine. Especially with the ever-attentive Jamie holding the door open for her, a slight smile on his smooth, attractive face.

And the clothes Nicholas had chosen for her only made matters worse. She was wearing a suit in soft burgundy leather, which was far too warm for the time of year. It seemed he deliberately wanted her to be as hot and bothered as possible. The round-necked jacket was fitted and clung to her body, and the skirt, whilst not quite mini, was quite short and slim. Underneath, she wore nothing but her harness, and on her feet, the same toweringly uncomfortable shoes he'd made her wear back in her studio. Cleaned back up again to a high and brilliant gloss. On her long legs, he'd allowed the sheerest hold-up stockings.

'Good morning, Mrs Sutherland.' Jamie's smile had widened now. 'That's a beautiful suit.'

The young swine! He knew! Nicholas must have told his right-hand man what his plans were.

'It's too hot for the time of year,' she snapped, hesitating at the car door as Jamie retreated to let her pass. How on earth was she going to get inside with any elegance? How on earth was she going to get in without the dildo fucking her?

'If you get too warm, my dear, you can always remove your jacket,' said Nicholas smoothly, from just behind her. Oblivious to all this by-play, the silent chauffeur was loading the last of their luggage into the boot.

Suppressing a retort, Christabel continued to hover. How could she do this? The darkened interior of the car beckoned like a fantasy cave of danger, and the *faux* penis seemed to swell inside her body. A hand curled under her elbow, lifting and urging.

'Allow me,' said Jamie, propelling her into the limousine.

Christabel almost choked as the dildo jostled an exquisitely sensitive zone inside her. She was unable to stifle a grunt of pleasure and, when she sat down, the sensation ballooned perilously and she gasped.

'Are you all right, my dear?' enquired her husband urbanely. He sat down at her side, and Jamie took the jump seat that faced her.

Christabel swallowed, fighting for control, feeling as if the top of her head were about to come off. It was difficult to sit properly without incurring an even deeper ravishment, and she tried as best she could to perch elegantly on the leather upholstered seat, her full weight supported on one cheek of her bottom.

'I'm fine, Nicholas,' she said primly, already needing to adjust her pose. The dildo was somehow both pushing and pulling on the root of her clitoris and she would have given anything to reach beneath her skirt and finger herself.

'Are you sure?' Her husband laid his hand on her thigh. The gesture might have been purely the action of a kindly man concerned for his mate but, as he rocked her slightly, Christabel silently and explicitly cursed him.

The demon! He knew exactly what she was going through, and he had told his pretty-boy toady about it too. There was no other explanation for the lascivious smirk on Jamie's face, and the way he kept glancing at her crotch with eyes wide open.

Inwardly wailing, Christabel snapped her thighs closed, awfully aware that Jamie probably didn't even need to be told about her plight. The way her skirt had risen, he could most likely see it!

'Would you care for some water, Mrs Sutherland? You look a little flushed.'

You're just as bad as he is! thought Christabel, trying to concentrate hard enough to give Jamie a venomous look. 'No, I'm fine, thanks, Jamie,' she murmured. A drink was the last thing she needed, feeling like this. The other night had been quite enough, thank you. Jamie Carlton would never see her wet herself again.

Her breathing was shallow, and she was teetering on the point of sensations she could barely keep from showing on her face but, with a supreme effort, Christabel asked, 'So, Collingwood? Does somebody want to tell me all about it?' She turned to Nicholas and, despite her trials, she held his grey glance boldly. 'Is it some great pile you've gone and bought? And just forgot to mention?'

'No, I'm simply leasing it,' he said amiably. She could see that, inside, he was laughing at her puny efforts to resist what she was going through. 'I don't even know much about the place ... Jamie made all the arrangements through an agent.'

'Good for Jamie.'

Her husband didn't reprove her – even though, at the end of her tether, she'd virtually snarled. But he did reach for her hand and hold it in his own. An arrogant mockery of a spouse's sweet regard.

Jamie seemed unmoved. 'Collingwood, yes ...' he said, as if beginning to read from a prepared statement. Which he might well be. Nicholas had once said his assistant had a photographic memory. 'In Sussex, near Summerdean, it's a large, red sandstone house, Gothic in style, built towards the beginning of the last century. Set in extensive grounds, with various outbuildings, woods and water features –'

'Dear God! You sound like an estate agent!' exclaimed Christabel, irritated by the stodgy description, on top of everything else.

'Jamie's only trying to give us a good general picture of the place,' said Nicholas, squeezing her hand. 'There's no need to lose your temper!'

'No need to lose my temper!' Christabel's voice cracked as the tension inside her transmitted itself downward, tightening her deliciously around the dildo. 'Jesus Christ, Nicholas! You'd lose your temper if you had –'

Flushing purest crimson, she stopped. Waves of shame and lust surged through the cradle of her pelvis, and she came furiously, almost crushing the small bones of Nicholas's hand and gouging the car's carpeting with the high, sharp heels of her shoes.

'Oh, God,' she groaned, slumping back against the upholstery and closing her eyes to shut out the smiling faces of the two men.

'Are you sure you wouldn't like a glass of water?'

'No, Jamie, I fucking well don't want a glass of water!' she hissed, her eyes snapping open again. Both he and Nicholas were watching her closely, and she was obscurely pleased to see that Jamie was clearly affected by her little show. His eyes were brilliant, he looked slightly pink around the ears and, though she dared not let Nicholas see her looking, the younger man showed the clear bulge of an erection at his groin.

Nicholas, however, seemed as impassive as ever, although he murmured an almost silent 'bravo' as he twisted his hand and raised hers briefly to his lips.

Christabel turned away, unable to face them again. She felt hot and sweaty and her beleaguered vulva was swimming with her juices. She pursed her lips as her vagina fluttered again around the thick dark prong inside it.

Cool, cool fingers touched her face and urged her not to hide. 'Come on, Christabel, my sweet, there's no need to be embarrassed,' her husband whispered, making her look at him. 'Jamie is fully aware of what's going on beneath your skirt.' He squeezed her hand again, very delicately. 'And I think we all three of us know why such measures are necessary, don't we?'

'Why *are* they necessary?' she asked, her lips parched. She took a sip of the water that she had so vehemently refused. It seemed that Jamie was becoming as proficient as Nicholas was at reading thoughts rather than words.

'It's an issue of respect, my dear,' said Nicholas simply. 'The time has come for you to respect my wishes. My desires . . . I know I don't own you, Christabel, but you're my wife. If you can't give me total fidelity, then you can at least indulge me in other ways.' He paused in answer to her mute, questioning look. 'Ways like this.' He loosed her hand and reached down to cup her leather-covered crotch with his fingers, pressing the silk lining of her skirt against the protruding base of the rubber penis.

'Agh! No! Nicholas, please!'

The vile thing rocked, and Christabel pulsed again, clasping it involuntarily within her churning, rippling belly. Beating the seat beside her with her fists, she cried and climaxed.

Chapter Three
The House of Long Shadows

*E*leanor! My Eleanor!

The clothes were wrong. The hair was wrong. Even the face wasn't quite right. But Ethan Vertue knew his lover had returned to him . . .

Daniel Ranelagh slid from where he'd been crouched behind the sturdy old oak, studying the beloved but shabby façade of Collingwood, and sat down, leaning heavily against the tree's trunk. Laying down his binoculars, he rubbed his aching temples.

It was tiring to fight the fantasies and, most of the time, he welcomed them, but now that the latest lessees had arrived, he knew that he'd have to be more careful. He was going to have to find a way to intersect with reality, without losing a grip on the dreams that sustained him. It was going to be difficult, but he'd have to do it. Because, if word of his 'peculiarities' got back to the rest of the family, Father might well carry out his threats, and persuade one of his medical cronies to get Daniel committed.

Which Daniel was sane enough to know would send him really mad!

For all his present phobias and foibles, Daniel loved

Collingwood. He had to be here, breathing in the air and the resonances of Ethan and Eleanor. Healing his soul by living simply, walking in the woods, and by his writing.

The idea of that made him feel better. Father had called him a weakling, a wastrel and a jessie for becoming an author, and had been even more furious and uncomprehending when he'd discovered what it was that Daniel wrote. But, for Daniel, there was a perverse delight in the fact that the overblown historical romances his parent so despised were the first thing in life that had ever earnt Daniel any money of his own. He even made his *oeuvres* more outrageous than ever, just to get up his father's nose!

Screw you, Pater! he thought mildly, pulling out the thong that held back his hair. He gave his shaggy locks a good shake, then kneaded his scalp to try and unravel his inner tensions. Eyes closed, he settled back more comfortably against the oak. There was one pastime that always relaxed him, even though, in some ways, it was a part of his problems too. Like a drug that gave a marvellous high, then plunged you down again. Like alcoholic euphoria, with a hangover lying in wait.

It wouldn't hurt to take some brief solace, though. A charge for his batteries, an indulgence for his inner self . . .

Almost immediately, Ethan slid into him. Or became him. Or he became Ethan. He didn't know which. Opening his eyes again, he seemed to look out upon the light of a different age.

And Eleanor.

He imagined her as she'd looked this morning, giving him his instructions for the day's garden work under the cool, watchful eye of Charles Woodforde, her husband. It would have been nice to make a sketch of her then, to preserve such beauty for all time.

Her gown had been primrose yellow, fresh, pure and innocent. Her hands were so slim and fragile, and her skin so white against her rich hair. She looked like a faultless, untouchable princess, so refined that no one would think she knew anything of country matters.

Ethan chuckled to himself, unfastening his trousers as he pictured his beloved – and the secret sweetness beneath her elegant, expensive gown. He'd dared her to stop wearing her fine French drawers, and to steal away and play with herself whenever she could, whilst thinking of him. He could tell by the coins of rosy colour in her cheeks, as she'd spoken to him, that she had accepted his challenge. Perhaps before taking breakfast with her dour but handsome Charles?

That was it! She'd stolen away to the linen closet, or to the privy, or some such hideaway, and once there she'd whipped up all that lemon-coloured cotton and lace and worked on her own privates with all the luscious abandon of a sophisticated courtesan. He could just imagine the expression on her face, the vermilion tints of the shimmering flesh between her legs, the flash of fingers that were growing ever more skilled under his tutelage. He seemed to smell the rich, ripe muskiness of her womanly sex, and he could almost taste her on his tongue as he ran it around his lips.

Oh, dear Jesus, he felt hot. He felt hard. His penis was a great truncheon rearing up from his crotch, pointing skyward as if scenting the air for some evidence of the presence of his beloved Eleanor. He wanted to bury himself in her immediately. To take her roughly, without any of the preliminary niceties. He wanted to ram his flesh into any part of her that would receive him. Her fanny, her sweet mouth, her tight, gripping bottom.

Ah, yes! That tiny ruddy place that expanded so bravely to receive him ... God, he could almost hear her ecstatic yelps and groans as he worked in that narrow, clinging channel. She loved it! She loved all sex. She even loved *him*.

And he loved her. Her fine, sharp wit and her mercurial pride, as well as the ineffable delights of her aristocratic body. It could never be, but he knew that if she were to be his – entirely – he could die a happy man.

But, for now, what he could have of her would suffice him. Her presence in his thoughts as he shot his load of seed.

'Eleanor!' groaned Daniel Ranelagh, as his lean hips pumped and his white come jetted out of the tip of his penis. He almost laughed as it landed stickily on his jeans.

What a slob I am, he thought, as he got his breath back. His hair was tangled and scruffy and needed a trim; his flapping satin coat had been a hopeless case when he'd picked it up in Oxfam; and his jeans had been faded and torn long before they'd become stained with spunk as well.

He'd better clean himself up before he met that beautiful creature who had just arrived, he decided. The one in the leather suit the colour of Crozes Hermitage, who he assumed was the wife of Nicholas Sutherland, the man who'd just leased Collingwood for the rest of the summer.

I don't want you to think that I'm a disgusting, unwashed hobo, Mrs Sutherland, he said to the handsome woman, in her absence. I'd like to impress you . . . Even if everybody has already told you that I'm mad!

After fastening his fly, and doing his best to rub away the mark of his own semen, Daniel got briskly to his feet and retrieved his abandoned field glasses. He felt himself smiling involuntarily, a sensation that cheered him up immensely.

It came as no surprise that the tension headache had gone.

'God, what a weird place, Nicholas,' whispered Christabel as they entered the long, shadowy front hall at Collingwood. 'Whatever possessed you to lease a gloomy old heap like this?'

She was exhausted. The broad, uneven steps leading up to the front door of the house had been an agonising trial to her, but her body was too tired now to find the torment stirring.

I don't think I can bear another orgasm, she thought, groaning silently as the dildo jiggled inside her. If she climaxed again, she'd collapse on the spot, she was sure of it.

'It's fascinating,' Nicholas said, steering her by the elbow, making her stride out smartly. 'And it's actually a lot less dilapidated than the photographs suggested.' He looked around him, his aura fresh and lively. He was full of all the energy that Christabel now lacked, thanks to *his* perversity. 'Yes, I really think this place will suit us well.'

Any goddamned private place at all will suit me, thought Christabel, contemplating murder. Just somewhere I can squat down and get this terrible thing out of me. Always providing that you'll let me have the key, you swine! Her knees buckled; she could barely take another step but, with a towering effort, she managed to stay alert and look around her. Try to concentrate on this dismal old dump, dire as it is, she told herself. Just do anything to distract your mind and keep from coming.

At that moment, a plump but elegant middle-aged woman appeared in the gloomy hall before them, a genuine smile of welcome on her face. Christabel realised that this must be their housekeeper, or whatever such women were called here in the backwoods, and that she hadn't just materialised, but had popped out from a curtained alcove beneath the elaborate winding staircase.

'Hello, Mr and Mrs Sutherland,' she said, holding out her hand and shaking Nicholas's. 'Welcome to Collingwood; I'm Paula Blake. This is my husband Sylvester. And this is Hetty, who helps out around the house.' From behind her, a man and a woman moved forward:

the man thin, with receding hair and a bright twinkle of humour in his eyes, and the woman pretty, young and blonde, with a busty figure.

Oh, please say this isn't going to be a long drawn-out welcoming committee, pleaded Christabel silently. She felt as if the newly appeared trio knew everything that Nicholas and Jamie did about her. That they could see and smell and savour her parlous state.

Whilst the usual introductions were made, and all the Collingwood staff were shaking her perspiring hand, Christabel caught sly glances passing quickly between them.

They probably think I'm some slut of a call-girl he's brought along to have fun with, and that the real Mrs Sutherland is back in London. She twisted her wedding band and wished that Nicholas had allowed her to wear some of her more impressive jewellery to arrive in. Anything other than just a leather suit and a sex-plug made of latex.

'I'll show you to your room, Mrs Sutherland,' said Paula Blake after a moment and, gritting her teeth, Christabel prepared to mount the staircase.

I can't go on, she thought, almost tripping on the first step, aware that eyes both knowing and speculative were upon her. Could Blake and the sharp young Hetty see up her skirt? she wondered, looking back at them when she reached the landing. Were they staring up, in awe and horror, at her martyred pubis?

'Are you all right, Mrs Sutherland?' her companion enquired, brown eyes curious as she paused to let Christabel catch up. 'You look a bit hot and bothered. I can run you a bath straight away, if you like . . . There's always hot water.'

'No, thanks. I'm fine,' Christabel said, thinking quickly. She couldn't undress in front of this woman, no way! 'I'm just tired. It's been a rather hot journey . . . Air-conditioning on the blink, I think. I'll maybe just have a lie-down, then have a bath later.'

36

'Just as you wish, Mrs Sutherland,' said the other woman imperturbably. 'You'll find towels in the bathroom, and more in the linen chest, if you need them.'

Within a few moments, Christabel had achieved the blessed sanctuary of her bedroom. A room, it seemed, that she would not be sharing with Nicholas. Looking around, she liked what she saw, in spite of everything. Like the whole of Collingwood, the room was rather dark in character but, despite this, and its genteel shabbiness, it was also welcoming. It had a certain distinction, a faded, off-beat opulence; and, what was more, there was a wide and comfortable bed.

'Is there anything else I can do for you?'

Christabel spun around, then caught her breath, wishing she hadn't. Had there been a hint of suggestiveness in the Blake woman's voice, just then? As if she knew what was making her new employer's wife so red-faced? Surely Nicholas hadn't phoned ahead and told her?

'No, thanks very much. This is all lovely.' Christabel gestured around the room, but with more care this time. 'I'll be fine.'

'Well, just ring if you do need anything.' Paula Blake nodded to an old-fashioned tapestry bell-pull that hung beside the bed; then, as she made to leave the room, there was a sudden rap on the door.

I'm the mistress now, I suppose, thought Christabel, and called, 'Come in!'

Sylvester Blake brought in her cases, then fished in his pocket and produced a small silver key.

'Your husband thought you'd be needing this, Ma'am,' he said, passing it to Christabel. 'And he says if there's anything else you want him for, he's three doors down the landing.'

Was she imagining things, or had Blake really winked as he'd handed over the key?

* * *

37

There was a knock at the door.

Nicholas Sutherland, who had been lying on his bed, lightly aroused and picturing the black dildo sliding wetly from the body of his wife, sighed and sat up. 'Come in,' he called, bracing himself for company.

'I just wondered if you needed me for anything?'

Jamie looked delicious, Nicholas thought, hoping his hunger didn't show too much on his face as he studied his personal assistant. The younger man was freshly bathed, that was clear, and looked fit and rested, despite the fact that it was less than an hour since they'd arrived. He wore blue – as he so often did, because it suited him – a pair of mid-blue chinos and a long-sleeved polo shirt, two shades darker. Nicholas's heart thudded and, beneath his thin silk robe, his cock stirred restlessly.

'I don't know, really.' Nicholas rubbed his face, his weariness half feigned, half real. 'I feel tired. But edgy, too. I can't relax . . .'

Jamie gave an odd little half-smile. 'Yes. I'm not surprised. It was all rather . . . er . . . intense, wasn't it?'

Nicholas smiled and nodded. Jamie was a sweet boy, and the soul of discretion. He never referred overtly to anything to do with his employers' private lives, but it was clear he wasn't unmoved by all the drama. And Nicholas was well aware that his PA admired both women *and* men.

Could I have been as cool as he is, at his age? thought Nicholas, beginning to sweat beneath his robe. Jamie had appeared superficially unaffected by Christabel's gyrations in the limousine – even when Nicholas had asked him to unfasten a button on her jacket, and reach in and fondle her breast – but Nicholas had noticed the younger man's sturdy erection.

Did you masturbate in the shower, my friend? Nicholas wondered, staring intently at the boy's crotch. And if you did, who was it for? My wife? Or me?

'I could do with a massage, actually, Jamie,' he said,

flexing his shoulders. 'Would you care to do the honours? You've been threatening to show me your technique for long enough now.'

'For sure. I'd be happy to.' Jamie sounded a little nervous: not quite so poised as usual. 'I have some oil in my bag. I'll go and get it.'

Massage? Oils? Oh, it was all such a cliché, Nicholas reflected, spreading bath towels out on the carpet while he waited. It would have been nice to employ a more innovative gambit, but he really was tired and, for the moment, elaborate mindgames seemed too wearying. Watching Christabel writhe and climax had primed his fires, yet somehow also been a drain on him.

Satisfied with the disposal of the towels, Nicholas shucked off his robe, amused and relieved by the reliable way his cock sprang up. The years were passing all too fast, but there seemed as yet no diminishment in his powers. In fact, the reverse seemed to be operating. He was more libidinous these days than he'd ever been as a teenager, and he had the life-experience now with which to better enjoy it.

Is it too early for candles? he wondered, drawing the heavy curtains and shutting out the light that was just beginning to mellow into evening. Striking the match, he tried to imagine what Christabel was doing. Had she bathed after she'd freed herself from her harness? Had she masturbated again, or been so wrung out that she'd only wanted rest?

For a moment, he considered changing his tactics, and going to her room to make quiet, tender love to her. It wasn't her fault she was promiscuous; in fact, he himself did everything he could to promote her sensuality. It was part of his game plan, the simplest of steps on the complex path ahead . . .

A soft knock at the door snapped his reverie, and he shouted, 'Come in!'

Jamie's eyes widened at the sight of his employer's naked body. Nicholas was proud of his physique and, even apart from his prodigious erection, he knew that, for his age, he was impressive.

'Don't worry, I haven't started without you,' he said mildly. 'We need the oil . . .' He glanced towards the patterned blue toilet-bag that Jamie was clutching, which he presumed contained the younger man's massage accoutrements.

'Something's already started.' Jamie's voice sounded a little reedy and he licked his lips. He seemed stripped of all the confidence and *savoir faire* that typified his daily efficiency. His blue gaze was zeroed squarely on his employer's stiff penis.

'Merely the anticipation of a pleasant, relaxing experience,' Nicholas lied creamily. They both knew well enough what lay before them.

'Why don't you undress too, Jamie?' he went on. 'You don't want to get oil on your clothes and have to change again for dinner.'

'Good idea!' The younger man had already abandoned his toilet bag and was tugging off his polo shirt whilst still speaking. Within seconds, his shoes were off, too, and he was out of his socks and his elegant trousers, flinging everything on the floor with a fine disregard for his usual meticulousness. He hesitated, though, with his underwear. Nerves suddenly seemed to strike him, even though he was sporting an erection that threatened to split the white cotton of his boxer shorts.

Nicholas gave his assistant a steady look, trying to instil confidence. Jamie was magnificent, his physical promise making him more desirable than ever . . . But they were about to take a step that might just be further than Jamie had ever been before.

'Just a massage, Jamie,' he said softly, nodding for his companion to continue. He brushed his fingers against his own cock, as a further spur, then suppressed a groan at the intense degree of his own excitement. Maybe

Jamie wasn't the only one who had something to be afraid of.

His effort to quash his fears touchingly visible, Jamie slid off his shorts and let his penis spring up and bounce enticingly against his flat, washboard stomach. He was circumcised, Nicholas noticed, refusing to give in to his own impulse to lick his lips. Cut men were his preference. Jamie couldn't have been more perfect for him, and he made a snap decision to move ahead more quickly than he'd originally planned. Feeling his heart rate accelerate, he lay face-upward on the towels, his cock presented.

With his own member swaying, Jamie reached for the toilet bag and unzipped it. 'Er . . . I thought we might start with your neck muscles. Where the tension is . . .' He moved closer, sank to his knees, and set out his oils, all the time staring fixedly at Nicholas's groin.

'I think we both know where the tension is, Jamie.' Nicholas lifted his hips slightly as he spoke, making his erection move in a swaying, dancing circle. He suddenly felt totally wanton. Sluttish, almost. Sympathy for Christabel darted through his mind, and he smiled. Dear God, the sexual imperative had a hell of a lot to answer for!

'Massage me, Jamie,' he murmured, jerking his pelvis again, commanding with the stiffness of his flesh as well as with his voice.

'Of course,' said Jamie, quietly submissive. There was no need for the words 'sir' or even 'master'. But Nicholas could still hear them, and their fugitive echoes made his cock even harder.

Having coated his fingers with oil, Jamie tentatively raised both hands towards his target. A drop of oil dripped on to Nicholas's thigh, then another. Jamie seemed frozen, his expression half of greed, half of fear as his grip hovered just inches from the tip of Nicholas's penis.

41

'Go on,' urged Nicholas, aware of a tremor in his own voice now. He was valiantly resisting the compulsion to buck upward again and force the issue. His entire cock felt as if it were expanding, especially the glans. He longed to scream out, 'Touch me, you bastard!' but managed to refrain.

At long last, though, the desired contact was made. With caution and reverence, Jamie laid hands on Nicholas. His grip was light, yet not too light to elicit a response.

'Oh, my God,' groaned Nicholas, the breath shuddering from his lungs at the two-fold caress. A finger and thumb circling the tip of him and stretching his frenum; the palm of a hand, curved like a cradle, lovingly fondling his balls. Gouging at the towels beneath him, he pushed his hips upward, knowing it was unlikely that he could ever have stopped himself anyway. He wanted to come, and he wanted to come quickly. Why on earth should he wait? There'd be plenty of time to recover and take a second turn . . .

Fingers twisting wildly on thick folds of terrycloth, he growled, 'For pity's sake, man, suck me!'

I ought to be off sex for life after this thing, thought Christabel, hiding the newly cleaned dildo along with the vibrator, beneath her undies, in a drawer. Unlikely as it seemed, though, she felt a strange nostalgia for her ugly black tormentor. The way it had stretched her and possessed her, without effort, or human guile, or complications, was at least perfectly honest.

Perhaps I ought to wear it all the time? she mused, selecting a pair of thin white silk panties and stepping into them with some care. She still felt extraordinarily sensitive down there, and the urge to reach down and touch herself was so strong it clouded her mind.

'For God's sake, woman! You're not an animal,' she told herself, slamming the drawer shut, and walking quickly to the window, seeking distraction in the uncomplicated beauty of nature. Collingwood's grounds and gardens weren't the best-tended she'd ever seen – in fact, they were downright scruffy – but there was a compelling verdancy, almost a brooding quality about the scene.

Evening was falling, and bringing down with it a shimmering veil of gold across the overgrown shrubs and the flower beds that straggled away into the equally ill-kempt park. As she scanned the tree line in the middle distance, Christabel spotted a movement close to a particularly gnarled old trunk.

At first she thought it was an animal, something small and wild, moving in the undergrowth but, after a second, a man straightened up from a crouching position. As he came to full height, he lowered a glinting pair of field glasses.

'My God,' murmured Christabel, 'a real live country bumpkin peeping Tom!' The thought amused her. She was still half naked and she felt like putting on a show.

Throwing her weight behind the stiff catch, she opened the deep window and leant out a little way, enjoying the soft whisper of the sun-warmed air against her nipples. She did not look directly at the man who stood amongst the trees; in fact, she had no idea if he was even still looking at her, but just the idea of being observed reawakened her passions.

Take a good look, Jethro or whatever your name is, she instructed him silently. Clinging firmly to the window frame with one hand, she let the other hand drift carelessly over her body, making sure that one artfully flexed finger grazed the tip of her breast. As if in sympathy, between her legs, her clitoris leapt. Turning her head slowly, and glancing obliquely, she looked for the watcher.

He was still there, and still looking in her direction, even though his field glasses now hung around his neck, no longer in use.

Too shy, turnip boy? she challenged, noting that he

was youngish, and, though she could not make out details of his features, that he had long hair which curled on his shoulders, and a body that was slim. He was also dressed in a long, flapping, rather odd-looking coat, that seemed to have a sheen to it, as well as jeans, and a shirt that also seemed to gleam.

Silk and satin? Well, whoever her admirer was, he clearly wasn't a farmer, in those fabrics. He looked more like a rock star. A sense of fascination added piquancy to her lust, and she had a sudden urge to make a dash for her camera and take a picture of her watcher.

To leave the window now, though, would break the momentum of her desire, and might make him leave. And it wasn't as if she had a sufficiently powerful zoom, or telephoto, to capture him anyway.

Widening her thighs as best she could on the narrow window ledge, she chose to proceed, and let her travelling hand slide downward. After hesitating just one heartbeat, she let it move on, and further down – inside her panties.

Distance denied Christabel the expression on the young man's watching face but, when he tipped his shaggy head a little to one side, she recognised a reaction. She would have liked to have seen him raise his field glasses again, and perhaps clutch his own groin as he did so, but at least he was still observing her, after a fashion. Perhaps he was afraid she was just an erotic daydream?

Oh, God, this isn't going to last long, she thought, lightly fingering her clitoris. The tiny organ was still perfectly primed, and even the most minuscule amount of pressure was likely to affect it. Unable to help herself, Christabel wriggled her bottom against the edge of the window sill, enhancing the pleasure she was already experiencing with a pressure on her anus.

It took just one rock of her hips and one flick of her finger, and she was coming immediately . . .

* * *

44

Dear God!

The fabric of Daniel's reality seemed to rip in two again. It was Eleanor! It was! And she was touching herself. Right there in the frame of the window, defying Collingwood itself in order to glorify and proclaim her womanhood.

'Oh, Eleanor,' Daniel/Ethan whispered, agonised with desire and awe.

She was the most beautiful creature he'd ever seen, an exotic temptress, flaunting her lush body in just her little drawers. The shape of her breasts, high and round, was clear, even from this distance, and in his imagination, he fancied he could see the nest of her crisp yet silky pubic hair through the thin fabric of her undergarment. That he could see her graceful fingers dividing the lips, and rubbing, rubbing, rubbing . . .

'My love!' he cried, almost collapsing as she jerked, stiffened and seemed to collapse herself, still iconified in the dark, mysterious mouth of the window. She'd just spent, he realised, right there, at one with the soft evening air. At one with him, because he knew that she'd seen him watching. Opening his mouth, he breathed in deeply, almost tasting her.

His gaze still directed at the figure in the second-floor window, Daniel suddenly blinked as the whole scene wavered in his vision.

'Christ Almighty!' he whispered, experiencing a drawing back together of his wits and senses. He wasn't bloody imagining things again . . . What he'd just seen was real! That was no shade of Eleanor Woodforde he'd conjured up; that was a living woman he'd just watched masturbate herself to orgasm. That was Mrs Sutherland, the one that Hetty had said was called Christabel.

She was there, now, rising from her seat in the window sill, stretching hugely, as if she'd just woken like Sleeping Beauty. As she turned away and disappeared from her eyrie, Daniel sighed, but not unhappily, and lowered himself to the copse floor, lying facing downward. Then, filling his mind with thoughts of women with golden-red hair and a perfect, rounded bosom, he began to grind his aching crotch against the hard-packed earth.

Chapter Four
Foreshadowings

*T*he oak-panelled dining room was equally as dark and brooding as the rest of Collingwood and, now that evening had fallen, Christabel almost expected members of the Addams family to turn up as guests at their table. Indeed, some of the family portraits even seemed to be of them!

'Who on earth owns this place?' She gestured with her wineglass. Nervous tension made her want to drink more than was good for her, but caution slowed her down. When Nicholas was in this odd, charged mood, anything could happen and, already having secrets from him, Christabel decided to keep her wits about her.

Nicholas looked up from his meal at her and, even though he didn't frown, or express displeasure in any way, Christabel was instantly reminded of an icy Victorian patriarch who ruled his family with a firm, unwavering discipline. His eyes were steady as he laid down his heavy silver cutlery and blotted his lips with a damask napkin. Formality was the order of the evening, it seemed, at Collingwood. They were sitting within touching distance, but subtly divided by barriers of form.

'Collingwood is the property of a brother and sister,

Jamie tells me,' he said, his glance flashing to his assistant. 'The Honourable Daniel Eugene Ranelagh and the Honourable Augusta Nemone Ranelagh, to be precise . . . Younger son and daughter of the Earl of Silchester, who lives in the next county.'

'You're kidding!' Her nerves temporarily forgotten, Christabel laughed at the extravagance of the names, then took a long sip of her wine. What the hell!

'No, that's quite correct,' said Jamie, chipping in. He too was close, sitting directly opposite her at one end of the long polished table, with Nicholas at the head of it, presiding. 'Apparently the Earl gave this house free and clear to the Honourable Daniel and Honourable Augusta because, well, he can't abide having them live with him!' The younger man smiled, his smooth face lighting as he glanced back towards Nicholas. 'They're both a bit of a disappointment to him, it seems. What you might call a brace of genuine black sheep.'

My God, they've done it! thought Christabel suddenly. She took a longer swig at her wine, barely tasting its strength and complex flavour. Her husband and his PA had had sex together; it was obvious to her now. The whole dynamic between the two men had changed, at least on Jamie's side. He was looking at Nicholas with a dreamy longing in his eyes, an expression of almost fawning adoration. It wouldn't have surprised Christabel if Jamie had suddenly reached for Nicholas's hand, then kissed it.

Bastards! Bastards! Bastards! Between them, they'd dragged her down here in the most ignominious of circumstances, and Nicholas had reproved her for her sexual appetites . . . And now he and Golden Boy here were fucking each other. It was so unfair that Christabel hated the pair of them.

'Black sheep, eh?' she said crisply, not letting her resentment show. 'They sound like my kind of people. Am I likely to meet them soon?'

'I shouldn't think so,' said Nicholas, picking up his

fork. His eyes were narrow as he looked in Christabel's direction and, despite her anger at him, she felt her belly flutter. The cooler he was, the greater his self-control, the more he stirred her. 'The Honourable Augusta spends most of her time in London, so the staff say, and the Honourable Daniel lives in the dower house, and keeps himself very much to himself.'

'But surely he comes up here sometimes?' Christabel felt a sudden frisson of excitement from a different source. The man she'd seen at the tree line, the one in the long coat, with the flowing hair – was that the mysterious Daniel Whatsit Ranelagh? 'To sort out estate business and stuff . . .'

'Well, actually . . .' Jamie began, a little diffidently, as if he felt he was speaking out of turn, 'the young woman who helps the housekeeper told me that the Honourable Daniel is . . . how shall we say? A bit strange. He's phobic about the house and won't ever come inside it, for some reason. She doesn't really know why.'

'He sounds interesting,' said Christabel, crossing her knife and fork and putting aside her plate. She had been hungry, but other appetites were rousing now, piqued by Nicholas's poker-player eyes – and the hypocritical mind that lay behind them – and the fleeting sight of the Honourable Daniel Ranelagh.

'Now why doesn't that surprise me?' said Nicholas evenly, pushing away his own plate and inclining a little way across the table towards Christabel. He was wearing a beautiful black shirt, very plain and cut from a very fine silk jersey material, and she had never seen him look more impressive. His body language was both alert and almost insultingly relaxed, and Christabel was more certain than ever he'd recently had sex.

'It isn't a crime!' She was defending herself, she realised furiously, even though all she'd done was express an opinion.

'Have you forgotten why you're here?' Nicholas's voice was silky, and he didn't turn from her, even when there was a knock at the door, and Mrs Blake came in, carrying a silver tray bearing what was obviously their dessert. Christabel noticed detachedly that it was something with lemon and cream, and that it looked and smelt absolutely delicious.

'That looks beautiful, Mrs Blake. And it probably tastes twice as good,' she said brightly, as the plump woman smiled and set the dish on the table, along with their dessert bowls.

'Would you like me to dish it up, ma'am?' There was a vaguely intimate note in the housekeeper's voice that made Christabel shudder, even though the evening was warm and balmy. Had Nicholas said anything to the Blakes about his reasons for bringing his wife down to the country? Had he explained her blushes, on her arrival, and her over-cautious walk?

'No, thanks very much,' she said, 'we'll help ourselves.'

The other woman nodded and swiftly cleared the main-course plates but, just as she was almost through the door, Nicholas said, 'Could we have some coffee in a little while, please, Paula?'

'Of course, Mr Sutherland,' replied Paula Blake, visibly simpering.

Christabel felt anger and desire seething in equal parts. She mustn't even speak of other men, yet it was perfectly OK for her husband to flirt with the staff, and even go to bed with that goddamned male slut Jamie! She wanted to rant and rage in protest, yet just one look at Nicholas's face kept her silent. He was observing her, monitoring her expressions, impassively judging her.

'Don't you want to please me at all, Christabel?' he asked, making her bristle even more. He was talking to her as if she were a naughty child.

Part of Christabel was so incensed that she wanted to storm from the room, find the nearest man – preferably the mysterious Daniel Ranelagh – then demand that he roger her. But another part of her was growing more and more excited. The part that had found pleasure in being humiliated back in her bedroom and her studio. Within her abbreviated lace and satin briefs, she felt moisture begin to gather and, though she hated it, her nipples peaked and hardened. Something that both her companions could probably see through her thin silk slip-dress.

'Yes.' She pursed her lips, aware that even they were betraying her now. Growing fuller and pinker, as if she were anticipating a kiss.

'Yes what, Christabel?' her husband persisted, while silent Jamie set out the dessert bowls and served the pudding.

'I want to please you, Nicholas.' She couldn't help the touch of facetiousness in her tone, and felt her dread and excitement thicken as dark humour stirred in her husband's slate-grey eyes.

'To please me, you must obey me, Christabel. Do exactly what I say . . . and refrain from what I forbid you to do. Do you understand?'

Christabel's chest and throat grew unbearably warm, and she felt faint in a way that was also vaguely pleasant. The same twisted forces that had moulded her in the studio and in the limousine were coming into play. New parameters were governing her mind and body, making her conform to her husband's subtle perversions. Free will seemed to have quit the room, unnoticed.

She could not speak but, as her head went light, she nodded.

'In that case, my darling, show me your breasts.'

The serving spoon clattered against the dish but, to his credit, Jamie didn't spill any of the creamy lemon pudding. His eyes upon her, he continued to fill the bowls.

Oh, no, Nicholas, don't do this! wailed Christabel silently. Paula Blake would be back any instant with the coffee, and she would see the display. The older woman's manner had been almost insulting to start with, and this would give her even more on which to speculate juicily, back in the kitchen.

'Your breasts, my dear,' said Nicholas quietly, nodding thanks to Jamie who had just set his dessert before him. 'Help her, Jamie,' he went on, lifting his silver spoon.

Turned to stone, Christabel endured in silence while Jamie came up behind her and unzipped the back of her dress. His hands were warm but pleasantly dry as they brushed against her, peeling down the shoestring top and letting it settle around her waist. Unclipping her strapless bra, he drew it off and laid it on the table.

I can't bear this! thought Christabel, wondering why being so casually exposed was such an aphrodisiac. Her breasts ached and felt twice as heavy as they normally did, as if Nicholas's stare was a physical burden bearing down upon them.

'You're quite aroused, I see,' he said, tasting a spoonful of the lemon dessert, and making a small, appreciative sound before speaking to his assistant, 'Feel her, Jamie, will you, please?'

Although she couldn't look him in the face, Christabel sensed the younger man's confusion and her horror escalated. What now? What now?

Nicholas laughed, and ate another spoonful of his pudding. 'Her nipples, Jamie. Just her nipples.' Touching his tongue to the centre of his top lip, he appeared to sweep up an errant fleck of lemony cream and savour it lasciviously. 'For now, that is.'

Protest froze in Christabel's throat. She wanted to shout, 'How dare you do this?' but she couldn't because the voluptué in her longed for Jamie's touch. For any man's touch. Nicholas's would be the most welcome, no matter how outrageously he treated her; but, failing him, perhaps Daniel Ranelagh's would do? The weird man who lived alone in the dower house. Arching her back, she thrust her breasts forward.

52

'Christabel,' Nicholas warned, but it was too late. Jamie Carlton's fingers were already closing around her nipples, his thumbs strumming her as he exceeded his remit.

'She's very erect, Mr Sutherland,' the younger man reported, not faltering. Now that he'd been given sanction to make free with her, it seemed that all his reticence had dissolved. He was making the most of his chance to grope his employer's wife.

Not that she wasn't enjoying the experience . . .

Christabel bit her lip as Jamie delicately rolled and pulled both her teats in a slow, impertinent rhythm. The fact that Nicholas was allowing such a manifest overstepping of his instructions only aroused her more. Transferred sensations in her clitoris made her shuffle in her seat and, closing her eyes, she tried to fight it, but she couldn't.

Becoming aware of movements around her, she spluttered when she felt something cool against her lips.

'Open up, my dear,' instructed Nicholas and, as she opened both her eyes *and* her mouth, she was fed some pudding. The luscious lemonyness caressed her tongue while Jamie continued to fondle her. All the while, Nicholas watched the process closely.

'Eat up, Christabel,' he said, putting another spoonful into her mouth. 'It's good for you.'

It was syllabub, or something similar and, despite the distractions, Christabel enjoyed the unctuous taste of it. The creamy dessert was cool and smooth and, for a moment, she imagined how soothing it would feel smeared on to her nipples or into her vulva, which was growing ever hotter and needier by the moment.

'Touch yourself, my dear,' whispered Nicholas into her ear, as he pressed the loaded dessertspoon against her lips again. 'Be a good girl, and put your hand between your legs.'

Christabel clamped her jaws shut, and tried to wriggle away from Jamie's tormenting fingers. Mrs Blake would be here any minute with the coffee, and to have her see this would be mortifying, unthinkable. To have a man see her abused and handled like this was acceptable, somehow, but not a woman. Oh, no! Never! She just couldn't.

'Christabel!'

Nicholas's voice was quelling and his hard, fiery glance even more so. Christabel felt her clitoris leap, as if it too demanded her compliance. She could not believe how much passion her shame could rouse in her. Even the imminent arrival of the housekeeper couldn't suppress it. With a small moan, Christabel reached down and cupped her crotch through the thin layers of her clothing.

Her sexual channel was a furnace. It seemed to gape a mile wide. Even through the silk and lace of her dress and panties, she could feel the slipperiness of her labia. The frock was a Chloe, and it was probably already stained.

'Squeeze yourself,' said Nicholas, still insisting against her mouth with the syllabub. As she swallowed another spoonful, Christabel felt, as she'd suspected, that her skirt was damp and warm against her fingers. Past caring, she wriggled and burrowed between her legs.

The pleasure was intense but complicated. Almost in orgasm, she could feel the scrutiny of both Nicholas and Jamie pressing down on her. They were watching her face for signs of her weakening and, when she tried to purse her lips, her husband pressed the spoon against them.

'Please, no! Nicholas! I can't eat now!' Her whole groin was gathering itself, collapsing inward, ready to pulse and grab at emptiness.

'One more spoonful.' His voice strangely kind and coaxing now, as if he were a kindly uncle and not a grim Victorian tyrant. She sensed him nod to Jamie, whose fingers immediately tightened on her nipples.

The taste of lemons filled her mouth and, between her legs, she reached the moment of criticality. Her vulva leapt as the silky dessert slid down her throat, and the rising heat within her seemed to melt the cream. Diverse stimuli fused and warped in her singing senses.

Suddenly, there was a knock at the door and, still riding the waves of her ebbing climax, Christabel was catapulted right back into shame and confusion. The coffee had arrived – and she was bare-breasted and clutching her crotch.

'Just one moment.' Nicholas's voice carried, but sounded as cool as an ice floe. Edging aside Jamie – who appeared just as drugged and eroticised as Christabel felt – Nicholas pulled Christabel's dress back over her breasts and quickly zipped it. 'Leave your hand where it is, my dear,' he murmured to her, his grey eyes molten, then neatly he flipped the tablecloth over her lap. Her bra, which lay on the table, he left in plain sight.

'Come in!' he ordered, nodding to Jamie to return to his seat.

The air in the dining room was thick and unnaturally silent when Paula Blake bustled back in again with her silver tray. Christabel didn't know where to look, for fear of giving herself away. Her throat and chest already bore the hot stigmata of orgasmic mottling and, even over the scent of coffee and lemons, she could clearly smell musk. It was unmistakable, and Paula Blake was bound to recognise it. Even if she didn't, there was always the accursed bra, just sitting there – not being worn.

Christabel also had no idea what she would do if she was expected to be 'mother' and pour the coffee. She would have to disclose exactly where her hand had been.

'Thanks, Paula. I think we've got all we need, for the time being,' Nicholas said personally, indicating the coffee tray. 'That dessert was glorious, perfectly delicious . . . Don't you think so, Christabel?'

With Paula Blake looking curiously at her, Christabel had no option but to lift her glowing face and attempt politeness. 'Yes. It . . . it was fabulous. Thank you.' She forced the words out through lips that seemed tight and unnaturally dry. Her chest grew even hotter and pinker when Paula Blake gave her a knowing little grin, then flicked a glance towards the brassière.

'Are you sure you have everything you need?' said the housekeeper, sounding to Christabel's ears exaggeratedly innocent. It was obvious that the Blake woman knew everything, or at least something, and found the situation, and Christabel's predicament, riotously amusing.

It was Nicholas who answered, even though the question had been aimed at Christabel. 'Yes, thank you, Paula. We're all fine. We won't need to bother you again tonight.'

When Mrs Blake was gone, he poured three cups of coffee, without speaking, and passed Christabel and Jamie theirs. The scent rising from the tiny porcelain demitasse was as evocative, in its way, as the other lingering odours and, as she sniffed it, Christabel's mouth began to water. She prepared to withdraw her fingers from her groin, and reach for the cup, then instinctively she froze and stayed her hand. Something deeply female in her wanted to ask her husband for permission.

Nicholas laughed quietly, as if he had psychic powers and had been monitoring her frequency. 'Go ahead,' he said, his fine eyes crinkling with amusement.

Raising the cup between her musk-anointed fingers, Christabel took a sip of coffee and almost gasped at its pungent, reviving strength. Coffee was normal, a constant from the real world of London and the life she was accustomed to. It was doubly welcome here in the peculiar universe of Collingwood.

'At last! We're getting somewhere,' said Nicholas, when Christabel put down her coffee cup and it clattered in its saucer. 'Now take off your panties and show Jamie how you masturbate.'

But if you *wanted* me to do it then, why can't I do it now? thought Christabel, staring down at her hands where they lay like two prostrate white birds against the counterpane. The light of a summer moon streamed in on to her through the open curtains of the bedroom window, its soft radiance a subtle invitation.

Thinking back over what had been done, and said, around that dinner table, Christabel could barely credit either. What Nicholas had proposed, and what she'd agreed to, was incomprehensible. It all just seemed like a silly, preposterous dream.

She was to refrain from all sexual activity except that sanctioned by her husband, and under his close supervision. She mustn't even masturbate unless he told her to . . . Which was ridiculous, because he had no way of knowing whether she did or she didn't. She supposed he must be relying on her word of honour.

I must be mad. He must be mad. Jamie must be as mad as the pair of us: for playing along with it all and keeping a halfway straight face. Maybe it's just this house driving anyone who lives here clean off their rocker?

Like poor Daniel Ranelagh, she thought, tantalised once again by the idea of this mysterious 'black sheep' of an aristocratic family. She imagined him roaming the grounds of Collingwood, tortured and broodingly poetic in his eccentric clothes, just waiting for the right, willing woman to alleviate his sufferings.

Don't be bloody ridiculous! she told herself, already halfway to seducing him in her mind. The intriguing figure she'd seen watching her might not actually *be* Daniel Ranelagh. The real misplaced scion of the Ranelagh family might be a hideous, sexually inept chinless wonder who lived a solitary life for a good reason. Which was because he was a geek!

Even so, she couldn't turn off her romantic imaginings. Pictures of sex with a delicious, dark misfit in a dappled woodland grove.

What am I doing? she asked herself, looking out of the window and watching the moon sail high amongst some thin and scrappy cloud. Aren't I supposed to be having pure, clean, non-inflammatory thoughts instead of lurid sexual fantasies?

Although why she should curb her natural tendencies, when she was as sure as hell that Nicholas wasn't curbing his, was a fascinating question. Shifting uncomfortably beneath the cool, laundry-fresh sheets, she wondered if he'd meant what he said, then wondered if she'd even just imagined him saying it. The tableau back in the dining room had certainly been bizarre enough.

She seemed to remember Jamie sitting and watching smugly while she'd pushed her chair away from the table, slid off her knickers and lifted her skirt, then rubbed herself. Jamie and Nicholas, glancing complicitly at each other, both of them seeming to know as much about her sexuality, these days, as she did herself.

Despite the tumble of thoughts in her mind, and the growing ache of frustration, Christabel suddenly realised she was getting tired. Maybe it was the moon's light getting to her? Lulling her. Beckoning her to a Freudian place where she might understand her own twisted psyche and that of Nicholas.

As she closed her eyes, she seemed to see that new location. It was a dream and, though she knew that, she slid right in . . .

She was in a schoolroom. She was young again, perhaps nineteen, or at least she seemed that age. She had a woman's body but she was wearing the clothes of a girl. Green blazer, green skirt, white shirt and school tie.

My God, I'm at St Trinian's, thought the adult, dreaming Christabel, standing apart from the scene and silently laughing. This is priceless. I'm the ultimate naughty girl!

Behind her, a door swung open, and Christabel turned around to see who had joined her in this odd, private world of hers.

Three figures strode into the room, all male, all wearing the long, dark, elegant scholastic robes that teachers rarely wore these days. They were all handsome, all stern-looking, and they all had a disquieting air of purpose. Two of the faces were very familiar to her, the other less so.

'Now, Beaumont, I assume you know what you're here for,' said Mr Sutherland, standing before her desk – which was on the front row – with his subordinates at either side, flanking him.

My maiden name, thought Christabel, unable to look Mr Sutherland in the eye, but glancing first at one, then the other of his cohorts. Mr Carlton was having a hard time looking serious now, and his blue eyes had a most unscholarly twinkle. The third man was impassive but enigmatic, and had far longer hair than Christabel had ever seen on a schoolmaster. It was dark and wild, and hung in curls to his black-clad shoulders. His unknown face was gaunt and pale and beautiful, and reminded her of that of a television actor she had once had a crush on.

'I've asked Mr Ranelagh to join our little tribunal,' said Mr Sutherland, when Christabel looked back at him. 'He's very interested in my methods of pupil control. I hope you don't mind him sitting in?'

Why ask me? thought Christabel, I clearly have no say in things. Nevertheless, she nodded and hung her head. Mr Ranelagh's eyes were a brilliant, burning green.

'Very well, Beaumont, time to begin,' said Mr Sutherland crisply. Was there a hint of humour around his fine mouth? Christabel wondered. Was this a joke? An elaborate hoax? A grown-up shadowplay?

'Stand up, girl!' he went on, his voice more magisterial now. 'At the side of your desk. Hands behind your back. Let's hear about your crimes, so we can assess an appropriate punishment.'

Punishment? thought Christabel, obeying. And panicking. What were they going to do to her? These three men . . . Were they *all* going to punish her?

'I . . . I'm guilty of the crimes of lewdness and unfaithfulness,' she began, launching into a catalogue of her adult misdemeanours. It took quite some time, and her three judges asked for details.

'But why would you do such a thing? If you care for the man,' asked the newcomer, Mr Ranelagh. His voice was deep and soft and husky; a young man's voice, but still experienced.

'I don't know, sir,' said Christabel, feeling the beginnings of some very inappropriate sensations. The recital of her own sexual philanderings had excited her. 'I don't know,' she said again, 'I suppose I just couldn't help myself . . .'

'I suggest a short lecture on the finer points of self-control.' Mr Carlton's tone was round, his smile full of anticipation. 'Followed by a brisk chastisement to enforce it in the memory.'

'Ch . . . chastisement?' Christabel stammered, more astonished by the stirrings of her own body than anything else.

Mr Sutherland looked at her as if she were rather dim. 'Yes, Beaumont. A chastisement. Surely you agree that you deserve it? You've listed your own shortcomings. Your licentious behaviour . . .'

'Yes, sir. I'm sorry, sir,' she muttered, feeling yet more licentious by the second. Dire as her straits were, she was beginning to desire these black-clad men before her. Especially Mr Ranelagh, who appeared intriguing and exotic.

Lifting slightly from the deepest layers of sleep, Christabel wondered why on earth she didn't change this scenario, and make it one she was more likely to enjoy. One where she could get to know the sphynxian Mr Ranelagh a little better.

Sinking again, she looked around the schoolroom – which was bare now, apart from her own desk, and three throne-like chairs into which her inquisitors had sunk – and the observer in her laughed at her own untutored foolishness.

This *is* what you want, you ninny. Get on with it!

'Well then, Beaumont. Get on with it!' echoed Mr Sutherland. 'Remove all your clothing and be quick and neat about it!'

This wasn't school as Christabel remembered it, kicking off her shoes and tugging at her tie simultaneously. Part of her didn't relish the idea of being naked for her lecture and her punishment; but the deeper, truer part was silently cheering. She *wanted* them to see her lush breasts, her trim bottom, and the soft, abundant curls between her legs. She wanted them to see her desire – and to want her for it.

When she was naked, there seemed to be no place to tidily leave her clothing, so she just stood there, clutching it to her in a bundle.

'On the floor, Beaumont,' Mr Sutherland directed, twirling a ruler – which had appeared from nowhere – between his fingers. 'Come on! Be quick about it! Chop chop!'

As Christabel bent down to place her clothes on the dark, polished floorboards of the schoolroom, she was aware that she was presenting her bottom and her privates to the tribunal. Pushing away her crumpled blouse, she slyly widened her stance a little, so she could flex and part her thighs. She was wet now, very wet, and she wanted to display it.

'Wicked girl,' said Mr Sutherland, suddenly at her side and dragging her to her feet. 'This is a prime example of what I've been talking about ... You can't resist showing off, can you?'

But I couldn't have shown anything, if you hadn't made me take off my clothes, Christabel wanted to protest. She knew it was useless, though, and pointless. This was still a dream and the laws of logic were redundant.

To further demonstrate the perversity of his reasoning, Mr Sutherland laid his long, cool hands upon her. Holding her against him with one hand – her naked back against his immaculately suited front – he hooked his other hand beneath one of her thighs and made her lean against him, while she stood on just one leg.

'See, gentlemen,' he said, raising the captured limb and forcing her, albeit very gently, to thrust her opened vulva forward, 'see the condition of her ... The way she's wet and swollen ... She has no control over this. She constantly desires ...'

'Very true,' said Mr Carlton, rising from his seat, and approaching. 'She's actually dripping. Do you see it, Mr Ranelagh?'

'Yes. Yes, I do,' said Mr Ranelagh, joining the others, and actually sinking to his knees to observe her at close quarters. 'Her sex is vermilion ... I can almost see it twitching.'

Christabel felt tears dripping from her, as well as lubrication. Both men were crouching now, and staring at her pudenda. She had never felt so mortified in all her life; or so unequivocally and unbearably female.

Take me! Have me! And if you won't do that, just touch me or lick me or something! she wanted to cry out, wafting her crotch forward in helpless invitation.

'See? See what I mean?' said Mr Sutherland again, his voice disparaging her, while his body – with an immense hard-on – pushed her forward.

'It's unseemly,' said Mr Ranelagh.

'It's unladylike,' said Mr Carlton.

'It should be severely punished,' said Mr Sutherland, his voice like honey in her ear.

What? What now? thought Christabel, trying to regain some control over her own subconscious. Instead of lying her on her back, over the desk, and making love to her, the three men were manhandling her into position, face-down over it. She still hoped that one of them might be so overcome with lust that he would enter her from behind but, as the moments passed, the atmosphere in the schoolroom became portentous.

They would not take their pleasure now, she realised. They would do that later, possibly together, possibly apart. What they were going to do now was punish her, just as they had warned they would. All that remained now was for her to discover whether she could bear it.

But I don't know anything about this. How can I dream about it?

'Oh, don't worry, my dear,' said Mr Sutherland, her husband, as if he'd heard her, 'you will take as naturally to this as you have done, and will do, to any number of dark, forbidden pleasures ... You are a natural voluptuary, my love. You cannot help but rouse.'

'But I'm afraid!'

How true that was. A sprained wrist. A grazed knee. A burnt finger, on a saucepan. She was terrified of all pain, and cried on every occasion she was forced to endure it. It was difficult to see how it could ever excite her, but her irrational body was running counter to all her fears.

'Will you secure her, gentlemen?' Mr Sutherland said pleasantly to his companions, and Christabel trembled at visions of chains and shackles and ropes.

But that was not to be. Mr Carlton stood in front of her, gripping her wrists against the wood of the desk top; Mr Ranelagh crouched against her legs, his face just inches from her pouched and dripping sex, and held her thighs. She could not move. She could barely breathe. Her husband made ready, shucking off his gown, rolling up his sleeves.

The first blow, when it came, was both a shock and a relief to her. It hurt like hell but, to her astonishment, she relished the swelling, stinging heat, and, as more slaps fell, she raised her rump towards them.

'Wicked girl,' her husband repeated, as he whacked her wriggling buttocks, and his friends tried in vain to keep her still.

'Wicked girl,' whimpered Christabel, waking up with both her hands between her legs.

She was having an orgasm and the high bright moon was laughing . . .

Chapter Five
Yellow Light

Someone had obviously swept the terrace recently, but they hadn't done a particularly marvellous job of it. Christabel could see the imprint of brush strokes in the fine film of soil that coated the uneven flagstones. The stained, lachrymose stone angels that stood at the corners of the enclosing parapet didn't look too impressed, either.

This morning, she'd woken full of delicious, terrifying memories, and an even more disquieting sense of dislocation. The dream had seemed real; but, while it was past now, it felt like a fragment of her future. She didn't think Nicholas would go to quite the lengths that his alter ego, the donnish Mr Sutherland, had; but with him, you never could tell. He was well capable of creating such a scenario and, if he did, she didn't know whether to dread it – or long for it with all her heart.

Because, in her dream, the pain of her spanking had made her climax.

'Don't be an idiot,' she told herself, strolling past a large, white-painted wrought-iron table that was already partially laid for breakfast. 'And don't brood, either,' she added, looking around her for distraction.

It was still quite early, even though dawn was well

past, and, assessing the light, Christabel decided to make the best of it. There was a soft, almost yellowish aura to the scene, perfect for taking pleasantly touchy-feely shots of nature in all its glory. Very Edwardian Lady, she thought as she checked her camera, then descended the broad stone steps that led down to the park itself. Although, if there was anyone less like a prim, repressed female naturalist than she was, she'd yet to find them!

The grass was still damp as Christabel struck out towards the tree line, and the circle of wild, unkempt copse that surrounded Collingwood and its gardens. The legs of her jeans were soon disgustingly soggy at the hems, and her trainers squelchy, but it didn't seem to matter because her spirits felt clear and light.

Turning on impulse, she looked back at the dark, vaguely gothic silhouette of Collingwood, and raised the camera. To give the old place its due, it didn't look anywhere near as grim and forbidding in the cheerful softening light of morning. Just kind of eccentric and forlorn. A little neglected. The Honourables had clearly invested some money on the interior fittings, but hadn't had enough to spend on the exterior. Which was a shame, she thought, feeling surprised by an unexpected interest in heritage. Perhaps Nicholas could be persuaded to invest? she mused. It would all depend on how memorable this summer was for him.

She reeled off a few shots of the house, making rapid minute adjustments for each one. Patting the pocket of her baggy artist's smock, she checked that she'd brought extra film with her. In a venue as photogenic as this, she'd get through loads, and a major problem would be how to get it processed. She was a long, long way from both her own darkroom, and a reputable commercial developers.

I'll worry about all that later, she thought, capping her lens, and striding forward towards the tree line.

When she reached the copse, Christabel realised she'd

been walking with a subconscious purpose. She found herself standing on exactly the same spot that her mysterious watcher had yesterday. Once again, she turned and peered towards Collingwood.

How good had those field glasses been? Raising her camera to her eye, she extended the zoom lens to its most powerful setting. The image this produced was small, but quite big enough. With even a halfway decent pair of binoculars, the watcher – Daniel Ranelagh, she presumed – would have had a pretty good view of her antics on the window sill. There was no doubt he would've known exactly what she was doing.

Oh, my God, what will I say when I finally meet him? she thought. Then an even more worrying notion struck her. What if it hadn't been Ranelagh? There had certainly been a man here and, if it wasn't the honourable landlord, then it must have been an estate worker of some kind. A gamekeeper. Oh, Lord, what if I was doing a Lady Chatterley?

Pursing her lips, Christabel debated whether to return to the house, or go on, plunging into the darker, wilder tract of the copse beyond. The house would be safer, Nicholas and Jamie notwithstanding, because in the woods she might encounter her observer. The Honourable Daniel, or the Collingwood version of Mellors . . .

God, woman, what is the matter with you? she thought sternly, lowering the camera and turning towards the shaded woodland. You're taking everything too seriously. So what if you do meet a man? So what if you become friends, or even have sex with him? Just how fairly is Nicholas playing this game of his himself? He's got Jamie, and he's probably got him now! He's being just as unfaithful as you are!

She found herself on a path. Overgrown, almost formless in places, but a track nevertheless. She followed it carefully, dodging between handkerchiefs of golden light, listening for forest sounds as she waded through undergrowth.

Born and raised in various urban environments, Christabel suddenly wished she knew more about the country. She would've loved to be able to identify bird calls, and to recognise the different wild plants and flowers. She resolved to scour Collingwood's library for books on local flora and fauna, and perhaps even create her own record of her finds. The Country Diary of a Millennial Woman, she thought, grinning; because she certainly couldn't call herself a lady.

Nearly falling head over heels, over a straggling root, shook her out of her mood of bucolic romanticism.

Get real, Christabel, she told herself, sitting on a fallen tree-trunk to get her breath back, and check she hadn't knocked her camera. You're no chaste, tweedy country woman, and you never will be. Nicholas was joking when he suggested there might be a book in this.

Having assured herself that no harm was done – either to herself, or her precious Nikon – Christabel got up and on the move again. She'd walk for another five minutes, she decided, then she'd head back towards the house. Rural rambles were all very well, but she was already hot and sweaty, and rather muddy.

Then, without warning, she found herself in a wide, oval clearing – and laughing with delight at the strange, fey structure that stood in it.

Stone me, it's a Hansel and Gretel cottage! she thought, as she approached the homely little building. It was a kind of summer house, constructed from honey-washed stone, with a shaggy thatched roof, and a ram-shackle, low-browed veranda of weathered timber. Christabel fell instantly in love and began taking a slew of photographs. In the yellow morning light, she could almost believe the fairies had built it.

This is going to be *my* place, she informed her absent husband, making an instant decision. If Nicholas didn't know about this cottage, she wasn't going to tell him. This could be her hideaway, her secret neutral zone.

'Up yours, Nicholas, my love,' she murmured, feeling

an insane urge to giggle and make the 'V' sign. Lowering her camera, she made her way to the cottage door.

The latch operated smoothly, suggesting frequent use, and it suddenly occurred to Christabel that she was trespassing. Bedraggled as it was, this dwelling was presumably just as much the property of the Honourable Ranelaghs as Collingwood and its dower house were, and it probably wasn't included in Nicholas's lease agreement.

The cottage was pleasantly light and airy inside, due to a pale wash on the walls and several surprisingly generous-sized windows. Not really a country workman's dwelling, then, she thought. More likely a sort of rustic folly, a retreat for the idle young rich from the main house. The presence of comfortable furnishings and signs of recent habitation seemed to confirm that.

An empty wineglass stood on the scrubbed oak table and, beside it, the bottle, equally empty, that had once held a very decent vintage. There was also a square of crumpled tinfoil, scattered with crumbs, that suggested someone had eaten a packed lunch in the last day or so.

Further investigation revealed that the cottage was just the one room, with a wood store and a rather primitive lavatory around the back. There was running water, but it was cold and raised by hand pump.

Back in the living quarters, the rumpled bed drew Christabel's attention. Someone had clearly slept here lately, as the blankets were clean-looking and there was a body's indentation. When she bent towards it, she smelt the echo of a musky cologne.

Opium pour Homme, possibly, she thought. Or maybe something hand-blended, and unique, but with the same strong notes. Whatever it was, it was certainly a man's fragrance, and quite a sophisticated one. The only person she could imagine it belonging to was the Honourable Daniel Ranelagh.

But why would Daniel Ranelagh sleep here? By all accounts, he was the sole inhabitant of the dower house, so it couldn't be an issue of privacy. What would possess him to doss down in a glorified stone hut with medieval plumbing when he had a perfectly good home, all to himself, with modern amenities?

Because he's weird, that's why, she told herself, more intrigued than ever. Effortlessly, she pictured the Mr Ranelagh from her dream here in this room – even though he was purely an imaginary construct – lying on the disordered bed, his long hair spread across the pillow. An insanely funny notion suddenly occurred to her.

I bet he comes here for the same reason I'm planning to, she thought, laughing aloud as she lay down on the bed and breathed in his perfume. It's the perfect place to fantasise and masturbate.

What do you really look like, Honourable Daniel? she mused, flexing her limbs and staring up at the ceiling with its cracked and yellowing plaster. The long-haired observer of yesterday might not have been Daniel at all. The mad black lamb of the Ranelagh family might be quite conventional to look at. Short-haired and clean-cut, like Jamie, or Brad from the other night. Dear God, so much had happened since then that she could hardly remember her young conquest's face; and yet her time with him had been a catalyst of sorts. Surely she owed him more?

But Brad was the past, now – and, whether Nicholas liked it or not, Christabel had a feeling that Daniel Ranelagh might well be part of her future. She just hoped he wasn't a witless Hooray Henry with the sexual imagination of a doorstop. Once again she tried to summon a possible image of him.

Tall and dark; long-haired; gaunt and wild and pale. These were the characteristics that immediately reasserted themselves. And if he wasn't like that, she knew she'd be surprised – and disappointed.

Turning her face into the pillow, to better scent him, Christabel wondered for a moment whether her mystery man ever brought women here. It was just as perfect a spot for a tryst as it was for solitary pleasure. The bed was wide and well sprung, if a little basic. There was no reason why the Honourable Daniel hadn't had a hundred women here on this mattress, exercising a modern *droit de seigneur* over all the local beauties.

Maybe he's had Mrs Blake here? And Hester? She imagined the plump housekeeper squirming and bucking beneath the lean but still hypothetical frame of her blue-blooded employer; then she pictured Hester, doing the same, but with the gymnastic ability of youth. She seemed to hear echoes of the voices of both of the women, bouncing off the uneven, flaking walls; two different voices producing the same shrill, excited squeals.

How good a lover are you, Daniel? Christabel pondered, experiencing a sudden, tangible longing to sample him. It seemed a long, long time since she'd had straight, uncomplicated sex with a man. The last one she'd made love with in even a remotely conventional way was Brad, and even then the way she'd behaved with him hadn't been entirely normal for her. It had been as if she'd already been changing that night; as if her own actions had prefigured those of Nicholas.

But what she wanted now, she realised, was something simple and uncomplicated – rustic, if you wanted to call it that. A nice, down-to-earth, no frills fuck. The missionary position, with the lord of the manor, would suit her perfectly. Right here, in the magic cottage, her sexual refuge.

And if she couldn't have that, she would make her own amusement. Nicholas could go to hell and back and get screwed by the traitorous Jamie while he was there!

Kicking off her trainers first, Christabel unbuttoned and unzipped her tight blue jeans, then wriggled out of them, admiring the smooth, sleek shape of her bare legs as she unveiled them. She would have to take more

71

walks, and do some exercises if she were to keep in shape down here, she thought absently. There was probably no gym or health club to be found for miles and miles . . .

Not bad though, old girl, she thought, raising her legs from the bed and pointing her toes at the faded ceiling. Running her hands down the backs of her thighs, she slid them around over the curves of her buttocks, letting her fingers tentatively flick beneath her panties. She wanted to take things slowly and tantalise herself a little, not go straight for the obvious, sensitive places.

What would happen if the Honourable Daniel came in now? she wondered. How would he react to the sight of a pair of long, shapely female legs, and a rounded bottom only slightly hidden by a pair of lace knickers? Would he stiffen and want her immediately, without even so much as a civil 'how do you do?'

Visualising the scene as if through the Nikon's view-finder, she layered image upon image. Herself, thighs and buttocks presented. Daniel Ranelagh, prising his rampant member from his trousers and pushing it into her, her underwear dragged roughly aside. At the other side of the small room, Nicholas calmly watching her impalement as Jamie sucked his cock, blond head bobbing.

Dear God, it was so hot, so soon! Her resolution to linger faltered as her vulva seemed to contract and grab at nothing. Silky fluid oozed into her furrow and she felt it trickle down the groove between her buttocks. Lowering her legs, she hooked her thumbs into her knickers and pulled them off, revealing a damp patch the shape of a diamond, slowly spreading. She studied it a moment, then flung the garment on to the floor.

Spreading her thighs, she again fought to resist the *coup de grâce*. She wanted to savour these forbidden moments, all the more so because she was stealing them from two different men. Her husband, by defying his perverse dictates; and Daniel Ranelagh, by pleasuring herself clandestinely in his cottage. Taking a firm grip on the inside of her knees, she opened herself wider, thrusting up her pelvis to push her sex into greater prominence.

The sight of her own wet, red pudenda made her shudder. Seen like this, her desire was crude and blatant, without finesse. She was just a hungry maw, a distended clitoris, begging for friction.

On the point of reaching down to touch herself, and replace the caress of her eyes with that of her fingers, she froze. There were sounds outside. Unfamiliar, yet recognisable. Footsteps and the soft, vibrant tones of an unknown voice. She couldn't make out the words, but they had a strange, almost sing-song cadence, as if they were part of a reading or a drama of some kind.

Just outside the door, which was still slightly ajar, the steps faltered, but the voice went on, with more energy.

'Lady Lucinda's heart pounded in her bosom like the beating of a captive bird's wing. She saw the burning heat in McGuire's dark eyes, the insolent passion he felt for her . . . Against everything she held dear, she longed to surrender her body to him.' There was a pause, and the voice came again, but sounding quite different: 'Full stop. End chapter.' A distinct click sounded, and the unknown speaker murmured, 'Yes!'

In the portion of a second it took for the door to swing open, Christabel thought, 'My God, he's writing a romantic novel!' and, when the writer entered the cottage, he was carrying a dictaphone.

Legs akimbo, fingers almost digging into her own crotch, Christabel could not move. The newcomer was most definitely the man who'd watched her from the tree line, with field glasses, but that distant view of him had not done him any justice. He was lean, strange, young and quite beautiful; and if he was Daniel Ranelagh, he was uncannily close to the picture she'd imagined of him. He also had a scruffy, bohemian look which she supposed was very much that of an outcast writer.

Wearing a long, dark duster coat, a pair of tightish black trousers festooned with a variety of zips and buckles, and what looked like a crushed velvet T-shirt, he would have looked more at home in a London literary café than he did in the heart of the country.

So eloquent a moment ago, the young man now seemed, like Christabel herself, completely lost for words. He stared at her from across the small and claustrophobic space of the cottage, his eyes – which were an intense emerald green – locked on to her vulva. A clear sequence of emotions flickered across his pale, narrow features. She saw shock, amusement, plain, honest lust, and last, and strangest of all, a sense of recognition.

He thinks he knows me, she thought, beginning to close her thighs. And it isn't because he saw me through his field glasses.

Immediately the young man – Daniel? – launched himself forward. 'Oh, please, no, my dear!' he cried, flinging the dictaphone carelessly aside as he approached her. Before she could move again, he was on the bed, crouched between her legs, lowering his handsome face towards her naked sex.

Oh, dear Lord! thought Christabel, starting to squirm as a hot mouth pressed firmly against her sex, lips parting to allow a tongue to lick her clitoris. A couple of curling strokes brought her almost instantly to climax and, without thinking, she wound her hands in his long curly hair.

Waves of intense feeling blanked out all Christabel's questions and qualms. Her vulva leapt and pulsed and she dug her fingers fiercely into her supplicant's scalp. Nothing mattered but his tongue and the way he sucked her.

'My darling,' he murmured indistinctly against her, and the delicate air pressure produced an exquisite new sensation. Her sex-flesh rippled in another piercing orgasm.

After an indeterminate period of gasping, panting and trying to connect, unsuccessfully, with reality, Christabel felt her pleasure gently ebbing. Daniel was no longer sucking her, but simply nuzzling her with closed lips now, rubbing his entire face along the length of her, pressing occasional tiny kisses against her labia. 'My love,' he whispered repeatedly, 'my darling love . . .'

Unable to summon either the words or the will to break the spell, Christabel felt sudden, unaccountable tears fill her eyes. Whoever the woman was whose place she'd been fortunate enough to take, this man clearly worshipped and adored her. The way he handled her was supremely loving and respectful. She relaxed her hands and stroked the tangle of his hair.

Suddenly, he looked up from his affectionate ministrations and met her eyes with a strange, disjointed look. His lips, which were wet and glossy with her juices, parted as if to speak, then curved beautifully into a sweet and boyish smile.

'Look. I –' Christabel began, not really knowing what she was going to say, and glad when Daniel rose from between her legs and laid his hand lightly over her mouth.

'Hush, Eleanor, my darling, there's no need to speak . . . We have so little time. Let's make the most of it. Let's love each other.'

Eleanor?

Christabel tried again to speak, but a renewed pressure in Daniel's fingers, and a pleading, almost panicked look in his eyes kept her silent. She got a strong impression that for her *not* to be Eleanor would be agony for him.

OK, I'm Eleanor, she thought, feeling an arousing blend of fear and curiosity. This was the 'weird' man, the eccentric rejected by his father; who could know what he might be capable of if she didn't fulfil the role that he'd assigned her?

But if she was 'Eleanor', was this man really Daniel Ranelagh? Could it be that he too was playing a part? Maybe they were characters in another fiction he was planning? The next novel after 'Lucinda and McGuire' . . .

A passionate kiss silenced her cogitations. She could taste her own pungent flavour on his tongue and, though it wasn't new to her, it tasted strangely different. She didn't know Eleanor, but suddenly she became her.

'My love, who are you?' she murmured as he released her mouth and started browsing on her neck. His long hands explored her thighs in possessive strokes. 'You took me so beautifully by surprise that I can barely remember my own name, let alone yours.'

His entire body stilled and he lifted his head, looking at her worriedly for a second.

I've blown it, thought Christabel. I've spoilt it all. He's either going to be very embarrassed, or very angry, or both. And whichever it is, I could be in serious danger.

But then he smiled again, the same sweet, boyish smile, and she immediately felt safer.

'My Eleanor,' he said. 'You're trying to flatter me, aren't you?'

Ironically aware that she was playing yet another man's game, Christabel nodded, and watched Daniel's smile broaden happily. His hands slid under her top, and the light silk camisole she wore beneath it, and as he squeezed her breasts, he said, 'Well, then, my sweet? Do you recognise these? Rough, workman's hands . . . Hands accustomed to hard labour, in your husband's garden . . . Ethan Vertue's hands?'

Ethan Vertue? Who the hell was Ethan Vertue? Another book character, obviously . . .

'Of course; how could I mistake them?' she said, then gasped as he gently flicked her tumescent nipples. Completely at odds with his own description, Daniel's – or perhaps she should say 'Ethan's' – hands were soft-skinned and well kept. The hands of an aesthete or a gentleman of leisure.

'Oh, yes! Oh, God, Ethan, yes!' she moaned as he took the tips of her teats between his fingers and his thumbs. The pressure he exerted was light and delicate, distractingly perfect. She had no idea who 'Ethan' was but his erotic skills were consummate. Still working on her breasts, he leant over her again, kissing her deeply.

In the heart of her sex, passionate desire rekindled urgently. As she pushed her hips upward, trying to find some part of this strange new lover to work against, Christabel allowed her husband to surface briefly in her consciousness. She felt one quick pang of guilt, knowing she did care for him and did love him after her own fashion – but, almost as swiftly, her anarchic libido took her over.

This wasn't Christabel betraying Nicholas. This was Eleanor, who was also being unfaithful, but under different circumstances. Perhaps Eleanor's husband was cruel? A tyrant, but not in the erotic sense, like Nicholas. Whoever he was, or had been, or might be, Christabel sensed that Eleanor's husband did not deserve fidelity, and that she was entitled to the healing love of Ethan.

Feeling a lurch of sensation between her legs, she purred with pleasure. Now that the mitigation was out of the way, it was time to enjoy herself!

'Do you want me now, my darling?' enquired 'Ethan', lifting his mouth from hers, but not releasing her tingling nipples. Swivelling under him, 'Eleanor' jerked her hips in answer.

'You must tell me what you want, my love.' He tweaked and rolled the sensitised peaks. 'You must say it to me . . . Use the words. I long to hear them.'

They're not so different, after all, thought Christabel, becoming herself for a moment, and laughing softly. But it was no hardship to answer this man's simple request.

'I want you to fuck me, my dear Ethan,' she said archly, removing his right hand from her breast, raising it to her lips and kissing his fingers. 'I want you to place your cock right here inside me, and give me an orgasm.' Drawing the kissed hand down her body, she pressed it to her.

'Ethan' gave a low, surrendering moan, then stiffened his fingers so he could rub her and paddle in her wetness. 'God, you're a horny little bitch, my lady,' he murmured.

'Eleanor' laughed, then choked with surprise, unexpectedly impaled. Within the space of seconds, she was riding his right hand, her interior hot and clenching.

'And you're an insolent, provocative monster, Ethan Vertue!' she gasped, when the power of speech returned to her. 'And you still haven't fucked me!'

He drew back then, and looked down into her eyes, his own vaguely puzzled, and questioning. Christabel wondered if she'd gone to far and misjudged the mood. A moment ago, he had seemed to want her raunchy . . .

Then 'Ethan', Daniel, or whoever he was, smiled again, suddenly and broadly, making Christabel feel that the bright yellow sun had just come out inside the cottage. 'Well, I can soon put that right, my dearest,' he said, tugging off his long coat and flinging it away behind him. Within seconds the rest of his clothing had followed it, apart from a pair of tight black briefs, made of cotton, which were revealingly tented.

Laughing, he threw himself back on to the bed, and grabbed Christabel's hand. 'Oh, my, look what you've gone and done to me!' he said, pressing her fingers to his bulge.

Christabel could not help but caress him through the cotton, loving the heat and the solid, reassuring feel of his erection. There was nothing effete or imaginary about such a well-developed penis.

He made a low, growling sound in his throat, and his lean hips bucked eagerly towards her. His body was very pale, Christabel noticed, and looked strong, but there was a touch of slackness about the quality of his flesh, a minute lack of tone. He didn't have quite the same iron-clad, disciplined musculature that her husband had, but what he did have, she found strangely attractive in an almost motherly way. He even had the beginnings of a little pot belly, but that just made her want to cuddle him more.

On his peeling off of his black underpants, it was Christabel's turn to growl, at least inwardly. The Honourable Daniel's cock was a splendid object, and more than made up for any shortcomings in his general physique. Again, he did not have quite the elegant length of Nicholas, but compensation came in the form of a genuinely impressive girth.

He's going to stretch me, thought Christabel suddenly, her entire body shuddering.

'Come here, you!' she commanded him, lightly gripping his cock and urging him forward.

'Oh, God, yes!' he answered, climbing over her, and pushing up her top and camisole so he could kiss her breasts as she held him. Bucking his hips, he jabbed himself teasingly against her belly, then moved into position.

Christabel did not cry out as he entered her, even though the sensation itself was stunning. It was a wonder to her how the same basic piece of anatomy could continually surprise her. Every man felt different; every cock that possessed her felt exciting and new.

They lay still for several seconds, locked together, then Christabel flexed her inner muscles and laughed with delight as Daniel howled in response.

'Oh, dear heaven, that's exquisite!' he shouted, tossing his head and setting his long curls flying around their faces. With a mighty heave of his narrow white pelvis, he began to jerk and thrust.

Their copulation was frantic, rather mad, and completely lacking in finesse – but it was exactly what Christabel wanted. She felt as if she were being pummelled, pounded, beaten against the mattress by the plunging force of Daniel's long pale body, but within seconds she was flung up heavenward into a long, blinding climax.

'Oh please,' she heard herself whining, but her wits were so addled that she had no idea whether she was begging for more, or pleading for cessation. Daniel Ranelagh seemed to have the staying power that belied his poetish looks.

At last though, he gave a strangled shout – half muffled against Christabel's shoulder – then he shuddered and bucked in climax. Christabel clawed him, coming herself for what felt like the dozenth time, then gasped and subsided in a boneless heap beneath him.

It had all been too much, like being in a whirlwind; she had to pant for air. But, like the gentleman he actually was, Daniel quickly eased his weight off her. Giving her a smear of a kiss, he too collapsed, equally insensible, along her hot and sweaty side.

'I love you, Eleanor,' he breathed, his narrow hand drifting over her thigh for a moment, before slipping off on to the mattress.

Then to Christabel's astonishment – and her amusement – he began to snore.

Lurching abruptly out of a dream she couldn't remember, Christabel sat up and realised she too must have nodded off, moments after sex.

The light in the cottage was brighter, and more golden than ever and, after a fleeting glimpse at the sleeper beside her, she checked her watch.

Jesus wept! It was twenty past eleven!

Nicholas will be wondering where the hell I am, she thought, feeling alarm beat at her innards. The breakfast table had already been half set when she'd left the terrace, but by now her husband and Jamie would have had the opportunity to consume even the most lavish of English country house spreads. They had probably discussed her absence at great length too, and had a thoroughly enjoyable time deciding how to punish her for it.

But, as she looked again at the unconscious young man at her side, she knew that whatever penalty they imposed on her would be worth it. She could not remember the last time she had felt so free during sex. So uninhibited. In spite of the fact that they had both, apparently, been playing the role of someone else, the act itself had been relaxed and joyously natural. Not a sophisticated joust for power, the way it was with Nicholas. Or a throwaway, purely sexual interlude of rapaciousness, the way it was with the likes of Brad.

She and Daniel had shared a quickie, it was true, but there had also been a wealth of tender meaning to what had happened. A peculiar bond had been forged between them, even though they didn't even know each other yet. It seemed a dreadful wrench to have to get up and leave him.

A short while later – when she'd cringed over the archaic lavatory, washed in cold water, and dragged all her clothes back on – she stood looking down at him. She would have liked to have tapped her new lover on the shoulder, and said, 'Thank you. That was marvellous. I'm Christabel Sutherland, by the way . . .' but she was increasingly conscious of the passage of time, and she knew that what they had to say to each other could not be got through briefly.

Even so, she was still tempted to linger. Daniel – if indeed it was the Honourable Daniel Eugene Ranelagh – looked so young and tranquil lying there. He'd turned over, and was no longer snoring, and there was a smile of angelic perfection on his gauntly sculpted face. Not knowing how she knew it, Christabel got the impression that this peaceful state was something he hadn't enjoyed for quite a while. And it made her feel better about herself that it was she who'd helped him achieve it.

81

You were amazing, your sweet, randy Honourable-ness. We must do it again – although I really don't know when that will be.

With reluctance, but a good deal of haste, Christabel quietly left the cottage and began backtracking at a cautious run through the woods towards Collingwood. Once or twice, she had a close thing, and nearly tripped, but a guardian angel seemed to be looking out for her and keeping her upright. It took just a few minutes to retrace her steps and reach the open park.

Pausing for breath, she looked towards the terrace and, to her dismay, saw two figures sitting at the white-painted table, beneath a large garden parasol that had been erected in her absence. Two heads, one dark, one blond, turned uncannily in her direction. As she'd suspected, her husband was waiting for her, in the company of Jamie.

Christabel's belly fluttered.

She had no doubt they'd want a full explanation.

Chapter Six
Shades of Pink and Red

*S*lowly surfacing, Daniel squinted as the sun through the cottage window assaulted his eyes. Sometimes, when he awoke, he wished he hadn't, and that he could stay in dreams that were soft and comforting. Right now, though, he knew there was cause for optimism.

Eleanor!

No, Christabel, actually.

Had he really made love to her? It seemed he had. He was certainly naked ... And he could smell a woman's perfume, and the pungent odour of a woman's sex.

Dear Heaven, what a happening! It was wilder than anything he'd written about in even the steamiest of his novels and it had the forbidden quality of the world of Ethan and Eleanor. It had *been* Ethan and Eleanor. The edges were blurred, but in a warm and fuzzy way that was deeply soothing. He had identified with Ethan at the time, but somehow, looking back, he'd also been Daniel too. And in control of himself.

He thought back to the mad split second when he'd walked in and found himself faced with such an exquisite but unexpected sight. He'd almost flipped out, believing himself to have finally lost his grip on reality altogether; but then a surge of power and lust had brought decisiveness.

And what a decision! It had been the most lunatic gamble he'd ever taken – but it'd paid off. She hadn't rejected him. She'd played along. She'd played his game.

Oh, dear God, how marvellous she'd been! Her body yielding yet tight, and capable of the most awe-inspiring inner contortions. He felt as if she'd wrung him out like a cloth.

'Well, not quite,' he murmured, unwinding the blanket that had twisted itself around his hips, then looking down at his cock, which was surprisingly stiff and perky.

'Wow!' he breathed, touching himself in admiration. He'd had sexual intercourse for the first time in ages and, instead of knocking the stuffing out of him, it had revivified his energies. If Christabel Sutherland were to walk in again right now, he could easily be ready for her. Be up to a full, woman-pleasing stand in the space of seconds. In fact, just thinking about her had already almost done the deed.

Was I any good? he wondered. Suddenly, he wished that he could have been completely himself – Daniel, that was – that he could summon up his memories with rather more clarity.

She'd made plenty of noise, he was sure of that. Moans, cries, whimpers; they were usually reliable indicators. The women in his bodice-ripping novels always screamed and groaned with pleasure, and his publishers got nothing but letters of praise for his love scenes. Not one of his fans had ever guessed, it seemed, that 'Danielle Dangerfield' was actually a man, lived as a semi-recluse, and was mostly celibate.

But not any more, thought Daniel, closing his eyes, stretching in the shambles of the bed, and taking his penis firmly in his hand. He'd had Christabel, and Ethan

84

had had his Eleanor. He just hoped there was a way for both his 'selves' to continue to get what they wanted . . .

'Wanking again, brother dearest?' said a familiar voice from the doorway.

Daniel's eyes flew open and his fingers missed a stroke, lost their rhythm, and slipped from his cock.

'Augusta! How delightful to see you,' he said, sitting up and giving his visitor a despairing look as he flipped the blanket over his erection.

'Now, you don't really think that at all, Danny,' purred his sister, Gussie, coming across to sit on the bed and twitching back the blanket again. 'It looks to me as if you and your right hand were about to have a meaningful relationship . . .' She reached out and pressed her forefinger to the tip of his still straining cock. 'Or are you Ethan today? And this is *his* dick.'

Daniel stirred in the bed, his hips lifting automatically to Gussie's experienced touch. There was a familiar comfort in letting her handle him, an echo of their adolescent experiments. Although they'd always had the good sense not to go too far, he'd learnt all he knew about women and sex from his sibling.

'No, Gussie,' he said, letting her grip him more firmly. 'Astonishingly enough, I'm "me" today . . . and being "Daniel" hasn't felt so good in ages.'

Without releasing her hold on him, his sister studied him closely. Daniel watched as realisation dawned in her brilliant green eyes, and her lovely smile widened. Gussie was a year his junior but, with the same long, dark, curly hair and sculpted Ranelagh bone structure, he and she could almost have been twins. Although Gussie possessed an incredible pair of breasts.

'Goddamnit, Dan, you've been with a woman, haven't you?' she demanded, giving him a playful, yet also menacing squeeze.

Daniel made a soft sound in his throat, detachedly comparing the technique of his sister with that of Mrs Christabel Sutherland. Both had exceptional hands, and both knew where to grip and precisely how hard to do it. This was rapidly becoming the best day he'd had all year.

'Daniel! Give! Tell me who you've been with!' Cupping his balls, she squeezed again, this time more carefully.

Still held, Daniel sat up a little and looked into his minx of a sister's eyes. 'This isn't fair, Gus,' he said, reaching for the skimpy buttoned top she was wearing. It was soft pink cotton, and it adhered to every contour. 'I'm showing my all, and you're still covered up. Now be fair.' She didn't protest when he undid the buttons and unveiled her breasts.

'Oh, all right!' said Gussie, her exasperation clearly feigned. She released his cock for a moment, then peeled off not only her top, but her matching skirt too. Kicking off her canvas shoes left her naked, but not in any way vulnerable. Before he could stop her, she had him securely back in hand: balls firmly cupped, and a finger and thumb around his glans.

'Now, brother dearest, tell me who you've had sex with. Immediately!'

'The lessee's wife. Mrs Sutherland.'

'You dog, Dan! You absolute dog!' she cried, giving him a tweak that made him groan and jerk towards her. 'They were only supposed to be arriving yesterday, weren't they? That's incredibly fast work . . .' She hesitated, and gave him a gentler look. 'Especially for you.'

I must seem such a sad case to her, thought Daniel momentarily, feeling his mind begin to muddy.

No!

Immediately, he lifted himself towards her again, acting, rather than reacting, coaxing her into increasing the stimulation. He felt better now, and he was going to enjoy the moment!

'It *was* amazingly fast work!' He gasped as Gussie got his message and began doing the cleverest things imaginable with her fingertips. 'I was incredibly bold, though I say it myself . . .' Spreading his thighs, he lay back, admiring his sister's smooth-skinned, perfectly toned body in the detached way that had long been the custom between them.

'Do tell,' encouraged Gussie, delicately massaging.

'I took an opportunity that presented itself. Without having to think twice . . . Oh, Lord, Gus, that's good! Have you been learning some new tricks?'

'Nope,' his sister said matter-of-factly. 'It's maybe just that you're in the right mood to appreciate the old ones . . . Now come on, tell me what happened!'

'Well, I didn't have to do any seducing or anything really,' he said, trying to relax, and just accept the delicious sensations that were pooling in his pelvis. 'In fact . . . you could say . . . she just offered herself to me on a plate. She – Agh! Gus! I thought you wanted me to tell you everything? I can't tell you all the details if I'm coming, can I?'

'Sorry, bro,' said Gussie contritely, giving his penis a little pat, and then relinquishing it. 'It's just that most of the men I've had hold of recently haven't been nearly as nice as you.' She shrugged, then adjusted her position, hutching backwards to rest against the foot board. Opening her slim legs wide, she offered him a perfect view of her luscious sex nestling in pubic hair trimmed in a heart-shape. 'Let's watch each other, shall we? That way, it's easier to talk.'

'If you say so,' murmured Daniel, remembering some cherished teenage nights. 'Anyway, as I was saying,' he began, taking a grip on his own erection.

'It was a couple of hours or so ago . . . I just walked in here and found her right here on the bed. Doing what we're doing!'

'You're kidding!' said Gussie, squirming her trim bottom against the blankets, but not missing a beat of her steady rhythm between her legs.

'No, I'm not . . . She was here. Just where I'm sitting.

Stark naked from the waist down and holding her thighs wide open. She was soaking wet, too.'

'Wow, that sounds so hot,' Gussie said indistinctly. She had brought her heels in closer to her body now, and was lifting her crotch in time to the action of her fingers. Daniel's semen began to gather, ready to fly . . .

'What did you do?' Gussie's voice was faltering now.

What had he done? He could hardly remember. What the woman before him was doing was grabbing his attention . . .

Yes! That was it!

'I . . . I just dove across the bed, got down between her legs . . . and licked her. What else could I do?'

'Oh, Dan, you bastard! Oh! Oh, God!' Gussie's pelvis lifted, then jerked repeatedly, her buttocks clenching.

Daniel sobbed, 'Oh, Gussie!' then he, too, happily lost control.

'So you never actually introduced yourself?' said Gussie, taking the kettle off the little Calor stove and pouring boiling water into two old pottery mugs. She was dressed now, but still looked foxy and alluring in her tiny pink outfit. Her full breasts jiggled as she prodded each tea bag with a bent tin spoon.

'Well, no, I suppose I didn't,' replied Daniel, tucking in his T-shirt, then bending to retrieve his dictaphone from the battered old armchair where he'd thrown it. He was relieved that the device had made a soft landing. He was always breaking the damned things, or losing them. 'Although I'm sure she realised who I am,' he added thoughtfully. 'It wasn't strictly the first time we'd seen each other.'

As Gussie served him his tea, he described the vision he'd seen through his field glasses.

'Mmm . . . She sounds so absolutely my kind of person,' his sister enthused, gesturing delightedly with her teacup and nearly saturating both herself and the bed, where they were sitting. 'Do you think she goes for the female of the species, too? That would be so cool!'

For a moment, Daniel felt himself flip out, and he seemed to see a picture of two female bodies writhing. Eleanor and Christabel Sutherland? Christabel and Gussie? He didn't really know . . .

There was a snap of fingers, and Daniel flinched, glad he'd already put down his tea.

'Dan! Come back to me!' Gussie's voice was curt with alarm.

'Sorry.' Rubbing his face, he pushed his hair back out of his eyes. 'Just lost it again for a minute, there . . . What were we talking about?'

Gussie still looked concerned. She cocked her head on one side. 'Are you all right? Really, Daniel . . . Tell me.'

'Yes. I'm fine . . . Better than I've been for ages,' he said, happy that he could be honest with her. 'Must be getting my leg over at last. It's done me a power of good!'

Gussie grinned. 'Obviously,' she said. 'But what about my leg? Do you think I might get it over the sumptuous Mrs Sutherland, too?'

Daniel considered. Then nodded. 'I think you might well be in with a chance there, sis. I mean . . . She's obviously pretty uninhibited.' He reached out and stroked Gussie's cheek, then let the caress trail down to her breast. 'And you're pretty gorgeous . . .' Feeling the little crest of flesh harden to his touch, he thumbed her nipple vigorously.

'Oh, Danny, Danny, Danny . . . Don't do that! You'll get me started again.'

Daniel grinned, and continued. His sister was already swirling her bottom against the mattress. She was the most libidinous creature he'd ever encountered – with the single possible exception of Christabel Sutherland. He wondered what it would be like to see the two of them together.

'Well, you'd better do something about that, hadn't

you?' he said crisply, giving her breast a last squeeze. 'And, as I'm totally knackered for the time being –' he glanced down significantly at his groin '– and I've also got a lot of transcribing to do, you'll have to go elsewhere to get your jollies.' He shuffled off the bed and retrieved his dictaphone. 'Is your stuff back at the dower house?' Gussie nodded, idly fingering her own nipple, where Daniel had roused it. 'Right, I'm off back there now then ... Why don't you go over to Collingwood and introduce yourself? By all accounts, the husband is quite impressive, too.'

Abandoning her breast, Gussie looked at him levelly, her green eyes dark with concern. 'Why don't you come over to Collingwood with me? It might be interesting to confront your latest conquest ... See how she reacts.'

A cold hand gripped Daniel's heart and, for a moment, his hard-won confidence started to slip. Digging his nails into his palm, he quickly regained control, though. 'I'm not quite ready yet,' he said quietly, then gave Gussie a reassuring smile. 'But I might be soon. I've got a good feeling about it. Really I have.'

'So have I, Daniel,' said Gussie. Rising from the bed and standing beside him, she inclined upward and chastely kissed him on the cheek. 'So have I.'

Together they left the cottage, making a parting of the ways, then waving fondly to each other as they drew apart.

As Gussie disappeared from view, Daniel smiled to himself, and felt a rush of optimism.

He hadn't lied. He did have a good feeling: About a lot of things.

'Now what on earth do you think she's been up to?' said Nicholas, as Jamie topped up their coffee cups. It was almost noon but, beneath the parasol, out on the terrace, they were still enjoying a lazy breakfast.

The sun was high now, and benevolently brilliant. Christabel looked flushed as she strode across the grass towards them, and Nicholas had never seen her look so abundantly desirable. He had an urge to dismiss Jamie on some fabricated pretext – an Internet link be set up immediately, or whatever – then grab his wife, bend her over the parapet and thrust right into her.

It was a tempting prospect but, as Christabel came closer, something in her walk, leonine and sensual, alerted his senses. Was that luscious glow about her solely due to the sun? Or did her aura of physical awareness have other causes? Nicholas's spirits rose, as did his penis, at the prospect of discovering them.

'Mrs Sutherland looks very well this morning.'

Jamie, as always, was circumspect, but Nicholas noticed the younger man was watching his wife with close attention. Had he too seen the invisible sex-spoor on Christabel's body? The tell-tale evidence that would give him an advantage in their games?

Nicholas's mind began to seethe with possibilities. Scenarios. Seductive dispositions of his wife's fabulous flesh. Activities and arrangements to which he longed to introduce her. He felt a sudden desire for everything, all at once, but he knew he had to be patient. The gradual conditioning was equally as important as the ultimate goal.

'Mrs Sutherland looks to me as if she's had sex, in some form or another,' he said softly, experiencing a rush of delicious excitement.

He'd promised to punish her if she defied his wishes again.

'Good morning, my dear,' he said as she reached them and took a seat at the table. 'You must have been out early. Have you had any breakfast?'

'No . . . No, I haven't.'

Nicholas was glad of the tablecloth and his loose, casual trousers. There was a superb, breath-catching wariness about Christabel at the moment, that made him want to cross his legs, his cock was so swollen. She knew she'd done wrong, and it was clear she knew that he was poised to come down on her; but she was still dancing on the very cusp of freedom.

'You seem edgy, Christabel,' he remarked, enjoying the piquancy of teasing himself, as well as her. He imagined her naked, in the sunshine, ready for punishment. Her silky skin agleam with a film of sweat . . .

Dear God!

Under the guise of taking a sip of his coffee, Nicholas fought to contain his passions. He was good, indeed a past master, at projecting a cool, unruffled persona, but there were times when, just as now, the façade was difficult. The act of suppression was an arousal in itself.

'I'm all right,' his wife said. Although she was unaware of the more extreme fates his subconscious was concocting for her, it was obvious that she was gradually getting more anxious. She was fiddling compulsively with the canvas carrying-strap of her camera.

'I wonder,' he said, tearing his eyes away from her as he prepared to start the drama.

'I wonder,' he repeated, when she remained silent, 'if you have anything to tell me, my dear? Any small, inconsequential details that might have some bearing on the matters we discussed last night?'

'Oh, don't give me all that silly, oblique double-talk of yours, Nicholas,' she flashed at him suddenly, her blue eyes like summer lightning. 'If you want me to tell you what I've been doing, just ask me.' Her breasts rose and fell as she took a breath, some of her confidence obviously deserting her. 'Or *order* me to . . .'

Oh, she was wonderful. 'What have you been doing, Christabel?' he asked quietly. 'What have you been thinking?'

He could see her inner conflict on her face. In the tense lines of her body. He could see her nipples, hard and distinct, even through the substantial fabric of her smock-like top. Was she going to lie to him? he wondered. Did it even matter if she did? All he needed was a hint, to give a context.

'Shall I leave, sir?' Jamie's voice was hushed and Nicholas silently applauded the man's discretion. Clearly, the younger man was prepared to give up the chance to see a spectacle.

'No. Stay.' He reached over, and made a deliberate show of squeezing his assistant's hand, watching Christabel's eyes all the time as he did so. Her flare of interest was both exciting and revealing, and he filed the fact for future use. 'Stay,' he said again, stroking his thumb across Jamie's knuckle. 'I may need you ... This might be something you'll enjoy.'

Jamie smiled brilliantly, and shifted a little in his seat. Nicholas imagined that fine young cock getting rapidly stiffer.

'Well?' he prompted, looking at his wife's pinkening face and darting, avoiding eyes.

'I ... I've been thinking about sex. I couldn't help myself. It's only natural,' she blurted out, the colour in her cheeks increasing. 'I can't control my subconscious, Nicholas!'

'Can you not distract yourself?' he suggested silkily. 'Perhaps you could consider the beauties of nature? Read a book? Listen to some music?'

'In the middle of the night?'

'In the middle of the night, you should be asleep,' he said, 'getting your beauty sleep. Like the rest of us.' He saw her look of disbelief, and her quick glance towards his PA. Ah, but I slept alone, he wanted to tell her. Which was the literal truth, in spite of the temptation of sharing a bed with Jamie.

'I can't help myself,' repeated Christabel, shuffling in her chair again.

'"I can't help myself",' mocked Nicholas, although he couldn't keep the humour from his voice. 'Do you know what this means?' he asked. 'Do you recall our agreement?'

'Of course,' said Christabel. He saw her bite her lips.

She was afraid, but she was excited too. And as full of expectancy as he and Jamie were.

'I shall have to punish you,' he offered delicately.

'Isn't wife-beating an offence?' Her head came up with spirit.

'Oh, Christabel, Christabel, Christabel, don't be obtuse. You know full well how things are . . .' He looked her right in the eye. 'Don't you?'

For a moment, there was perfect communication between them. His wife did know, and she signalled the fact to him without giving even the most infinitesimal physical indication. Nicholas felt so elated that he understood how people could say that their hearts sang. But he too gave not the slightest sign of joy.

'I . . . I suppose so.'

'In that case, get up and take your clothes off.'

Christabel's eyes widened then, as if a real fear had suddenly kicked in. Her eyes flicked quickly to Jamie, then back to Nicholas himself, and he felt a moment of compassion for her. Even the bravest and the long-initiated felt anxiety, when they stepped up to the mark. He held her look, transmitting not only his steadfastness to her, but also his encouragement.

With exceptional gracefulness, she rose and began to strip.

Oh, God, oh, God, oh, God, I'm letting it happen again, thought Christabel as she pulled her smock off over her head and flung it to one side. I'm revealing myself to Nicholas and Jamie again – my real self, not just my body – and I'm doing it right here. Out in the sun. Where anyone can see me.

And voluntarily.

Which was the most bizarre thing of all, she realised, unlacing her shoes, then removing them and her socks at the same time. If she had chosen to back out now, Nicholas would have let her, she knew that. And yet she was proceeding, struggling out of her jeans and kicking them away, feeling the warm air on her suddenly naked legs.

This is sex, she thought as she peeled off her camisole. As valid as intercourse, but just different to it.

Sliding her thumbs into the elastic of her knickers, she considered the presence of Jamie. A threesome then, if not a conventional one. Though what was a 'conventional' threesome? She'd never had one of those either.

When her panties were off, she stood and waited. She knew what was coming, and what her role was, but the protocol, and the way to play the scene were new to her. The sun was very warm on her naked skin, and she began to sweat again. It would have been some small comfort to move in beneath the parasol, she thought, looking longingly at the shade. Her nudity would have seemed less highlighted there, but she knew instinctively that her husband would not allow that.

'I . . . I might burn.' She hung her head, not sure if she was even allowed to speak now.

Nicholas laughed, but it was a soft, young laugh, completely without malice. 'There's no doubt about that,' he said, then made a swift, imperious gesture to Jamie. 'But if you're worried about the sun, my dear, we'll proceed beneath the parasol. And Jamie will go inside and fetch some sunscreen.' The younger man nodded, then rose and went about his errand.

Christabel felt almost disappointed. 'Isn't he going to miss the fun?'

'Fun?' Nicholas looked at her steadily. He looked perfectly relaxed where he sat, but Christabel sensed that some of this was merely accomplished play-acting. 'I doubt if you'd really consider it fun, my dear.'

'Whatever,' said Christabel tightly, feeling her nerves shriek red alert as Nicholas pushed his chair back.

'Come here,' he said, making a slight curling gesture with his finger, then beginning to clear a space on the surface of the table.

Christabel's stomach did a flip. She felt weak at the

95

knees. It was one thing to talk about punishment purely as a notion, but this was the crunch, the moment of truth; it was going to happen. She moved forward but it seemed as if she were floating.

'Were you ever punished as a child, Christabel?' her husband asked as she reached him. Placing his cool hand on her lower back, he tipped her forward.

As if she'd done it a hundred times, Christabel went straight over as he propelled her. She felt like a doll; as if there were no will in her, no fight. The damask tablecloth was cool and it chafed her nipples.

She was only in her early thirties, but her childhood seemed an aeon ago. Even this morning, with Daniel Ranelagh, felt like decades past. Displaying her bottom, she was in another time and space.

Fighting for concentration, she framed an answer. 'I used to get slapped on the thighs now and again. For disobedience. And, at school, we used to get the slipper, from the prefects. They weren't supposed to do it. I think it's illegal . . . But they still did it.'

'So you're accustomed to chastisement in one form or another?'

Christabel flinched, and suppressed a moan. Nicholas was stroking his fingers up and down the crease of her bottom now, and it felt so voluptuous that she wanted desperately to wriggle. Let him do anything, she thought, anything he wants, if he'll just do this for a while. She could feel her vulva beginning to rouse and delicately moisten.

'You're aroused.' Nicholas sounded as calm as if he were commenting on the weather. 'Are you thinking about sex again, Christabel?'

She didn't know what she was thinking about, really. She was doing more feeling than thinking but, even so, she supposed it was about sex. She nodded, then jerked forward violently when Nicholas touched her anus.

'And have you been masturbating too?'

She nodded again.

'Many times?'

Christabel felt a sudden, overpowering desire to tell her husband about her strange time with Daniel Ranelagh. She got as far as opening her mouth to speak the words, then hesitated. That secret wasn't entirely hers to divulge. It was something not between Mrs Christabel Sutherland and a handsome young aristocrat, but between the mysterious 'Eleanor' and a man called Ethan Vertue. Feeling a strange boost, she closed her mouth again. But opened it on a gasp when she felt a fingertip push against her rear.

'Many times?' Nicholas repeated patiently, entering her to the first joint of his forefinger.

'Twice!' she croaked, trying to wriggle away from the intrusion, but unable to, because Nicholas had taken a firm hold on her hip with his other hand. The finger seemed to swirl a little and, despite the fact that she wasn't sure if she was going to choke or have an orgasm, Christabel understood that she was being asked another question.

'Once in bed, last night. And once while I was out walking, this morning,' she said, panting for breath as she rode the infernal stimuli. Her own fingers dragged like claws across the tablecloth.

'Tut tut,' murmured Nicholas, and the finger was withdrawn.

Christabel didn't know whether to sob with relief, or with disappointment. She had always been afraid of the way she responded to having her bottom touched, and had almost tried to resist the pleasure it gave her. But Nicholas knew the full extent of her weakness, and she felt a shudder run through her, thinking of how he might use that knowledge. How he might use *her*, when the initial punishment was over.

'Are you ready?'

She felt him adjusting his footing as if he were judging distance and force.

'Yes!' She spoke up boldly. How terrible could a few

smacks be? Her youthful punishments hadn't been particularly traumatic.

'Very well, then.'

When the first blow fell it was a stinging, jolting impact that made her cry out, 'Bloody hell!' and try to scoot across the table.

Her memory had served her badly, it seemed. The pain was fearsome and extraordinary, and it seemed to increase exponentially with each swift strike. By the time she'd taken ten she was sobbing freely, her pelvis working.

Then the spanks stopped, and Nicholas bent over her, and whispered in her ear, 'Would you like to rest a minute?'

'Can't we stop now?' pleaded Christabel, reaching around to clasp her bottom's tingling lobes. Some instinct seemed to have suggested the burning would be assuaged that way but, when she held herself, she wasn't so sure. The fire felt worse but, in a weird way, also better. 'It hurts!' she muttered, squeezing very gently.

'Don't be foolish, dear,' said Nicholas, his voice beautifully forbearing as he took her by the wrists and prised her fingers off her buttocks. 'It's supposed to hurt . . . And we've hardly started yet.' He pressed her hands flat to the tablecloth and, because she couldn't touch herself, Christabel felt compelled to wiggle her bottom.

'Keep still, Christabel,' he said, placing a hand quite forcefully on the small of her back and pressing her down, 'or everything will be much worse for you, I promise.' The words were menacing, but the tone was light and loving.

How can it be? she thought, the imposed stillness and the pressure of her pubis against the table acting like an aphrodisiac upon her. Her sex seemed to be burning in the same flames that were slowly toasting her bottom, only, down there, the fire was worse. And better. And gorgeous.

The slaps began again. Firm, focused, regular, systematic. He was setting both her buttocks alight with perfect equality. She could easily imagine their brilliant colour was uniform. The pain had certainly invaded her whole lower body.

But just when she thought she had the measure of the experience – when, although she could hardly believe it, she was actually enjoying herself – Nicholas changed tack.

The spanks moved not only from side to side now, but also up and down. First, Nicholas's palm was acting like a scoop somehow, lifting and belabouring the underhang of each bottom-cheek, then it angled another way and came down almost diagonally across her anus. And it was this particular stroke that disturbed her most. It was more severe, but it was also an incredible turn-on. She suddenly longed for the vulgar intrusion she'd feared just minutes ago.

Without warning, Nicholas stopped hitting her; and it was as if the world had also stopped turning, the very same instant. Everywhere was quiet. Even the subliminal sounds, like chirping birds and sighing trees, seemed to have been silenced. Christabel held her breath, even though she'd been panting.

Her husband's hands settled on her buttocks, making her wince. She tried not to respond too much, but it was difficult. He was gripping her hard, agitating all the mad sensations within her. She could feel each one of his fingertips individually, where it made contact with her simmering flesh. The touch was so distinct that she fancied she could almost read his fingerprints.

Then he parted her cheeks and she let out a high, sharp cry.

Oh, God! Oh, God! she thought, wailing inside, mentally pleading for the forbidden penetration. But, instead, she felt him feather his breath across her, blowing gently on the tiny, contracting hole.

The stimulation was subtle but ravishing and, before

she could contain herself, Christabel was writhing and flailing her legs. Nicholas's only response was to bear down harder and hold her firmly against the table, widening the gape of her beleaguered anus with an increase in pressure. The exposure was so maddening that the stinging in her bottom was inconsequential beside it.

'Have you ever been sodomised, my darling?' Nicholas's voice was a salacious purr as his face moved parallel to her body, almost reaching her ear. 'Have you ever had a cock inside this beautiful peach of a backside?'

Overwhelmed by a paroxysm of desire, Christabel moaned and shimmied her body against the table. Her vagina was a streaming, hungering maw, but against all reason it was her behind she wanted him to pillage. She wanted to feel his long, elegant penis forging its way into her untried rectum. No matter what the price, she wanted him to take her, to possess her last virginity.

'Christabel . . . Answer me,' he demanded, kissing her neck and, at the same time, digging his thumbs more firmly into the inner cheeks of her bottom.

'No! No, I haven't!' she whined. 'I've never done that!'

'Would you like to?' His thumbs were circling, massaging, opening and closing her.

'Oh, yes! Oh, God, yes!' she cried, torn between pushing up against the tormenting attack of his hands, and grinding downwards, to rub her pubic mound against the table.

'Are you sure?' he persisted, really going at her now, playing with her bottom and her anus as if they were his latest toys. 'It's not for the faint-hearted, my love. Believe me, I know.' He chuckled – a round, rich sound that spoke evocatively of a wealth of personal experience – and, even despite the state she was in, Christabel was astounded. She had always believed that Nicholas was the protagonist, not Jamie. Imagining her cool imperious husband as the writhing victim was simply extraordinary.

'Could you cope with it, I wonder?' he went on, still working her. 'The feeling of complete vulnerability. The violation. The terrifying belief that you're going to soil yourself, and your master, at any second. Believe me, Christabel, your innards really don't know what's happening to them ... That is, until you come so hard you think you're going to faint!'

'I can cope! Please! I want it!' said Christabel, feeling she was going to faint if she wasn't sodomised. 'Have me now, please, Nicholas ... Please do it now!'

'Shall I?' her husband said musingly, his hands stilling on her flesh. 'It would be easy enough, I suppose ... We have butter here. I could grease you up like a randy little piglet and just do you right here across the table ... Would you like that?'

'Oh, yes! Oh, God! Please!' She swirled her hips, imploring physically as well as vocally. She could hardly bear the stillness of his fingers.

'But you're supposed to be learning restraint, aren't you?' he said, lifting his hands away entirely and causing her to protest. 'I can't give you exactly what you want ... It would defeat the object, my love.' There was a wickedly convincing regret in his soft, soft voice.

'For pity's sake, Nicholas, please,' Christabel gasped. She was at her wits' end. She had to have something ... Reaching around behind herself, ignoring the heat and pain in her buttocks, she held herself open, offering him her anus.

'No, my dear, you can't have that,' he said quietly. 'Not exactly what you want ... Tempting as I find your display.'

Christabel began to cry. She hated herself for it, but she seemed to have no control over her body or her emotions. Sobbing bitterly, she continued to stretch herself open for him.

'Poor baby,' murmured Nicholas, coming up close

again, 'poor tormented baby ... Let me make things better.' Sliding one hand beneath her belly, he dug into her crotch and found her clitoris; with the other, he pushed a finger into her arse.

As her orgasm finally erupted, Christabel screamed and kicked and rolled around the table. Through the waves of pleasure, she heard the tinkling crash of china, and the rattle of cutlery tumbling on to the flagstones. The sounds seemed strangely distant, as if in another country.

The first thing she became aware of afterward was the slow, sly withdrawal of Nicholas's finger; the second was a definite sense of company. She was too spent to worry at all about the latter, though; all she could do was lie amongst the dishes and catch her breath.

'Time for a little sun now, Christabel,' said Nicholas. When he grasped her wrist and pulled her to her feet, it shocked her horribly. She felt the tears well again and her whole body begin to tremble but, with a superhuman effort, she stood up straight and held her head high. There was as little point in trying to hide the pink, orgasmic flush on her chest, as there was the spanked red soreness that covered all her bottom.

Jamie was standing just a few feet away, holding a tube of sun cream and a straw hat. His expression was awe-struck, and it seemed that, in spite of everything, he'd arrived in time for the 'fun'.

Chapter Seven
Under the High, Bright Sun

'*A*h, Jamie, just in time,' said Nicholas, his voice almost merry as he looked from Christabel to his personal assistant. 'Christabel is about to take the sun for a while, and her skin needs ... ah ... buttering up, for protection.'

Mention of butter made Christabel blush even harder, and she felt a spike of pure hatred for her husband. Being teased was far, far worse than any kind of spanking.

'I think I might go in,' she said, trying to shake off Nicholas's hold on her wrist, but not succeeding. He was gripping her like an industrial vice, although not actually hurting her.

'Surely not?' he said lightly, giving her a look that was far more steely than his tone. 'Now Jamie has gone to the trouble of fetching your sunscreen, it's only polite to stay out here and use it.'

It seemed she was to be allowed no retreat, even though she was naked and her bottom was dully throbbing. 'Just as you wish.' She stared away, across the park, towards the trees, looking for tranquillity and quiescence. 'May I at least put my underwear on?' she asked, attempting to sound unconcerned about his answer.

Although she wasn't looking at him, she sensed that Nicholas made a show of debating the question. 'I'd prefer you not to,' he said, after several moments, 'for your own good, as much as anything ... Your panties are lace; they might irritate your spanking.'

Christabel shrugged, and Nicholas let go of her. 'Well, in that case, I'd better put on some sun cream,' she said, holding her hand out towards Jamie for the tube.

'Jamie will attend to that.' Nicholas returned to his seat. 'He's a good masseur. He won't miss an inch of skin.'

I'll bet he won't! thought Christabel, looking across at her husband's young blond assistant. Jamie's hands were large, but also sensitive-looking, with tapered fingers that she could imagine getting nimbly into nooks and crannies. She closed her eyes a moment, imagining those same hands touching Nicholas.

'Stand over there, please, my dear,' said Nicholas, indicating a spot a couple of yards away, out in the sun, 'where I can get a good view of you.'

You and Jamie and the staff and anyone else who happens to be strolling by, thought Christabel mutinously as she moved into position. Even so, the idea of being displayed excited her. It took her back to that night in her studio, which had been so pivotal.

Without being told, Jamie placed the tube of sun cream on the table; then, in a deft movement, looped Christabel's hair up in a twist and covered it with the straw hat. Christabel felt ridiculous, wearing a sunbonnet whilst she was naked, but she was grateful to get the sun's rays off her head. Events were dizzying enough, without adding heat stroke.

With the same perfect efficiency that he no doubt shafted Nicholas, Jamie then commenced to coat Christabel's body with sunscreen. She felt confused and reluctantly excited, and had no idea what to do with her hands, but her awkwardness didn't faze Jamie in the slightest. His own hands first positioned her limbs assuredly, then swept and skimmed like the wings of a bird, or a butterfly. Light as it was, his touch was deep, yet had a reverence that took Christabel's breath away. The cream in itself was a sensuous experience, too: smelling deliciously of lemon and bergamot as it warmed up on her skin. Jamie spent many, many minutes applying it to each breast in turn – and, by the time he'd finished there, her nipples were like cherry stones.

Jamie took a pause, and almost thirty seconds passed with no more touches. Christabel's eyes, which had been tight shut, snapped open, and she looked across at Nicholas, just in time to see him nod to Jamie.

Christabel watched, both aghast and yearning, as Jamie loaded his hands with sun cream, then stood to one side of her, setting their bodies at right angles to one another. Nicholas nodded again, and his assistant laid his hands on her: one on her pubic mound, the other on her bottom. He didn't pause, this time, but began massaging immediately.

The pleasure was instant and massive. The heat in her bottom was a different kind of warmth now, and it blended perfectly with the tension in her vulva. Moaning, she flung her arms around Jamie's well-turned shoulders and supported herself, feeling a perverse delight that her greasy body was ruining his clothes. In a vulgar jerking motion, she rode his hands to climax.

'Not exactly what I had in mind, but there's nothing I can do about that now, I suppose.'

Nicholas's voice nudged Christabel from a stupor, and she realised she was still clinging shakenly to Jamie. His hands were still on her, too: cupping her crotch and lewdly wedged against her bottom. She could feel a finger positioned, with insulting accuracy, right on the tip of her clitoris, and there was another poised to slide into her anus. The slightest body movement and she'd be masturbated, by default. Taking the risk, she lifted her head, then gasped with feeling.

Nicholas was still sitting calmly in the shade of the

parasol. His face was expressionlessly serene, and his posture relaxed; it was only the glint of his eyes, and the fact that he was smoking one of his thin, black cheroots that gave away how moved he was by what he'd seen.

He enjoyed the display, thought Christabel, her heart dancing in her chest. It turned him on to see me handled by another man. Between her legs, a stab of fresh arousal pierced her.

And what of Jamie?

She twisted, giving vent to a slight whimper at the friction that created, then looked down the body of the man who was still touching her. The helpless bulge in the crotch of his trousers made her smile, and she would have liked to have groped him just as thoroughly as he was groping her, only she didn't think Nicholas would approve of that. He was probably reserving his assistant's erection for himself.

It didn't, therefore, surprise her when Nicholas stubbed out his cheroot unfinished, then stood up and walked across to her and Jamie. 'I've seen enough now,' he said, his voice mild, but with an edge. 'We have matters to attend to, Jamie. Arrange Mrs Sutherland over the parapet – to take the sun for a while – then meet me inside. I'll be waiting for you in the usual place.' He gave them both a significant look, then walked away.

Dumped with Jamie again, thought Christabel as her husband disappeared from view. She looked at the younger man, and he stared back at her, his expression just as neutral as his master's. For one so young, his *sang-froid* was impressive, and she wondered how he'd cope if the tables were turned. Would he blush as brightly as she had? Would he protest?

'I suppose you've had prior instructions about all this?' she challenged him, as he relinquished her privates and led her by the elbow towards the broad stone

106

parapet that surrounded the terrace. When they reached it, he turned her to face it, inclining her forward.

'Yes,' he said, pressing gently on her back. 'Mr Sutherland has acquainted me with his wishes.' The pressure became implacable and Christabel was forced to go over the warm, toasted stone. The texture was rough against her belly and her nipples, but not abrasive, and the edge was conveniently level with her pubis.

'Don't you think that the things he asks you to do are a bit weird?' she quizzed, as he took a light hold on her glowing buttocks and seemed to 'dress' her position. He adjusted her thighs and calves too, then arranged her arms straight out beside her, along the stone.

'No, not really.' He repositioned the hat on the back of her head, so it was shading the vulnerable area at the nape of her neck. 'In his place, I'd probably be doing something very similar.' He took a step away then, and Christabel sensed that he was assessing his handiwork.

'I find that hard to believe,' said Christabel tightly, as the heat from the stone began to rearouse her existing fires. She wanted to push herself against it, but her pride kept her still. 'How long am I supposed to stay here?' she demanded fractiously.

'Mr Sutherland said "a while",' replied Jamie, and Christabel sensed he was on the point of leaving.

'And how long, pray, is that?'

'You must use your own judgement, Mrs Sutherland.' He sounded as deliberately ambiguous as Nicholas now, and Christabel experienced an intense desire to leap up and slap him. 'But if you leave too soon, I don't think your husband will be all that pleased.'

'Go to hell, Jamie!' she said savagely, listening to the sound of his brisk, retreating footsteps. 'Go to hell and take my bloody husband with you!'

Jamie paused, then laughed softly, sounding more like Nicholas than ever. 'Cheerio, Mrs Sutherland.'

'Just go and screw yourself, you limp-wristed little

pervert! And the same goes for that arrogant faggot that you're shagging!'

The only reply was further laughter, fading into nothingness.

Christabel counted to a hundred. How long was 'a while'? How soon dare she get up, put her clothes on and retreat to the dubious sanctuary of her bedroom? There was nothing to stop her going now, really. Nothing except the most perverse and invisible bondage. A desire to obey the husband she'd just this minute called an 'arrogant faggot'!

What must I look like? she mused, feeling herself grow trance-like, as the high, bright sun beat down on her reddened buttocks. She imagined herself a sacrifice, an offering to some Central American solar deity. Then she giggled. Weren't they all supposed to be pure, undefiled virgins? It had been a long, long time since that had described her!

For what she supposed was 'a while', she fantasised along Amerindian lines. Envisioning bronzed warriors wearing enormous, prosthetic cocks of clay and wood, lining up to take her on the altar. But suddenly the sound of footsteps broke the spell.

For pity's sake, who is it? she thought, desperate to leap up, but also too embarrassed to. The most likely candidates were either one of the Blakes, or Hester, come to clear the breakfast things, and Christabel could have kicked herself for not remembering this sooner. If she'd had any sense, she'd have gone an age ago, and to hell with Nicholas!

The steps closed in on her and, as they did, she felt certain it wasn't either her husband or Jamie. The tread was light, almost a skip, definitely feminine.

'Er . . . Hello. Are you all right?' enquired a very beautifully articulated and strangely familiar woman's voice.

Apprehensive, and yet intrigued, Christabel steeled herself, then straightened up and turned around.

She found herself facing a young and very lovely woman of about her own height – and detecting familiarity again, but in face and body this time. The woman was slim and pale-featured, with a mass of long, dark, wildly curled hair and a soft, sweetly shaped mouth that appeared naturally crimson. She was wearing a skimpy pink two-piece and reminded Christabel very much of a certain American singing star, who was noted for her raunchy performances and barely decent costumes. But there was also another resemblance that she couldn't quite put her finger on. Either way, the handsome young woman was smiling broadly.

Christabel didn't know where to put herself. It seemed a nonsense to try and cover herself with her hands, as the newcomer had already seen everything anyway. All she could think of was to pull off the stupid hat and fling it away from her.

'I'm ... I'm sorry, you must be wondering what on earth's going on,' she said, meeting the other woman's brilliant eyes with all the insouciance she could summon. Which wasn't much. 'I don't normally greet people like this but ... Well ... It's a kind of game my husband and I are playing.' She shrugged, feeling a minute increase in confidence. 'You know how these things are ...'

'Tell me about it!' said her companion, whose smile softened, becoming deliciously complicit. 'I know quite a few chaps who like those sorts of games ... I used to play them all the time with my older brother.'

'Your brother?'

'Yes. My brother Daniel.' The other woman's expression was waggish, and her eyes amazingly green. 'Look, I'm sorry, I know who you must be, but you're probably wondering who the heck I am.' She held out a slim hand. 'I'm Augusta Ranelagh. Charmed to meet you ... Please call me "Gussie".'

'Christabel Sutherland. It's a pleasure.' Christabel put out her own hand, and they both laughed wildly.

'It certainly is, I can tell you!' said Gussie Ranelagh, still chuckling as she tracked a detailed, approving glance up and down Christabel's body.

My God, I'm being leered at by another woman! thought Christabel, feeling shockingly excited. She experienced a sudden, astounding yearning to kiss Gussie on the lips.

Dear God, what's happening to me? It's women now! Her face blushed as crimson as her bottom. 'Look,' she said, 'let me get dressed, then we can go inside and have some tea or something ... Maybe even a drink? I think I need one.'

'Amen to that!' Gussie responded cheerfully. 'But why bother to dress? You're all sticky with sun oil. You'll only spoil your clothes...' Something very naughty seemed to flicker in the emerald depths of her eyes, and she suddenly looked far more like her brother than she did the sexy American singer. 'You could take a bath and I could mix some cocktails for us to swig while you're in it.'

I'm not mistaken, and I'm not imagining things, thought Christabel, feeling her pulse race. She *is* coming on to me.

'That sounds great,' Christabel heard herself saying, as she reached for her abandoned clothing, but didn't put it on. 'A bath and some drinks would be perfect ... Exactly what I need.'

'Come on, then, let's get to it,' said Gussie, her eyes naughtier than ever.

Carrying a bundle of clothing and Christabel's camera, the two women walked into the house together. Christabel felt as if she were floating, part of yet another fantasy. She was naked yet, with Gussie beside her, it didn't bother her. She almost wanted to meet Hester or one of the Blakes.

'I hope your husband doesn't mind me turning up like this,' said Gussie, as they mounted the stairs. 'It's bad form to loiter around the old place while it's let.

Intrusion of privacy and all that, especially when your old man has paid us such a lot . . . But, after what Daniel said, I simply had to meet you.'

'You've spoken to Daniel this morning?'

They were on the landing, and Christabel stopped in her tracks. Well, at least it confirmed that the man from the cottage was the Honourable Daniel Ranelagh . . .

'Oh, yes, didn't I tell you?' Gussie took Christabel by the arm and urged her onwards. 'I saw him just before I came up to the house. At our little folly in the copse . . .' She laughed softly. 'He was in a terrifically good mood and he spoke very highly of you.'

'Oh,' was all Christabel could say, as they reached her room and Gussie threw open the door and walked in as if she owned the place. Which, of course, she did.

'This used to be my room, before we started leasing,' Gussie said, walking to the window and opening it wide. She turned around, and gave Christabel a significant look, and Christabel had a horrible feeling that Daniel Ranelagh had mentioned what he'd seen through his field glasses, too.

'It's very beautiful,' Christabel said noncommittally. 'Very comfortable . . .'

'Yes, I liked it. Even though I never actually spent a lot of time here.' Gussie had begun to prowl the room now, picking up Christabel's things: cosmetics, books, camera paraphernalia. 'We were lucky, I suppose. We were able to start letting fairly quickly after we'd spent the piddling bit of money we had to bring the place up to scratch . . . We've had some Americans and Japanese here, and they're terribly pernickety . . . But, on the whole, this has been the best idea Dan and I ever had.' She paused then, and stared very intently at Christabel, from under her eyelashes. 'Well, on the money-making front, that is.'

Christabel wanted to ask a thousand questions, yet somehow she felt constrained not to. There was a very delicate mood building between her and Gussie.

Something totally new: as alien as the new realm she was exploring with Nicholas, yet just as welcome. Fresh opportunities seemed to open up with every breath she took, yet she was aware that it was still possible to miss them.

'I feel so grungy,' she said, pushing her hair away from her face. 'I really need that bath!'

'Let me help you.' Gussie darted towards the *en suite* bathroom. 'I'll run the water while you sort out some clothes.'

'Thanks . . . You are kind,' said Christabel, smiling at her new friend as the other woman looked briefly back over her shoulder.

'Think nothing of it.' Gussie's smile was slow and seductive – unlike any other smile Christabel had ever received from a woman before.

Christabel was glad of a moment or two of breathing space when Gussie disappeared into the bathroom. Am I going to do this? she thought, sorting through the undies she'd brought from London, and looking for the prettiest items. Do I really want to make love with a woman?

Thinking how much Gussie's pink top and skirt suited her, Christabel chose pink underwear, too: a deep rose set of lace-encrusted bra and panties. She didn't give any thought to what she might wear over the lingerie; her brain couldn't seem to process further decisions. Clutching her lacy bundle, she followed Gussie into the bathroom.

The room was already redolent with the luxurious scent of jasmine. She must have put half a bottle of essence in that water, Christabel thought, her eyes drawn to the sight of Gussie bending over the side of the huge, old-fashioned white bath, stirring the perfumed water to create a mountain range of foam. The younger woman's thighs were long and sheer and sleek, disappearing under the very briefest of skirts, and Christabel didn't doubt that the revealing pose was

112

quite deliberate. Designed to set the viewer wondering whether Gussie was wearing underwear or not. Christabel thought not. Where the thin cotton jersey was stretched over Gussie's slender haunches, there was no indication at all of a visible line.

'Sorry.' Gussie lifted her shoulders as she turned and straightened up. 'I got a bit carried away with the bubble bath.'

'No problem,' said Christabel. Her skin was so sticky that Epsom Salts would have been adequate. 'I like it frothy.'

Gussie's green eyes flashed. 'Well, at least you get a bit of privacy, under the bubbles, for ... you know?' She shrugged again and made a very slight, but telling little rubbing gesture.

Christabel stared at her. Was there nothing this wild creature wouldn't bring out into the open? She realised that her surprise must have shown, because Gussie laughed.

'Well, surely you do it? If you play sex games with your husband and all ...' She gave a little shimmy, as if the thought of that delighted her. 'I certainly do. In fact, I feel very much like a little session right now.'

What does she expect me to say? thought Christabel. Go ahead. Fine by me. I'd love to watch you. Feeling her heart flutter madly beneath her breastbone, she realised how ridiculous she was being. She was behaving like a blushing, prudish matron who disapproved of anything other than the missionary position, with lights out, when she'd probably had far more experience, over the years, than Gussie herself had.

'Don't let me stop you,' she said softly, trying to sound more comfortable than she felt.

'Oh, it's all right,' said Gussie breezily. 'I'll hang on for a bit. I promised you a cocktail, didn't I?'

Christabel had forgotten about drinks, but suddenly realised she was ravenously hungry. 'I'm not sure I should be having alcohol,' she said cautiously. 'I haven't eaten anything today yet. I went out before breakfast, and then when I got back . . . well . . . I got side-tracked.'

'Don't worry, I know just the thing to sop up the booze. You just hop in here, have a good languish, or whatever –' Gussie winked broadly '– and I'll be back in two shakes with absolutely everything we need!'

Everything? What did that mean? thought Christabel as she lifted her leg tentatively over the side of the bath to test the heat of the water. It was just right, so she slid in until she was submerged up to her shoulders.

She felt tempted to just float in the moment, looking neither forward nor back. Collingwood might be miles away in both space and time from the hectic grind of London but, since she'd arrived here, her sex life had become unexpectedly complex. Nicholas. Daniel. Jamie. And soon, Gussie too, no doubt. Was this really what Nicholas had wanted? Collingwood was supposed to be an escape from temptation, but she got the definite impression he'd intended it to be just the opposite. She still couldn't believe all the things that had happened so far.

Sliding her hands beneath her, she cupped her buttocks and realised that the soreness from her spanking had almost dissipated. There was a tantalising echo of it when she gripped herself, but it wasn't pain any more; in fact, it was pleasant, and almost reassuring. She wondered what Gussie had thought of the residual redness.

Maybe she and Daniel played spanking games with each other all the time? she mused. It was a tantalising thought. She imagined beautiful Gussie yelping over her brother's knee; Daniel's long, pale hand impacting on a bottom Christabel had no doubt was as well-nigh perfect. She imagined Gussie squirming and grinding herself against the long bone of Daniel's thigh, getting closer and closer to climax with every stinging smack.

'Oh . . . Oh, please,' Christabel found herself moaning.

She too was shifting her thighs and writhing now, and her hand had gravitated, unbidden, to between her legs.

Water slopped and sloshed, and Christabel watched a tiny cloud of froth detach itself from the mass. She felt dreamily aroused, but she couldn't bring herself to rub her sex in earnest. There had been too much commotion there already today and, as there was more to come, she decided it would be prudent to try and pace herself.

'Have I missed anything?'

More water went over the edge, as Christabel withdrew her hand and turned sideways in the same motion. Gussie was standing in the doorway, holding a tray laden with drinks and food.

'I don't know what you like,' the dark girl went on, 'but Paula's done us proud. She's an incredible cook. Marvellous at baking.' Gussie set down the tray on the thick chenille bath mat, and started pointing out the various delicacies. 'Sausage rolls, cheese straws, cheese puffs, quiche wedges ... She cooks for an army and ends up eating it all herself. I suppose that's why she's got such voluptuous boobs.' Exquisitely slender herself, Gussie nevertheless loaded first one plate, then another, with a mountain of goodies, then held one out to Christabel.

'I can't eat all that in here,' Christabel protested, nevertheless feeling her stomach growl in approval.

'It's the best way!' Gussie waved the plate. 'All the crumbs go in the water and not on you.'

'I can't,' said Christabel, wondering why it should feel so embarrassing to eat in the bath after everything else she'd done. 'It just doesn't seem right.'

Gussie laughed and shook her head, but put the plate back on the tray. 'Get out and eat, then,' she said amiably, then shrugged and took a bite of a sausage roll. 'At least your hands are clean.'

Christabel sloshed her fingers around under the water, keenly aware of where they'd just been, then rose cautiously out of the foam and reached for a towel.

'Ooh, Venus emerging from the waves,' Gussie murmured, licking flakes of pastry from her fingers. She was looking directly at Christabel's crotch – and her eyes were full of a hunger that had nothing to do with baked goods.

Christabel felt herself blushing again, and wrapped up very tightly in the towel before sitting down on the large bath mat with Gussie. Taking a cheese puff from her plate, she took a diffident bite, then another when she discovered how glorious it was.

'This is fabulous,' she said, trying not to gobble. She was starving, she suddenly realised. So hungry she could've eaten everything on the tray. 'But what's that?' she said, greedily licking stray crumbs of pastry from her fingers.

'That' was a tall jug full of brilliant, almost salmon-pink fluid. Ice cubes glittered like gems in its lurid rosy depths and condensation was gathering and trickling down the glass.

'Codswallop!' announced Gussie, with aplomb.

'Pardon?'

'That's its name.' Gussie laughed again and set out two highball glasses. 'It's called "Codswallop" and it's a cocktail made from gin, Campari and raspberry liqueur, topped up with lemonade. Absolutely scrummy and nowhere near as sickly as it sounds.'

Christabel frowned. She wasn't at all sure ... She mainly drank wine, and believed that gin was married inviolably to tonic.

'Here! Live dangerously! Just try it and I guarantee you'll love it!' Gussie held out a well-filled glass towards Christabel.

Christabel hesitated, then took it and tried a tiny experimental sip.

The drink was surprisingly delicious. It was sweet, but not cloyingly so. The bitter herbal tang of the Campari seemed to cut the syrupiness of the lemonade and the fruit liqueur, and the chemical bite of gin added

116

a cleansing after-kick. Drinking more deeply, Christabel wondered exactly how strong it was. Its pleasantness on the tongue could be dangerously deceptive.

'What are the proportions?' she asked as the drink seemed to sweep through her nervous system. It was so pink, she thought. So pink and intoxicating, like Gussie in her skimpy cotton outfit.

'Oh, I don't know!' Gussie gestured blithely with her glass, spilling a little of the drink on to the bath mat. 'I just bung it in 'til it looks the right shade.' She took a sip. 'It tastes the right shade to me ... What do you think?'

'It's good. I like it,' said Christabel, licking her lips. 'I didn't expect it to be my sort of thing ... but it is.' Absorbing the taste of the drink, she became aware that she was talking about more than just a cocktail with a silly name.

'It's good to try new things,' said Gussie quietly. As if it were the most normal thing in the world, she dipped her fingers into her own glass, and held them out, dripping, towards Christabel. 'Experiment a bit,' she finished, making the most infinitesimal gesture of encouragement.

This is it, thought Christabel, leaning forward. She touched the tip of her tongue to the very tips of Gussie's fingers, tasting not the drink but the enormity of the moment. Taking one, then two and three fingers into her mouth, she began, very tentatively, to suck.

It was a strange thing to be doing with a woman, she thought, drawing harder on the three slender digits, and laving them slowly with her tongue. Men loved it, of course, because of the symbolism. But Gussie Ranelagh had no penis between her legs to refer this to. She was a woman, and she had a clitoris. An erogenous area of far greater finesse and subtlety.

And yet, as she continued to suck and salivate, Christabel could clearly see the caress was having an effect. Gussie began to sway, and her eyes closed, making her long eyelashes into tiny fans of raven-black. Her beautiful face became a mask of abandonment; she was clearly aroused. She wanted . . .

But do I want her? thought Christabel, unwilling to relinquish her new friend's fingertips, even though all trace of the cocktail was long gone.

'Ooh, yeah,' sighed Gussie, her free hand settling delicately on her own rounded breast, fingers pincering her nipple.

She's gorgeous! The realisation hit Christabel like a piledriver and, in the shock of it, the fingers slipped from between her lips. Still cradling them, she raised Gussie's whole hand back to her mouth and kissed the palm wetly and messily, sucking and licking in an instinctively more appropriate action.

'Ooh, yeah, yeah, yeah!' repeated Gussie, her green eyes snapping open and fixing on Christabel's face. She gave a slow, sultry smile and said, 'New things, eh?'

'Ooh, yeah,' said Christabel, laughing against the skin of her lover's palm.

Gently extricating herself, Gussie took hold of the hem of her soft, pink top and peeled it off over her head in a sinuous, serpentine motion. As she shook her mass of dark hair out of her face, her high breasts shook in an hypnotic rhythm.

She *is* gorgeous! thought Christabel, almost giddy that she could take pleasure in the sight of another female body without feeling threatened, or jealous, or making comparisons. She just loved the way Gussie looked. Loved the pure curves of her, the size and the thick, stubby shape of her dark nipples. Her sleek ribcage and the ideal flatness of her midriff and stomach.

'Take your skirt off too,' she heard herself order, hardly recognising the harsh, hungry note the words carried. 'I want to see everything.'

Without a sound, but with an houri-like smile, Gussie complied, again snagging fingers into a waistband, but this time tugging downward as she came up on her knees to facilitate the manoeuvre. Granting Christabel a brief glimpse of night-dark pubic hair, she then sat back down on to her bottom to wriggle the skirt off over her feet. With a twirl and a flourish, she flung the garment away, halfway across the room.

Christabel found herself staring hard at the other woman's crotch. Gussie's bush was as black as the hair on her head, and trimmed and plucked into a heart-shaped motte of exquisite neatness. It gave an impression of chastity somehow; it was sweet and maid-enly. Christabel felt like a dirty old woman, just looking at it. Gussie caught the look, and the expression, and rearranged herself.

Cleverly avoiding kicking over the cocktail jug and the plates of food, Gussie spread her legs like a centre-fold – and the impression of purity vanished. The membranes of her vulva were puffy with desire, as rosy-pink as the Campari and as silvery as the gin with her running juices.

'Now you,' she said, looking straight into Christabel's wondering eyes.

Now you . . .

Oh, dear heaven, it was so scary.

Chapter Eight
Campari Rose

*I*t wasn't as if she hadn't done it before.

Long before Christabel had walked naked before Gussie, she had played 'you show me yours' games as a schoolgirl. She even remembered sitting almost exactly like this with another sixth-former, one night in the bathroom at her boarding school. They hadn't touched each other – unless her memory was playing tricks on her – but they had masturbated: first together, then taking turns so they could watch each other.

So what was so different between the then of youth and the now of adulthood? It had seemed naughty but natural, then; now, she felt suddenly inhibited.

'Are you afraid?' Gussie's voice was soft and kind. 'Because if you are, we don't have to do anything . . .' She made a slight, ambiguous movement with her shoulders. 'It's just that you're so beautiful. And so sexy. And I can't resist you.' She put her hands down between her legs and touched herself. 'See?' She held out her fingers, showing Christabel that they were gleaming.

What's wrong with me? thought Christabel, still hesitating. She could feel her own body stirring in answer to Gussie's display and yet, somehow, she still couldn't move forward.

What do grown women do together? she thought, realising that her own ignorance was the stumbling block. She'd been with enough men, but this was another world. And she was even discovering her experience with men wasn't all she'd believed it to be . . .

Gussie's green eyes were as bright with pleading as they were with outright lust, and Christabel felt angry with herself for resisting. She wished she could step out of her own body and shake herself.

But then Gussie appeared to have a revelation. 'Don't worry, Christabel,' she said, leaning forward earnestly, her fingers still lodged in her furrow. 'There isn't a set way to do this . . . No form. No sequence of events. No pressure. Women just do what they like together. There aren't any rules.'

Christabel felt a weight lift off her. Her fingers went to the tucked under corner of her towel, and she cocked her head on one side. 'But how do you know I haven't already done this a thousand times?' she said, then laughed at Gussie's pop-eyed look. 'No! I haven't . . . I've had plenty of lovers but none of them women.'

'I thought not.' Gussie appeared to have recovered from her momentary surprise. She seemed unshakeable once more. 'And I hoped not, too. It's wonderful to be the first . . . The teacher. Although I suppose that's true for virgins of either sex.'

This is my virginity with a woman, thought Christabel, her heart welling with feeling. How wonderful that her initiatrix should be so young, and so beautiful. She couldn't imagine wanting Gussie if she'd been a brusque, clumpy-shoed, stereotypical dyke. It was narcissism, she supposed, but she wanted to make love with a woman like herself.

Unhitching her towel, she let it slide away, uncurtaining her nudity. She felt a moment of silly fear – as if Gussie hadn't seen it all before, and might not be attracted to her – then a glow of pride. Arrogance, even.

Moving around sideways to the bath, so that she was facing Gussie, she spread her thighs just as the other woman had, then tilted her pelvis to better exhibit her genitals.

Aware that her untrimmed pubic curls were bushier than the younger woman's, Christabel reached down and combed them apart with her fingers, separating the slick, spongy leaves of her labia to complete the display. As she leant back on one arm, she had never felt so exhibited, even in the wildest of her recent scenes with Nicholas. Revelation to female eyes – to desiring eyes rather than those of nurses and gynaecologists – was an entirely new dimension of disclosure. She wished she had a mirror, so that she too could see the same sight that Gussie was seeing. The membranes between her legs felt hugely engorged, and her clitoris as swollen as a hothouse fruit; she wondered if she was as wet as Gussie appeared to be, or perhaps even wetter.

'My God, Christabel, you're lush,' murmured Gussie. 'Your fanny is the same colour as the Campari . . . No! It's redder. Campari Rose . . . That's the colour I'll always imagine when I think of you.' Her fingers darted to her own vulva and, quite without embarrassment, she slowly began to rub. 'I want to touch you Christabel,' she said, her voice growing lower and less perfectly articulated as her middle finger flicked and circled, 'but I know you're still finding your way, so I'll just do myself. I'll show you what *I* like . . .' Her thick black eyelashes drooped, and she seemed to go away for a moment, into some hidden world of memory, then she opened her eyes and chuckled softly. 'It's weird,' she murmured, 'how often I end up doing this!'

About to launch herself over the precipice, and mirror what Gussie was doing, Christabel paused. Something about the younger woman's voice, some delicate edge, made her focus for a moment on Gussie's face rather than the way her fingers were ceaselessly moving between her legs.

What does she mean? thought Christabel, seeing an inkling of the complete picture even as the question passed through her mind. Not so long ago, she'd casually considered the outrageous notion that Daniel and Gussie Ranelagh might be closer, far closer, than a lot of sisters and brothers usually were ... But now, with every second that ticked past, she became convinced of it.

Gussie had spoken of games that she and Daniel had played. Had they been playing them this morning? Making love to each other? Right after Daniel had been making love to *her*? Gussie had very pointedly referred to Daniel's 'terrifically good' mood.

For a moment, the implications were so far out of Christabel's own world view that they alarmed her – then, a second later, she found that she was laughing at herself.

I'm jealous! she thought, letting her hand slip away from her body for a moment. I only met the pair of them today, and now I'm jealous of them both! Over each other!

'What is it?' said Gussie, her expression curious but unfazed. Her hand remained where it was but fell still. 'I know sex is a hoot sometimes, but what is it about it that's suddenly so amusing?'

'I'm sorry, Gussie, it's me ... I'm ridiculous,' said Christabel, pushing both hands through the front of her hair, then shaking her head. 'Here I am, sitting naked with one of the most beautiful women I've ever met, and finally realising that I really do desire her ... And what do I do?' She gave Gussie a shame-faced look. 'I start getting jealous of ... of her other lovers!'

Gussie beamed. 'Wow, that's rather flattering, actually!'

'Well, it's sweet of you to see it that way.' Christabel felt marginally relieved. 'But it's a bit rich, coming from me. Considering my own sexual peccadilloes ... I've no business getting jealous over anyone else's lovers!' She

123

reached for her abandoned glass and took a sip to cover her nervousness.

'That's good to hear.' Gussie's voice was more sultry again, more intimate, and she suddenly seemed to be a lot closer than before. 'The fact that you consider me your lover. Does that mean you'll let me touch you soon? I promise I'll tell you anything you want to hear ... If you *want* to hear it, that is? Otherwise, I promise to be as quiet as a mouse.'

Christabel considered this, still sipping cautiously. The drink was stronger than its fruity taste implied.

'I – I think I'd like to know some things,' she said at last, putting down her glass. She wanted to move closer to Gussie, and not operate by remote control any more; but, somehow, she still couldn't yet bring herself to.

Gussie gave her a long, steady look. Then she stood up in one complex, comprehensively elegant motion that made Christabel absolutely certain she was looking at someone else who either had been, or was still, a fashion model. Once on her feet, the younger woman inclined forward and held out her long, pale hand. 'Come to bed, Christabel. Come and lie with me. And I'll tell you everything.'

Leaving their picnic and the cooling bath water behind, Christabel allowed herself to be led into the bedroom. She noticed that, at some time while she'd been bathing, Gussie had turned back the bedcover, and the linen bed sheets looked excitingly cool and pristine. Gussie urged her between them, then shimmied in beside her. Sliding her arm round Christabel's shoulders, she said, 'There ... Is that all right?'

It was more than all right. Gussie's skin was smooth and soft, and the enfolding warmth of her was so strangely reposeful that Christabel felt the unfamiliar prickle of tears. She felt comforted; and, after all that had happened to her in the past few days, the embrace of a woman – even though it was new to her – felt reassuringly and peculiarly 'normal'.

'It's wonderful,' she muttered thankfully against Gussie's neck. 'Great . . . I can't think why I haven't tried this before now.' She breathed in deeply, enjoying Gussie's scent – which was basically woman, but overlaid with a subtle, spicy cologne not unlike the fragrance she'd smelt earlier in Daniel's bed. The siblings were so close that it seemed they used the same, or a very similar perfume.

'Because you were waiting for me.' Gussie's other hand came across Christabel's body and gently smoothed up and down her back. 'And believe me, sweetheart, I'm going to do everything in my power to justify that wait.'

'We don't have to rush, though, do we?' said Christabel, feeling a residual echo of anxiety as Gussie's hand settled, very lightly, on her buttock.

'No, no rush at all,' replied Gussie, shifting her hand a little further up Christabel's back. 'I didn't hurt you then, did I?' she enquired. 'I noticed that you'd been spanked . . . Is it still sore? Shall I keep my hands off your bottom?'

'No, it's not sore,' said Christabel, reaching behind her, taking Gussie's hand and reinstating it. 'I'd more or less forgotten about all that . . .' She paused, gnawing her lip, and feeling glad to be able to hide her face in the cloudy mass of Gussie's wild hair. 'It's not weird to you, is it? Spanking and such, I mean . . . You said you understood.'

'I do,' said Gussie, beginning to knead the curve of Christabel's bottom-cheek, and inducing a delight that Christabel barely knew how to master. 'I've been spanked myself many a time. In the sexual sense, that is . . .' Her strong fingertips curved inward, approaching Christabel's sex. 'And I like it. I like it a lot . . . Even if sometimes it is hellishly painful and embarrassing. In fact, the embarrassment's part of the fun for me.'

Feeling a strong urge to squirm, and to twist around and make Gussie touch her vulva, Christabel understood perfectly what the other woman was telling her.

125

Shame, vulnerability and embarrassment were intensely exciting to her now, far more thrilling than all the so-straight sex she'd coasted through over the years. Pandora's Box had opened now – and from it had sprung some new and surprising pleasures.

'Yes,' she said, 'I know exactly what you mean.'

'Bless you,' purred Gussie, rolling forward and pushing Christabel on to her back, her hand still cupping Christabel's buttock. 'Now we understand ourselves, it's time you let me kiss you!'

Kissing? Kissing a woman? Why did that seem stranger than the fact that they were in bed together? That Gussie's hand was on her bottom? Christabel was almost afraid to let it happen, and felt deeply grateful when her lover took the initiative.

Gussie's lips were firm and mobile, as strong as a man's and just as demanding. Christabel felt her own lips part compliantly for Gussie's tongue, while her arms slid naturally around the younger woman's back.

Kissing, they were breast to breast, belly to belly, pubis to pubis. The contact was complete along the whole line of their torsos. Her mouth deeply invaded, Christabel felt almost frantic with passion. She churned her hips, demanding in silence what she couldn't ask for in words.

'Open your legs, darling,' mumbled Gussie, still kissing messily and jabbing with her tongue. 'Open your legs, then you can rub your clittie on my thigh.'

Christabel complied, then almost shouted with relief at the pressure. Scissoring her legs and jerking her bottom, she rubbed and swivelled, feeling her juices spreading and smearing across Gussie's skin.

'Yes, baby, do it!' groaned Gussie, her mouth sliding across Christabel's face in a series of scrappy kisses. 'Bring yourself off on me! I want to feel you . . . I want to feel you come!'

Try and stop me! thought Christabel, feeling her hips tip upward and inward of their own accord, bringing the entire length of her quim against Gussie's thigh. As she began to rock, with all her strength, she felt Gussie set up an equal and opposite action. Without benefit of words, their movements were in synchrony – and the friction was exactly what she needed.

'Oh, God! Oh, God!' she shouted, her pelvis rearing up as she came, her ecstatic form arching convexly now, instead of curving inward. She felt Gussie grip her tightly, keep up the gorgeous pressure, ride her body like a rodeo-rider mastering a wayward mare.

'Oh, God,' whispered Christabel presently, drifting back into normal consciousness. She felt as if Gussie had mopped the floor with her. She felt totally exhausted. She felt gloriously happy and fulfilled.

'So, how was it?' enquired Gussie, who was lying beside her now. The other woman's voice sounded throaty and indulgent. 'Marks out of ten for your first time with a woman?'

'Twenty,' said Christabel, coming up on to her side, and looking down at her companion. 'But what about you? You haven't come ... Let me do something for you.'

'Bless you,' said Gussie again, looking up at Christabel from beneath heavy-lidded eyes. 'It won't take a second...' Gripping Christabel's wrist, she drew the hand down between her legs, then separated the forefinger from amongst its companions, and settled it on her clitoris. Christabel tried to rub, but Gussie said, 'Stay still!' and moved the digit herself instead.

It took just a couple of brief, light strokes. Gussie went rigid, snarled a harsh profanity, then kicked her legs and thrashed her head. A second or two later, she relaxed completely and let out a long whistle. Then she whispered, 'Wow ...' as she released Christabel's hand, and pulled her back into her arms.

'I told you it would just take a second,' she said, chuckling fondly and stroking Christabel's back.

Enjoying the gentle, non-threatening caress, Christabel

sighed with contentment. This unexpected female companionship was almost as new and special as the woman-to-woman sex had been, although the lovemaking itself had been a revelation. She would never have believed that being with someone of her own gender could feel so natural, and be so satisfying. It was just something she'd never considered until now.

'Was that enough for you?' she asked tentatively, comparing how much time and attention Gussie had invested in giving *her* an orgasm, with the brief, almost perfunctory efforts she'd been required to make. 'I mean . . . If you want more, I'm here. Just say so.'

'Don't worry, sweetheart,' replied Gussie, giving her a quick hug. 'Sometimes I prefer my jollies short, sharp and to the point. And I've already had some fun today. I don't need any more . . . For now.'

Christabel liked the sound of 'for now' but was grateful for the lack of compulsion to perform. She'd had her own share of 'jollies' for the time being, too. But she was still curious about what Gussie had got up to earlier.

'This fun,' she said cautiously. 'Was it with Daniel?'

There was a short silence, and Christabel wished she could have taken back the question. She'd spoilt things.

But Gussie continued the slow, soothing stroking.

'Yes, it was with Daniel,' she said, eventually. 'Does that bother you? I suppose it might do . . . Although it's never bothered Dan and me.'

Christabel thought for a minute. 'No, it doesn't bother me . . . I don't think I really have an opinion.' She frowned, wondering why she wasn't even a little bit repulsed. 'If anything, I find it exciting rather than alarming,' she finished, voicing her sudden and most powerful impression.

'Good. I'm glad you're cool with it,' said Gussie, sitting up, her hand settling comfortably on Christabel's waist. 'You're one of the very few people who knows . . . actually –' she hesitated, looking down on Christabel, her mass of black curls a bizarre halo in the sunlight that streamed in through the window '– and it's something I've wanted to talk about for quite a while now.'

'Go ahead,' said Christabel, sitting up too. 'You did say you were going to tell me everything.'

Gussie laughed. 'So I did, before I got side-tracked . . .' She grabbed the counterpane and flipped it up. 'And I will when I've had a pee and we've got some more food and drinks. I'm starving, now, and so must you be if you didn't get any breakfast.'

Christabel hung back. 'OK. That sounds good . . . I need to use the bathroom too, but you go first.'

'Oh, come on, Miss Prissy,' cried Gussie, taking hold of Christabel's hand and drawing her up naked from the bed. 'There're no secrets from Gussie, now, you know . . . This is just like school. We're all girls together, here.'

Dubious, but excited nevertheless, Christabel followed her. She didn't know where to look when Gussie blithely sat down on the big throne-like toilet, and she blushed pinker than at any time previously on hearing the urine splash and tinkle.

'Now come on, girl,' said Gussie, giving Christabel a sly sideways look, and wriggling provocatively, 'don't tell me that you don't think this is sexy?'

Christabel was on the point of saying 'No! Oh, no!' but then reconsidered. Gussie looked extraordinarily cute and brazen just sitting there, peeing, and, though she didn't want to admit it, Christabel found herself thinking of what had happened only a few nights ago, with Jamie. Looking back on it, she felt a jolt of sharp desire.

'OK, I do,' she admitted, laughing. 'As you say . . . It's always good to try new things.'

'Right then, your turn!' Gussie announced, jumping to her feet after neatly wiping her crotch. 'You said you need to go.'

It was true, Christabel realised. Very true. After

drinking Gussie's Codswallop, and having her bladder irritated by vigorous sexual activity, she really did need to urinate urgently – but she had some doubts as to whether she could perform with a lover present.

'Come on. Don't be shy with me,' said Gussie, leading her forward and installing her, with some reverence, on the throne.

Christabel felt her urethra close, and heat surge through her face and neck and chest. 'I can't go,' she whimpered, feeling as if she'd been returned to infant-hood by this girl who was some years her junior. 'I want to go, but I can't . . .' She felt pathetic.

'Hey! Relax! Don't worry . . .' As she spoke, Gussie crouched down at Christabel's side, then reached deftly between her legs and began to massage the tense area around the tiny orifice.

Almost instantly, and with an uncontained gasp of relief, Christabel began to pee, the release of fluid so needed it was blissful. As her waters poured out of her she came again, but with an exquisite lightness. It lasted only an instant yet it was complete, and sweetly grati-fying. Resting her hot face against Gussie's hair, she murmured, 'Thank you.'

'You're welcome.' Gussie turned her face so that they could kiss, then withdrew her wet fingers from between Christabel's thighs. After Christabel had blotted herself, and stood up again, Gussie hauled the chain.

'We could both do with a bath now,' she said, study-ing her hand ruefully, then wiggling her fingers at Christabel, 'but I bet the water's gone cold . . .'

They sufficed with a brief wash, each sponging off the other's body with a lot of giggling and very little decorum, but eventually they were both clean and wrapped in bath towels. Loading the food and drink back on to the tray, they adjourned back to the bedroom and set out their picnic on the Persian rug beside the bed. The Codswallop was rather less strong now that the ice cubes had melted, but was lighter and more refreshing as a consequence.

'Daniel and I have always been close to each other,' said Gussie presently. 'We're a lot younger than our elder brother and sister – both of whom are crushingly boring and thoroughly approved of by Daddy – so we sort of naturally fell into being partners in crime from an early age. We were always left to our own devices ... and when sex came around, it seemed equally natural to experiment together ...' She took a sip of her drink. 'I think Daddy had suspicions about us ... Which is probably why he thinks we're such a bad lot, and has gone to great lengths to keep us out of sight and mind. He never liked Collingwood, and there were tax advantages to dumping us with it, too. I don't understand the details, and really I don't care!'

Christabel stared at the younger woman. Her own family life had been middle-class, ordinary, but happy, on the whole, as she remembered it. She and her sister had always been treated kindly, and with equality; and, though they rarely saw each other these days, their occasional meetings were always fun. She couldn't begin to imagine how damaging Daniel and Gussie's upbringing had been. It was no wonder Daniel had become eccentric. Gussie, being a woman, and emotionally stronger, had clearly coped better.

The more Christabel heard though, the more curious she felt.

'And ... and when you're both living at the dower house, do you –' the ultimate question jammed in her throat '– do you sleep together?'

Gussie looked up, over the rim of her glass, her eyes questioning. It was almost as if she were asking what answer Christabel would prefer to hear.

'*Sleep* together? Yes. Sometimes,' she said, placing heavy emphasis on the verb. 'Daniel has nightmares occasionally. He tends to get overwrought – although he's been a lot better in recent months, I must admit –

and human contact in the still of the night is reassuring.' She hesitated again, giving Christabel the impression of an inner debate. 'But if by the term "sleeping together", you mean intercourse . . . Well, no, we've never done that. Strange as it sounds, we both feel that that just isn't right, somehow.' She rolled her eyes, as if she found her own logic slightly batty. 'Kissing. Mutual fondling. Having orgasms together and discussing each other's separate sex lives in the most graphic and disgusting detail . . . That's all OK. Fabulous, even . . . But the ultimate? No. We've never wanted it.'

Christabel wasn't sure if she was relieved or vaguely disappointed. But at least it seemed to make the situation easier to discuss. And it did, somehow, do away with her own jealousy. She'd had something of each of the Ranelaghs that neither one had shared with the other.

But she still had questions. She understood Daniel's relationship with his sister, but not his relationship – or lack of it – with reality.

Gussie pre-empted her.

'I suppose you're a bit curious about Daniel's other, what you might call, "peculiarities"?'

'Yes, I am . . . But if it's not something that you and he talk about, please don't feel you have to explain anything to me,' Christabel said, denying her own intense interest.

'Well, he lives quietly, so not a lot of people are aware that he's . . . um . . . a bit different,' said Gussie thoughtfully, 'but I think he'd want you to be in the picture . . . Whatever *that* is. Anyway, fire away!'

'Well, really, I suppose I'm desperate to know who Ethan Vertue and Eleanor are,' said Christabel, taking a bite off the end of a cheese straw and barely tasting it. 'When he and I were together, earlier, he gave the impression that he believed I was someone called Eleanor and that his name was Ethan . . .' She hesitated, chewed, knowing that Gussie deserved the same hon-

132

esty she'd been so forthcoming with herself. 'It was strange. But not scary or anything. He was so totally in the role that it seemed quite natural for me to slip into a new character too. Especially when we were making love.'

She looked sharply at Gussie, fearing an adverse reaction. But there was none. The other woman's face remained tranquil, but interested.

'I never actually got around to telling him who I really was,' Christabel finished.

'Don't worry,' Gussie abandoned her loaded plate and reached across to squeeze Christabel's hand. 'My brother might be weird, and a bit doolally sometimes, but he hasn't lost contact altogether. In fact, I think that a lot of the time the whole thing's nothing more than a performance for him now . . . Artistic temperament and all that.' She gave Christabel a wolfish grin, her green eyes looking devilishly like Daniel's. 'He certainly knows who *you* are . . . And he was very specific about what a fabulous lay you are!'

'The cheeky bugger!' exclaimed Christabel, deeply flattered.

'It sounds as if you two had a pretty horny time together, actually,' said Gussie, retrieving a stray crumb of pastry from her bare leg.

'We did.' Christabel looked intently at her companion once more. 'You're not jealous, are you?'

'Goose! Of course I'm not!' cried Gussie, laughing. 'I'm *grateful* to you. Daniel hasn't had the opportunity to make love to a woman in ages, and I think that's part of what's made him act so strangely . . . Being with someone as nice as you has done him a power of good!' She leant over and gave Christabel a hug, crushing several cheese pastries in the process. 'You're the best thing that's happened to either of us in ages!'

'Thanks. I think . . .' said Christabel, brushing away crumbs when Gussie allowed her to extricate herself, 'but you still haven't explained Daniel's problems . . . or who Ethan and Eleanor are.'

Gussie's beautifully moulded face became serious. 'Well, I suppose, in some ways, you wouldn't say Daniel actually had a problem. He's sorted out a life that suits him and his foibles, and I think that, by and large, he's relatively content. It's just that, sometimes, he seems to think he's someone else.'

'This "Ethan Vertue" character?'

'Yes. That's right.'

'But why? And who is Ethan Vertue when he's all at home?'

'Was. Ethan Vertue died almost a hundred years ago,' Gussie said solemnly.

'Oh dear,' said Christabel, at a loss for further comment. Was Gussie trying to hint that there was a supernatural element to Daniel's strange belief? Christabel had never personally encountered any paranormal phenomena, but she kept an open mind, and somehow *wanted* to believe in them.

'Don't worry,' said Gussie, 'I don't think he's possessed by demons or anything. He just has a vivid imagination – which is great for him, because he's a writer and he can make up fabulous stories, right off the top of his head.' She grinned, obvious pride in her expression. 'Anyway, I keep digressing . . . The main thing is that Dan had a sort of minor nervous breakdown a few years ago, and it left him prone to fits of depression, and a bit what you might call delusional. There were a few different factors at the bottom of it, but no one thing you could pin it on . . . The ongoing bust-up with Daddy; Mummy's death; a girl that Dan was really keen on doing a bunk . . . Stuff like that. In the main, he got over it quite quickly, but then he began telling me about these fantasies he'd started having.'

'About being Ethan?' Christabel prompted.

'Yes. Ethan Vertue was a groundsman who worked

134

here at the turn of the century. A bit of a rough diamond, by all accounts. Highly intelligent, even though he had no proper education, and a gifted artist, apparently, although none of his drawings have survived. He fell in love with the lady of the house at that time, Eleanor Woodforde, and they had a mad, passionate affair . . . but her husband ended up shooting him. Or so the local lore says. The official verdict was accidental death, but you know how people like to embroider.'

'It sounds like a high drama,' observed Christabel, intrigued by the story itself as much as by the unknown characters involved. She imagined for a moment how it would be if Nicholas had chosen to mete out old-fashioned violent justice. He would have been locked away, for the rest of his life, as a serial murderer. 'How come the lady of the manor was called Woodforde when your family name is Ranelagh?' she asked.

'Oh, Eleanor was a Ranelagh by birth. She married beneath her, as Daddy would say,' Gussie said, pulling a face. 'Charles Woodforde had quite a bit of money, but it was from industry . . . "Trade". Apparently, Eleanor's father gave them the house for the same reason Daddy fobbed it off on Daniel and me. To keep them out of the way because they were a social embarrassment.'

'So what happened to the Woodfordes, if Ethan Vertue was killed?'

'Eleanor disappeared. Just upped and went one night in mysterious circumstances . . . Completely disappeared, never to be heard of again. It's not certain whether she went before Ethan was killed, and he was supposed to join her; or whether she did a runner because there was nothing to keep her here after his death. Local stories conflict.' Gussie shrugged and gave a wry smile. 'But, then again, they so often do. I'd hate to think what they say round here about Daniel and me.'

'What became of Charles Woodforde?' enquired Christabel, taking the opportunity to share the last of the watery Codswallop between their two glasses.

'He lived on alone at Collingwood, and drank himself to death. He only outlived Ethan by a couple of years.'

Christabel shuddered, feeling a cool, ghostly finger tickle her spine. 'It's a sad story, really, isn't it?' she said, looking at the other woman. 'A bit of a tragedy. No one was happy in the end.'

Gussie's smooth brow puckered. 'I don't know ... I honestly don't. Ethan obviously lost the one he loved, and died before his time, and the same thing happened, more or less, to Woodforde ... But Eleanor might have found happiness somewhere. A new life? Who knows?'

Christabel considered the idea, clutching her towel more closely around her. Without being asked, Gussie dragged the counterpane off the bed and swathed them both in it. 'There, that's better,' she said, her voice solicitous.

'But what if she didn't?' said Christabel, following her previous thread. 'What if Woodforde killed her too? And buried her somewhere in the grounds? Perhaps Ethan knew that, and that's why he had to die too?'

'Shit! I never thought of that,' Gussie said, looking genuinely alarmed. 'Maybe there *is* something in this "Ethan" thing of Dan's, after all? Maybe he's roaming the park and the copse, looking for the burial site?' She pleated a bit of the counterpane with her fingers. 'And he never goes in the house, you know ... I assumed that was because that was Woodforde's domain, and he would never allow the outdoor servants in there, but it could be because he's afraid ... Afraid of having to re-live his death somehow, just as he relives his life, outside, and in the cottage?'

It was all very bizarre, and not, to Christabel's mind, in the least bit consistent or logical. But one thing very frighteningly suggested itself.

'Maybe it's not a sham at all, Gussie?' she said in a small voice, edging instinctively closer to the younger woman for reassurance. 'Maybe he really *is* convinced that I'm Eleanor Woodforde?'

Chapter Nine
In the Warm Light of Day

'*S*ome of the time, perhaps ... Not all the time. I'm sure of it.'

Gussie's response had been ambiguous – and even now, the next day, Christabel still pondered. Was Daniel Ranelagh really delusional, or was it just, as his sister had first said, that he was highly imaginative?

As the previous afternoon had worn on, and the two women had found no reason to part, they slipped back almost playfully into lovemaking, and afterwards Gussie had spoken more about her brother. Including one fact that was both surprising and impressive.

'My God! Of course, I've heard of "Danielle Dangerfield"!' Christabel had exclaimed on hearing it. 'I've even read a couple of her books. I mean, "his" books ... This is amazing! I heard him dictating something this morning, outside the cottage. And I suppose it did sound sort of ... "tempestuous" ... But I didn't realise who he was, of course.'

When Gussie had finally left – with a promise to return soon – it had occurred to Christabel that there might be copies of Daniel/Danielle's novels in Collingwood's library. She had been just on the point of dressing and going down there to look, when she had suddenly stopped to wonder what Nicholas and Jamie were doing.

Apart from times when the conversation had touched briefly on her husband and his PA, she hadn't thought about them too much in the hours she'd been with Gussie. The experience itself had been too all-encompassing to allow much in the way of distraction. And, when it had been over, she'd felt too relaxed and replete to seek out further confrontations.

Eventually, come evening time, when renewed hunger had driven Christabel out of her room, she'd discovered what had happened to her husband from the surprisingly well-informed Paula Blake.

'Oh, he and Mr Carlton have been working, Mrs Sutherland,' the housekeeper had said, somewhat smugly. 'They've been in the library all day. Doing things with computers and the Internet and suchlike . . . They looked ever so busy when I took them in their lunch, and your husband said not to bother with a formal dinner this evening. Unless you wanted one, that is . . . He said that he and Mr Carlton would be working through, and that I should just prepare them some sandwiches.'

What the hell is he playing at? thought Christabel now, eating her solitary breakfast on the terrace, just as she'd eaten a solitary evening meal whilst watching television in the sitting room. Is this a punishment for me taking up with Gussie? Which he must know about . . .

She looked around her in the soft morning light and tried to recapture memories of what had taken place on the terrace yesterday. She'd bent over this very table to be spanked. She'd stood just over there, naked, being oiled and fondled by Jamie. She'd been bent over that parapet, displaying her bare bottom, when Gussie had found her.

It was like a scene from another lifetime, made remote by the intervention of Gussie and the revelations about

139

Daniel. Christabel still hadn't seen Nicholas at all this morning, and even the thought of him seemed obscurely distant.

She was sure of one thing, though. She couldn't believe that Nicholas and Jamie had spent all that time alone together working.

'Internet, my arse!' she muttered, chuckling to herself and reaching for more toast. The connection to her life with her husband suddenly grew strong again.

Fortified by her breakfast, Christabel felt clear-headed. After returning briefly to her room for her camera, she made her way to the library to beard her husband in his den.

I wonder if they'll be all over each other, already, she thought, then turned the handle and walked in briskly – to give them no warning.

Both men were seated at the large oak library table, with the remnants of a scratch breakfast at their elbows. Nicholas was deep in contemplation of a multi-page document, his brow furrowed, and his grey eyes intent behind his spectacles; while Jamie was typing busily at a laptop, his fingers covering the keyboard with a sure and dazzling speed.

At the sight of her, Nicholas laid down his papers, pulled off his glasses, and rubbed his eyes as if they were tired from all night working, and Jamie's hands stilled after executing a swift, automatic keystroke.

Surprised by the ordinariness of the scene, Christabel spoke sharply. 'I thought we were supposed to be on holiday? Have you two been working in here all night?' She hesitated, a little fazed by the combined intensity of both Nicholas and Jamie looking at her simultaneously. 'I asked Mrs Blake and she said you were here all yesterday, too.'

'Not *all* of yesterday,' said Nicholas as both he and Jamie rose politely to their feet. 'All work and no play makes Jack a dull boy, et cetera et cetera . . .' He exchanged a brief, expressive glance with Jamie, then zeroed back in on Christabel again. 'We have managed to find a little time for ourselves, thank you, my dear. Although when I looked for you, it seemed impossible to find *you* anywhere.'

Christabel had a sudden feeling of disquiet. Was she really supposed to have waited there on the terrace until Nicholas gave her permission to move? Was she in trouble now? His steady grey eyes seemed to suggest as much and, as they panned over her, with insulting slowness, she felt driven to fidget.

Then she mentally shook herself.

Get a grip, Christabel! This isn't the Victorian age. Nicholas doesn't own you; he isn't a tyrant or a bully, like Charles Woodforde was. If you choose to obey him, or let him spank you, it's just that. A choice. If you hadn't even wanted to come here, he couldn't have forced you.

'Oh, I got fed up of the game after a while,' she said lightly. 'The Honourable Augusta turned up all of a sudden and we got talking . . .' She gave him a straight look, hoping it seemed as insolent and unwavering as the one he'd given her. 'And you know how it is when two women get together.' Flicking her eyes momentarily to Jamie, then back again to her husband, she flashed a message.

Nicholas's eyes widened, and Christabel felt a wild urge to punch the air in triumph. Gotcha! she wanted to shout. I've given *you* a shock now. You thought you were the only one who could do that, didn't you?

Her husband's recovery, however, was immaculate. He gave no further sign of perturbation, and his face returned to that smooth, cool state that she found so perversely arousing. Christabel saluted him inwardly, and took pleasure from the fact that, across the table, Jamie was showing considerably more emotion. A victim of his own youth, he looked quite agitated.

'Yes, I can quite imagine what it is like when two women get together,' answered Nicholas suavely after a moment. 'But that doesn't do away with the fact that you left the terrace without permission.'

'But –' she began, then felt the protest die in her throat.

He was playing the game again. Still playing it. Maybe he'd always been playing it, even in the earliest days of their courtship? Feeling her heartbeat accelerate, Christabel nervously swung her camera bag on its strap, and fiddled with the ribbon on her old straw sun hat.

'Is it so difficult to remember why I brought you here?' he said, his voice lowered to a whisper. A lover's whisper, the sort she might hear while beneath him in bed, feeling his rigid penis stretch her. For a moment, she wanted to fall down on her knees and beg him for sex. Right here. On the table. With Jamie watching.

'No. No, it isn't. I just forgot . . .'

'Well, then.' He held out his hand towards her, and she thought how sophisticated and tempting he looked. A sovereign, even in jeans and a casual, fine-knit black polo shirt.

Abandoning her hat and camera case, Christabel crossed to the table and stood before her husband. She could feel her nipples puckering beneath her light voile top, and her vulva moistening against the gusset of her panties.

'How feminine you look today,' he said, laying the fingers of one hand momentarily against her cheek. The words were loaded and suggestive, and she knew that inside he was laughing. His fingers curved a little, and their eyes met and held and passed messages. He's laughing *with* me, not at me, she thought, with a sense of wonder.

'Yes,' she said, breathing in and loving the way her bra-less breasts lifted, 'I *feel* feminine . . . Perhaps that's Gussie's influence.' She touched her own fingertips to the sheer floating outfit she'd chosen to wear today, and it dawned on her that her flippant words were true.

'"Gussie?"'

'It's what Augusta Ranelagh calls herself,' she replied in a soft voice, trying to fit the pattern of dulcet, compliant femininity.

'And does Gussie make you feel *completely* female?' The hand that had touched her face slid down her body now, the backs of the fingers flirting over one hard nipple, then over her belly, then pressing gently against her crotch.

'Yes!' she said defiantly, jutting her hips forward, pressing herself against the contact.

Nicholas withdrew his hand, laughing quietly. 'Oh Christabel, Christabel, Christabel, what are we going to do with you?' He stepped away from her, giving her a look of appraisal that made her shake. She experienced a desperate sensation of need: something ancient, unreconstructed, but very powerful.

'What do you want, Christabel?' her husband said, his grey eyes strangely full of light.

He wouldn't give it to me now, even if I told him, thought Christabel suddenly, smiling inside. Even if I knew precisely what it was, and could name it.

She looked beyond the men, and their worktable, and out through the casement window to where the sun was shining. Its light was simple and straightforward and enticing. She found herself wanting that.

'I want some fresh air,' she said crisply, spinning away from Nicholas and feeling her thin skirt billow around her. 'And I'm going out to get some.' Not waiting for his response, she snatched up her camera and her straw hat and almost ran from the room, taking with her the respect that she'd seen in both men's eyes. Veiled in Nicholas's but transparently clear in Jamie's.

He wants me, she thought, cramming the straw hat on her head in protection from the already bright rays of the sun. There had been disappointment in Jamie's look as well as admiration.

She imagined the possibilities as she set out again, across the warm and fragrant turf of the park.

143

What would it be like to be with Jamie? How would he behave if their lovemaking was autonomous, undirected by Nicholas? She flashed to a fantasy of being bent over the back of the leather-covered chesterfield in the library, and shafted, with farmyard vigour, by the naked Jamie. She was still clothed, with skirt up and pants down, but he was perfectly bare and golden. His muscular buttocks tensed as he drove into her, then twitched convulsively as he grabbed her, froze, and climaxed.

'Oh, for crying out loud!' she snarled, her steps faltering. What was it about this place that filled her head with such thoughts? She'd considered herself sexual and liberated in London but, looking back, she'd been a model of continence compared to the way she felt here in the country. It must be something in the air, she mused. All that growing and ripening and burgeoning going on.

Once in the shade of the copse, Christabel felt better, and more rational. There was nothing so dreadful about what she was feeling; it was only her true nature reasserting itself. Something that her husband Nicholas understood with a perfect clarity.

Just enjoy, Christabel, she told herself. Just enjoy! Her heart seemed to lift as she picked her way along the path.

In the clearing, she found Daniel Ranelagh stretched out on an old sun lounger on the veranda of his enchanted creamy-yellow cottage.

Jesus Christ! What now? How should she greet him? Were they an item? Star-crossed lovers? Or total strangers? Perhaps they were all three, and there was a thing!

'Er . . . Hello?'

'Hello!'

Daniel's face cracked into a smile as they both spoke at the same time, and Christabel felt the irresistible urge to giggle.

'This is weird,' she said, moving towards him and holding out her hand as she succumbed to the compulsion and laughed.

With adroitness and grace, Daniel leapt to his feet and advanced to meet her. He was, as far as she could tell, wearing little more than a pair of disastrously ripped jeans. His pale chest gleamed like ivory in the sunlight, and she could almost feel it smooth and warm against her breasts again – even though it was only their fingers that made contact.

'Isn't it?' Daniel said. 'We haven't even been introduced yet.' He grinned, looking seductively young and cheerful and not in the least bit haunted and strange – apart from his lack of clothes and the straggling length of his hair. 'Daniel Eugene Ranelagh. At your service,' he said, bending over her hand and kissing her fingertips decorously. When he straightened up again, his eyes were fiery and deliciously green.

'Christabel Sutherland,' she answered, just as formally. 'Although I'm not quite sure *I* should be at *your* service this time. At least, not until we get to know one another a little better.'

She laughed again, and Daniel joined in, shaking his head in mock despair. Then, lifting her hand again, he repeated the finger-kiss with a great deal more energy and fervour.

'I do beg your pardon for yesterday,' he said, releasing her, and gesturing that she sit down beside him on the wooden step. 'As I remember it, I did leap on you in a rather peremptory manner. It wasn't a very gentlemanly thing to do, and I know I should say I'm sorry –' he gave her a sly look out of the corner of his eye '– but I'm afraid I'm not. I enjoyed myself immensely.' He frowned. 'Or at least, I think I did.'

Don't you *know*? Christabel wanted to demand, as she sat down, and put aside her hat and camera case. Then, as she looked at Daniel closely, she felt alarmed. He seemed to have drifted away somehow. He was worrying a loose thread on his tattered jeans, his eyes unfocused. She wondered, suddenly, who she was watching: Daniel Ranelagh or Ethan Vertue?

It was impossible to be angry with him, Christabel realised. Whatever Gussie's opinion on the matter was, her own instinct was that Daniel's problem – and the way it affected his emotions and his behaviour – was totally real to him. He believed in Ethan, and whether it was his own mental fabrication, or some kind of paranormal phenomenon, mattered not one whit. He was affected by it, and sometimes frightened by it, and she felt sorry for him. And with that pity came an extraordinary wave of tenderness.

'Well, I enjoyed it immensely, too,' she said, reaching out to take his hand again. 'And that's something I *know*!'

His hand closed around hers like a drowning man's grabbing at a life-raft. He looked up at her, then away again, gnawing his lip. Lifting his free hand, he rubbed his face, then combed back his hair, where it was flopping forward. He gave a gusty sigh, then shuddered as if he had a fever.

'Daniel?'

Christabel felt afraid. Afraid for his fear. She shook the hand she was holding, then chafed it as she would a swooning girl's. 'Daniel? Are you all right? What is it? Are you . . .' What the hell did one call it? 'Are you regressing? Are you becoming Ethan again?'

He took several deep breaths, his pale chest rising and falling while he slowly shook his head.

'Oh, shit! This is so embarrassing,' he said at last. 'I thought I was pulling out of all this. I seemed to be getting to be able to control it . . . But seeing you seems to have stirred things up again.' He turned to her. 'You really do look like Eleanor did, you know,' he whispered, his face whiter than ever, 'or at least how I imagine her to look . . .'

'I'm sorry,' said Christabel, still rubbing his hand.

Was she really making things worse for him? 'I'd better go,' she added, feeling a ridiculous urge to kiss his long, cool fingers.

'No!'

His face was suddenly haggard with horror, and the rising wave in Christabel suddenly crested, breaking through her in a way that was as confusing as it was powerful. She felt the tenderness she'd experienced before, but transmuted into a shocking surge of lust. It seemed inappropriate, but also irresistible. She drew Daniel's shaking hand to her breast and held it there, creating a cup of it with her own hand, making him enclose her. His green eyes grew dark as she looked into them, like emeralds seen through smoke. He licked his lips and suddenly his face was transformed too. As his fingers flexed around the soft flesh of her breast, and his thumb flicked across her nipple, she wondered again if it was Ethan Vertue who was with her. Not a scared Ethan, but one who was full of desire and confidence. When she moaned, this new creature laughed with mischief.

'Is that good?' he murmured, his thumb still circling and arousing. Her light top was no barrier whatsoever.

Christabel made a rough sound in her throat. He was caressing just her breast, and her nipple, but he was bringing her whole body burningly alight. Hot blood rushed through her face and her neck, and she felt deliciously embarrassed. How could she feel so wanton after such a simple caress? She shifted her position on the edge of the veranda, in an attempt to gain some comfort; and immediately Daniel chuckled wickedly. Looking into his knowing face, she saw a fugitive echo of Nicholas, her husband. Same power trip, different man, she thought dreamily. Maybe it was the trip itself that ultimately turned her on?

'Are you aroused?' Daniel enquired. The words were solemn, but the spaces between them filled with silent

147

mirth. 'Does my touching you this way make your cunt get wet?'

The sound of the explicit word seemed to act directly on the very organ it named. Christabel felt her vagina suddenly grab at empty air, responding to the promise in Daniel's voice, and in his body. She was desperately uncomfortable but the sensations thrilled and plagued her. As her hand dropped away from his, she made a fist – two fists – her fingernails pressing hard into her palms.

'Are you wet?' he persisted, taking her nipple between his finger and thumb and drawing on her whole breast, making it stand out like a pointed cone from her ribcage. The feeling was almost painful but, to Christabel's surprise and horror, the ache of it made her even more excited. Her clitoris twitched in its niche like a beast in its lair.

'Yes!' she gasped, not sure whether she was answering his question or applauding what he was doing to her. She wanted him to play with her other breast, too, to make it tingle and ache and, as she imagined that, she rocked against the wood beneath her.

'Very wet?' he queried, his handsome young face looking more Mephisphelean, and more like Nicholas's, by the second. And when she nodded, her throat too clogged with mounting lust to allow speech, he chuckled again and began unfastening the tiny buttons down the front of her top, using his left hand with the same deftness as he used his right. The buttons undone, he brushed aside the thin, gauzy garment and bared her unmolested breast. 'Fondle yourself,' he ordered, nodding towards her nipple.

It felt very strange to be caressing one breast at the same time her other was being handled by someone else. She began with light touches, but that didn't seem enough, somehow, so she started to pinch and tug a little harder.

'Does pain excite you?' Daniel asked, pincering her

nipple more firmly and rolling it between his fingers as if he were attempting to elongate the flesh.

Did it? She recalled the fiery electric impact of Nicholas's hand cracking against her bottom and she couldn't suppress a moan. Mauling her own breast, she tilted her pelvis so she could press the whole length of her congested sex against the wooden floorboards of the veranda. Beneath her, her skirt was soaked but she didn't care.

'Does it? Does it excite you?' Daniel prompted, his face so wild that Christabel had to look away. She felt rather afraid of him, but more so of herself. She wanted him to hurt her, and that was making her hotter and hotter.

'Yes! Oh, God, yes!' she gasped, eyes tightly closed as she rode the swell of the gathering distress.

'Oh, my beauty! My beauty!' crooned Daniel in reply, and a clearer part of Christabel's mind felt a flash of fear. This was Ethan speaking now, she sensed, not Daniel. Ethan, who was freer and more primal, perhaps, even, more cruel. But then the fear was gone, lost in a maelstrom of dark arousal.

Still gripping her breast-tip in the living clamp of his fingers, Daniel suddenly leant forward and thrust his other hand at her crotch. Burrowing with his fingers, and working the thin stuff of her skirt and her panties in between her labia, he clasped her and pressed in hard against her clitoris. Gripping her firmly, he used one finger in a fatal rhythm.

Her legs kicking madly, Christabel wailed in rapture. She experienced an orgasm so acute and so instant that she wasn't quite sure whether it, too, was a form of pain. Daniel's slim, caressing hand seemed to be crushing the very warmth of the sun against her. The pleasure was so intense she felt her head begin to swim.

When she knew what was happening again, Daniel's hands were no longer plaguing her body, and she was slumped backward against one of the veranda's sturdy uprights, one leg on the ground and the other stretched across the veranda itself. Opening her eyes, she saw that Daniel was leaning against another of the supports, both legs pointing inward, towards the cottage, across the boards. His own eyes were closed and he had one hand pressed against his groin. His face was tense and his tautly cupped fingers were moving compulsively.

Poor baby! thought Christabel, laughing within and full of fondness. Strange as the experience just past had been to her, she was sated – while the man before her suffered.

Breasts still swinging free between the opened panels of her top, she came up on her knees and moved towards him. 'Hey, you,' she said softly, placing her hand over his, 'why don't you let me do that?'

Daniel's eyes flicked open, but his expression was still distracted. For an instant, Christabel thought that he was going to shake her off and tell her that she wasn't like Eleanor at all, but then his face cleared and he let his hand slip from his crotch. The tiny action was both casual, yet provocative.

The ragged jeans Daniel wore had a button fly, but it took just an instant or two to open them up and reveal his treasure. Christabel smiled at the paradox of his underwear. Daniel might believe that he harboured the spirit of a man who had lived decades ago, but his taste in underclothes was unashamedly contemporary. His cotton thong was snowy white and designer-labelled, an incongruity that only increased his odd allure.

'How very modern,' Christabel murmured, running a fingertip along the logo-embroidered elastic that spanned his lower belly. His dark pubic hair was escaping profusely from beneath the familiar name of an Italian couturier, and the shape of the pouch was massively deformed by the erection beneath it.

Daniel looked confused again, spaced out for a moment, but then he snapped back to lucidity. 'They were a present . . . From Gussie. She likes the labels.'

'They look good,' said Christabel, hooking her fingers under the elastic, 'but they're in the way.' With an impatient drag, she pulled down the thong and his cock bounced free.

Daniel groaned and closed his eyes, the automatic jerk of his hips making the thick, reddened shaft sway enticingly. Christabel felt a moment of *déjà vu*, remembering Brad, the stud she'd been playing with when Nicholas had ambushed her in her studio, but then she forgot him. He was insubstantial, a shadow beside the complexity and layers of the troubled Daniel Ranelagh. Reaching back into his underwear, she eased Daniel's testes into the air and daylight, too, making his entire genitalia a presentation, raised to prominence by the tension of the elastic.

Oh, gorgeous, she thought, her fingers tingling and her mouth filling with saliva. His flesh was hard, yet had a quality of succulence. She wanted to lick and suck and drain him of his juiciness.

But in a minute . . .

Displayed, Daniel made a husky purring and moved his hips slowly from side to side, making his penis sway in a reciprocal action. His hands fluttered against his thighs, as if he wanted to touch himself, but felt constrained not to. He moaned again, licked his lips, then muttered, 'Please . . .' His eyelids flickered but he didn't open his eyes.

Casting around behind her, Christabel quickly found her camera bag, and took out the Nikon. Her fingers flew over the various adjustments, then she raised it to her eye, focused adroitly and began to take pictures. Pictures of Daniel's cock, bare and magnificent, in the warm light of day.

Crouching and swooping, she framed him and snapped him from many different angles; mindful always, despite her passion to capture the perfect erotic image of him, that she kept his face, and thus his identity, either out of focus, out of frame, or hidden by shadow. He wasn't Brad, or any of her other willing models, and she held him in respect.

Obviously frustrated by the delay, Daniel opened his eyes; then grinned when he saw what she was doing. 'Oh my,' he murmured, bringing up his hands as if he meant to touch himself and add another element to the subject of her studies.

'No!' instructed Christabel, lowering the camera a second and looking at him intently. Hands didn't feel right somehow . . . 'Don't touch yourself. I don't want that . . . I just want your prick.'

'My prick, eh? Is that what you usually call it?' He let his hands fall again and looked down at his own sex with what Christabel could only interpret, to her amusement, as inflated male pride.

'Prick. Cock. Penis. Shaft. Rod. Whatever.' She lifted the camera again and carried on snapping. 'A rose by any other name, and all that . . .'

Daniel laughed, and his flesh seemed to swell and stiffen even further in her viewfinder, as if he found being a sex object a potent turn-on. Christabel took yet more photographs but, after a short while, the film was done, and the camera stalled and began to rewind automatically. She reached for more film, but Daniel sat up, laid a hand on her wrist, and stopped her. With a look of great eloquence, a look that clearly said 'enough already', he silently reminded her of more urgent priorities.

Christabel laid aside the camera and knelt in front of him. His penis and his balls seemed to invite all her senses, not simply her vision. She could scent the rich, gamey aroma of aroused man; she could imagine the slick, velvety feel of him against her fingertips; she could taste him already, so fine and rich and salty. 'You're beautiful,' she murmured, reaching forward to touch his glans, and capture the fat droplet of pre-come that was balanced upon it. As she smeared the fluid over the minute aperture at the very tip of his penis, he responded with a growl, his lips drawn back.

The heat in Daniel's flesh was astounding and, as she caressed him, smoothing her thumb around the head of his cock and into the sensitive groove below it, he seemed to grow hotter and ever harder as a consequence. His eyes were tightly closed once more as she manipulated him, and she could see sweat gathering along his collar bone, and the tendons in his neck standing out like steel cords.

'Oh, God, you're killing me!' he accused her, laughter and acute arousal in his voice. 'You're killing me. Please don't stop!'

Still delicately fondling the plum-like glans of his penis, she slid her other hand lower and formed a cup around his scrotum. She felt him jerk, a primal act to protect himself, then she went on the offensive by ever so lightly squeezing him. It was barely more than holding, but she could still feel a residual tenderness in her nipple where he'd twisted and pinched it. He deserved to feel a taste of his own dark medicine.

As she commenced using both hands on him – one gently palpating his tip, and the other in a long, dragging stroke moving repeatedly up and down his shaft – Daniel began to shout at her, using impassioned praise and profanity. His hands alternately clawed at the boards beside him and wound themselves into his own hair as he tossed his head from side to side. His hips began to buck and his shoeless heels kicked against the wooden boards. The effort of not coming was a clear test of his endurance.

As more fluid oozed out of the eye of his penis, and Christabel dutifully massaged it into him, he seemed to lose his self-imposed battle to remain silent. 'Kiss me!' he ordered, his pelvis rising to invite her.

Hiding a smile, Christabel inclined forward and pressed a closed-mouthed kiss on his grimacing lips.

'Not there, you evil, tormenting whore!' he cried,

laughing again. 'There!' One hand closed momentarily around hers, over the tip of his penis.

'Are you sure?' she whispered, leaning over him, over the scene of the delicious crime, to press similarly chaste kisses first on his jaw line, then on his throat, and then on his sweating chest. 'It might have a rather drastic effect,' she murmured, planting two more kisses, one on each male nipple.

'That's what I'm counting on! For Christ's sake, do it! I want to come in your mouth!'

'Well, when I'm asked so nicely –' for a moment, she rocked back on her heels, still holding him, but at the same time suggesting she might withdraw '– how can I do anything but comply?'

Moving forward again, and looking up into Daniel's eyes, which were now open, Christabel bent right over him and touched her furled-up tongue-tip to the very end of his penis. Working as neatly and precisely as she was able, she began to worry the tiny orifice and lap his juice.

The taste was quite bland really, she thought, but nevertheless she savoured him. His desperate cries were a delicious compensation. Still holding him closely she pushed and worked and jabbed at the delicate little hole, ignoring his yelps and imprecations that she suck him. With a careful pressure beneath his glans, she kept him hovering.

I wonder who he thinks I am? she mused suddenly, flattening her tongue and starting to use it in a broader, washing action over the whole of the rounded end of him. Christabel or Eleanor? she wondered, feeling his balls begin to crawl and rise precursively. He was going to come at any second; his seed was gathering . . .

'Who am I?' she said, lifting her face just an inch or two from his penis and looking straight up at him.

At a moment when even the most rational of men would barely be able to remember their own names, let alone debate the identity of a lover they hardly knew,

Daniel looked at her with eyes of perfect clarity. There, in his emerald gaze, was a far greater knowledge of her hopes and her dreams and her nature than she herself had ever possessed. An answer was superfluous, but he gave it anyway.

'Why, you're Christabel, of course,' he said, his voice as urbane as if they had just been introduced, over champagne, at a cocktail party.

A couple of heartbeats later, he was howling like a savage as he climaxed in her mouth.

Chapter Ten
In Sepia Tone

*I*n the aftermath, over a welcome but very odd-tasting cup of tea, made with powdered milk, they told one another a little about themselves. It didn't seem at all odd that the sex should have happened first.

Even to her ears, Christabel's own story sounded at least as outlandish as Daniel's. She was just as much a rebel as he was – abandoning an academic future to become a model and a dancer, then marrying one rich, older husband after another – and it seemed that both of them were familiar with the realms of fantasy. Hers in the present; his in the past. Hers in technicolour and his in sepia tone.

'I think I could break free if I knew what had happened to Eleanor,' he said, cradling his cup and staring into it as if his answers were in there.

'But surely there are clues ... Something you could follow up on?' suggested Christabel, tasting her own tea and grimacing. 'Letters perhaps. Diaries. Eleanor's address book. Anything like that.' After the intimacy and the pleasure they'd shared, it troubled her to see him beginning to get unhappy again. She didn't know whether to be sorry for him, or to grab him by the shoulders and give him a damn good shaking.

'Oh, there is some stuff of Eleanor's. Clothes and suchlike,' he said, his brow furrowed beneath the wayward curls that were straggling forward over it. He was decently dressed now, and had put on socks and shoes and a long silk shirt with his patched and tattered jeans. 'I saw it once when I was a teenager, and Gussie and I were exploring.' For a moment, he rubbed his eyes with his fingers. 'It was probably seeing it that started this whole business ... Or at least partially ...' He sighed heavily. 'But I don't know where any of it is now. It's stored somewhere, out of the way of the lessees. Probably gathering dust up in one of the attics.'

The urge to shake him grew stronger than ever. 'Then, for heaven's sake, why don't you go and find it?' Christabel exclaimed. 'I'll help you look through the attics or whatever. I've got precious little else to do, except get into more trouble for Nicholas to use as a lever over me.' She put down her cup, having had sufficient of the dried-milk tea. 'It'd be nice to be doing something that has nothing whatever to do with him ... That would really flummox him.' She chuckled, already enjoying the challenge. 'And there's no way he'd object to you spending time in your own house ... He's not like that. He won't stand on ceremony about having paid for exclusive access, or whatever!'

'I can't go in the house.' Daniel's voice had lost all its rich timbre, all its cadence. Christabel looked at him more closely. She hadn't altogether believed Gussie's claim that Daniel couldn't enter Collingwood but, studying him now, Christabel realised it was true.

'I'll be with you, you know,' she said, aware that part of her was losing patience with him, and wishing that it wouldn't. 'And Gussie, too. We'll all search!'

'It doesn't make any difference. I can't go in there!' he said angrily. 'I get a panic attack if I step over the threshold ... I've tried and tried. I was even sick once. Helluva mess ... It would have been embarrassing if it hadn't been so ghastly.'

'But why?' Christabel heard the harshness in her own voice, and immediately felt sorry. He was white as milk again, shaking, almost having one of the attacks he described. And that was just from thinking about going in the house.

'I don't know! I don't bloody know!' He took a long breath. 'Well, not precisely . . . It's something to do with Ethan, of course. I do know that. Maybe he went into the house himself, looking for Eleanor, and that's when that bastard Woodforde shot him.'

Christabel had never had a child, or even wanted one, but, at that moment, she understood how a mother would feel, trying to reason with a beloved but irrational son. She took hold of Daniel's hands and made him look at her.

'Daniel, you are not Ethan. You can do anything you want. There are no constraints on you.'

His well-shaped mouth thinned to a stubborn line. 'I've told you. I've tried. Again and again. I just can't do it!'

'What about Gussie, then? Can't she look for the stuff for you? Surely she wants to help? I'm amazed she hasn't done anything before now.'

'She's never had the opportunity . . . The house has been let all the time, and she does have a life of her own, you know.'

'You're afraid to find out the truth, aren't you, Daniel? If it'd been me, I would've tried a damned sight harder!'

He gave her a weak smile that should have irritated her, yet didn't. She still felt cross with him, but bizarrely turned on, too. It was novelty, she supposed, because Nicholas was always so strong-willed and unwaverable.

'You've got more backbone than me, Christabel,' he said softly. 'You're powerful –' he shrugged his wiry shoulders '– no matter what kind of submissive role you play when you're with your husband.' He freed a hand, reached around, and ran his fingers down her spine.

'There's steel in there. You only submit because you want to.'

'Look, it's you we're talking about, not me,' said Christabel, enjoying his touch as she acknowledged the truth in his words. 'Have you ever considered attacking the problem from another angle? Perhaps going up to London and hiring a private detective or something, to try and trace Eleanor that way?'

Daniel pulled another of his lost-boy faces.

'Don't tell me,' replied Christabel exasperatedly, 'you can't go there, either. And Gussie's always been too busy to try!'

'Sort of . . .'

'Dear God, if you weren't such a fabulous lover, and a halfway decent writer, your Honourableness, I'd say you were one of the most pathetic specimens of humanity I've ever encountered!'

They both laughed then, the tension of the moment dissipating – only to give way to a different kind of tension. Daniel's hand began to exert pressure on her back.

'Am I really a fabulous lover?' he asked, shaking his other hand from hers so he could enfold her in his arms.

'Yes!' she said emphatically, as his mouth grew closer and closer. 'A total wimp in most departments, but first class both between and out of the sheets.'

His mouth reached hers and bore down upon it savagely, imprinting her lips with his singular, but very welcome dominance. She allowed him in, greeting his muscular tongue with hers.

After a couple of minutes battling like Titans, they broke apart, laughing again. Christabel touched a finger to her lower lip and found it tender.

'OK, you're not really a wimp,' she conceded, examining the soreness with her tongue, 'but will you let me help you find out what happened to Eleanor? Do you dare?' She watched his face closely, trying to assess the tangled feelings underpinning his current desire. 'I want to know for myself now, too. I feel I have a stake in this, and not just because of you.' She brought a hand between them, and laid it on his warm, smooth chest. 'If I look so much like this woman, I want to know what became of her.'

A kaleidoscope of feelings passed quickly across Daniel's face, his extreme closeness making the intensity of them dazzling. But, finally, he gave her a shy and cautious smile.

'Yes,' he said at last, his expression clearing and lightening.

'Yes, what?'

'Yes, you're right,' he said, prising her hand from between their bodies and lifting it to his lips so he could kiss the tips of her fingers. 'Yes, you have a right to know about Eleanor too, and, yes, it's time I faced up to my demons.' He renewed the kisses, then started slowly sucking each digit, one by one.

Christabel felt a thrill of pleasure. Not only because of the titillation of what he was doing, but because she'd finally managed to get through to him on a rational level. She wanted to reward him for these first signs of grown-up bravery, and it seemed he was already thinking along the same lines as she was.

'Before we start on any searches and investigations and what have you,' he said, then paused to suck deeply on her pinkie in a way that reminded her of another, more intimate suction, 'do you think we could possibly run over one or two of my better qualities again? You know, the thing you said was fabulous?'

'If we must,' she replied, attempting to sound as if she were indulging him, but succeeding only in revealing how much she desired him.

Daniel released her fingertip from his mouth, then rose briskly to his feet, pulling her up beside him. 'Splendid!' he said, taking her hand and turning towards the cottage door. 'But let's try it *between* the sheets this time, shall we?'

Without waiting for further comment, he led her quickly inside the cottage.

It was gone lunch time when Christabel finally returned to Collingwood, carrying copies of two of Daniel's books, and a bunch of wild flowers, as well as her camera bag. She felt physically weary, but in other ways surprisingly energised. Daniel's problem had given her a sense of purpose. She was determined to find out what had happened to Eleanor Woodforde.

Looking down at the books she held caused her to smile. *Lucifer's Mistress* and *A Brigand's Bride*. Priceless! She'd quizzed Daniel at length as to why he wrote flagrantly romantic bodice-rippers, rather than the psychological thrillers or techno-adventures that seemed more suited to a male storyteller but, what with all the distractions, she hadn't obtained a definitive answer from him. She supposed it was him having a psyche so firmly rooted in the past, and in a romantic past at that, which drove him to pen his overblown historicals.

The lurid covers suggested amusing reading within, but Christabel decided not to dip into Daniel's novels just yet. The first order of the afternoon was a shower, then she supposed she ought to find her husband, and see if he had even the slightest interest in what she'd been doing all morning. She tried to imagine Nicholas's reaction if she told him that she'd not only been to bed with Daniel Ranelagh, but that they'd also played the sort of games *he* favoured. Touching her nipples through the thin voile of her top, she seemed again to feel the burn of Daniel's fingertips.

En route to her room, she saw no sign of anybody. Nicholas, Jamie, and even the staff seemed to have vanished. The library had been abandoned, and the entire house seemed drowsy and deserted. It wasn't even worth seeking out Gussie for company, as Daniel said that, while on holiday, his sister rarely rose before noon.

With no one to rush for, Christabel took a long leisurely shower, then put on an old smudgy-printed T-shirt and pair of soft jersey shorts in thin grey marl. It was no use wearing pale, flimsy clothing for grubbing around in attics that were knee-deep in spiders and dust.

Returning to the ground floor, Christabel still found neither sight nor sound of anybody. Nicholas and Jamie could be anywhere, she supposed. The house itself was sizeable, and they might even have followed her example and gone walking. Dismissing that idea, she thought about knocking on either one of their bedroom doors, but then decided this wasn't the moment for confrontation. She didn't feel like games this afternoon.

Ending up in the kitchen, Christabel discovered that Collingwood wasn't completely deserted. Hester was there, chopping vegetables and listening to the radio. The younger woman immediately offered to prepare some lunch for Christabel.

'Don't worry about me. I'm not particularly hungry, thanks,' said Christabel but, on being pressed, she allowed the girl to make her a sandwich.

As she ate, and sipped a glass of chilled wine, Christabel asked the younger woman how she could get up into the attics.

'If you go up the back stairs, at the end of the kitchen corridor, and just keep going up until you can't get any further, you'll find a little landing with a locked door on it. That's how you get in . . .' She rose and took a key from a row of hooks by the kitchen window. 'There's a door to the back stairs on the first-floor landing too, if you want to go that way, instead.'

Christabel took the key and slipped it into her shorts pocket. 'Thanks . . . Although I think I'll try and find my husband first. Have you any idea where he is? I did wonder if he'd gone off for a walk with Jamie, but it's not really his style.'

'Well, I took them their lunch in the conservatory,

162

Mrs Sutherland,' said the girl, returning to her sharp knife and her carrots. 'About an hour ago, I'd say ... It's very likely that they're still in there. Have you looked?'

'I didn't even know there was a conservatory,' said Christabel, finishing her wine, then dabbing her mouth with a napkin.

Furnished with instructions on how to get to the conservatory, as well as the attics, Christabel took her leave of Hester and returned thoughtfully to the entrance hall. Whatever Nicholas and Jamie were doing, they were doing it very quietly, because there still seemed to be no sound of life in the house.

When she eventually found it – after a trek through the sitting room, a back corridor, and the flower room – the door to the large, sub-tropical conservatory was standing open, so Christabel was able to slip in without making a sound. The foliage was surprisingly lush and dense, and at first she thought that Nicholas and Jamie must have already left; but, after a moment, she heard the faint sound of a voice, and saw a flash of movement amongst the thicker greenery at the far end of the room. Almost not breathing, she crept on forward, her nerves on red alert.

The sight of her husband and his personal assistant naked, *in flagrante*, was a shock to her system, even though she'd been expecting it. Feeling a strange fluttering in the region of her chest, she crouched down, assuming a better position for watching.

Nicholas, she had always known, had a beautiful body; but Jamie, crouching over her husband and massaging his shoulders, was a revelation. The young man was muscular, almost the shape of man idealised, but not to the extent that he appeared a parody. He was just a perfect human male animal – and possessed of a perfect human male penis. His prodigious erection kept brushing against Nicholas's back and buttocks from time to time as the massage progressed, although both men seemed curiously oblivious to the contact. Or at least superficially so . . .

As her own body shuddered with excitement, Christabel acknowledged that the two men made a stunning tableau. Jamie was strong, golden and athletic; while Nicholas was finer and paler, his bodily power more subtly expressed. She admired the tight, indented cheeks of her husband's buttocks, where he lay face-down on the padded massage mat, and saw them quiver a little as Jamie's penis nudged them. When Nicholas moaned softly, flexing his back and torso, an astonishing revelation was immediately made clear.

Her most far-out speculations had been correct after all! What Nicholas had hinted to her on the terrace . . . Far from being the active, aggressive partner, her husband was the receptive one. *He* would be the one fucked by Jamie.

'Oh, my God!' she breathed, then clapped her hand over her mouth, even though it was too late to call back the sound. She need not have worried, however; the two men were too deeply absorbed in each other to be aware of her.

Jamie's skilled fingers had moved on from Nicholas's shoulders now and, after very lightly skimming his employer's mid-section, he began to manipulate the older man's bottom. Circling the lightly oiled cheeks, he dug in his thumbs and moved the firm flesh in a strong, ruthless action.

As Nicholas began to moan, and to rise up to meet the assault of Jamie's sinewy fingers, Christabel felt almost faint from the impact of what she was seeing, and from the heat of the conservatory itself. Making a dogged effort, she gritted her teeth and dug her finger-nails into her palms. She must not spoil the moment by coming crashing out of the undergrowth in a swoon. Not so much for fear of retribution for her spying, but because what was happening between the two men before her was too precious and too sacred to interrupt.

She looked into her heart for jealousy, but found it just wasn't there. The sight she was seeing was beautiful, and she wanted only enjoyment for her husband and his lover.

Not that she wasn't aware, as Nicholas came up on to his knees, revealing his stiff penis, that knowledge of this relationship was advantageous to her. The playing of power games was addictive, she realised, and intoxicating. How nice it would be to have some levers of her own.

It was also gratifying to see the tables turned on Nicholas. Never, in their entire relationship, had she seen him in a state of vulnerability. And, right now, he looked willing, submissive, almost feminine as he went over on to all fours and offered his naked buttocks to Jamie. He was abasing himself; yet, even so, he retained a certain dignity. She couldn't imagine herself looking as poised as he did in similar circumstances.

But Nicholas had further to sink, it seemed. As he pitched forward, his cool patrician face looked hot as he pressed his cheek against the mat. Christabel found his fall irresistibly exciting. She clutched her own crotch, through her shorts, as she watched with fascination. And she almost moaned, in counterpoint to her husband's cries, when he reached around behind himself and parted his own buttocks.

'Jamie! Oh, please, Jamie,' she heard him entreat the young, blond god, who seemed to loom over him like retribution for so many years of arrogance and dominance. Adding to her husband's pleas, she silently implored the gilded Jamie to comply.

The personal assistant, however, seemed too inured to his role of service to deny his employer. He moved forward immediately, and drew a fingertip up and down the stretched crease that Nicholas was offering him. It was a teasing action, Christabel could see that, but basically he was obeying, and doing exactly what Nicholas wanted him to. Her husband clearly relished a little tantalisation before the *coup de grâce* and, as she often did, she applauded and approved of his preference. Waiting for a splendid lover like Jamie Carlton, she knew that she too would be inclined to elongate the moment.

'Oh, yes! Oh, yes!' cooed Nicholas, rocking and thrusting his bottom in response to the cruise of Jamie's fingertip. 'That's it, baby. I love it when you do that!'

Baby?

Christabel had to bite her own lip in an effort not to giggle. Did all men resort to such girlish language when they entered this new continuum of sexual pleasure? This was the first time she'd ever seen two men together, so she had no way of knowing. Yet, peculiar as it sounded, she found the gentle, almost womanly language both endearing and arousing. She felt privileged to be seeing this private world, and watched enthralled as Jamie continued to practise its rites.

Still granted complete access by Nicholas's grip on his own buttocks, the young man began to vary his caresses and strokes. His fingers first glided up to the small of his lover's back, then slipped back down again, circling Nicholas's anus, then fondling his balls. He performed the action several times, slowly, lingeringly, reverently, and though Nicholas seemed to be enjoying it, Christabel could also sense some impatience. Her husband's bucking and writhing was becoming more and more emphatic. 'More, Jamie, more!' he suddenly urged, jerking upwards.

Consummate servant that he was, Jamie, as ever, complied immediately. Reaching for the massage oil, he anointed his fingers with it, then poured a measure of the slick golden fluid into the crack of Nicholas's bottom. Christabel saw her husband shudder finely throughout the whole of his body as the oil hit him, then welled and flowed down between his thighs and on to the mat. As Jamie applied more, it trickled down over Nicholas's scrotum and dripped off the end of his rampant penis.

Christabel experienced another great wave of lust and dizziness. Staying still, and in hiding, suddenly grew into an enormous effort; but, with resolute steeling of her will, she held her station. Even though her own body was oozing and seeping too, as if matching every oily droplet that slid hypnotically from her husband's member.

Jamie was bent right over Nicholas now, weight on one arm, while the other continued to slowly knead and caress. 'Do you want it, Nick?' he whispered in his companion's ear, his voice breathy and seductive. 'Are you ready? Are you relaxed enough yet?'

'Nick', was it? She had never called her husband 'Nick'; had never been encouraged to. Yet it seemed that in private moments, between these two, that was the name he preferred. She tried to imagine how he might react, if she ever called him 'Nick'.

Regardless of pet names and intimacy, however, her husband looked far from relaxed. He nodded his head in answer, and seemed to be bracing every part of himself – for something.

Christabel had assumed that Jamie would sodomise her husband straight away, but another second or two revealed that this wasn't so. The younger man doused his fingers in yet more oil, then slid his hand back between Nicholas's bottom-cheeks. After just a tiny pause, he began to push against his lover's anus with just one digit.

Stretched as it already was, the rose-like aperture yielded easily. Within the space of a pulse-beat, Jamie's finger was buried right up to the knuckle – and Nicholas was panting like a racehorse as he appeared to fight desperately to retain control of himself.

'Jesus Christ!' he wailed as Jamie began to pump him.

The scene was too much; so hot and so gloriously dirty that Christabel wasn't sure she could watch any more without ripping down her shorts and panties and masturbating furiously in time to the strokes of Jamie's forefinger. When Nicholas grunted and pulled at himself, then gasped, 'More! Another finger!' the impulse spiralled.

But, just as she turned, and her hands flew to her waistband, a tiny, fugitive sound made her freeze and catch her breath. She realised to her horror that she'd been caught red-handed in the act of peeping.

When she turned around, though, she found not Hester, nor one of the Blakes, unexpectedly returned, but Gussie Ranelagh, just behind her, green eyes popping.

Christabel couldn't think what to say – or even mime – but at least she retained the presence of mind not to look down guiltily at her own hand. Surreptitiously she allowed her fingers to relax, then did the only thing she really could do under the circumstances. She lifted a forefinger to her lips in a 'shushing' gesture, then nodded to Gussie, indicating that she too should observe what was happening.

As lightly and silently as a native guide, the other woman moved up and positioned herself at Christabel's shoulder. The only indication of her excitement was the slight raggedness of her breathing.

Beyond them, the drama continued to unfold, the protagonists as mercifully unaware of Gussie's arrival as they had been of Christabel's existing presence.

Jamie was working Nicholas with the requested two fingers now and, though the harsh twist of her husband's elegant features against the mat beneath him suggested that such a dilation was agony, his delirious whimpers of happiness told quite the opposite story. With undisguised hunger, he was lifting up his rump to meet every downward stroke. His swinging penis looked red and inflamed, as hard as a poker.

He's going to come. He's going to come. He must come soon, thought Christabel, acutely aware of Gussie's warm presence just beside her. Her every nerve-end was picking up the waves of the other woman's excitement, and she could barely imagine what the pair of them might do when Nicholas reached his climax.

But, just when Christabel was convinced that her husband was on the very point of ejaculating, he stopped all movement, and held himself still, his body trembling on the skewer of Jamie's fingers.

'I want it. I want it now, Jamie.' His teeth were gritted, his voice as hoarse as if he'd been shouting for an hour, against a gale. 'I want your cock inside me. I want to feel it. I want you to fuck me.'

'Oh, Nick,' murmured Jamie, removing his oily fingers and reaching around underneath Nicholas to gently caress his chest and his belly. Christabel noticed how very carefully he avoided her husband's cock, clearly unwilling to risk a premature crisis when neither he nor his beloved were ready.

The two men remained curved together for a few moments: poised on the brink of the next giant leap, as if they both felt trepidation in and amongst their intense desire. Then, with an exquisite grace, and a palpable sense of ceremony, Jamie began to oil himself.

Christabel experienced a feeling of trepidation too. She had felt awed and enthralled and aroused by what had passed between Nicholas and Jamie so far, but all of a sudden she realised she could not watch any more of it. She wasn't ready to see her husband in so profound a state of surrender. It was too much a mystery, too intensely male, too exclusively his and Jamie's. With some lingering reluctance, but knowing she was doing the right thing, she began to draw back. And, as she did so, she felt Gussie retreating too, and blessed the girl's intuitiveness.

When the two women had put a safe distance between themselves and the scene in the conservatory, they stopped and looked at each other, then flopped down, side by side, on an antique sofa that stood in the shady hall.

'Phew! Well, that was pretty interesting,' said Gussie, fanning herself. It was such an understatement that Christabel started giggling and, after a few seconds, she realised she couldn't stop. A reaction – mad hysteria – had set in; but not from horror, just the relaxation of tension.

'Hey, are you all right?' she heard Gussie say, but wasn't able to answer because of the grip of helpless mirth. 'Christabel! Please! Stop, you're frightening me!'

The alarm in the other woman's voice acted as a regulator and, dragging in a few deep breaths, then holding them, Christabel was finally able to control her hiccups and giggles.

'I'm sorry about that, Gussie,' she said, still smirking a little and fighting the odd outbreak. 'I'm all right, really . . . It's just a reaction.'

Her beautiful face a picture of concern, Gussie took Christabel's hand. 'Are you sure?' she said, beginning to stroke, gently, with her thumb. 'I . . . er . . . take it that that must be the first time you've seen them together like that.' She pursed her lips, looking far more perplexed than Christabel felt. 'That *is* your husband, I assume? And Jamie? I've never actually met either of them, you know.'

'Yes, that was Nicholas and Jamie,' answered Christabel, enjoying the touch of Gussie's fingers. Thoughts of the time she'd spent with the younger woman were already beginning to rise up and drive out images of her husband and his lover.

'Which is which?'

Christabel looked at her in surprise, then realised that, although she'd spoken of her husband and his friend to Gussie, she'd never actually described them. She laughed again, and Gussie looked worried.

'It's OK! I'm not going to have the screaming ab-dabs again,' she said reassuringly. 'And I don't know why I should automatically assume you'd know which man is which . . .' She shrugged. 'The darker, older man is Nicholas, my husband, and the young blond about to have his evil way with him is Jamie . . . Although I suppose they're probably doing the deed by now.'

'Phew!' said Gussie again, and it was her turn to giggle. 'That's what threw me, I suppose. From what you'd said, and what I'd assumed, I was rather expecting your Nicholas to be on top.' She puffed her lips expressively. 'But that just shows you, you should never make assumptions.' Her green eyes narrowed. '*Are* you all right?' she said again, more seriously. 'I mean, does it upset you to see your husband with another lover?'

Christabel thought for a moment, searching for absolute inner honesty within herself. But the answer was clear.

'Well, yes, I do feel jealous, I suppose, but it also excites me. Well, more than that, actually . . . It's a turn-on, but it's also appropriate somehow, in a sort of moral way, if that makes any sense?' She pulled a hopeless face, wishing she could express herself more elegantly. 'I feel a bit more at ease with my own . . . um . . . "experiments", if I know that Nicholas has peccadilloes of his own.'

'Well, that's the most rational and sensible thing I've heard anyone say in a long time,' said Gussie roundly, patting Christabel's hand. 'Now, what do you want to do while your hubby and his toy-boy are at it? Do you fancy a bit of that "experimenting" of yours?' Her green-jewel eyes sparkled seductively, and the patting hand settled and began to stroke.

Christabel was powerfully tempted. Gussie was radiant, an icon of womanly sexuality. Her glorious breasts strained unbrassièred against a thin, overwashed white T-shirt, and her tight denim cut-offs seemed to delineate explicitly the pudenda that lay beneath them. It would be so easy and so delightful to accept her offer.

'I want to,' said Christabel woefully. 'But I sort of

promised myself I'd do something . . . Something to try and help Daniel.'

'Daniel?'

'Yes. I thought I might hunt around through the attics, and see if I could find any of Eleanor Woodforde's belongings. Papers. Letters. Journals. Anything that might offer some clue to why she disappeared, and where to.' Christabel felt a sudden qualm of disquiet. Suppose Gussie saw this as futile or, worse still, a form of insult? 'Although, if you think that's a bad idea, or hopeless, or whatever . . . Or you think I'm sticking my nose in where it's not wanted, I'll leave it, of course.'

Gussie leant over and kissed Christabel very softly on the mouth. It was all the answer that was needed, but Christabel was happy to hear the younger woman's words too.

'Bless you,' said Gussie, her voice sounding a little teary somehow. 'You're only wanting to do what I should have done ages ago . . .' She frowned, bit her lip, then kissed Christabel again. 'But I kept making excuses. Lessees. Work. Telling myself that it might not be the best thing for Dan, when I really knew that it was probably the very thing that would finally sort him out.' She looked as if she might cry, and Christabel felt compelled to return the kiss, and stroke Gussie's wild black curls. 'Thank you, Christabel, you're an angel! You're exactly the catalyst that Daniel and I need!'

Drawing away a little, Christabel felt a mad urge to laugh again. 'Look! You'll have me in hysterics again if you keep calling me an angel,' she said. 'I can't think of anyone less angelic than me.'

'Oh, you are one, believe me,' said Gussie, giving Christabel a wink as she rose from the sofa, and held out her hand in invitation. 'And, when we've turned over every goddamned box in those attics together, I'm going to show you that I can be pretty heavenly, too! Just you wait!'

Chapter Eleven
Grey Areas

The conditions up in the attics made Christabel feel as if she were in the sweatbox of some Third World prison camp. It was no wonder people had been reluctant to explore. Especially as, at first, there seemed to be very little of the sort of evidence they were seeking.

The things of Eleanor's that Daniel had spoken of comprised mainly of a small selection of her clothing and some innocuous domestic papers. Orders for kitchen implements, furnishing fabrics, special foodstuffs. They found no diaries, no personal letters, nothing at all to throw light on her personality, her emotions and her relationships. There was certainly nothing whatsoever to indicate where she might have fled to. Everything seemed to indicate a settled, ordinary, married, English country gentlewoman, not a sensualist, and adulteress and a runaway.

The only items that had any bearing on Eleanor's inner life were certain items amongst the clothing – which was all neatly folded and wrapped for storage, within chests of camphorwood.

'Look at this,' said Gussie, folding aside layers of yellowed tissue paper and lifting up a delicate camisole of ivory silk and lace. She held it against her, for effect, and Christabel thought that she looked like a ghost or a hologram in the inadequate light. 'It's definitely hers,' she went on, lowering the exquisite garment and studying its stitching. 'Look here. These are her initials . . . They've been embroidered.'

Christabel abandoned the household ledger she'd been studying, and went across to where Gussie was kneeling over the open trunk.

On a tiny label, stitched into the back of the camisole were a painstakingly embroidered entwined pair of initials, 'E. W'. 'It must have been part of her trousseau,' said Christabel, wanting to touch the fine workmanship and handle the sensuous texture of the fabric, but feeling reluctant because her fingers were grey with dust. 'It's a "W" for Woodforde, not an "R" for Ranelagh.'

'My God, I'd love to try some of these on. They're beautiful,' murmured Gussie, setting down the camisole and reaching in for more garments.

'Why don't you?' asked Christabel, trying to imagine the pale silks and satins with Gussie's dramatic colouring. She would look wonderful, and she was a Ranelagh – these garments were meant for her. 'Surely these things belong to you? They're in your house, and Eleanor was part of your family.'

'I suppose so,' said Gussie, lifting up what appeared to be a voluminous pair of knickers, of peach satin, trimmed with frothy lace. As the fluid fabric unfurled, they could see that the bloomers were made almost in two parts, completely split up the length of the crotch. 'This's handy!' Gussie's voice was more suggestive now, as she put her hand through the aperture and wiggled her fingers.

'I wonder if she wore things like this when she went to see Ethan?' mused Christabel, trying to envisage the scene. She had no real idea what Eleanor looked like. Daniel's imaginings were her only guide. She used her own image, clad in antique clothes and lingerie.

She'd go into the copse, clad in a long, sensible gown

174

of some kind, and laced boots, but, beneath, she would be wearing these exquisite, hand-stitched, satin and lace fripperies. Ethan – who she imagined a twin of Daniel – would come to her, kiss her hurriedly, then rummage beneath her mass of skirts as he crushed her back against an oak tree. Layers of serge, or wool, or whatever her sensible gown was made of, would be lifted to expose the shimmering cobweb finery beneath. His work-hardened hand would find its way easily into the long slit in her drawers, searching for her heat, seeking out her moisture, finding her clitoris.

'This is gorgeous stuff, it really is!' Gussie's enthusiasm broke the spell of regression, and once again Christabel snatched her fingers surreptitiously from her own crotch. The heat and the flying grey dust in the confined space around them was beginning to have an effect on her. She felt dizzy and confused. And more than a little alarmed.

She supposed that the cumulative effects of the last few days might be telling on her. She had always believed herself a libertine; but now she'd discovered she'd only been skimming on the surface. And it was a shock to the system. She wasn't sure yet whether she was going to sink or swim in this new environment. So many others surrounded her, reaching for her, drawing on her . . .

Nicholas. Daniel. Gussie. Even the constant, peripheral yet unignorable presence of Jamie. What they wanted, and what they gave, seemed overwhelming somehow. She felt a grey wave begin to close over her: not cold and wet, like the ocean, but hot and dry and choking, like the desert. She lifted her hands, reaching out to Gussie, but somehow unable to make the other woman hear or see her. Gussie was absorbed, digging in the trunk, her beautiful face lighting up, even though Christabel's vision of it was rapidly becoming obscured.

'Bingo! What have we here?' Daniel's sister cried,

snapping open what looked like an evening bag she'd pulled from the depths of the clothes trunk.

The last things Christabel saw, before she fainted, were photographs.

Unable to concentrate on his work, Daniel closed the document he had open, then abandoned his laptop for the day. He simply couldn't get a grip on his characters or their world.

No. That wasn't it. Not really. He could get into the lives of Lady Lucinda and McGuire just as well as he'd been doing since he started the book, but the trouble was that those lives kept intersecting, in his mind, with other lives. Ones in his imagination, and also far more real ones.

Would Christabel be able to find out anything in the house? Gussie would help, but even his sister didn't know for certain that there was anything useful in the attics at Collingwood. He recalled seeing clothes, himself, all those years ago, and a whole mountain of household stuff, but that had been long before the time he'd felt any need to look for anything more illuminating. Before the time of his obsession, before he'd been in love with a woman long dead, but who seemed to live on in his mind, irresistibly real and sensual.

Was history repeating itself? What if Nicholas Sutherland was as murderously jealous as Charles Woodforde had been, but simply expressed it in a more perverse and modern way? What if he, Daniel, was putting Christabel in just as much jeopardy as Ethan had put Eleanor?

Questions whirled in his head, and he stared out of the window of his tiny study in the dower house, looking for answers in the view of the tiny garden plot that surrounded it.

Shadows were lengthening, and he realised evening was already beginning to fall. He looked in the direction of Collingwood – although he couldn't see it for the part of the copse that stood between the two dwellings – and wondered if Christabel and Gussie had found anything useful. Then, despite his worries, he smiled. Knowing Gussie, the investigation was quite likely to get interrupted. Especially in the heat, and the intimate proximity of the attics . . .

As it was evening, and his nerves were fraying, and there was no likelihood of any more productive work today, Daniel decided to have a drink. In the fridge, he found a couple of bottles of Chenin Blanc that Gussie must have brought with her, and he opened one and poured himself a tall, cool goblet of the light, fruity wine.

Returning to the study, he set his glass beside the chaise longue then threw himself down on the cushions to ponder and brood.

And if Christabel and Gussie did find something useful, what then? He might know, at last, what had happened to Eleanor. Ethan would know, too; if, in some obscure way, he really did exist somehow in Daniel's consciousness.

And that raised a big question. What would happen then? Would he lose Ethan, and just be himself? On his own, driven to seek a real life so he could continue his writing?

It was confusing. Not black and white. He didn't know what he felt. His imaginary world was a cocoon, a place of safety, yet in his heart of hearts he knew he longed for freedom. It would ultimately serve his writing much better if he got out, met new people, saw new places – and he couldn't do that until he had a closure of the mystery of Eleanor.

Although Christabel was 'new people', he supposed. And what they'd shared was so unexpected that, even as he thought about her, his penis began stiffening in his underwear. The only trouble with Christabel was that, when it came to it, she was deeply in love with her husband, and Daniel knew that he himself could only ever be a distraction for her.

He thought of what Christabel had said about her spanking. How it had aroused her, and how, almost against her will, she'd felt 'in place' being humbled and subjugated. Daniel supposed that they'd skimmed the edge of that feeling when he and she had been together on the veranda, at the cottage; but it could never fully work for her with him, and he knew it. He didn't have the still, implacable centre that her husband did. Or at least the ability to seem that way, as Daniel sensed that there would be very few men who weren't stirred to some kind of madness by Christabel. And that probably included her husband.

But a comparison of his own shortcomings with the qualities of a man he'd only seen from a distance didn't interfere with Daniel's imagination. He suddenly saw a picture of Christabel – or was it Eleanor? – in the library at Collingwood, as it had been when he'd last been able to enter it.

She was wearing dress from the turn-of-the-century era, clothing such as Eleanor would have worn, even though, as he thought about her, he became more and more sure the woman he was seeing was Christabel. In his fantasy, her manner was agitated, and as she prowled the room, her long, dark skirts were swishing. She was biting her lips, chafing her hands together; she was worried. She was a penitent wife awaiting her husband's retribution.

Daniel sat up, took a long swallow of the delicious wine, then slumped down again. He closed his eyes, reconfigured the fantasy in his mind; and then, using the technique that made it so easy for him to write, so credibly, as a woman, he allowed himself to sink into the scenario until he became a part of it.

He became Christabel Sutherland awaiting her husband Nicholas . . .

* * *

She supposed she should have known this day would come. Mr Sutherland had been most particular about what would happen if she transgressed again and, like a fool, she had agreed to the terms, blithely convincing herself that she could resist temptation easily.

But, of course, she hadn't. Instead of devoting herself to quiet country pursuits, as she'd intended, she had succumbed to the allure of other 'country matters' – and taken a tumble, in a woodland cottage, with the Honourable Daniel Ranelagh. Who was young and lusty, and delightfully *dis*honourable.

Biting her lips, and rubbing her fingers against each other, she felt nervous, worried, and alarmed. And yet, within her, a rather different excitement was brewing.

What would her husband say if he discovered she was also looking forward, in a perverse way, to the proceedings? Pacing again along the exquisite Persian carpet runner that lay behind the leather chesterfield, Christabel felt an intense urge to touch herself, and to hug her arms around her chest. Her breasts were aching now, and her swollen nipples chafing against the constraints of her stiff-boned corset. Every part of her seemed to be repressed and constricted by the many layers of her clothing; she felt like an effervescent fluid straining for freedom from its bottle.

'So much energy, my dear,' said her husband's voice. 'But then again, I suppose, that has always been your problem.'

Christabel spun around, almost knocking over a delicate table, with her vast skirts, in the process. Her husband was a gentleman, but sometimes he moved like a cat burglar. It was so typical of him to come upon her silently, and thus immediately command the advantage of surprise.

'Nicholas! You startled me,' she protested, smoothing her skirts and feeling the crimson rush of embarrassment flood her face.

'Why so?' He advanced into the room, his eyes steady

179

and intent upon her, accusing her although she hadn't yet – on this occasion – done anything wrong. 'Surely you were expecting me? We agreed on this, did we not? Please don't tell me you wish to go back on your word.'

'Of course not,' snapped Christabel, feeling more and more confusion. Nicholas looked so beautifully handsome in his elegant grey coat and trousers. The cool lines of his face were enhanced, as ever, by the snowy brilliance of his high white shirt-collar, and the elaborate embroidery of his waistcoat seemed to hint at the sense of whimsy which Christabel well knew lurked beneath the surface of his stern persona. Considering him now, she had no idea how she could ever have let him down and succumbed to the temptations of other men, no matter how personable they were. When she was with Nicholas she belonged to him completely.

'Well, then. Shall we proceed?' he said equably, bringing his hands, which she had believed clasped behind his back, into view. She felt her innards shudder when she saw what he was holding.

It was a strap of leather. A lovingly polished, nut-brown length of it. A device specifically designed and wrought for the punishment of the human backside. And, in this case, the female human backside. Nicholas had shown it to her, on several occasions, when their discussions of her shortcomings had become serious; but he had never used it, only threatened it. Until now.

'It's simply the item we agreed on, my dear,' he said, running his fingertips over the leather. His expression was patient, forbearing. Christabel knew that she must be clearly showing her fear.

If only I could be detached in all this, she thought, making every effort to keep her posture straight and her face as untroubled as her husband's. She felt pulled in any number of different directions: pride compelled her to project an image of composure and stoicism; fear urged her to beg for mercy, to plead with Nicholas not to strike her; and lust, a dark, sweet and almost incomprehensible passion, drove her to invite the kiss of the lash, and the mysterious fire that lay beyond it.

'Indeed it is,' she said, moving forward yet unsure of what to do, and how to position herself. Nicholas had informed her that, in order to be effective, and sufficiently memorable, her 'instruction' would be carried out on an unprotected territory. That she would have to offer up her bottom, white and bare.

He seemed to sense her hesitation, and her questions.

'First we must make you comfortable,' he said, laying the strap on the fine walnut library table, then holding out his hand to her as if he were asking her for a dance. 'Remove your corset, perhaps?' He gave her an almost flirtatious little smile. 'I think you will soon have enough to contend with, without having your poor insides crushed and flattened by strips of whalebone.'

Christabel stood where she was, frozen and horrified. She had anticipated lifting her skirts, and the mortification of having to lower her drawers and uncover her rear – but to have to undress completely would compound her shame to a hideous level.

'But . . . but I'll need my maid,' she stuttered, feeling her face grow pinker and pinker. 'I need assistance with all the laces and fastenings.'

Nicholas closed upon her, then took both her hands in his, and looked into her eyes. His face was an icon of unexpected sympathy. 'Don't worry, my dear,' he said, gently chafing her with his thumbs, 'I'll be your maid. You'll be safe with me. Let me help you.'

This doesn't make sense, thought Christabel as her husband turned her around like a doll and began to undo the hooks down the back of her gown. He fully intends to punish me, to strike me repeatedly on my bare bottom with a lash of leather until I scream with the pain of it; and yet he's being kinder and sweeter to me than he's ever been. There seemed to be no logic at all in what was about to happen to her, what was already happening, and yet, on a deeper level, she understood it perfectly.

Bowing her head, she allowed Nicholas to unfasten her dress, then ease it from her shoulders and down her body, so she could step out of it. She shuddered as she stood there in her petticoats, feeling far more exposed than she had ever done when she'd been naked in bed with him, with her legs spread and his cock inside her. Her lingerie, and its mechanics, she had always kept a secret from him, and this undressing was as intimate a revelation as the act of sex itself.

'So many layers,' he murmured, coming around to the front of her and releasing the fine fastenings of her camisole. As he slid the garment's delicate straps down over her arms, Christabel gasped. The starched cuff of his shirt had brushed momentarily against her breast, and had felt like a caress through the thin muslin of her shift.

Flinging aside the camisole, her husband gave her a long, assessing look, then touched her breast again, where it bulged over the rigid edge of her corset. A single fingertip touched first one nipple, then the other, pressing, then circling lightly. As Christabel whimpered, she heard him murmur, 'Have a care, my dear.'

As he repeated the gesture, and little darts of sensation shot from her breast to her groin, Christabel knew implicitly that Nicholas had full knowledge of her desire and its convolutions. Every stage and facet of this procedure was purposefully designed to bring her to the highest pitch of helplessness and yearning. Every demeaning action was performed to make her needy.

'Let's have these off, too,' he said after a moment, first plucking at the abundant flounces of her many petticoats, then swiftly untying them and pushing them down over the swell of her hips. Like an obedient little girl, Christabel once again stepped clear of the layers of lace-frothed fabric, then looked on nervously as Nicholas threw them aside with her other things.

'And how much more might there be?' he enquired, pressing a hand to her firmly corseted waist and slipping a finger beneath the upper edge of her drawers.

Christabel felt speared by desire and confusion. She wished he would beat her and be done with it. This protracted study of her undergarments was making her so desperate she almost felt giddy.

'Christabel?' he prompted when she didn't answer immediately.

'My . . . my drawers. The corset. Chemise underneath . . . Stockings and garters. That's all.'

Nicholas smiled. He was thoroughly enjoying himself, she realised. Building up the layers of his own titillation, just as she was removing layer after layer of clothing. He seemed in no great hurry to rush towards the denouement.

'And all very lovely,' he said, his hand rising languorously over the ramparts of stiffened cloth and whalebone, then curving around one muslin-veiled breast again. He gave her a quick squeeze there, then issued an instruction as he released her, 'Lower your drawers to your thighs, Christabel. Then hold them there.'

With a dry mouth and a pounding heart, she obeyed him, fumbling with first the button and then the fullness of the lace- and ribbon-trimmed muslin of her knickers. She felt silly and awkward clutching them in a bundle at her hips.

With a deftness that suggested it wasn't the first time he'd performed such an operation, Nicholas then unlaced her corset and lifted it free of her chemise-clad body. Christabel was slim enough not to have required the garment over-tightened, but even so the sudden lack of it left her dangerously unsupported. She felt as if the strictness of the boning had been sustaining her not only physically but mentally – and that now she had no more armour whatsoever against Nicholas's personality and his cool-as-ice eyes.

'Very good,' he said, setting the corset aside, and

standing back to peruse the effect. 'Now, lower your drawers a little further, and at the same time gather up your chemise and hold it folded above your breasts.

'But Nicholas –' she began, feeling the power of anger rise to replace the protecting corset. They had agreed on a punishment, not a humiliating display. Or, at least, that was what she had believed to be the case. A quick chopping gesture of her husband's hand suggested otherwise.

'Please obey me,' he said. His voice was quiet and silky, exhibiting no vexation or perturbation of any kind; but, risking a quick glance at him, Christabel saw his eyes were passionate. The peril of collapse, and her physical yearning for him, grew suddenly stronger.

Feeling deeply inept, and possessed of twice as many thumbs as she should have had, Christabel struggled to obey him. Sweat seemed to trickle over every pore of her skin as she exposed it to him, and to pool, along with other, muskier fluids, in the hot folds of her groin.

'Knickers a little lower,' her husband instructed, when she tried to shield her pubis with the rucked-up lace and muslin. It seemed that she was to be allowed no shred of defence whatsoever.

Above the thick bunch of white fabric and lace around her upper chest, Christabel knew that her shoulders, neck and face were now completely scarlet. Every part of her body that modesty decreed should be guarded from the male gaze was now exhibited, in the rudest and most embarrassing fashion, to her husband. And, more than that, she realised unhappily, her parts were also revealed to anyone who might be either passing the library window or inclined to enter the room without benefit of a knock. Breasts, belly, bottom, and crotch – they were all on show for the delectation of the casual observer.

But if this is so terrible to me, she thought, closing her eyes and adjusting her stance a little, why do I feel more and more aroused by it? Her nipples were as hard as stones and the tension in them seemed to drag tantalisingly on the unfettered globes of her breasts. Between her legs, her sex was heavy with the weight of her desire, and she felt sure that her lubrication must now be so copious that it would be visible to the sharply acute gaze of her husband.

And as if he'd read her mind, at that very moment, he said, 'Please part your legs a little, my dear, will you?'

Even though the adjustment was minor, the cost to Christabel was enormous. She felt a horrid, welling sensation and her juices trickled out of her betrayingly. A distinct wet patch was forming on the muslin that was bunched between her legs.

'Now, move forward, my dear,' Nicholas went on, his voice still steady, although perhaps containing just the slightest undertone of salaciousness. 'Stand here.' He indicated the centre of a finely worked oval rug that stood in the open area in the middle of the room. 'I want to enjoy the very best view of you with your lovely bottom unmarked.'

So deeply was she sunk into the rites of humiliation, that Christabel had almost forgotten the primary purpose of this meeting here in the library. She felt choked with shame and fear and a luscious, belly-melting helplessness that made her sway on the heels of her buttoned boots. If Nicholas were to touch her right now, in her most intimate place, she was quite convinced she would have a crisis immediately.

'My dear. I'm waiting,' he reminded her.

Tottering and deeply uncomfortable, Christabel managed to obey him. The need to keep her shift and knickers held carefully in place made her progress laughable and ungainly.

And yet Nicholas seemed enchanted.

'Beautiful,' he breathed, beginning to circle around her once she was in place. 'Quite breathtakingly. You are a perfect Venus, my dear. Lewd. Sluttish. But like a goddess and exquisitely adorable.' As he passed to the front of her, she saw him pass his tongue, just once, across his upper lip. 'If it wasn't absolutely essential that I strap you, for your own good, I would like nothing better than to open your legs now and fuck you immediately.'

The sound of the explicit word seemed to echo his licking of his lips. It was like his tongue being drawn not across his lips this time, but across her clitoris, and Christabel moaned softly at the spontaneous sensation this invoked in her. Her knees sagged and, in an instant, Nicholas was holding her by the elbows and supporting her. 'Bear up, my dear,' he murmured. 'Be brave and stalwart, for both our sakes.'

Rallied by his words, Christabel braced herself. Difficult as it was, she stood proudly again, drawing back her shoulders and presenting herself to him as elegantly as she could in her parlous situation. Making her face into a smooth, impassive mask of beauty, she acknowledged the fact that, even though what she really wanted at that moment was for him to pass his long, elegant fingers between her legs and bring her to an instantaneous and screaming climax of pleasure, that was not about to happen until she'd been through a spiritual mill for him. He was going to make her suffer – and she was going to bear it. For him. It was as simple as that, and only when it was over, would she get – and deserve – her final release.

'That's better, Christabel. So much better.' He released her, but she still stood tall and straight, offering him her breasts with their twin, prominent peaks, her nipples. Her crotch, too, she willingly tendered, along with the swell of her hips and the tight round globes of her bottom. Which, in quivering apprehension, she knew he would make use of first.

As if divining her thoughts, he gently turned her, then took hold of each soft globe in one of his hands. Moving them around, in circles that were robust and completely unmindful of her modesty, he made a low sound of appreciation in her ear.

'Your bottom is a delight, my dear,' he said quietly, his breath a threatening zephyr across the back of her neck and her shoulders. 'But I want to see it reddened and hot and inflamed. I want to see your buttocks moving, compulsively, because the flesh is so tormented that you can't keep yourself still . . .' His hands gripped, pulling her this way and that, creating a tension that seemed to her more agonising than any amount of anticipated pain. 'I want to hear you groan, my dear. I want to hear you sob. I want to hear you scream.'

Unable to prevent herself, Christabel began to groan already, her desire burgeoning. She thrust her backside into Nicholas's grip and then waggled her hips to try and alleviate the distress between her thighs. Her fingers gripped her clothing so hard she almost tore it.

'You're ready, aren't you? Oh, so ready,' he purred, his wicked evocative tongue touching her neck, just beneath her ear lobe. 'You're wet and hot, aren't you, my dear? So randy that you'd let me do virtually anything to you . . . Aren't you?'

Christabel groaned again, bending her knees, bearing down.

'Answer me, my love,' he commanded, licking her again and stretching her buttocks wide apart.

'Yes! Yes!' she gasped, her entire body a column of desperation. She wanted something from him – anything from him – she cared not what, only that they move on from this plateau of frustration.

'Are you ready to be beaten?' he persisted, adjusting his grip and brushing her anus with his thumb. 'To be punished? Severely?'

'Oh, yes! Oh, God, yes!' she cried, her voice rising and cracking as he delicately prodded the tender entrance to her rectum.

The probing ceased. 'Excellent!' he said approvingly, then he released her bottom entirely and took her by the arm and guided her to the back of one of the deeply upholstered leather chesterfields. 'Then we'll begin, my dear. Lie across here, and make sure your bare skin is pressed against the leather . . . It's smooth and cool and you might find it soothing.'

Cool as it was when she initially lay down across it, there was nothing in the slightest bit soothing about the back of the chesterfield, Christabel quickly discovered. The slick kiss of the leather against her hard, puckered nipples only increased her longing to have them pinched or sucked, and her sweaty lower body seemed to adhere immediately to the surface of the hide. Fluid oozed out from between the lips of her vulva and, within seconds, it was pooled in a slippery, shimmering patch beneath her pelvis. Every last aspect of her disposition seemed expressly designed to betray her. She longed to cover her face, and hide her shame, but Nicholas would not allow that. In quiet, patient tones, he instructed her to stretch out her arms across the chesterfield's well-padded seat, then he performed a final dressing of her position – adjusting both the set of her limbs and the way her lingerie was tucked and folded.

'You're exquisite, Christabel . . . A vision of loveliness,' said Nicholas, making a final adjustment to the angle of her hips. 'I feel so proud of you. I feel almost smug . . . I would love to exhibit you like this before a small, select group of friends. Connoisseurs, who would truly appreciate your shame, and the pain that lies ahead of you.'

Horrified by such a prospect, but unable to prevent herself imagining it, Christabel felt her body rouse to an even higher pitch – if that were possible. She could almost feel the lascivious scrutiny of perhaps a dozen pairs of eyes. They would be intent on studying the most critical areas. The cleft of her bottom, her anus, the juicy purse of her sex, swelling beneath it. As she listened to the discrete sounds of Nicholas shrugging off his jacket, loosening his collar, and rolling up his sleeves, she also began to imagine that he would allow his hypothetical audience to examine her, as well as observe her.

In the theatre of her overactive mind, she seemed to feel fingers searching her body. Examining, exploring, boldly entering her every niche and cranny. She began to wriggle across the chesterfield, her damp skin squeaking and squelching against the leather.

'I'm too cruel to you, aren't I, my darling?' said Nicholas, suddenly close to her. His voice was no longer arch and mannered, but soft and genuine, almost loving. 'Would you like me to just get on with this, and stop teasing you?'

Unable to speak, Christabel nodded, her every sexual feeling way beyond overwrought. She longed for resolution now, even if it cost her bottom dearly. She wanted to show Nicholas her new-found fortitude before it was lost to her completely.

'My dearest,' he murmured and, before she could hardly draw another breath, he had spun away, and raised the instrument.

Just as she drew in another breath, a gasp of the purest fear and excitement, the long strap of leather fell across her. In the first instant of the impact, she seemed not to feel anything at all, her body was so shocked by the sensation and its suddenness. But a half beat later, she screamed out passionately, her bottom flaming. The heat and pain scoured her soul and left her unable to reason. There was no way she could endure a second stroke and her heart continue beating . . . Yet, a moment later, that stroke arrived, and her heart tripped onward.

As more blows fell, lining up in bands of parallel crimson intensity across her buttocks, Christabel became aware of a strange, loud, animal wailing and, to her horror, she also realised she was producing it. Even as she inwardly berated herself for her lack of stoicism, she continued to caterwaul and, at the same time, she jigged and bounced against the chesterfield. The whole of her rear had gone up in flames – she was scarred for life. She couldn't bear it.

And then, just as abruptly and as violently as it had begun, her chastisement was over. For several minutes, though, it might as well have been continuing, the distress in her buttocks was so great. Her flesh seemed unable to relinquish the sensations. It was like a lingering physical echo, a reverberation. She wasn't screeching now, but she couldn't stop herself from sobbing.

That was until a gentle hand slid nimbly beneath her belly ... and she was howling again. With an ecstasy that negated all the pain.

'Jesus Christ!' shouted Daniel as his body jack-knifed up off the chaise in a mighty orgasm. Semen was jetting, white and silky, from between his fingers – which was amazing, considering he couldn't for the life of him remember releasing his cock from his jeans.

'Jesus,' he muttered again, as he swung his feet to the floor, preparing to begin the hunt for tissues. His legs seemed insubstantial as he tried to get up but, after a moment, he managed it, and spotted the box he required amongst the junk on the sideboard. Once marginally clean, he poured himself another glass of wine – he'd drunk the first one without remembering doing that, either – and settled down to try and understand what it was that'd just happened.

Had he fallen asleep? It didn't feel that way; there was no drowsiness, or real dislocation of his senses. Yet the vision, fantasy, scenario, or whatever it was, had been as clear, if not clearer, than any of his Ethan and Eleanor experiences.

Had it been one of those? With the perceptions skewed somewhat? he wondered, then thought not. The characters he'd been with – or simply been, in the female case – were definitely Christabel and Nicholas Sutherland, the lessees of Collingwood.

And, what was more, he had a deep, almost frighteningly strong gut feeling that what he'd experienced was a true representation. That it *was* the dynamic between them ... Which was all the stranger for the fact that he wasn't convinced that Christabel actually understood it herself yet. She would do, in time. He sincerely believed that. But, for the moment, she had only touched its leading edge.

I'll never have that with her, he thought again, sipping his wine and suddenly feeling like drinking the whole bottle, then another and getting entirely drunk and disgusting. It was a bitter irony, he reflected, that after this long arid period of sexual drought, the woman he'd thought he'd found for himself was really the lifelong love of another man. He supposed that, if he'd really been Ethan Vertue, he might have tried to steal her away, persuading himself that it was for her own good. But he was Daniel Ranelagh and, for all his sins, he was a gentleman. He just couldn't do it.

Which left him alone with his fantasies, his solitary ramblings – and the writing of his novels. Abandoning his wine with some reluctance, he returned to his laptop and opened the latest chapter of the saga of Lady Lucinda and McGuire.

As the white letters stared at him from their blue background, he shrugged and experienced an unexpected surge of enthusiasm.

He couldn't use any of the details of the wild episode he'd just enjoyed, but maybe the mood and the relationship could enliven a little of what he was writing.

His spirits rose as he put his fingers to the keys, and began a new paragraph.

Chapter Twelve
Some Light on the Matter

Ma petite, you must come to me. You will be safe here. Mr Woodforde has too volatile a temper for you to remain any longer at Collingwood. In a little while, we can send for your friend Ethan. There should be no difficulty in our finding a suitable position for him, and failing that ... Well, my income is secure. One more soul beneath my roof will make no difference. Please come soon, chère Eleanor, for your own sake. Fondest regards, your devoted amante, Marie-Ange Chamfort.

'I know that name,' said Gussie, turning over the thin, slightly yellowed sheet of paper as if further illumination might be found on its blank reverse. 'Chamfort. I know a woman called Chamfort ... only very slightly, mind you. She lives in London sometimes, and also in Paris ... She runs a magazine, quite a racy one, actually. Her name's "Marisa". I'm sure she must be related. I mean "Marie-Ange" ... and "Marisa". Both "M" names ... It's too much of a coincidence.'

They had found the letter, along with several very old and discoloured photographs, inside a delicate beaded reticule, which someone – most likely Eleanor herself – had hidden away right in the bottom of one of the camphorwood trunks. Or at least Gussie had found the reticule, just at the moment when Christabel had done her fainting act, overcome by the oppressive, dusty heat of the attics.

When she had come to again, moments later, it had seemed pointless to go on searching, as the box Gussie had been examining was the last one anyway. So, clutching the evening bag and a small selection of the clothing, the two women had come downstairs again, back to the relative coolness of Christabel's bedroom.

'Well, if this is Eleanor, Daniel's all wrong in imagining that I look like her,' Christabel said, picking up one of the brownish-toned Edwardian photographs for a closer look. Considering the limitations of the technology of the time, and the social conventions that had prevailed, it was a surprisingly telling likeness of a delicate-featured, dark-haired woman.

Eleanor Woodforde was an enigma. Though her clothing was prim and decorous, a neat pin-tucked and high-necked blouse worn with a long flowing black skirt, there was a suppressed, yet unmistakable sensuality to her. Her eyes were as dark as her hair but, even in the smudgy image, there was an evident fire in them. A wildness quite at odds with her Sunday School-marm clothing. Christabel supposed this was the streak of voluptuousness that Ethan Vertue had recognised. And then tapped into.

'She looks more like me than you,' said Gussie matter of factly, leaning over to study the photograph again. Christabel felt a momentary frisson of excitement at the other woman's nearness. Gussie's white T-shirt was heavily smeared with dust, her hair was all over the place, and there was a distinctly musky, sweaty fragrance to her; but all this only added to her attractiveness. Her primitive sexiness.

And Eleanor Woodforde had possessed the same thing, only censored by her era.

'Yes, I suppose she does . . .' Christabel felt her own body, which was just as hot and sweaty as Gussie's, begin to stir again. 'But that isn't surprising, is it?' She turned to look at Gussie, trying to imagine her in a prim blouse and with her curls severely tamed. 'You said that she was a Ranelagh, too. It must be a family resemblance ... I suppose, in some ways, you could say she looks a bit like Daniel, too.'

Gussie's brow crumpled, expressing deep thought. 'She was our great-aunt, actually. So if you think about it, it isn't surprising that we have a similar look.' She shrugged. 'The gene for grit and pluck and jolly old Britishness and all that must have skipped a generation with Dan and me, I think. But the Ranelagh good looks seem to show up fairly consistently, don't you think? Even Pa's pretty fit for his age ... It's just a shame that he's such a boring old fart with it!'

Christabel laughed and felt like giving Gussie a hug of sheer affection. The youngest Ranelagh was wonderfully entertaining company, on top of everything else.

'And these were the men in her life, we have to assume,' Gussie went on after a moment, picking up the two other photographs from the bag.

The first of the pair showed a young man, about Daniel's age, wearing a high collar and a rather roughlooking country suit of clothes. This could only be Ethan Vertue, Christabel assumed, studying the image that Gussie held. He'd been tidied up rather drastically for an official estate photograph, by the looks of it, with hair slicked down and boots highly polished, and, both ominously and prophetically, he was holding a broken shotgun.

'Cute,' observed Gussie succinctly, and Christabel had to agree. It was easy to see Ethan's attractiveness, even though, like Eleanor, he seemed constricted by both his clothing and the pose. Like his lover, there appeared to be an undisguisable eroticism simmering beneath the surface of him – a charm and lustiness that sparkled in his eyes and suggested that his firm mouth was used to smiling.

Gussie replaced Ethan's photograph with that of another, much older man. 'Not cute,' she said thoughtfully, 'but there's something there.'

Charles Woodforde had a serious and refined face, elegantly angular and hauntingly pale and troubled. Christabel realised he must have loved his wife, but that he'd had terrible difficulty showing it. For a split second, she seemed to see Nicholas in Woodforde's stead.

But Nicholas isn't cold, she told herself, refocusing on the solemn visage of Charles Woodforde. He's just perversely subtle, and that's a very different thing.

'He's striking, certainly,' she said, comparing the two photographs, 'and Eleanor must have loved him too, in a way. Or she wouldn't have married him in the first place, or have kept his picture in secret, along with Ethan's.'

'I think you're right,' said Gussie thoughtfully. 'But, as the stories go, he was a bit mad ... You know, unstable. He was probably violently jealous, because he loved her far too much.'

The two women fell silent for a moment, and Christabel considered the strange ménage represented by the photographs. There's a present-day parallel being played out too, she thought suddenly, feeling thankful that Nicholas didn't take jealousy to such murderous extremes. His reprisals were devious but they were also darkly pleasurable.

And it seemed that Gussie was thinking along the same lines as she was.

'You're living a sort of contemporary version of all this, aren't you?' she said, indicating the photographs set out between them. 'Only it's a bit better balanced. Because your Nicholas has got his Jamie, to your Daniel ...' She seemed about to say more, but didn't do so. Christabel watched, feeling a shimmer of anticipation as Gussie fidgeted, pleating the bedspread.

'Ah, but it's not all that well balanced, is it?' Christabel said, wanting to smile. It was quite easy to read

Gussie's unspoken hints. 'I've got *you*, as well as Daniel, haven't I?'

'Yes. You have,' said Gussie, her beautiful face serious beneath the smudges of grey dust that only seemed to enhance it. 'If you want me . . .'

Caught on the edge of her spontaneous desire for the other woman, Christabel felt confusion. She looked more closely at Gussie and saw, along with the sensuality, a wry and almost childlike wistfulness. Daniel's bold and gorgeous sister looked unexpectedly unsure of herself.

'Of course I want you, Gussie,' said Christabel, reaching out to touch Gussie's grimy face. 'Who wouldn't? You're beautiful and clever and exciting.'

Gussie gave her a twitchy little smile, then turned her face so she could kiss Christabel's caressing palm. It occurred to Christabel suddenly that this was a *young* woman she was with. Gussie's worldliness and confidence had conspired to make Christabel feel the younger one, until now; but, in the face of this strange moment, the true order began to reassert itself. Christabel felt a sudden visceral urge – a need even – to be kind and nurturing, as well as raw and passionate.

Pushing Gussie's thick, wild hair away from her face, Christabel traced the pure sweet lines of the other woman's face with her fingertips.

'I do want you, Gussie,' she said. 'I want you now. Dust and all. Please let me make love to you.'

'Really?' said Gussie, her voice small. Like her brother, she was infinitely empathic, Christabel sensed. The young woman was conspiring with her, reverting to girlishness to please her.

'Really,' said Christabel, full of determination. She took Gussie's delicately pointed chin between her fingertips and brought the younger woman's mouth to hers. Gussie's lips yielded like bruised petals, totally acquiescent; her tongue lay quiet, stirring only as Christabel probed it.

'But I'm all dirty and sweaty and horrible,' Gussie said, as Christabel freed her mouth. She looked down, as if ashamed of the dust of honest toil. 'I ought to shower first.'

'Don't you dare. I want you now,' said Christabel. Not giving the momentum the chance to lapse, she put her dirty hand on the area of equally dirty white T-shirt that covered Gussie's left breast, and the girl moaned and immediately thrust her chest forward.

'We'll mess up the sheets,' protested Gussie, her voice, in character, a little whiny.

'Then we'll do it on the floor,' said Christabel, rising from her seat on the bed and urging Gussie up, too. She gave the firm full globe enclosed in her fingers an encouraging squeeze.

'I'm not your husband. Or Dan. I'm just a woman,' said Gussie, clearly fighting the pleasure of the simple, earthy caress. 'Do you really like women, Christabel? Or are you just trying to be kind?'

'Don't be a fool, Gussie,' Christabel replied, surprising herself with the roughness of her own voice. 'I never do anything that I don't want to. Not really.'

And I don't, she thought, thumbing the younger woman's engorged nipple and enjoying the way Gussie's legs almost seemed to buckle.

It was true. Even the trials that Nicholas had put her through – the shaming and the exhibition, the spanking on the terrace – were things that the wiser part of her had been longing for. She longed for them now, even though she also desired Gussie. If Nicholas were to come in this instant, and bend her over the bed and spank her, she would welcome it. She'd welcome worse. She thought of her dream of the schoolroom. Rulers and canes and whatever else there was that could be used to punish and humiliate. She imagined standing out on the terrace, naked, her bottom thrashed and throbbing, while her husband – not Jamie! – manipulated her clitoris until she orgasmed.

That was it. That was the crux of it. She wanted Nicholas. His mouth. His fingers. His cock. She couldn't remember how long it had been since she'd had him inside her, and him not fucking her was a far worse punishment than any beating or indignity.

A small sound of distress brought her back to the moment. Her hand was still on Gussie's breast, and she realised that the other woman had sensed her sudden absence.

Guilty, Christabel kissed Gussie again; messily and with much clashing of teeth and tongues, rolling and mashing the firm orb of her breast at the same time. She could feel Gussie almost melting against her, and taste the heat of her sighs, straight from her mouth.

'Get down on the rug, Gussie,' she said as they broke for air. 'Lie down and take off your shorts and your knickers . . . Nothing else.'

Gussie's green eyes widened, then came alive with delight and fearfulness. With nun-like grace, she sank to the antique rug and began to comply with Christabel's command. Her shorts were stranglingly tight, and she struggled to get them off, losing her elegance as she wriggled and tugged and shimmied. She was wearing a pair of cream lace bikini briefs, Christabel saw, but they came away in a tangle with the denim cut-offs. Her face pink with effort and mock anguish, Gussie dragged both garments off, with some difficulty, over her trainers.

But yes, I do want her! thought Christabel feeling a strange yet gratifying sense of lightness as she stared down at the archetypally wanton sight of Gussie, half naked and looking as if she desperately wanted to touch herself. The younger woman's legs were flexed and parted, and her moist juiciness was evident and displayed by her neatly trimmed corona of pubic hair. Christabel could clearly see her inner labia and clitoris.

'That's it. Legs wider, though. Touch yourself.'

Hearing the brief instructions, Christabel suddenly

wanted to look around in surprise and see who'd issued them. But it had been her. She had stepped up to the mark, assumed the mantle, taken ascendancy. Behind her cool face, she smiled and said a silent thank you to the absent Nicholas. How marvellously he'd taught by example, helping her to refine her own techniques by showing her how a master worked. She thought back to her brief episode with blond Brad, in what seemed like another lifetime. She'd only been mimicking dominance then, even though it had seemed real enough at the time. Now she was living it. She'd flipped over her own dual nature with barely any effort at all. It was so easy, she felt like laughing out aloud.

'Touch yourself,' she repeated softly, kneeling over Gussie and feeling like a dark and powerful angel. The girl obeyed her at once, slipping a hand between her legs and beginning to work herself.

'Good, Gussie. Now, tell me how that feels ... Is it nice?'

'Oh, yes! Oh, yes!' murmured Gussie, treating Christabel to a virtuoso performance of squirming and rubbing and humping her own hand. Her creamy, honey-coloured bottom was lifting up from the jewel-patterned rug beneath her, the muscles in her thighs and buttocks working compulsively. To Christabel, the sight was delectable, inciting sweet tremors in her own excited flesh. She wanted to reach down and worry her own clitoris in just the way Gussie was pounding hers. But that would undermine her now – it was not the moment.

She moved closer. Knelt down. Studied the delicate, pulsing entrance of Gussie's sex from a distance of little more than inches. Watching the snug orifice twitch and pulse, she had an idea, and rose immediately to her feet, standing between her younger lover's thighs.

'Keep doing yourself,' she ordered, looking down into Gussie's stricken face. She smiled to reassure the girl she wasn't abandoning her completely. 'I want to try something. I won't be a moment . . . Try not to climax.'

Turning from the stunning sight of Gussie caressing herself, Christabel went to the oak dresser which now contained her lingerie and other clothing. Opening a drawer and lifting aside a pile of silk frippery, she took out the vibrator she'd stowed away just the other day. How opportune that she'd decided to bring it with her. She supposed she had Nicholas to thank for that, too. She might not have bothered with it if he hadn't taunted her, back in London.

On returning her attention to Gussie, Christabel found the younger woman still stroking herself, but in a lighter, more circumspect manner. She was taking good care to obey her instructions – not to come.

'Good girl,' whispered Christabel, sinking down again between Gussie's outstretched thighs. 'You can stop now, if you want to . . . Just hold still.'

Gussie let her hands slide away from her body and lie beside her, like a pair of wilted lilies, at her side. Her sex – perfectly exposed now – was still too, but at the same time looked strangely vibrant and volatile. As if dynamic energy were somehow contained within the juicy, crimson membranes – a volcanic power which waited only for a trigger.

'Oh, Gussie, you're so juicy . . . so rude,' murmured Christabel, using her tone of voice, and her warm breath in proximity to Gussie's even warmer sex-flesh, to leave her companion in no doubt as to which aspect of her anatomy she was referring. 'So swollen and excited . . . Can you part your legs a little wider for me? Spread yourself with your fingers . . . But without touching anything between them?'

Gussie nodded, then swallowed as if her mouth were dry. Using the very tips of her fingers, she reached down between her legs again, and drew her outer labia apart, revealing the crinkled inner flesh and the stiff red button of her clitoris.

'Well done, my sweet. That's gorgeous,' murmured Christabel, uncapping a small tube of lubricant that she'd brought with her to the rug. She smoothed a couple of drops of the clear, silky substance over the pink head of the vibrator, then poised the tube itself directly over Gussie's genitals, where the younger woman was still holding herself wide open. 'Now I'm going to anoint you with a little bit of clear gel ... To make you nice and sticky for me. So I want you to try and continue to keep as still as you possibly can.'

Gussie's green eyes snapped open and she looked downward. Christabel saw her take in the position of the lubricant tube, and the string of clear jelly already snaking its way downward. As the substance hit her, Gussie groaned very softly and the muscles in her thighs twitched a little; but, to Christabel's delight, the younger woman's body remained quite still.

A devil took hold of Christabel. Or at least took control of her fingers. She squeezed hard, and continued to squeeze, exhuding the entire contents of the tube of gel on to Gussie's quim.

'What are you doing, you mad thing?' demanded the younger woman, giggling at the sight, and obviously also the feel of the slippery deluge.

Christabel laughed too. 'Well, I never like to skimp on things,' she said, crushing the tube and watching the silky mess trickling and slithering, its slip-slidy progress causing Gussie to tense and contract her anus and the inner muscles of her bottom-cheeks. The mouth of her sex made a vulgar slurping sound.

'Oh, God! Oh, please ... I don't think I can hold on! I'm going to come!' bewailed Gussie, releasing her saturated labia and gouging at the patterned rug beneath her. Christabel could see the tendons in the young woman's legs tightening like the control wires of some fabulous mechanism. Gussie's bottom began to lift, and her bare belly to ripple.

'Don't,' commanded Christabel, injecting as much

fierceness as she was able into her voice, whilst still laughing. 'Don't come! You little slut, control yourself!'

Gussie appeared to tense every muscle and sinew in her body. 'Yes, ma'am,' she spluttered, biting her lips, her heels scrabbling. 'Oh, God, this is just like being back at girl's school!'

Christabel was taken aback, and lost the beat for a moment. 'So you did ... um ... *things* at boarding school too, then?'

'Oh, yes; we played some horribly dirty little games. Some of them a lot worse than this,' replied Gussie, panting with the effort of governing herself. 'It was fabulous fun though ... I learned nearly all I needed to know back in that dormitory, I can tell you.'

Christabel smiled inside, thinking again of her own rather less extreme explorations. 'Then that's all the more reason for you to learn a little self-control now, my girl!' Still fighting laughter, she reacquired her stern persona. 'And if you cannot, I'll most probably have to punish you.'

Almost before the words were out of her mouth, Christabel saw Gussie's sex clench again. Ah, so it was that way for Daniel's dishonourable sister too, was it? Christabel felt a little flame of fellow-feeling and satisfaction. She tossed aside the spent lubricant tube and took up the fabulous pink staff that bestowed so much pleasure.

Should I punish or please? she wondered, exploring the slick shape of the vibrator with her fingertips as Gussie continued to squirm and shimmy in ever greater expressions of frustration. Perhaps a little of both?

'Could you bear to be punished, Gussie?' she asked softly, setting the vibrator purring, but not applying it. 'If I promised you a little of *this* –' she touched the humming tip to the inside of Gussie's thigh and watched the girl jerk and try to manoeuvre her crotch towards the misplaced stimulation '– would you let me smack you? And make you cry?' She moved the vibrator an inch or two upward.

'Yes. Oh, God, yes,' murmured Gussie, her head beginning to thrash from side to side, setting her wild black curls in motion. 'Do anything you want, my darling. But do something!'

Christabel turned off the vibrator and removed it. Rocking back on her heels slightly, she reviewed the composition of female flesh before her. Gussie's large breasts were lolling slightly beneath the grubby white T-shirt, but they were still enviably firm and well shaped, even when she was lying prone. Christabel felt an overpowering urge to see their gloriousness naked and exposed again.

'Push up your T-shirt, Gussie,' she said, striving to emulate the impassive tone that Nicholas used to such effect. She heard a little tremor in her voice, but not much, and she felt pleased. 'Show me your tits,' she went on, revelling in the crudeness, but still trying not to reveal as much.

Gussie stilled, gave Christabel a sudden, knowledge-filled look, then reached for the loose hem of her T-shirt. She's playing the game just as much as I am, thought Christabel, her heart filling with affection for this beautiful and wild-spirited woman. Bless you, Gussie, she told her, in silence.

Rolling up the white cotton, Gussie revealed herself – a stunning sight, naked from her upper chest to her trainer-clad feet. She was like a gift, freely given, that Christabel relished. Her skin was honeyed and gleaming, her pubic bush as black as night, her saturated sex tumescent. Crowning her stunning breasts were her dark and thickened nipples, standing like little corks, rude and insolent. Inviting. Christabel leant over them, and briefly mouthed each one.

Wriggling and gasping, Gussie grabbed her and, for a moment, Christabel allowed it. She could taste the salt of sweat on Gussie's skin, and she found it intoxicating.

Using her teeth very delicately, she gripped the nipple in her mouth between them and tugged on it, drawing up the whole breast from Gussie's sleek ribcage. The younger woman groaned and kicked her legs, clearly rapturous. Christabel tightened her grip, but infinitesimally. Nevertheless, Gussie thrashed harder and began to pant, intoning, 'Oh, God! Oh, God! Oh, God!' in a mantra.

Christabel released her immediately and knocked away the hand that Gussie had clamped to her own crotch.

'I told you not to come yet,' Christabel said, finding her role and injecting steel into her voice.

'I can't help myself!' wailed Gussie, still in motion. 'I'm almost there ... Please let me come! Christabel! Please!'

'Not yet,' reiterated Christabel, enjoying herself, and enjoying the way Gussie was clenching her teeth, screwing her hands into fists at her side, and waving her slender hips to and fro. 'And try to stay still, will you?'

Gussie obeyed, though the effort seemed to cost her as much energy as her frustrated movements had. Christabel moved around, so that she was kneeling by the side of the younger woman; then, before she really had time to dissect her own strategy, she grabbed one of Gussie's nipples with the fingers of her left hand and, with her right hand, laid a sharp resounding slap across the pale expanse of Gussie's inner thigh.

Gussie squealed.

Christabel hissed, 'Silence!' and somehow managed to maintain her iron-clad persona, even though the blow had as great an impact on her, she suspected, as it had upon Gussie's tender skin. Without pausing for further analysis, she struck again – and again – finding the growing bloom of the rose-pink marks she'd made hypnotically fascinating. She felt an intense, almost dizzying urge to extend the stigmata, to redden the entire length of both Gussie's inner thighs, then turn the girl over and begin working on her bottom and the backs of her thighs. But her hand rose and fell, rose and fell, rose and fell, the target constant. With her other hand, she twisted Gussie's nipple.

Gussie was sobbing now but, judging by the way her pelvis was helplessly weaving again, she found the hot sting of her slapped thigh a source of arousal.

She's nearly there, thought Christabel, ever more fascinated. Gussie's glistening quim gaped, completely abandoned, yet the girl was on the very point of climax. It was the dual pain – in her breast and thigh – that was taking her higher.

Once again, Christabel drew back and regrouped. She released Gussie's nipple, and ceased the spanking. The younger woman, however, still continued to jerk and grunt, her movements and her utterances uncouth yet beautiful. Christabel wanted to reward her for such a lubricious exhibition.

'Hush now, Gussie,' she whispered, crouching low and cooing into her female lover's ear. 'If you're a good quiet girl now, I'll let you have an orgasm . . . In fact, I'll give it to you myself, if you behave yourself. Do you think you can keep still? And not make a noise?'

Pursing her lips, Gussie rolled her eyes, but nodded compliantly. She stilled her body of all gross movement, obviously to the very limit of her own ability, although Christabel could still see the younger woman's tense and sweat-streaked skin trembling finely; and there was a frantic pulse beating in her creamy, unpunished thigh.

Christabel looked around on the rug, then retrieved the almost forgotten but still gel-smeared vibrator. Smiling, she showed it to Gussie – demonstrating its function with a quick, low-power buzz in front of the young woman's face – then added a slick of her own saliva to the neutral-tasting lubricant. Gussie remained silent throughout this, but her huge green eyes seemed to be begging even more fervently for sexual mercy. Christabel wasn't quite sure whether this was a plea that she use the vibrator, or withhold it; but, choosing her own course, she lowered it to within an inch of Gussie's streaming quim. 'Do you want it?' she asked, knowing that the answer, to her, was purely academic. Nothing would stop her now from using the appliance on Gussie.

Daniel's sister nodded, her exquisite face contorting with the effort of remaining silent and motionless, and, with a nod of her own, Christabel slowly began to effect the insertion.

A single tear ran down Gussie's cheek as the vibrator went into her. It slipped in with no effort whatsoever, Christabel was delighted to discover; not because Gussie wasn't tight and snug down there, but because the plastic was smooth and riding an overflowing well of moisture. The only effort was made by Christabel, trying to work slowly. As she carefully manoeuvred the finely crafted object into position, she recalled with some happiness how such a measured penetration could feel.

She remembered the last time that Nicholas had made love to her.

Her husband was a master of the achingly slow and incremental possession. His cock was large and well formed, and his favoured way of introducing it into her body allowed for full and ecstatic appreciation of its qualities. It was more years than she cared to count since Christabel had been a virgin but, when Nicholas pushed into her, inch by breathtaking inch – exerting a self-control she could never have achieved, were the roles to be reversed – she found herself stretched in a way that reminded her poignantly of her innocence.

'Oh, Nicholas,' she murmured; then, with a shock of dislocation, she came suddenly back to the present. She glanced down at Gussie's agonised face and tightly closed eyes, but saw no indication that the girl had heard the clandestinely quoted name. She was clearly concentrating every last fibre of her will in the service of following Christabel's own instructions. She was fighting the urge to flail about and scream in the intensity of her pleasure.

'Oh, my God, Gussie, you're strong,' whispered Christabel, inclining herself more closely over the magnificent sexual martyr stretched out before her. 'You're far stronger, my sweet, than I could ever be.'

Letting the mass of her hair fall across Gussie's belly, she kissed the veiled bump of the younger woman's pubic bone – then backed off again quickly when Gussie's hips inevitably rose.

Ah, it was time to stop teasing now. Time to grant this glorious creature the reward she'd so richly earnt with her body and her pain. With a speed and dexterity which she found impressive even in herself, Christabel swivelled the vibrator bevel at the same time as she plunged down and in and pressed her tongue to Gussie's swollen clitoris.

Then, as the electronic dildo thrummed and hummed, and she did her best to suck and nuzzle in time to its fine, sonic rhythm, Christabel heard her happy lover lose the battle . . . and start to shriek.

'So, how are we going to do this, then?'

Christabel struggled to make sense of the statement. Her brain was numbed by pleasure and, for a few seconds, she had no idea what Gussie was talking about. Then everything seemed to rotate somehow and the meaning dropped into place. Gussie was talking about the mystery of Eleanor Woodforde and the significance of the letter signed 'Marie-Ange Chamfort'.

Pulling herself into an upright sitting position, Christabel surveyed the erotic tableau of which she was a part. Both she and Gussie were completely naked now, but they hadn't yet moved from the Persian rug. The last thing Christabel clearly remembered was crouching over Gussie's face, while the vibrator still trilled away merrily inside the younger woman's body . . . After that, everything had been a tangle of tongues, flickering fingers, and writhing, thrashing climaxes.

Christabel blinked, trying to clear the images. She had to pull herself together. Think. It was difficult, given the distraction of Gussie's naked body, but not impossible. Rising to her feet, she reached for her silk robe, which lay across the end of the bed, and shrugged it on.

'I'm not quite sure, really. If you know this Chamfort woman, would you approach her?' She felt dubious at handing over the task to Gussie. Not because she didn't trust her, but because it seemed that she was dumping the younger women with all the legwork. 'If you don't mind, that is?'

'Of course I don't,' said Gussie cheerfully, unwinding her graceful form from the floor, and getting up too. 'I *want* to do it. Eleanor was my great-aunt, after all. I only feel guilty at not doing anything about this sooner . . . Especially for poor Dan's sake.' She reached for her white T-shirt and pulled it on, over her head.

Christabel felt a pang of loss. Somehow, she'd been assuming that she and Gussie would shower together, then perhaps eat, and maybe spend the night in each other's arms, in the great bed they were standing beside. She had a feeling that Nicholas might be otherwise engaged.

'Would you like to borrow a robe? We could take a shower,' she suggested.

But Gussie was already wriggling into her panties and shorts.

'I'm tempted, sweetheart,' said Gussie, shrugging expressively, then dipping down to put on her trainers. 'You wouldn't believe how I'm tempted . . .' She straightened up, genuine longing on her face. 'But I have to go back to town tonight. I should have gone earlier . . . That's how irresponsible I am.' She came towards Christabel, and took her hand. Raising it to her lips, she kissed the palm passionately; then, with some reluctance, let go. 'But I've got a job tomorrow. An early start ... And, as it's the first decent thing that's come my way in ages, I owe it to myself to give it a shot.' She shrugged again. Looked about twelve. 'I'm so sorry, Christabel.'

'Don't worry, love,' replied Christabel, reaching out and hugging the other woman, and breathing in the rich, musky fragrance of what they'd shared together. 'There'll be other chances. Don't you worry. That's a promise.'

For a while, they simply held each other; and then, finally, it was time to part. Gussie agreed to attempt to track down Marisa Chamfort and approach her, then to report back to Christabel. It seemed wiser to keep it all just between the two of them until they knew more. Daniel's peace of mind was too fragile to have his hopes raised, then dashed. Marisa Chamfort might know nothing at all. She might even be an entirely different Chamfort altogether.

'And you, will you be all right?' Gussie's big green eyes were dark with concern as the two women stood, preparing to part, at the open door.

'I'll be fine,' said Christabel, aware that she was less sure of herself than she was trying to sound. Could she handle what she'd seen between Nicholas and Jamie? Now that she was about to lose the sweet distraction that Gussie's beautiful presence provided.

'Don't worry ... I can handle those two,' she went on. 'I have a bargaining chip of my own now. The balance of power is much more even.'

'But what about Jamie? Where does he figure in all this. He looked pretty ... um ... possessive to me.' Gussie still looked worried.

'Look, Gussie, when it comes right down to it, Jamie isn't even in the game. It's just me and Nicholas in the big equation. He doesn't take our marriage lightly, and neither do I. However it might seem ... Don't worry, sweetheart. Please. Everything will be all right.'

But as, after a last delicious and distracting kiss, Gussie left, Christabel began to wonder just who it was she thought she was kidding.

Chapter Thirteen
Different Shades of Black

'Mr Sutherland wonders if you would be kind enough to join him in the dining room.'

Christabel stared at the phone receiver in her hand and wondered whether it was her husband or Paula Blake who was pulling her leg. Maybe it was both? Either way, it seemed that the normal social niceties would continue to be observed at Collingwood – no matter how abnormal everything else had become.

Assuring the housekeeper that she would be down shortly, Christabel flicked quickly through the relatively limited selection of evening clothes she'd brought with her to the country, and selected a sleek black shift that made her feel strong and chic and in control of herself. The dress was modest in cut, quite restrained in comparison to many of her clothes, but its slim shape flattered her without making her a sex object. An image she had no intention of projecting on this occasion. If Nicholas ordered his grinning, sodomising minion to start taking liberties with her tonight, she would halt the proceedings by describing exactly what she'd seen in the conservatory.

'Good evening, Christabel,' her husband said, rising to greet her as she entered the dining room. To her surprise, he was on his own, a dark-clad figure enthroned at the head of the table. But, even alone, he seemed to fill the room with omens, an aura of power and presentiment that thrilled her.

'Good evening, Nicholas,' she replied, taking the seat he'd courteously held out for her. She looked around and saw that there were just the two places laid; his at the end of the table, hers next to it, but on the long edge.

Where was he then? Her husband's lover?

The absence of Jamie was disconcerting. It ran counter to all the scenarios she'd been planning and, irrational as it seemed, she felt more uneasy rather than less. It suddenly occurred to her that she saw Jamie as a moderator.

'So, where's laughing boy tonight?' she enquired as Nicholas poured wine for her, then lifted the lid from a silver serving-dish. The tantalising aroma of a light game casserole drifted up to Christabel's nostrils, and the silent growl of her empty stomach reminded her it was many hours since she'd eaten, and then only a snack.

'I asked Jamie to return to London. On a business matter,' replied Nicholas casually, beginning to spoon the fragrant meat concoction on to a plate. 'It wasn't something that required the presence of both of us, so I took the liberty of claiming *droit de seigneur*, so to speak, and remaining here with you.' As he swapped their plates, he gave her a strange, almost flirtatious look. 'After all, it is what I pay him for . . . To do my bidding, and make my life easier.'

Is that what you call it? Christabel wanted to retort. Doing your bidding? She felt that she needed another set of senses to listen to Nicholas when he was in this mood. Normal physical hearing wasn't sufficiently sensitive to pick up every nuance of what he said. There could be other meanings, hidden in the ones she'd thought she'd understood.

She took a sip of the substantial but not over-heavy

red wine that Nicholas had no doubt chosen himself to accompany the game. It was heavenly, but she was wary. She needed her wits about her so one glass was all she dare risk, to steady her nerves.

'Lucky you,' she said, noncommittally. She didn't want to take the chance of antagonising Nicholas, either. Why spoil a good dinner?

'Yes, I am.' Nicholas paused in the act of offering her vegetables. 'Aren't I? A beautiful wife. An efficient and talented personal assistant. What man could ask for more?'

Christabel's hands were shaking as she took some broccoli and new potatoes. She couldn't help but see ghostly images of her husband and his lover in the conservatory: the sculpted perfection of their bodies; quite disparate in appearance, yet each desirable in his own specifics. Nicholas looked cool, now: unflappably poised and, as so often, all in black. And yet, beneath the casual silk shirt and the fluidly cut trousers, there was a body that had sweated and writhed in the steamy, neo-tropical heat of the glasshouse. The lips that sipped fine wine had groaned and contorted as a man twenty years Nicholas's junior had borne down on him and buggered him relentlessly. There was no evidence now that Nicholas had ever been in anything but absolute control of whatever situation he found himself in. If anything, he seemed more confident and at his ease than ever.

Yet she wondered . . .

'Are we looking after ourselves tonight?' she asked, espying a stay-warm cafetière on the sideboard, along with a bowl containing what was obviously another of Paula Blake's demoniac desserts.

'Yes. I thought it would be nicer . . . More intimate,' said Nicholas before taking a bite of casserole. 'This is superb, don't you think? Perhaps we should try and prise the recipe out of Paula and pass it on to Mrs Gill?'

What the hell are you up to, Nicholas? she thought,

but simply agreed that the casserole was fabulous. She watched him eat – his actions, as ever, economical and elegant – and felt her own unease and sense of dislocation grow. She had been a fool to think she could ever give back as good as she got with Nicholas. He had her on tenterhooks and perspiring already, and all they'd done was enjoy the first few mouthfuls of their dinner.

'So, did you and Jamie have a productive day?'

Well, one has to try, doesn't one? she thought, listening to what seemed like an echo of her own leading question, and wondering what the odds were of getting a revealing answer.

Nicholas stared mildly back at her, his grey eyes as calm as a windless lake.

'Very much so, thank you,' he said, before continuing to eat. He seemed as immune to provocation as he always did, and Christabel's intuition told her that inside he was probably laughing at her efforts. She had made a tentative first strike but it had bounced off him, ineffectual.

'And yourself? Did you have a satisfactory day?'

Very much so, thank you! she longed to say, in a singsong fashion, in order to mock him. 'Yes, I did actually,' she said instead. 'I took some photographs in the park – for that nature book idea that you seemed to find so amusing – and then later on I did some exploring inside the house.' She paused and looked him boldly in the eye, challenging him to crack, to colour and look away. Not very surprisingly, he held her gaze, his own opaque. 'Gussie had an idea that we might find some interesting memorabilia of earlier owners of Collingwood. Something that might throw some light on – on certain problems that Daniel has. He has a fixation about someone who used to work on the estate, and he . . . Well, he can't come into the house, and he has visions and –' She stopped, realising how preposterous this would seem to a level-headed pragmatist like Nicholas. 'I suppose this all sounds rather pathetic to you?' she said, wishing she could explain Daniel's strange psychology in a way that expressed the younger man's strengths as well as his vulnerability.

'No. It doesn't ... Not really,' her husband said quietly. With a look on his face that appeared strangely nonjudgmental, he poured a little more wine for them both. 'I'd gathered from the Blakes that Daniel Ranelagh suffers from certain psychological problems, but I'd no idea of the details ... Has he undergone some kind of trauma?'

As they continued with their meal, Christabel found herself increasingly better able to describe Daniel Ranelagh's situation, and the background to it that she and Gussie had so far discovered. Nicholas listened thoughtfully, and without interrupting, although, when she paused to eat now and again, he asked the occasional, incisive question.

Finally, when Christabel had finished – outlining Gussie's intention to contact Marisa Chamfort and discover if she was related to the 'Marie-Ange' of the letter – Nicholas said, 'That's curious ... I believe I've heard that name before, too.' For the first time, his relatively unlined brow puckered. 'In fact, I've probably seen her magazine.'

Christabel dropped her spoon on to her dessert plate with a minor clatter. They had been eating Paula Blake's rich, boozy trifle, which was utterly sublime; but, intrigued by this new development, Christabel suddenly lost interest in it.

'You? You read sex mags?' she asked, astounded.

Nicholas laughed. 'Occasionally,' he murmured. 'Is there any reason why I shouldn't?'

'No. No reason ...' she replied, still bemused. 'It just doesn't seem like you, somehow. I thought you were above that sort of thing.'

'What *does* seem like me?' He wasn't laughing any more. He seemed as calm and controlled as ever, but not without a residue of humour.

215

'I don't know. I hardly know the real *you* . . .'

It was true. And he'd managed to wrong-foot her again. She felt a strange meld of emotions – fascination and anger. It made her weak; it made her giddy; it made her excited. It made her aware of something that her mind had so foolishly and inexplicably forgotten, but which her body was now deliciously recalling. That, with this man, she didn't always want the upper hand.

'I'm flattered that you find me so enigmatic, my dear.' Nicholas lifted his glass and swirled the wine in it contemplatively. Christabel found herself focusing on the sinews of his hand and remembering seeing them taut as he clenched his fist – or gouged convulsively at anything within reach as Jamie worked his fingers deep inside him. 'But as for me being above anything? Not really . . .' He glanced up from the ruby depths of his wine and looked straight at her. 'I'm as base as the next man, and I'm sure you know that.'

Should she tell him what she'd seen?

'I like games, Christabel. Any game, really, as long as it's not straightforward. Or easy.' His eyes glinted, but not coolly now. They seemed like polished gunmetal, and bright. Almost reflective. 'I want to scale heights . . . and to plumb depths. To experience every level . . .' He shrugged; just the most infinitesimal lift of his shoulders, but it told Christabel with perfect clarity that he knew what she'd seen. 'I like to play in the shadows, and the grey areas.'

It was the most revealing evocation of her husband's personality that she had ever encountered or imagined. And Christabel sensed that what he was showing her was a gesture. The offer of a conduit between them. She suddenly began to understand what it was about her that he'd found lacking . . .

'And me, I'm too one-dimensional for you, aren't I?' she said, taking a longer drink of wine. 'Not "grey" enough. Not "dark" enough . . . Always grabbing at simple, easy pleasures that would never interest you.'

216

She felt sad and abandoned all of a sudden, a thousand times more hurt than she ought to have been by her husband's liaison with his personal assistant. It dawned on her that her infidelities back in London had never truly bothered Nicholas. It was just the very ordinariness of them that made her husband feel let down.

'Don't denigrate yourself, Christabel,' Nicholas said softly, putting down his glass and taking her hand. 'Not everyone sees their own potential, or even understands their own nature, straight away.' He held her fingers lightly for a moment, then began to gently rub his thumb over them, as if he were testing the texture of a fabric . . . or perhaps the responsiveness of her skin?

'But I'm thirty-one, Nicholas!' she cried. The tiny stroking movement was muddling her, stirring up the weak feelings, the melting. The strange urge she had to give something very important away. A part of herself. Into his care. His dominance. 'Surely I should have known,' she went on uncertainly, 'realised sooner . . . Sooner than this?'

'But you know now, don't you?' he said, a note coming into his voice that somehow amplified her sense of weakness. She was becoming a reed, she realised, bending to a mighty force. 'You're beginning to understand?'

She nodded.

He gave her a smile, a warm, almost soft smile that she realised was the last she might see for a while. 'I was a middle-aged man before I understood, Christabel. Older than you. There is no right or wrong time to begin.'

There was a long heavy moment of silence. Christabel watched her husband kill the gentle smile, only to leave a faint essence of it, deep in the back of his eyes.

'Remove your dress,' he said, his voice as cool and grey and impassive as his eyes.

Again?

It seemed that there was a right time to begin playing after all.

Christabel's blue eyes flared for a moment, first with confusion, then with hot, intrinsically female defiance. Nicholas watched the process with fascination as she ignored the first, then tamped down firmly on the second. The completeness of her response now was so awesome it almost unmanned him. She had made a quantum leap in her comprehension of his ways. Before, when he'd played with her, she had understood and she had looked into the shadows. Tonight, as she rose smoothly to her feet and shucked off her dress without demur or commotion, she was there, in the magic darkness, right beside him.

And she was exquisite.

Beneath the classic black dress, her underwear was black, too. Stretch satin. A plainly cut bra, full briefs, sheer black hold-up stockings. Nothing fancy or over-done, just a subtle allure that connected directly with his need for her. 'Yes. Very good,' he said, while his mind and cock both thrilled to her beauty. She had swept her thick strawberry-blonde hair up into a pleat that perfectly complemented the understated lingerie, and Nicholas had a sudden mad urge to push her to the floor, kneel over her, and then come on to the tender exposed nape of her neck. She was magnificent, well worth the wait, the perfect mate for him.

'Lick your lips,' he said, taking a sip of his wine to steady himself. He was aware that the responsibility lay with him now. *He* must not disappoint *her*. There must be no sign of his inner turmoil, even if – as he suspected – she was just as aware of it as he was. The game must be played, and played immaculately, by both its parties. 'Step away from the table, my love, so I can see you a little better.'

Lowering her eyes, his wife moved away and stood on the rug that lay parallel to the dining table. Her slender hands hung loosely at her sides and, though her stance was superficially humble, he noted that her shoulders were braced and her spine straight, as if she were deliberately flaunting her lovely breasts at him. Her nipples were prominent beneath the shiny, silky bra.

'I have friends who would love to see you like this, Christabel,' he said. 'Connoisseurs. Gameplayers. People who appreciate the true beauty of a conquered will.'

He saw a fine shudder pass through her body, but she kept her eyes directed at the rug and did not protest.

'I should like to exhibit you to them soon, Christabel. Either naked. Or partially clothed, to begin with. I should like to give you over to them, your eyes covered with a blindfold, and let them handle you and play with you.' He paused, then rose himself, walked over to her, touched her nipple through the slick stretchy fabric that covered it. 'I mean really play with you, Christabel . . . Their hands inside your panties . . . Touching you everywhere. Perhaps inserting their fingers into you. Into your sex and your bottom . . . Both at once, maybe.'

She was shaking pronouncedly now, yet still maintaining her pose. He touched her nipple again, lingering longer this time, and he seemed to feel the little cone of flesh growing harder and more crinkled beneath the silk.

'Do you remember how Jamie massaged you when we were on the terrace? Rubbing both your entrances at once?'

She nodded, and he could see her gnawing her lips, making them redder and more luscious.

'You may speak, Christabel. I never said you couldn't express yourself.'

'Yes. I remember.' Her voice was low, but surprisingly strong. He found himself more impressed than ever. His penis leapt.

'Did it excite you that I was watching you?'

'Yes, it did . . . A lot. I like it. I never realised.'

219

'And if I were to take you to a party . . . A gathering. And these things were really to happen?' He left the question open.

'That would excite me, too,' she said, and he saw her sway a little, her fingers tensing. She was becoming aroused. Wet. She wanted to touch herself. And he wanted to control that urge.

'Good,' he said, and began to parade a few familiar visions through his mind. He pictured his wife bound. His wife shamed. His wife punished. His erection ached at the brilliance of the images; they seemed three-dimensional and alive in a way they never had before.

Taking a few steps this way, then a few that, he studied Christabel from all angles. He imagined her at one of the parties he'd just mentioned. The centre of attention, surrounded by the friends he met with from time to time to indulge his fantasies. There was a regular cadre, and the gatherings were discreet, open only to that select group. But he had no doubts now that Christabel would easily qualify for entry. More than that, she had the potential to distinguish herself.

He seemed to see the familiar faces, smiling at her lush, exposed beauty, and the pliancy made all the more delicious by the will that lay beneath it. How ironic, he thought suddenly, that she should have mentioned Marisa Chamfort. A member of the group, exalted in its hierarchy, and publisher of a remarkable but carefully circulated journal that expressed the quintessence of its activities. Not, he reflected wryly, the same magazine that Augusta Ranelagh had referred to, which was a far more innocuous but still admirable publication.

He came to a halt, immediately in front of Christabel, feeling eager to proceed with the game.

'Pull your panties down for me, my dear,' he said. 'Just to your thighs, though . . . I want to see your bottom and your pubis, and your knickers in a roll, just beneath.'

Christabel looked deliciously unsure of herself for a moment, but then her expression quickly cleared.

Minx! he thought. She knows this. The classic presentation . . . Is it just instinct, or has she secrets she's never told me? Are you the one who's playing games with me, my darling?

He almost smiled, but managed to keep the joy inside.

Using the tips of her fingers, Christabel eased down her shiny black briefs and arranged them how he had specified. She had to do a little bunching and tucking to get them exactly right, but the elasticity of the fabric was helpful. Nicholas had to hide another smile when she had finished. She looked extraordinarily pleased with her achievement.

'Excellent,' he murmured, then spun on his heel and walked towards the door which led to the entrance hall and the main stairs. When he reached it, he turned.

His wife's eyes were wide. Luminous with the same blend of fear and acute arousal that had filled them when he had exposed her and humiliated her on the terrace. Oh, she loved this! She really did! And he loved *her*, the feeling as fresh as if it were the very first time he'd experienced it.

'Come on, my dear. This is nothing. Just the beginning.' He held out his hand and, shuffling slightly, but still a goddess, she came towards him.

As she walked awkwardly behind Nicholas, Christabel felt more exposed than she would have done if she'd been completely naked. And that was his intention, she realised, hiding her comprehension. She was fast beginning to understand the dynamics of such displays and inconsistencies.

She loved this. She hated this. She loved it *because* she hated it.

At the top of the stairs, he stopped and kissed her fiercely, his tongue plunging into her mouth while his fingers closed on one breast and kneaded it through the stuff of her brassière. Her bare crotch was pressed against the fine fabric of his trousers, but he ignored her pubis as if it were nothing, a cipher of her gender. His hand circled and mashed, then he took her nipple between his fingertips and pulled on it. She experienced a fleeting mental flash of Daniel doing something similar, then the younger man disappeared from her mind altogether. At a moment like this, she could think only of her husband.

'Call me "master",' murmured Nicholas, attacking her neck with a quick, rough kiss while he continued to pinch her teat. 'It might sound absurd, but it's something of a tradition . . .' He kissed her again, wetting her skin with his tongue.

'Yes, master,' she answered. A part of her acknowledged the clichéd banality of the title, and the way she was just falling into line with another demeaning situation. But a different, greater part of her experienced a thrill so intense it felt like being hit by a truck. She moaned at the pain in her breast and felt a huge rushing urge to fall down at her husband's feet and offer him anything. Everything. Her body. Her mind. The annihilation of her ego. She wanted to press her face to the smooth cloth of his trousers, and feel the pulse of his throbbing erection warm against her cheek. She wanted him to unzip himself and thrust his penis into her mouth, using her crudely and with no thought whatsoever for her pleasure. She wanted him to beat her then abandon her, unfulfilled and yearning for him.

'Will you be my slave tonight, Christabel?' he said, holding her lightly at the nape of her neck, and – still – by her nipple. 'Will you abandon yourself to my will? My will alone, with no thought for yourself?'

Christabel swayed, feeling the weight of her own body drag on the sensitive tip of her breast. The rightness, the synchronicity of his words seemed to reroute the blood from her brain and make her dizzy. In a last moment of boldness, she looked into his grey, smooth-as-iron eyes, unable to believe that they could not see directly into her thoughts and comprehend them like written words.

'Master,' she breathed, lowering her eyes again – and knowing her own unworthiness to look at him.

With one last smear of his palm against her breast, he released her. 'Walk ahead of me, slave. I want to see your bottom. I want to see it move.'

Christabel obeyed him, nervous in a way she'd never been before about the rhythm and grace of her walk. The panties around her thighs constricted her. She felt ungainly, clumsy, without merit. Her buttocks were not the faultless objects of beauty she should have made them, for him. She could have worked out harder, longer, polished her skin and made it soft as satin, pale as milk.

'Stop!'

She halted, her chest and face and neck filling with the blood-blush of her own shame. She'd been right. She was undeserving. She wondered if her bottom was blushing too.

'You have a beautiful bottom, slave, but I want to see you move it around more. Make it sway as you walk . . . Invite me with it. Make me want to do bad, bad things to it, and use it for my pleasure.'

For his pleasure? Oh . . .

Did he want to beat her? Or to bugger her? Perhaps both. There was no reason he shouldn't. Just because she'd seen him being possessed and worked by Jamie's hands on one occasion, it didn't follow that it was always that way. She tried to imagine him in her there, but had no prior experience of such a penetration that she could draw upon.

'Why are you still standing there?' he enquired, his voice as low and dark as midnight silk. 'Are you giving up already? I thought you had more spirit, slave. More capacity for sensation.'

Christabel almost leapt forward, then tried to moderate herself. Acutely aware of the globes of her bottom, she swayed her pelvis as much as she was able, tilting her hips with every high-heeled step she took. She felt idiotic and embarrassed. The more she stuck out her backside, the worse it became; and yet the shame drove her on to further abasement. When they reached the end of the landing, she tilted forward, parted her hobbled legs and circled her buttocks for him, in a spontaneous display that plumbed the deepest well of shame.

'Very nice,' observed her husband, 'but did I tell you to do that?' His hand settled on one proffered cheek and gripped it momentarily. 'When I want you to waggle, slave, I will instruct you to do so. Until then, you must simply obey.'

Christabel trembled, afraid. She could feel herself willing him to strike her now, to spank her, but she couldn't imagine where the impulse was coming from. When he'd spanked her before, it had really hurt. Far more than she would ever have previously believed.

'No, my sweet slave,' he murmured, bending over her back and pressing his clothed body against her near-nakedness, 'I don't think I will beat you tonight.' He put his hand on her belly, so close to her pubic mound that she knew his little finger must be touching the bush of curls there, so far away that her whole sex seemed to leap in a convulsive effort to entice a caress from him.

Again he did nothing. Made no move to fondle her. Feeling hopeless, abandoned and denied, Christabel made a low sound of moaning desperation in the base of her throat.

'Yes, slave, I know you want me to play with you,' he said, his hand moving lightly across her abdomen, but not downward, 'to rub your clitoris and put my fingers inside you.' His hand rose up, gliding across her ribcage and around her, pulling her so close to him that she could clearly feel his erection. 'But I'm not going to oblige you . . . Not for a while; in fact, perhaps not even

224

at all, this evening.' It was his turn to circle his hips now, giving himself pleasure by massaging his contained penis against the crack of her bottom. 'I want you to be swollen, engorged and uncomfortable ... I want to know that you're suffering, and feeling that nasty gnawing ache of frustration – because I will you to.'

Even as he spoke the words – 'engorged', 'swollen', 'gnawing ache' – Christabel experienced the sensations. Her sex felt like a hanging, bloated weight between her legs, yards wide. There was nothing she seemed to crave more than just the benison of a touch there.

Yet she knew she would have nothing. No relief. No cessation of the ever-gathering tumescence. At least, not until she'd gone through the most hellish fires of denial.

When Nicholas released her again, her trembling knees failed her and she tumbled ignominiously to the floor.

'What are you playing at?' he enquired, his tone light, almost teasing. 'On your feet, slave. I want you in my room. Come on! Chop chop!'

Oh, the cruel, cruel man! He must know that, while she was on the carpet, she could perhaps squeeze her thighs together and get just a little bit of comfort.

And yet, as he helped her up, Nicholas made her feel like a visiting princess, he was so gentle and so courteous. 'Come along, slave,' he murmured, his deep voice thrilling.

Christabel had not yet been inside her husband's bedroom, and was surprised to find it was plainer and less elaborate than the one she was quartered in. He let me have the best one, she thought, for a moment almost forgetting her discomfort. Was there no end to the unexpectedness of Nicholas? They had been married almost two years, yet every day held as many surprises as the first.

She hung her head. When all was said and done, and even allowing for his indulgences with Jamie, she really didn't deserve this man who had followed her into the bedroom. She was unworthy of him. She had to be humble. She ought to be punished.

As Nicholas closed the door, and walked around and stood before her, his demeanour relaxed yet watchful, Christabel fell to her knees again. Intentionally, this time.

'Punish me, master,' she whispered, feeling faint with excitement as she studied the simple but elegant pattern on the rug.

Nicholas stepped forward. With delicate precision, he dismantled her carefully groomed French pleat, then slid his hand amongst the thick tresses of her hair to shake the style free. 'In time, sweet slave,' he said, exerting a light, yet unequivocal pressure on the back of her head. 'In time,' he repeated, pressing her cheek to the hardness at his groin.

I love you, Christabel longed to say, but she was not sure if he would permit it. Instead, she circled her face against him like a fawning, devoted pet.

'Good girl,' he said, stilling her and ever so delicately bumping his trousered erection against her lips. But when she tried to mouth him, he retreated nimbly and urged her to her feet.

'On the bed,' he said crisply. 'Arms above your head. Legs spread. No naughty wriggling to try and craftily get yourself off.'

The Christabel of a few days ago would have denied such an intention. The Christabel of a few weeks ago would have told him to sod off and done it anyway. But now it was impossible. The Christabel of tonight wanted only to obey, and suffer so it pleased him.

Constricted by her knickers, it was difficult to get on to the bed, and into position, but Christabel managed somehow. Lifting her arms caused her breasts to tauten and rise then loll to either side a little inside the stretchy satin of her bra. The blackness of the fabric made their shape obscenely prominent.

Nicholas didn't speak once she had arranged herself

226

but, instead, he flicked open his black attaché case which he'd set upon the plain, mahogany lowboy. From where she lay, Christabel could not see the contents of the case, but her imagination supplied a deliciously menacing manifest.

If the contraption of rubber and straps that he'd coerced her into travelling down here in was anything to go by, who alone knew what other toys he might have with him? She pictured giant dildoes, slithery and obscene in the sculpted shape of penises; more leather restraints with which to cincture and constrain her body; plugs and balls that inflated; things that throbbed and hummed like her own pretty pink vibrator.

The waiting became agonising, far more of a trial because she had to hold the pose herself rather than surrender responsibility to bondage of any kind. She groaned under her breath as Nicholas reached into the case, then frowned, and rejected whatever it was he'd chosen a second ago. She felt the heaviness in her groin grow yet more ponderous.

In the end he selected what appeared to be a number of medium-sized lengths of soft black cord, then came towards her, a devilish smile upon his face. 'The simplest props are always the best,' he said with quiet satisfaction, and set about securing her to the brass rails at the bed's head and foot.

It was so much easier when she was tied. At least it seemed that way, at first. Christabel felt able to relax once the black ties held her in place; her limbs grew pliant as her tautened muscles began to untense.

That was until Nicholas sat down beside her on the bed.

'Can you be what I want, Christabel?' His hand settled like down upon the side of her face, cupping her cheek.

Was he expecting her to answer? Maybe this was a test? Should she keep still and silent, or respond to him with the honesty he seemed to require?

227

'Speak, slave . . . You may speak.'

It no longer surprised her that he apparently had access to her mind, as well as to every other part of her.

'Yes,' she said, casting about not for the most subservient answer, but for the true one, 'I can be what you want –' she paused, knowing she must give him what was in her heart '– but not all the time.' His grey eyes didn't waver from her face; his hand remained still and warm against her skin. 'A lot of the time, maybe . . . But there's a part of me that doesn't fit into all this. A part that needs to have control, sometimes.'

Nicholas laughed, but the sound was kind, young, delighted. 'Better and better,' he said, rubbing his thumb over her parted lips. 'That's what I want . . . Exactly what I want.' He slid aside the thumb and kissed her, touching his tongue moistly and wantonly to her lower lip. 'Because there will be times when I want these particular roles reversed, my slave. Times when I'm the one who's deserving of abuse.'

Is that what you've been using Jamie for, my love? thought Christabel dreamily, as her husband sat up again and seemed to ruminate on his options. For those times when you need to be the vulnerable one?

She did not voice the questions, however, but she sensed that her husband read them in her eyes.

'But that's not tonight, my slave,' he said, his face still close to hers. Brushing her hair back from her brow, he sat up, then looked down at her body, with obvious relish – as if he were a gourmet selecting which of a number of choice dishes to consume first.

'No punishment tonight,' he said after a moment, his fingers going to the buttons of his own shirt instead of her flesh. 'We'll save that, shall we?' He parted the front of his shirt, showing skin that seemed paler than usual against the panels of dense black silk.

With swift, economical grace, her husband removed all his clothes. Having accepted that for the duration of this interlude she had no rights, no will, and no entitlement to any kind of gratification, Christabel nevertheless felt gifted by the sight of Nicholas's superb nudity. He was as lean and lithe as any man half his age, and his physique looked particularly athletic as he muted the lights in the room, and moved – once more – to lie down beside her. His cock swayed like a tower as he adjusted his position on the bed to increase his comfort. Bending one leg, and drawing his foot up towards his buttocks, he tilted himself until both his body and his erection were facing towards her.

Then, taking his penis in his right hand, he began to speak to her in soft and sultry tones.

Chapter Fourteen

Illuminations

*B*right yellow light seemed to illuminate a place of confusing but rather pleasant shadows.

Christabel woke up and found that she was in her own bed; that she felt strangely refreshed and full of energy; and that a shaft of morning light from between the imperfectly drawn curtains was what had roused her.

Even before she threw back the covers, she realised that she was still wearing her bra and panties from last night, although the rest of her clothes were nowhere in evidence. Rubbing her face, and realising that she was also still wearing the remains of last night's make-up, she tried to reassemble in her memory what had brought her to this.

Nicholas!

A rush of warmth washed away her disquiet. Last night had been strange, and perverse in an unexpected way, but the upshot of it was that she felt closer to her husband than she had at any time since they'd got married. Since they'd met, really . . .

He hadn't punished her, or made love to her in any accepted sense. He'd just stretched out beside her and talked to her – for quite some time, and in great detail –

while he'd masturbated. It had been a trial of desire to have to lie there and simply listen to him.

How long had she hung on every syllable of that seductive, bitter-chocolate voice of his? Endured his lyrical account of what it was like to be buggered senseless by Jamie? Listened to the precise details of what he would like to see done to her at certain private parties? He'd even enlarged lovingly on how he envisioned a tryst between her and Gussie might unfold.

Every word that had fallen from his lips – they had become increasingly distorted as his own passion escalated – had been like a caress against her ever-moistening, ever-engorging sex.

She had tried to turn away and resist at least the stimulating sights, if not the sounds. His increasingly meticulous and graphic descriptions had been interspersed more and more with soft, heartfelt groans and the slick, liquid sounds of his hand sliding to and fro on his penis.

But he had made her watch him. Compelled her to observe folded, gripping fingers flowing over man-flesh. His marvellously enlarged cock, thrusting through the collar of his own fist, first in a stately measured process, and then in a pumping, headlong rush.

She had wanted him in her: in her mouth, her sex, perhaps just the embrace of her smaller hand instead of his larger one. Even in her bottom she'd wanted him, even sodomy. Anal sex was a dark and perilous deed that she'd never ventured into before – but, with her husband, she knew she'd risk anything, dare anything.

He had not permitted any of those penetrations, however; and, when his moment came, he'd knelt over her to come. His creamy semen had spurted out on to her belly in thick celebratory gouts; and, when he'd got his breath back, he'd massaged it carefully into her skin. She could still feel a lingering, puckered tightness where it had dried and, murmuring his name again, she ran her fingers over the ghost of him.

And in the final hour, when she could take no more, he'd been kind to her. Delicately prising apart her labia, he'd blown on her clitoris and she'd climaxed so violently it had surpassed all previous experience.

She didn't remember very much of anything after that. Just Nicholas lifting her bodily in his arms and returning her to her own room. She had felt too dislocated, too out of time to object; and now, although by every right it should have bothered her, it didn't at all. A more memorable and significant notion was that Nicholas had walked through the house, with her in his arms, whilst still completely naked. She giggled at the idea of her dignified, self-possessed husband strolling along the corridors of Collingwood in the buff, but the greater thrill of it was that he'd taken the risk for her.

For her. Well, then, he must value her after all. Ought not she be doing something about that now?

When she looked down at her body again, however, she shuddered with distaste. She was still wearing underwear that she'd had on, and perspired in, for many hours now, and she could feel a patina of spent lust clinging to every single inch of her. An almost palpable film that made her fastidious nature cringe. The smells of sweat and musk and semen were evocative, even fabulous, in their place; but, as they became stale, they also lost a lot of their charm. Wrinkling her nose, she kicked off the covers and rushed gratefully into the bathroom.

After a long, indulgent shower, she moisturised her face and body, and dressed in clean, pale, lightweight clothes that seemed to her the very essence of freshness and summer. Catching her hair in a loose ponytail, she considered a little make-up, then abandoned the idea. Think immaculate and unsullied this morning, she told herself. Young. Sweet. Perfect. Even if she was none of those, she admitted, laughing again, aloud, for the sheer hell of it.

When she was finally satisfied with her appearance,

and with only the slightest pang of guilt, she left her tangled bedding to the attentions of Hester or Paula Blake, and clattered down the great staircase towards the terrace, and the mammoth breakfast which she hoped was waiting for her.

The prospect of confronting her husband, though, engendered a degree of trepidation. When she reached the hall, her hurrying steps began to falter.

What if he had merely been playing with her last night? Embroiling her in one of his little psycho-dramas, just to get a particular erotic effect? Much as she knew she loved Nicholas, she would not put anything past him. She had never met a person more calculating than he was, and in that census she included herself, an admitted schemer. What if he ignored her this morning, or was cool and dismissive? What if he was already gone, on his way back to London – and Jamie Carlton's bed?

Her heart plummeted when she saw Nicholas on the terrace, at the breakfast table. He was wearing a crisp white shirt, dark tie, and the trousers and waistcoat of one of his understated Italian tailored suits. London clothes. He was leaving. He didn't want her. His eyes, that had glowed so hot for her last night, were hidden beneath menacingly dark shades. She approached him, her spirits low.

Setting aside his coffee cup, he sat and watched her, remaining still and silent for some moments after she had arrived at the side of the table. Under his scrutiny, opaque and alien, she felt constrained to remain standing, like a servant, a supplicant, the slave she'd been last night. She felt a fool, and angry with herself for allowing the emotion.

Then, as if the odd, assessing moment had never existed, Nicholas pushed back his chair, stood up, and drew out an adjoining chair for her. When they were both seated, he pulled off his sunglasses and looked directly at her. His eyes were still an enigma, but at least she could see them. It was a start.

Then he laughed. As he had last night, and the dour planes of his lean face lightened.

'Don't look so worried, my sweet,' he said, reaching for the cafetière, testing its heat, then pouring her a cup, and adding milk for her. Just how she liked it.

Sipping the rich brew gratefully, Christabel didn't know what to say to him. The sun was warm and high, the colours around them bright and true and uncomplicated. There appeared to be no frame of reference for the shadowed, twilight games they had played last night. The see-saw of power that was the best and most meaningful hope for their relationship.

But Nicholas seemed to understand her, as ever, without the need for words. 'Christabel. Don't be afraid. We're all right.' He didn't reach out and touch her hand in any kind of conventional reassurance but, even so, she experienced the touch of his mind, and his presence, and that was better.

'If you say so.' She gave him a small, cautious smile, and he quirked his black brows as if to say, I *do* say so!

Nodding, he reached for a piece of toast, then snapped off a corner and popped it in his mouth. 'Last night was significant, my love. A development . . .' He shrugged, the movement infinitesimal, yet powerful. Christabel seemed to see again his body flexing against the sheets as he caressed himself. 'We're getting close now . . . Close to the place I've always planned for us.'

Oh, you arrogant bastard! thought Christabel fondly as relief raced through her. She felt the familiar burn of defiance, but knew it was right, and good, all part of the equation. She – that was, *they* – needed it to work against. Without her vein of resistance, the battle of wills – and her eventual acquiescence – just didn't function.

'You mean the one where you're up in London with

Jamie and I'm stuck down here in the sticks, photographing flowers and bunnies?'

'Oh, Christabel, Christabel, Christabel, now you're being pettish!' he said, grinning with huge amusement. 'And I do so love it.'

'Well?'

'I'm sorry. I have to leave,' he said, toying with his toast again. His sardonic face looked softer again, coloured with a regret that she knew, with a thrill, was deep and genuine. 'A deal that requires my personal presence. Excellent as Jamie is, he can't do this.'

Plenty of things he can do, though, thought Christabel, eyeing her husband over her coffee. She still felt magnanimous, however. It didn't matter how many times Jamie screwed Nicholas, or vice versa: the younger man just wasn't *her*; he couldn't be to her husband what she was. She experienced a glow of superiority that was supremely sexual. Her fresh pure image began to grow crumpled and deliciously grubby around the edges.

'I'm not sure you'll believe me,' Nicholas went on, 'but it's very difficult for me to leave at this juncture. I really don't want to. I'd much rather stay here and –' his surprisingly long black eyelashes flickered down, then up '– spend the whole day tormenting your fat, beautiful little clitoris until you've had so many climaxes that you can't see straight.'

Christabel gasped and, clearly satisfied with the effect he'd just had, Nicholas lounged back in his chair and studied her fast-colouring face intently.

'Which is more than you did last night,' she retorted at last, her voice a little choked as, between her legs, sensitive membranes answered his challenge. She could feel herself moistening, and she fancied she could almost detect the operation of intimate microscopic glands as they obeyed the imperative of her surging hormones.

'You came, didn't you?' he challenged.

'Eventually.'

'And in some splendour too, my love. Admit it.'

She compressed her lips: fighting the smile, fighting the necessity to admit he was right, fighting the yearning to moan, because she wanted again what he had done to her last night.

What had he done though, truth be told? That splendour had been so tumultuous, she still had no clear idea how it had come about. She seemed to recall his breath wafting across her clitoris, but had he done more? Had he licked her? Had he sucked, and sucked again, until she was screaming? She certainly hadn't been able to see straight, then.

'Are you wet, Christabel?' he enquired, leaning forward again, elbow on the table, chin on knuckle as he stared intently down at her groin beneath its covering of lemon and white seersucker.

Christabel looked away, her face unaccountably flaming now, hotter than ever. How was it that, even after all they'd shared, all that had passed between them, he still had the power to effortlessly embarrass her with a few simple words? It was completely irrational.

Of course she was wet. Very much so.

'Christabel?' he cued.

'Are we playing again?'

'I don't have much time. We might be.'

'I might be.'

'Oh, you are, my dear. I think you are.'

She said nothing, but continued to burn: with the source of the match, the fuel, and the accelerant sitting calmly beside her, his thigh just a few inches from her own. It was suddenly very very difficult to sit still, and the longing to be naked and lewd in a shadowed room with him was so powerful that she could almost see their twined bodies writhing in the air before her eyes. He was doing something exquisitely unthinkable to her, prising her buttocks apart, slathering her with grease, inserting –

236

'Good morning, Mrs Sutherland. Beautiful day, isn't it?' enquired a cheery voice from just close by.

Christabel turned abruptly, her vision of depravity fragmenting in the face of Paula Blake's broad, sunny smile. 'Yes ... yes, it is,' she agreed, desperately off balance, but trying not to show it. Was the housekeeper thinking of the other night? Was she aware of what she had almost interrupted?

'Would you like some breakfast, Mrs Sutherland? Eggs? Bacon? Sausages? We've got most things.'

Christabel's appetite, which had seemed hearty, now dispersed along with her fantasy. The thought of fried food made her feel both impatient and a little sick.

'Ooh, I don't think I could manage all that,' she said, giving the other woman an apologetic smile. 'Just some toast, please. That would be great.'

'Christabel, don't be foolish,' interjected Nicholas, in a stern voice. 'You can't live on toast. You need to keep your strength up. Have a proper breakfast.'

Christabel caught the tail end of a curious look on Paula Blake's round, handsome face. She must be wondering what we've been up to for me to require all that 'strength', Christabel thought, feeling more embarrassed than ever when her own skin conspired against her by going pinker than ever.

'Well ...' she began.

'How about scrambled eggs on toast with some mushrooms?' suggested the housekeeper. 'That's a bit more substantial, but not too heavy.'

'Oh, yes! That sounds wonderful. I'll have that, please,' said Christabel gratefully and, with a sly smile, Paula Blake sped away towards the kitchen.

When the other woman had disappeared, Christabel rounded on her husband. 'What on earth must she think?' she demanded, feeling yet more vexed by his cool, superior look. 'What the hell am I supposed to need my "strength" for? It's a wonder you didn't have my bra off me again, just to spell things out to her!'

Nicholas straightened almost imperceptibly in his seat, and his expression, whilst not changing in any gross way, suddenly seemed a hundred times more steely. 'You require your strength in the service of my will, slave,' he said softly. 'And what Paula Blake thinks or speculates about our relationship is of no consequence whatsoever, admirable though the woman is . . . At the moment, what *I* think, and what *I* want, are what matters, Christabel.'

Christabel bowed her head. Her blood seemed to be rushing about inside her, its helter-skelter flow a kind of inner caress that stimulated every nerve-end it touched. Between her legs, she felt a synchronous pulse begin to beat in the secret sticky niche of her sex.

'What if I were to order you up on to this table, right now, and tell you to take off your knickers and your skirt and be open-legged and masturbating when Paula returns with your breakfast?'

The thought was appalling, and yet had a hideous appeal to it: not least of all because there was no trace whatsoever of flippancy in her husband's voice. He was proposing a genuine possibility. He was quite capable of commanding her to lie down amongst the jam and butter dishes, and the condiments, and play with herself for his amusement, and that of others. And the worst thing was that a part of her really wanted to do it.

Christabel had always loved to display herself in private situations, for the titillation of her lovers, but this was a whole new universe of exposure and exhibition. Putting her hands on the edges of her seat, she began to rise out of it in readiness. Her heart was bashing like a steamhammer, and she felt faint, but this was a challenge.

Nicholas took her arm and made her stay in her chair. 'No. Perhaps not today,' he said, smiling and quirking his eyebrows at her. 'It would be a waste for so small an audience. You're too rare and delicious a specimen.' Reaching across, he gave her left breast a squeeze, and flicked the nipple with his thumb, making Christabel unable to suppress a groan of pleasure, 'When you perform, it will be as I told you. For connoisseurs, my darling. An assembly of specialists who'll really appreciate your sufferings.'

'Oh God, Nicholas,' she whimpered as he continued to fondle her briskly through her blouse and her cotton bra.

He released her immediately, denying her the benison of his touch. 'Are you wearing panties this morning, slave?' he enquired suddenly, reaching out and tapping his slim platinum cheroot case, which lay on the table near his plate. He looked intently at it, as if fighting a mental battle over whether or not to indulge himself. After a moment, he pushed the case away regretfully.

'Are you wearing panties this morning, slave?' he reiterated, with just the slightest hint of terseness.

'Yes, master, I am,' she breathed, thrilling again to the subversive, tenebrous pleasure of submerging her pride and will beneath his.

'Describe them.'

'They're white cotton. Full cut. Quite plain. With just fine picot edging to the elastic around the legs. They're . . . they're very pretty, really.'

'And their condition?'

She looked at him. It was no use trying to appear puzzled. She knew exactly what details he wanted.

'They're damp . . . At the crotch. B . . . because I'm excited.'

'Excited?'

'Aroused.'

'I see.' Devilish and assessing, he steepled his fingers and studied her.

'Raise your skirt. I should like to see these "pretty" panties of yours . . . Lift your skirt and tuck it into your waistband.'

Conscious of time passing, and how quick scrambled eggs were to prepare, Christabel complied, uncovering her white panties to the morning sun and Nicholas's scrutiny.

'You're right. They are very pretty,' he said mildly, still perusing her over the peak of his joined hands. 'Now rub yourself through them. A couple of strokes, just with your first two fingers.'

Christabel gritted her teeth at the pressure. She wanted so much more. The fine fabric was sodden against the pads of her fingers.

Breaking the triangle, he reached across, grabbed her wrist and drew her hand towards his face, breathing in deeply.

'Very fragrant, my dear,' he said, sniffing again. 'Very choice.' He thrust her wrist from him again.

Just then there was the sound of an opening door, then footsteps, and Christabel leapt in her seat, gripped by déjà vu, and sure that this time she was really about to be caught, by Paula Blake, with her panties on show.

But Nicholas was too fast for her. With an elegant, almost matador-like flick, he flipped the long white tablecloth across her lap and modestly covered up her thighs and her underwear. The only remaining evidence was the faintest odour of musk clinging to her finger-tips; which was soon swamped by the appetising aroma of cooked food.

'Thank you, that looks wonderful,' Christabel said, in all honesty, looking down at the perfectly cooked break-fast in front of her. In a great mouth-watering rush, her appetite suddenly returned to her, almost sharpened, it seemed, by the bizarre situation in which she once again found herself. Sex and food were fast becoming inextri-cably linked in her psyche.

'Thanks,' said Paula Blake, apparently oblivious. She turned to Nicholas, 'Would you like more coffee, Mr Sutherland?'

'Please. That would be wonderful,' he said, and the housekeeper left again, apparently none the wiser.

Christabel picked up her knife and fork.

'One moment; before you start . . .' Nicholas raised his hand to halt her.

She peered at him in alarm. What now? Another variation of the performance in the dining room, with Jamie? There seemed to be no end to the times Nicholas could watch her masturbate under duress.

'Nothing. Well, not really.' He gave her an impish little grin, then flicked aside the tablecloth again. 'Just tuck up your skirt again for me – all around this time – and pull your panties down as far as your knees . . .' For an instant, he eyed the cheroot case again, then pushed it even further away from him and returned his entire attention to her. 'And then you can get on and enjoy your breakfast. We can *both* enjoy your breakfast.'

'But what about the coffee? When Paula comes back?'

Nicholas seemed to deliberately wait several beats before replying.

'There's always the tablecloth,' he said nonchalantly; then he nodded towards her groin, as if to say: get on with it, then.

Awkwardly, and yet feeling wildly alive with a ridiculous anticipation, Christabel bunched up her seersucker skirt and tucked it in all around, then slipped her fingers into the waistband of her panties. She glanced quickly at Nicholas – to see if there was a reprieve, yet not really wanting one – and, when he shook his head, she lifted her bottom and peeled her knickers down her thighs. The cotton lining of the crotch was dark with moisture and, when Nicholas made a rough sound of appreciation, she hung her head. Was there no indignity he wouldn't put her through for his entertainment?

'Aren't you going to eat?' he enquired urbanely once she was settled, underwear at half-mast, with her pubis on show. 'It looks far too delicious to be allowed to go cold.'

Christabel looked sharply at him. Was that a *double entendre*? Was he going to reach across and caress her as

241

she tried to eat her scrambled eggs? She suddenly felt as if a single mouthful would choke her.

'Do I have to feed you again, slave?' said Nicholas, his voice deeper now, and infinitely sterner.

'No! No, it's all right. I can manage.' She lifted her knife and fork and began her breakfast.

The eggs and mushrooms and toast were all delicious; the eggs particularly so, making Christabel suspect that they were free range, and freshly collected. But it was extremely difficult to give her full attention to them. She was far too acutely aware of her sex and her partial nudity to do justice to food, no matter how appetising. The fine canvas of the seat cushion felt rough, yet vaguely caressing against the warm bare skin of her bottom, and she became increasingly concerned that the same copious sexual lubrication that had anointed her panties would now be flowing freely and betrayingly on to the seat cover. She thought about adjusting her position, and clenching herself somehow, to minimise the staining; but she knew Nicholas would see her moving and no doubt immediately deduce what she was up to. Her erotic instincts told her that he would not approve of any kind of prissiness or damage limitation – he might even insist on something even more grotesque, like opening herself wider, and pressing downward – so she remained as still as she could and just endured the evocative trickling. Which seemed to increase under the steel-grey fire of Nicholas's scrutiny, and grow to a flood when he casually hid her with the tablecloth during Paula Blake's brief visit to bring their promised coffee. The housekeeper stayed little more than a minute but, all the time, Christabel felt a horror of being discovered, and a fear that her dangling panties might be partially visible beneath the protecting damask. As soon as they were alone once more, Nicholas instantly put her on show again.

'See, my dear, you were hungry after all,' he said,

when Christabel had finally emptied her plate of food. 'Did you enjoy that?'

To her surprise, Christabel realised that, once she'd resigned herself, she really had relished her breakfast. Maybe she ought to eat all her meals this way? She felt a sudden mad flutter of glorious weakening fear. What if Nicholas compelled her to always dine like this – with her thighs and her crotch on show? He was quite capable of such a request, and it would be a perfect exercise of his power over her. She hardly dare frame the thought properly, for fear of him reading it in her, so open was her face to him.

'And are you still hungry?' he asked, his eyes glittering.

'No. Thank you,' she said, her throat tight with excitement and tension.

'Are you sure?' he persisted. 'Couldn't you just force another tasty morsel past those delectable lips of yours?' His dark eyes flickered momentarily downward, the glance so swift it was almost invisible.

But Christabel knew to which lips he was referring. She felt them swell and grow more engorged just from the thought of him.

How long was it since her husband had fucked her? It seemed like an aeon, but in reality it couldn't be more than a few weeks. He was withholding himself from her, denying her his magnificent cock in the service of this 'discipline' régime of his, and even though she'd found substitutes – of various persuasions – she still craved his flesh.

'Perhaps some particularly choice delicacy, then,' she said, astonished and almost dizzied by her own sudden daring. She felt her vagina pulse heavily, as if it called to him.

'On second thoughts, perhaps it would be unwise for you to overindulge.' He studied his fingernails, feigning an airy lack of concern for her, all of a sudden. It was such a pose that Christabel almost laughed out loud.

'One should always leave the table wanting more . . . Isn't that what they say?'

'I've no idea! I don't even know who the hell "they" are!' cried Christabel, her mood made volatile by her own frustrated lust. Her sex was awash, and her entire pelvis one grinding ache. 'Look, you bastard, I'm going to masturbate! I'm going mad here! I've got to come!'

'I'd rather you didn't touch yourself. Not just yet . . .' Nicholas's voice was mild, almost disinterested, and for a moment Christabel was tempted to rage at him. Then she looked at his long, beautiful hands and felt herself bend, rather like a bow – powerful, yet supple. She remained quite still, riding the torment of frustration.

They sat together in silence for a few minutes, and Christabel felt extraordinarily close to Nicholas in an affecting, spiritual way. It was almost as if she were giving him pleasure; and that the gift was becoming more and more meaningful as her discomfort escalated. Maybe she really was giving him pleasure, she mused, feeling light in the head as she did heavy in the loins. Perhaps he had a hard-on knowing she was suffering the torments of hell.

After a while, he picked up a white envelope from amongst the files and papers he had been perusing when she arrived.

'Daniel Ranelagh left this for you,' he said, handing it to her. 'It's the first time I've actually met him. He seems a pleasant enough sort of chap – if a little eccentric, perhaps.'

Puzzlement distracted Christabel from her more primal problems for a moment. 'Daniel came here?' she said, slitting open the envelope. 'That's strange . . . As far as Gussie says, he never comes to the house. He has a phobia about it.'

'Oh, he didn't actually come right up to the house,' Nicholas said with a shrug. 'He lurked about around the steps over there –' he gestured towards the break in the terrace parapet, and the flight of steps that led down towards the lower levels of the garden, and the paddock beyond '– and, as it was clear he wasn't going to come any closer, I went over to chat to him. He seemed rather distracted, but quite cheerful in a slightly manic sort of way. I –' Nicholas hesitated, which surprised Christabel, and made her pause in taking out the contents of the envelope '– I found him extremely attractive, although he's not my usual type.'

Plagued as she was by thwarted desire, Christabel mentally stamped on the image of Nicholas and Daniel together. She simply dared not think of it. They were both so beautiful and so irresistibly attractive to her. Instead, she took out her letter and swiftly read it. There were only a few lines.

Dear Christabel, it said. *Please forgive me, but I shan't be around for a few days and we probably won't see each other. This isn't through any lack of desire to see you . . . Quite the reverse. You are beautiful and adorable and you've made me feel much better about myself than I have in ages. You've regenerated me, almost. And that's it, really . . . I feel so inspired that I have to write. To really buckle down and do some good work. I must strike hard while I feel this way, as who knows how long it will last. I've sometimes gone for weeks when I've been so lacking in life that I haven't written a word. So, please be patient with me, and we'll get together as soon as I've finished this draft of my novel. Who knows: I might even be able to come into the house, and . . . well, you know.* It finished, *Yours longingly and thankfully, Daniel.*

When she looked up, Christabel saw that Nicholas was eyeing her with a kind of studious neutrality which, for him, was surprisingly unsubtle.

He wants to know what it says! she thought wonderingly. But he's too good-mannered, or perhaps too apprehensive, to ask. Without a word, she handed the letter across to her husband.

It took Nicholas but a few moments to read it. Then he looked up, gave her a small but complex smile, and handed the letter back.

'Ah well, "you know",' he said, with only the slightest of inflections, and Christabel had not the slightest doubt that he *did* know. About Daniel, and Gussie and everything. He knew and he was just biding his time and putting her through hoops, because of it.

'No, not my usual type,' Nicholas went on, picking up his earlier thread. 'But tempting, nevertheless.' He touched his forefinger to his lips, contemplatively. 'I think I'll try him some time soon . . . Is he any good? Will I enjoy him?'

The forbidden images resurfaced, creating waves of turbulence in their wake. Christabel bit her lip, gathered her will, and replied, 'Oh, I'm sure you will . . . And he's a public school boy. He knows the score. You won't be the first, I shouldn't think.'

'I don't doubt that you're right,' Nicholas replied, then glanced at his watch. He frowned slightly, then rose to his feet. 'Anyway, I have a car coming shortly, and there are one or two matters I have to attend to before I leave.' He paused and looked down at her, his eyes focusing, she was certain, on the lush and glistening curls at her groin. 'Now, if you're quite sure you've finished your breakfast, I'd like you to walk with me.'

Christabel was surprised. She'd expected a dismissal now. Nicholas was a supreme compartmentaliser, and she had no place in his business world.

'L . . . like this?' she stammered, following his eyeline directly to her crotch.

'Let your skirt fall, but leave your panties round the top of your thighs. Come on. Time is short. We have to hurry.'

Her surprise and confusion increased. Nicholas was never like this. He was never ruffled. The only time she'd ever seen him out of control was in the conservatory, with Jamie on top of him.

With some difficulty, she accompanied him inside, thinking that strolling around the corridors of Collingwood with her knickers around her thighs was rapidly becoming a habit. Perhaps, soon, she would be able to do it without shuffling and ungainliness at all?

In the hall, Nicholas took her abruptly and quite forcefully by the arm. 'One moment,' he said huskily, then steered her towards the deep, curtained alcove in the lee of the stairs. When they were in the shadows, but not completely hidden from view, he pressed her hard against the lumpy carved oak front of an old cupboard that was stored there, and began tugging at the cotton folds of her skirt.

'Help me! Pull the damned thing up!' he hissed, his voice strange and angry in a way she'd never heard before. For a moment, her heart surged, and she expected him to unzip himself; but instead, he thrust one hand between her thighs and with the other covered her mouth. With a deft twist of his wrist, he jammed three stiffened fingers urgently into her sex, and bore down heavily on her clitoris with his thumb. When she began to struggle, he drove upwards with his entire hand, forcing her up on to her toes, then started to thrust with it in a fast, relentless rhythm.

Christabel wanted to shout with both protest and triumph but, with her lips sealed, the power of the cry was bottled inside her. The energy with which she would have both cursed and cheered on her husband's efforts was directed downward, instead of outward, and seemed to intensify the sensations of her ravishment. Within seconds of being grabbed, she was climaxing thunderously, her muscles clutching and spasming around the fingers that impaled her and her clitoris jumping beneath the pressure of Nicholas's thumb. Her entire crotch was both melting and in motion, and against the hand that silenced her she drooled and gasped and sobbed.

'God, you're a delicious slut,' she heard him growl as her orgasm went on and on, 'always in heat, always wet, always so ready . . .' He pushed upward again, whilst she was still coming, and she had to dance, on

247

her toes, and hold helplessly on to him. 'Ready for this, you little whore. For this!' Her legs and arms flailed as the pleasure ramped up and up and up. 'Have as many men as you like, Christabel,' he hissed. 'Have as many orgasms with as many cocks as you can manage . . . But never forget *this*, my love, because *this* is what you really want –' his thumb circled, pressed, and circled again '– and you know it! Don't you?'

Christabel didn't know if she ever even tried to answer, but she was certain that her husband heard her anyway.

Chapter Fifteen

Bright

*T*hey've all abandoned me, the bastards! thought Christabel, not once, but several times over the next few days – hardly knowing whether to be irritated or relieved.

After some deliberation, she settled for the latter. Since coming to Collingwood, since that first confrontational night in her studio, really, she felt as if she'd been pushed through a psychological mangle. And this period of solitude was a blessed, quiet relief. Just what she needed to replenish her mental and physical resources.

Not that she wouldn't have much preferred Nicholas to stay.

She supposed she needed a breathing space from him as much as anything, but he had left her at such a critical juncture. After those astonishing moments in the shadows, he had reverted almost immediately to his Mr Cool and Imperturbable persona, pulling up her knickers for her and escorting her solicitously to her room as if she had merely fainted, like some feeble Victorian miss. He'd said not one word more about sex and, despite the fact that he'd sported a clear and present erection, he'd done nothing whatsoever to satisfy his own requirements.

The man drove her crazy, and yet she missed him almost as if she were missing a part of her own body. She had never realised quite how much she loved him.

Love? It was strange how extraordinarily fresh the emotion felt to her. Whether she would ever be able to be quite what Nicholas wanted her to be was debatable. Her old ways were far simpler, and less demanding. But she'd try to please him, because she couldn't go back now. Her deepest nature, she realised, was the twin, and complement, of that of Nicholas; and having seen a glimpse of that other world, the one where he lived, she couldn't rest without at least trying to be a citizen there.

To distract herself from thoughts of Nicholas, of Daniel and Gussie, and even of Jamie, Christabel took her camera out each day into the park and the woods that surrounded Collingwood, exploring far and wide in an exhausting search for photographic subjects. The only place she stayed clear of was Daniel's gingerbread cottage, in case he was working there; but, apart from that, she covered what seemed like miles and miles. Although the idea of being a wildlife photographer had initially seemed silly to her, she soon found that capturing fugitive images of flora and fauna had a kind of Zen quality to it. Absolute concentration freed her from the demands of counterproductive inner chatter, and so focused became she on her endeavour, that when she emerged from 'the zone' – elated by what she'd seen and recorded – her perspective on everything else seemed clearer and brighter. She felt profoundly sensual, yet neither needy nor frustrated. It was a kind of preparation for some as yet unknown denouement.

She even decided – despite the prospect of mockery from her jaded London circle – to go ahead and do the book of nature photographs, if only to show Nicholas she was capable of something creatively worthwhile. Something of her own, that had not one single connection to him. Using a courier service, she had roll after roll of her exposed film processed – although not the one containing the intimate studies of Daniel, which would have to wait until she had access to her own darkroom again – and, as she assessed each set of images, she began tentatively to design a suitable outline.

Totally immersed in the project, she neither made phone calls, nor worried about not receiving them. So it came as a shock when Sylvester Blake put a call through to her when she was in the library, poring over her latest batch of contact prints.

Gussie announced herself with a volley of playful endearments and kissy-kissy noises. 'Are you lonely, my sweet? I'm missing you. I haven't had any action at all since I got here! I'm thinking of becoming a nun!'

Christabel was forced to laugh. 'Oh, yeah?' she said, wishing for a moment that Gussie was with her and they could kiss and touch each other. 'I doubt if you're eligible, Gussie . . . No matter how elevated your intentions are.' She paused, then laughed again, nervously. What had Gussie found out? Christabel felt almost afraid to ask. 'So? Any news on the Chamfort connection?'

'Oh, God, yes! It's the same family! The woman I know slightly, Marisa . . . Well, she's actually the great-granddaughter, or possibly the great-great, I can't remember . . . But whichever, she's descended from the Marie-Ange in the letter!'

'And does she know anything? About Eleanor, I mean?'

'Even better!' cried Gussie, clearly high on the latest developments. 'She's descended from Eleanor *as well as* Marie-Ange . . . It seems that not only was Eleanor pregnant with Ethan's child when she left Collingwood, but that the daughter she eventually had married Marie-Ange Chamfort's son. Which makes Marisa a sort of distantly removed cousin of mine, and a living blood link between Ethan and Eleanor.'

251

'And Marisa Chamfort told you all this, just like that? Just because you know her slightly?' Christabel was astonished. She had a sudden sensation of being on a rollercoaster . . .

'Well, no, not really . . .' Gussie's high spirits seemed to temper. 'She was a bit reticent at first. Stand-offish. I suppose it's because she's half French and lives in Paris a lot of the time.' She made a little 'humph', as if to dismiss the entire French nation for lack of co-operation. 'I didn't make any headway at all when I called her, but then, the next day, *she* rang *me* back and she was much nicer. She said that a friend had been in touch and that had convinced her to speak to me.'

'What friend?' Christabel had a feeling that she already knew the answer.

'Your husband. Is that right? Does he know her?'

'Apparently yes, but I hate to think how well . . .'

Was this Marisa a lover of Nicholas's? Was that why he was helping? Was he even helping? These points occurred to Christabel even while Gussie was speaking.

'Anyway, she didn't elaborate about how she knew Nicholas, but she did tell me the most amazing story about Eleanor, and Marie-Ange, and how they lived together in a sort of sexual "free house" with various exotic friends and lovers . . . It sounds like a sort of cross between a luxury brothel and an ahead-of-its-time feminist commune. The house is still there, but it's a bit more sedate these days, and Marisa uses it mainly as a London base.' Gussie paused for breath, and Christabel got the impression that Daniel's sister was rather smitten with the mysterious Mademoiselle Chamfort. 'She's fabulously wealthy, would you believe? And beautiful and bi-sexual into the bargain. You'll love her, Christabel; just wait until you meet her!'

When will that be? thought Christabel when Gussie had rung off. She didn't even know when she would see Gussie herself again. The younger woman wouldn't be able to return to Collingwood for at least a week, she'd said. Right out of the blue, opportunities had begun turning up for her, she'd told Christabel happily. It was almost as if she'd suddenly acquired a fairy godmother whose wand could open almost any door. Christabel wondered. Nicholas knew so many people in business, and in the arts; the godmother could well be a godfather. But what were his motives? He was generous enough, but she'd never thought of him as a particularly philanthropic man, so what in heaven's name was he up to?

The morning after Gussie's call, Christabel awoke in an assertive frame of mind. She loaded her cameras in readiness to work, but decided she would also make a phone call to Nicholas at some time during the day. When she had organised her own schedule first, she would confront him.

He pre-empted her, however.

She was just finishing a scratch late lunch of sandwiches in the library, whilst studying a new batch of enlargements, when the door swung open and Nicholas, talking in soft, easy, conversational tones, ushered an unknown woman into the room before him.

In the seconds it took to rise to her feet, Christabel deduced the identity of their visitor. She was slender, dark, and casually but chicly dressed – she could only be the mysterious Marisa Chamfort.

Nicholas stepped forward. 'Christabel,' he murmured, taking her hand, 'you look well. Have you missed me?' He pressed her palm with his fingers, the caress evocative of other pressures, in other places. 'I've brought someone to see you. And to see Daniel . . . It occurred to me that, as I know Marisa slightly, I might be able to persuade her to come down here and shed some light on Collingwood's mysteries.' Releasing Christabel, he retreated again, and gestured for the rather soignée young woman with him to step forward. 'Christabel, this is Marisa Chamfort, the great-great-great-granddaughter of Marie-Ange Chamfort, and of your Eleanor Wood-forde,' he said, then turned towards Marisa. 'Marisa, this is my wife, Christabel.'

She's beautiful, thought Christabel, holding out her hand and feeling it taken delicately in the cool grip of Marisa's. 'Pleased to meet you,' she said, too nervous to think of anything remotely original.

'*Enchantée*,' answered the other woman, a smile warming her rather fine blue eyes. She had a sharp, short, rather sculpted haircut, and a pronounced air of Gallic elegance and worldliness, but she was quite young and there was something vaguely familiar about her.

It's the Ranelagh look, thought Christabel in wonder, as the two women took a seat together on one of the big chesterfields, and worked their way through the edgy minutiae of further introductions. Eleanor's genes were still as strong after all these generations, it seemed.

As Nicholas slipped away to arrange for champagne to be brought, Marisa launched into a series of questions about Collingwood and Daniel. Her voice was soft and captivatingly French, but full of authority.

'So, do you think that if Daniel finally learns what happened to Eleanor, he will be well again?' she enquired.

'If you want to call it "well",' said Christabel cautiously. 'He doesn't really seem ill in any way to me. He just has a sort of fixation with the past that seems to make the present difficult for him ... It seems unfair that he can't come into the house now and again, and enjoy his own heritage. And his life would be much less restricted if he could get out a bit, and meet people ...' She hesitated. 'Form relationships with real women, not just figments of his imagination.' Marisa Chamfort's clear blue eyes were bright and penetrating, and Christabel felt more uncomfortable and flustered than ever. 'You probably think I'm being arrogant, pontificating like this ... After only knowing him a day or two.

Perhaps you should be talking to Gussie about all this, not me.'

'She's of precisely the same opinion as you are about Daniel,' said Marisa calmly. 'It's obvious that you both care a great deal about him.'

The woman's softly accented voice was even and pleasant, and Christabel could detect no bias or overtone; yet somehow she knew that Marisa Chamfort knew everything there was to know about Daniel's relationships – with Christabel, and with Gussie.

'I do. I mean, we do. Gussie and I . . .'

'And these new relationships of Daniel's . . . Do you foresee one of them being with you?'

My God, nothing if not candid! thought Christabel, feeling sideswiped. Marisa Chamfort's expression was still intent, everything about it incisive and unambiguous – she wasn't joking. Christabel found herself glancing towards the door, through which Nicholas had left.

Marisa had followed the look. 'I know your husband well, Christabel . . . I have known him several years, and I know he is a man whose visions are, shall we say, not bound by convention.' She looked down briefly, as if seeking expression in her faultless manicure. 'Under certain circumstances, and conditions, he might approve of a liaison between you and Daniel. He might even wish to be a part of it.'

Momentarily distracted from Daniel and his concerns, Christabel experienced a sudden bright leap of intuition. 'Nicholas spoke about a group of friends, associates or whatever, of his that . . . I don't know . . . play games together. Share certain interests.' Facing the cool brilliance of Marisa Chamfort's eyes, she proffered her own challenge. 'Are you one of those "associates", Marisa?'

'*Touché*, Christabel. You are very astute,' murmured Marisa, her hard glamour softening and becoming infinitely more sensual. 'I am a member of what you might call that "association" . . . For my sins.' She reached out and put her hand over Christabel's. 'Perhaps I shall see you amongst us soon? When we next gather? I should like that.' Her hand slid from Christabel's hand to her knee and squeezed significantly.

Oh Lord, she fancies me! thought Christabel, her heart racing. There seemed more warmth in Marisa's hand than might naturally be attributed to body heat, and more passion in her touch than might be derived from emphasis alone. Nicholas suddenly seemed to have been away far longer than was necessary, and Christabel had a suspicion that he was conniving with Marisa somehow. Giving the Frenchwoman the opportunity to make a pass.

But just as Christabel had defined to herself what was happening, and accepted it, her husband returned and, at the same time, Marisa Chamfort released Christabel's knee and rose to her feet.

'I think, if you don't mind, that I would like to meet Daniel now.' An impish smile lit her cool, porcelain features. 'No need to trouble yourselves,' she said as Christabel got up too. 'I believe I can find the way to the dower house quite easily by myself.'

Christabel didn't know what to say. She felt wrong-footed by the sudden change in Marisa's manner and focus, and vaguely indignant. Although why she had assumed that she'd be the one to bring enlightenment to Daniel, she didn't know. From her it would only ever be second- or third-hand reportage. Marisa Chamfort was an intimate part of the story of Ethan and Eleanor; she was their flesh and blood. And, if the worst came to the worst, she could even be his new 'Eleanor'. His muse . . .

'No champagne first?' enquired Nicholas, indicating the bottle waiting in its cooler. To Christabel's eyes, he didn't seem all that disappointed with developments, and she experienced a rush of interest that made her forget her feelings of pique against Marisa.

'No, thank you, Nicholas,' said Marisa brightly. She

was already halfway to the door. 'But I'm sure Christabel would love a glass. Why don't you drink a toast to my meeting my long-lost cousin? *Au revoir, mes amis . . .* We must get together later!'

'I feel as if I just imagined her,' said Christabel, slumping bemusedly back into her seat when the other woman had gone. 'As if she was somebody out of one of Daniel's novels or fantasies.' She took the glass that Nicholas handed to her and sipped the creamy yet bone-dry champagne gratefully. It seemed sacrilege to swig down an obviously superb wine just for the sake of it, but she dearly needed a drink. Her brief encounter with Marisa had left her disorientated. She half finished the glass, then turned her attention to Nicholas.

'You misled me,' she said, setting the wine aside. 'You never said that Marisa Chamfort was one of these so-called "special" friends of yours. You just said that she edited a magazine.'

'Forgive me. It was wrong of me to keep you in the dark,' said Nicholas, his voice soft and thoughtful as he prowled away from her, as if unable to settle. 'I should have been more open.'

Christabel almost did a double-take. Was Nicholas sickening for something? He was as self-composed as ever, but there was a different, far milder note in his voice. She might be imagining things, but she had never before heard him sound so meek. The question of Daniel and how he might react to Marisa seemed to recede a little in her mind. The blackest of the Ranelagh sheep was in the hands of fate and of an enigmatic young Frenchwoman now, and there was nothing further Christabel could do for him. It was far better that she concentrate on the strange currents that were flowing between herself and Nicholas.

She looked towards her husband, seeking clarification, some kind of sign that her strange imaginings were either true or false. He was not drinking but just standing by the fireplace now, and watching her, the elegant lines of his face set and intent.

He wants something from me, she thought, feeling the beginnings of panic. But what is it? It isn't what we've had before; it's something different ... And I have to work it out, or I'll fail an important test.

Oh God, what is it?

The moment seemed to stretch out, elongated by the lack of words, and movement, on Nicholas's part. Christabel looked and looked at him, desperately trying to analyse his requirements and interpret his subtle body language. What was it about him that seemed so different, yet so barely discernible? He was still the same strong, straight, tall figure. So admirable and full of composure. And yet ... And yet ...

Peering into his eyes, even from half a room away, Christabel 'suddenly saw it. What he wanted, bright and true, in his face and body. There was an almost infinitesimal change in the quality of his bearing, his facial expression. The difference was minute but, now she'd detected it, she had no doubts. She found herself back in her studio, replaying the scene she'd had with Brad, of all people. Experiencing a sense of authority and empowerment. The feeling of being completely in charge of the situation – and loving it.

And, back in the library at Collingwood, she also seemed to hear her husband's voice. Almost as if he were the telepath he'd always seemed to be. You see now, my Christabel, don't you? he was saying. You see now what it is that I want from you ... Take the power. If you can handle it, it's yours.

What to do, though? He was so much more than Brad. The younger man had been a pick-up, a toy, a cipher. Nicholas was everything: a man of significance, experienced and discerning. She would have to be imaginative. Just being herself trying to throw her weight about would be no good to him. A scenario was required, a framework for the shadowplay.

258

Glancing around, and trying not to seem to be doing so obviously, she sought inspiration. Her attention settled on the champagne bottle and remaining glasses, where they stood on the small walnut table. Nicholas had brought the wine himself, on a silver salver, instead of letting one of the Blakes, or Hester, wait on them. This could be taken one step further, couldn't it? And developed . . . After all, what came next after a servitor, but a slave? Before she had time to dissect her plans, Christabel rose to her feet and spoke.

'I think I'll leave this for now,' she said, abandoning her champagne glass. 'I think I'd prefer to have some champagne later, in my room, at about –' she looked quickly at the antique clock on the mantelpiece, close to Nicholas's head '– eight o'clock.' Her confidence surged when she saw him lower his eyes in acknowledgement. 'Could you arrange for it to be brought to me? And perhaps some hors d'oeuvres too? Something light . . . Not too stodgy,' she added, extemporising her role as best she could.

Nicholas nodded, then looked up again, his eyes excited, almost pleading. 'Of course.'

'Good,' Christabel said crisply, already making for the door. 'I'm going to take a bath now. Relax a little . . . Get ready.' She paused. 'Perhaps I'll see you later?'

For a tall man in a room full of furniture, Nicholas moved to her side with uncanny speed. 'Yes,' he said, 'you will.' He cast down his gaze again and, to Christabel's astonishment, he appeared to be nervous. 'And I hope you won't be disappointed.' Oh God, he was actually blushing! 'Or feel that you have to hold back in any way . . . I – I can guarantee the endurance of the one who waits on you.'

Christabel dashed from the room before he could see the utter depths of her own confusion.

Christabel was pinning up her hair when he knocked and, even though it was second nature to her to create

259

an artistic twist in no more than a matter of moments, in this case she made the task last somewhat longer.

Stay calm, she told herself, surveying her image in the mirror. Completely calm. Remember how confident you were with Brad. With Gussie and Daniel, even. This is no different. He's just a man. Even if he is Nicholas.

Thinking of Daniel distracted Christabel from her trepidation for a moment. There had been no word from the dower house since Marisa Chamfort had left the library, and it was difficult to predict what might have happened between her and her distant relation. Did he know the whole story now? Was he free of his fixation? Had the two of them already slept together?

Not your concern at this juncture, Christabel, she thought, smiling wryly. You've got more pressing matters to deal with, so you'd better concentrate!

'Come in!' she called out, still assessing her own reflection – still checking out her face, her hair, and the smooth, sleek contours of her shoulders and her throat where they were revealed by the plunging bodice of her gown. As near to perfection as I can manage at this short notice, she thought, as the bedroom door was pushed open and, after a moment, the familiar tall, dark figure of her husband pushed in a laden and slightly squeaking trolley.

Almost ignoring him, she smoothed a finger along lines of her immaculately groomed eyebrows, then turned her chin first this way, then that, to check every detail of her make-up.

'Your supper, ma'am,' prompted the man behind her, a little tension in his deep and resonant voice.

Christabel remained still, not looking round. This was the moment of truth. Could she pull this off? Treat her husband, the man who had spanked her, and subtly and elegantly dominated her for so long, like a subservient underling? It was what he wanted, but he was used to the best. To women like Marisa Chamfort, who knew what they were doing, not novices like his own

260

wife, who was only just beginning to wake to life's deeper possibilities.

It was now or never. Taking a final deep breath, Christabel wiped all trace of consternation from her expression.

'Yes, thank you,' she said evenly, abandoning the mirror and moving gracefully towards him. Like any former model or dancer, she had long since perfected the art of walking in difficult shoes, and consequently she could almost glide in her slender, high-heeled mules. Thus elevated, she was still not as tall as her companion, but the height difference was lessened. They studied each other – over the varied contents of the trolley – and, being empowered by her own excitement and the novelty of the situation, her gaze was so unfaltering that he was forced to look away first. Vanquished, his glance skittered swiftly across the bed . . . and to what lay upon it, neatly arranged in readiness. He'd mentioned 'endurance', and now she dearly hoped she'd understood him aright.

'Very well. You may serve,' she told him, crossing the room, then taking a seat on a low settee.

As her husband busied himself with champagne flutes, hors d'oeuvres plates and suchlike, Christabel steadied herself by contemplating both the man and his carefully focused actions.

In lieu of a uniform of some kind, Nicholas was wearing a plain white shirt, unbuttoned at the neck, and a pair of black cotton chinos. His hair was slightly damp from a recent shower, but neatly combed backward from his broad, intelligent brow. He was a little tense, clearly, but his natural poise to some extent masked that. It was also apparent that he wasn't accustomed to dispensing food and wine in this type of setting. His movements were as deft and graceful as they always were, but he didn't have the slick, unctuous fluidity that would have typified experienced waiter service. Watching him, she formed the impression of an indomitable alpha male being made to act as a malleable, house-trained pet, and that notion made her hide a smile behind her hand. There were some interesting times ahead of them, she was suddenly certain . . . and a voluptuous anticipation began to dissipate her fears.

'Is there a problem? You seem to be taking a while,' she observed, injecting a slight impatience into her voice to remind him of his status. He didn't reply straight away and, to her satisfaction, she saw his back stiffen, as if he were fighting a powerful urge to break out of his role. Crossing her legs with a slow, considered elegance, she let her right slipper dangle from her right toe, its rhythmic swing a subtle sign of her growing displeasure.

'I'm sorry, ma'am,' he said, his voice flat and very controlled. 'It's almost ready.'

That's insufficiently respectful, my man, thought Christabel, as he presented her with a crystal champagne flute, then poured a little of the effervescing wine so she could taste it.

'Yes, thank you, very nice,' she said, holding out the glass after she had sampled the vibrant, but exquisitely dry wine, 'although I would have much preferred Krug.' She paused, enjoying his almost inaudible intake of breath. 'Still, no matter . . .' She took a long sip from the filled glass, loving its taste and wondering if there had even been any Krug in Collingwood's cellars. It had simply been the first name that had come into her head.

'Are you new to this?' she continued, feeling the sweet kick of desire low in her belly. 'Are you used to waiting hand and foot on women?' She took another sip of wine, her mind racing through possibilities like a computer. 'Or perhaps you're more accustomed to serving men? Do tell me.'

'I've waited on women before, ma'am,' he said, sounding a little less sure of himself, 'and on men. But not often. On either.' He hesitated, not looking at her, and she thought she heard him catch his breath again.

'I find it challenging, ma'am. Rather difficult. It's against my nature.'

Under the guise of savouring her wine, Christabel scrutinised him from beneath her lowered lashes. Her heart was racing and her body was growing hot and heavy, languid yet exhilarated. What a fine feeling this was! And what a fine specimen *he* was! Handsome and dark; tall and moody. Proud, sure of himself, and primally arrogant, but prepared – within limits – to bend to her whims. Suddenly, she plunged back into one of the wild fantasies she'd been having while she'd been bathing and preparing herself; it was the ultimate extension of a game that had so far barely started.

She saw this man – her wilful husband, Nicholas – kneeling naked before her, on his hands and knees, his mouth a thin, strained line as he grappled with a pain far more intimidating than that which he had briefly inflicted on her. There were livid marks of crimson across his firmly muscled buttocks, and a look of pure devotion in his eyes. At her negligent signal, he crawled quickly towards her, ready to suffer again, or perform some new, demeaning service.

'Would you care for something to eat now, ma'am?'

Surprised out of her dream, Christabel gave Nicholas a narrow look. Speaking before he was spoken to was another misdemeanour – another fault – and the thought of an appropriate retribution set her entire body alight with lust. Unable to help herself, she glanced towards the bed.

'Yes, just a little though ... Would you select something for me, please?'

This chore afforded Christabel another chance to observe her husband as he worked. Watching the careful way in which he moved, she concentrated on the shape of his backside in his well-cut black trousers. She imagined him lowering them, exposing his naked buttocks for her perusal. She imagined herself touching him, and feeling him tremble; then striking down hard, across the target, with an implement of some kind. The vision was so vivid in her mind that she seemed to hear him whimper; and the fancied sound of it made a tingle run down her spine.

Oh, dear God, she thought, watching him fill a plate with sundry items of Paula Blake's exceptional cooking, delicacies for which she, Christabel, had not the faintest appetite. Her hunger now was for new experience, for self-knowledge. For how many years had she been suppressing these complementary urges to submit and to dominate, not allowing her profoundest fantasies free rein?

Emptying her glass, she handed it back to him when he brought her food. Without a word, he refilled it, then stood back as she ignored the plate of hors d'oeuvres he had presented her with and concentrated solely on the glass of shimmering wine. The truth was that she was far too keyed up to eat, far too stimulated. She was voracious now, but not for paté or for whirls of fine smoked salmon.

'So why do you find it difficult to obey women, Nicholas?' she enquired, not looking at him, but watching the bubbles rise hypnotically in her glass. 'Is it because subconsciously you consider yourself their superior? That you prefer to exert your own will over that of a woman? To see them bend to your wishes? Perhaps suffer a little?'

He didn't answer, but Christabel sensed that there was no clear-cut reply to her question. The concept of obedience to a woman probably was chokingly difficult for Nicholas, and yet at the same time he craved it and it aroused him. Which was ironic, as it exactly mirrored her own experience. Pleased with the symmetry, she pictured him erect inside his elegant black trousers and could almost taste his own ambivalence towards his body. He was a prisoner of the way subservience roused his sex.

'Shouldn't you answer me immediately, Nicholas?'

she suggested, still intent on her glass, but peripherally aware of her husband, and his repeated darting glances towards her and towards the object on the bed. 'Isn't it being disrespectful to ignore me?'

Still he didn't answer. He seemed to be throttled by his own confused feelings, and that made Christabel want to shout and dance with glee. She couldn't believe how right everything felt to her, how beautifully the strange scenario was going.

'Don't you *want* to please me, Nicholas?' Christabel persisted, knowing that the thin silk across her nipples was hiding nothing. 'Don't you *want* to serve me? To do exactly what *I* want?'

'Y ... yes, ma'am ... No, ma'am ... I don't know, ma'am ...' he stammered, losing it completely in a way that was breathtakingly erotic. Christabel felt as if she was with a different man altogether. One who was just as arousing, intriguing and unforgettable as her cool, implacable husband, yet who touched her mind and body with an entirely new dynamic.

Enjoying his plight, she kept her face calm, even though she wanted to shout out aloud with exultation. He was trembling. At fever pitch. Turned upside down by his own desire. And it had been so easy! She turned, at last, towards him, and observed, with barely contained triumph, his bulging fly.

'Now, Nicholas,' she said softly, abandoning her champagne and her untouched food to rise from her seat and move slowly towards him. She was aware of her silk gown swirling around her ankles in a playful wave, and its slim contours moulding to her body like liquid plastic. 'If you really want to please me, and to obey me, I'd like you to take all your clothes off for me ... I want to see you naked, with your hands on your head ... standing quiet and ready.'

Nicholas's face grew pale and haggard, and once more he visibly hesitated.

'Nicholas,' she prompted, moving even closer, and for just one instant letting her hand rest on his crotch.

He moaned, his body rocking. His eyes closed like a martyr's as her hand withdrew.

'Nicholas, don't disappoint me,' she said, returning to the settee, and sitting down comfortably. Ready for the show.

He undressed quickly as if the process pained him acutely and he wanted it over with, despite its shaming outcome. Within a minute or so, he stood naked before her, his hands on his head as specified, his eyes closed, his stiff penis jutting from his groin like a living totem.

Christabel let the moment stretch out and out and out, the silence awesome. This was already all she had anticipated – and much, much more. Whilst she had been bathing, preparing and anointing herself, she had indulged in a variety of fantasy agendas, but she hadn't anticipated this depth of feeling and arousal. The real experience was far more thrilling, far more dazzling than any well-plotted scene. She supposed that it was her own very palpable fear of failure that had provided the edge, a fear that, when it came to the moment, she couldn't really dominate him. But now she knew she was stronger than she had ever anticipated.

'So you desire me?' she said suddenly, enjoying the way he flinched at the unexpected words. His erection jerked and quivered with the motion of his body. 'I'd like an answer from you, Nicholas, if you please.' She kept her voice steady, almost affable, with not the slightest hint of stridency or a shout. Undue histrionics would only undermine her poise.

'Yes,' he said, his own voice little more than a whisper.

'And do you think that I would allow a person who has waited on me . . . a slave . . . to take pleasure in my body?' She let her hand settle on her thigh, her fingers spread and almost touching what he craved. 'Do you?'

'N . . . no.'

' "No, ma'am", ' she prompted.

'No, ma'am,' he repeated, his head lowered.

'Then why allow yourself to get into such a state?' she plagued him, pointing her toe at him in its high-heeled, extravagant slipper. 'Have you no control over your body at all?' Looking up, she watched the muscles in his neck and arms twitch and flutter. The temptation to take his hands from his head was obviously maddening him. His carved and handsome features were a mask of torment.

I've hardly even begun, she felt like saying but, instead, she simply asked him, 'Well?'

'I . . . I can't seem to stop myself,' he gasped, reduced almost to a state of guilty boyhood.

For a moment Christabel imagined that Nicholas and she were in a book-lined office somewhere. She wore a slim, tailored suit, gold-framed glasses, an academic gown . . . and, with his trousers round his ankles in an ignominious tangle, her husband was bending over, ready for punishment, across her desk.

Oh yes! One day, she thought, returning her attention to the delicious present and her naked victim.

'Have you even tried?' she accused him. 'I think you're just standing there, taking pleasure in looking at me when you know I've forbidden it.'

His grey eyes widened; his mouth moved. He seemed to be struggling, with enormous difficulty, to speak up in his own defence.

'Nicholas!' she prompted, making her voice ring like steel wrapped in velvet.

'Yes, ma'am . . . I don't know, ma'am,' he admitted, as if the reply were being torn from him with pincers.

'And did you deserve to enjoy me?'

'No, ma'am . . .'

'In that case, I think you'd better bring me the implement, hadn't you?' She nodded towards the leather belt that lay on the bed, the object which they had both been aware of from the beginning. It usually held up Christabel's jeans, but now it was a strange and magical talisman.

'Yes, ma'am,' he murmured, awaiting her nod of permission before moving towards the bed.

'Yes, indeed,' replied Christabel. She closed her eyes, took a deep breath, and gathered her strength ... for the real business of the evening – which was yet to come.

Chapter Sixteen
New Vistas

Christabel opened her eyes and looked around her, realising that she had been dozing amongst the tangled bedding while she waited for her husband to return from the bathroom. Stretching luxuriously, she let the memories flood back in. Outrageous images of a sweet, alternative world . . .

Stroking her hand up the curve of her hip, and then her waist, made her think of the leather belt she sometimes wore with her denim jeans. She had always loved the thing, thought it stylish in a butch sort of way, but now its place in her affections was even more special. Working purely on instinct, she had applied the belt enthusiastically and repeatedly to Nicholas's backside, and received a tangible pleasure when he'd gasped with every stroke. Her technique had been far from what she supposed must be 'classic'; in fact, it had been all over the place. But even so, in the final stages, she'd managed to make him squeal. Reaching down to touch herself, she imagined the fun she'd have, learning to beat him properly.

A movement at the very edge of her vision brought her suddenly back to reality. Rolling, she saw Nicholas walking towards the bed from the direction of the bathroom. He looked every bit his normal, handsome and arrogant self, and it was to his credit that there was only the tiniest hint of hesitancy in his long male stride. He hissed through his teeth, though, when he slid into bed beside her. Even such a self-possessed stoic as he couldn't deny the results of her passionate extremes.

'Not too painful?' she enquired with joy as he seemed to be having difficulty settling comfortably.

'Not too bad. It's easing,' he replied, reaching across to flip back the covers and expose her breasts. He shifted position again, and cursed feelingly under his breath. 'Believe me, my love, I didn't know you had such savagery in you. For a first-time performance, that was a truly impressive thrashing. I didn't know I had it in me to put up with it so well!'

But you did, Nicholas, didn't you? she thought indulgently. And later, you had it in me, didn't you? She almost giggled at the silly play on words.

When she had finished meting out what she considered a fair measure of suffering and humiliation, Nicholas had responded like a gladiator when she had finally ordered him to bed. And it was his groans and his entreaties, as she grabbed his punished buttocks, that had gilded her enjoyment and lifted her to climax after climax.

'Well, we all have our hidden depths, don't we?' she observed, throwing back her shoulders and trying to entice him to play with her nipples again.

'True,' he said. 'I saw yours immediately. The moment I set eyes on you. I've merely been waiting for you to come to the same conclusions.' As if denying his pain, he sat up again, and reached for her. Cupping her right breast, he handled the flesh vigorously, pulling and rolling the swollen teat.

Shards of reawakened pleasure made Christabel squirm. Unable to stop herself, she parted her legs beneath the sheet. 'You're an arrogant bastard, Nicholas,' she said gruffly, riding her urges. 'Couldn't you have just spoken to me then? Told me what you wanted and saved me all that aimless dashing about after young men who really didn't know what they were doing?'

'I could have, I suppose,' her husband said, still mauling her breast. 'But it wouldn't have been nearly as much fun as doing it this way.' He released her, and kneeling up, pulled the covers off her completely. As he moved, Christabel noticed that he grimaced. Good!

'Where do you keep your sex toys, my dear?' he went on, rising from the bed and giving her a glimpse of his hard-muscled but vividly crimson bottom. 'I'd like to play with you for a little while.'

'So is that it? You're in charge again now, and all that –' she gestured towards the ruddy glow '– was just a one-off. A novelty, purely to show that you can take it as well as dish it out?'

'Not a one-off, my love,' said Nicholas, leaning over her and caressing her inner thigh. Exerting light pressure, he forced her to open her legs wider. 'Not by any means . . . With the skills you promise, I might become addicted to allowing you your way with me.' He slipped his fingers into her crotch, tested her, then sniffed her odour. 'But in general I enjoy a broad spectrum of sexual entertainments . . . Sometimes dominant, sometimes merely an observer, sometimes submissive. And, as you've clearly realised, I like to play with both the sexes.'

Sweating against the sheets, Christabel fought not to swirl her pelvis enticingly. She didn't want to seem as if she were begging for it, even if she was. 'Oh, I had no doubts on that score, my love . . . Even before I saw Jamie finger-fucking you when you were together in the conservatory.'

'You enjoyed that particular show, though, didn't you?' said Nicholas, his voice seductively creamy as he knelt and looked down at her open sex. 'Poor Jamie, he must be feeling rather neglected by me now.'

'My heart bleeds,' sniped Christabel, unable to help

herself. This was *her* time; Nicholas must not think of Jamie.

'Don't worry, my dear, you will always take precedence.' Nicholas straightened up. 'In fact...' He rubbed his chin, as if pontificating. 'How would you like it if I gave Jamie to you as a treat, sometime soon? He's quite an innocent, really. He thinks he knows everything but, in actual fact, he knows far less than you do about my preferences and my secrets.'

Really? thought Christabel, immensely cheered. She began to entertain kinder notions about Jamie. She had always fancied him. He was deeply good-looking. And she had so much for which she wanted to pay him back...

'And would I be allowed to play with Jamie in the way I just played with you?' Feeling at one with Nicholas's intentions, she tilted up her pelvis, widened her legs more and offered an even better view of herself to him.

'Of course,' said her husband, his grey eyes widening with interest. 'But you would have to master him, you know ... Through force of will. Do you think you can do it?' Still apparently considering the question of Jamie, Nicholas thoughtfully began to touch her, exploring her labia and her perineum with one fingertip.

'No problem,' she gasped, grabbing the bedding at her sides to stop herself writhing. His delicate explorations were as light as air and totally maddening. Her body was aching for something rougher, something rude and peremptory that would make her feel deliciously used and violated. The pendulum had swung now, with a vengeance, and she longed to submit.

'I wonder how all our young friends are getting on right now?' mused Nicholas after a few moments, as he bent low and close to Christabel's body. Using both hands now, he meticulously prised open her inner sexlips to create an even greater exposure. 'I have a notion that my Jamie is probably in the arms of your Gussie

'. . . I set them up together, you know. I thought their coupling would raise some interesting possibilities.'

'Jamie and Gussie? Together?' croaked Christabel as her husband began to scoop up her juices and smear them lasciviously over the length and breadth of her sex. She hissed through her teeth as his fingers dipped lower and anointed her anus.

'There seemed a certain appropriateness to it,' he murmured, still rubbing her and observing her privates from the closest of quarters. She could feel his breath on her engorged flesh, her trembling openness. 'Daniel with Marisa. Gussie with Jamie. You with me. Three elegant twosomes that can be rearranged again and again.'

'How do you know that your schemes have worked?' said Christabel faintly. Her knuckles were white now, white as the sheets she had grasped in her hands.

'Because Jamie has his orders, and there is no way on earth Marisa will be able to resist young Daniel. She's probably riding him, or sucking his penis, even as we speak.'

Christabel groaned, her own resistance shattered by the sudden images. She began to climax and, as she did so, Nicholas increased his ravages. His finger and thumb closed in to delicately pinch her clitoris and, further back, he pushed a single rude finger into the rose of her anus.

Her groan rose to an uncouth shriek as the pleasure she experienced increased in a dark, clasping spiral. The pumping finger inside her bottom made her legs and arms flail. She was vaguely conscious of both kicking and striking Nicholas in her ecstasy, but she heard him laugh and felt him simply increase his efforts. The finger moved faster, and his voice, when he spoke to her, was a deep laughing growl.

'You'd better get used to this, my darling,' he said, waggling his fingertip inside her. 'Because, any minute now, I'm going to flip you right over, and put my cock in there instead.'

273

Yes, my darling, oh, yes! cried Christabel silently and deliriously, her entire belly spasming in a hard, clenching rhythm. I'll love it. Whatever you do, I'll love it, no matter how gross.

Then, afterwards, we'll fall asleep together, she thought. The notion came to her clearly and calmly, despite the turmoil of her orgasm.

She'd always known they would finally sleep together at Collingwood. The knowledge of it had been there in her subconscious, even throughout their fiercest conflicts; the reality of it was inevitable now that they finally understood each other.

The time of trial was over. It was time to play. She reached for her husband, imagining a thousand new games . . .

Visit the Black Lace website at
www.blacklace-books.co.uk

FIND OUT THE LATEST INFORMATION AND TAKE ADVANTAGE OF OUR FANTASTIC FREE BOOK OFFER! ALSO VISIT THE SITE FOR . . .

- All Black Lace titles currently available and how to order online
- Great new offers
- Writers' guidelines
- Author interviews
- An erotica newsletter
- Features
- Cool links

BLACK LACE — THE LEADING IMPRINT OF WOMEN'S SEXY FICTION

TAKING YOUR EROTIC READING PLEASURE TO NEW HORIZONS

LOOK OUT FOR THE ALL-NEW BLACK LACE BOOKS – AVAILABLE NOW!

All books priced £6.99 in the UK. Please note publication dates apply to the UK only. For other territories, please contact your retailer.

DIVINE TORMENT
Janine Ashbless
ISBN 0 352 33719 2

In the ancient temple city of Mulhanabin, the voluptuous Malia Shai awaits her destiny. Millions of people worship her, believing her to be a goddess incarnate. However, she is very human, consumed by erotic passions that have no outlet. Into this sacred city comes General Verlaine – the rugged and horny gladiatorial leader of the occupying army. Intimate contact between Verlaine and Malia Shai is forbidden by every law of their hostile peoples. But she is the one thing he wants – and he will risk everything to have her. **A beautifully written story of opulent palaces, extreme rituals and sexy conquerors. Like *Gladiator* set in a mythical realm.**

THE BEST OF BLACK LACE 2
Edited by Kerri Sharp
ISBN 0 352 33718 4

The Black Lace series has continued to be *the* market leader in erotic fiction, publishing genuine female writers of erotica from all over the English-speaking world. The series has changed and developed considerably since it was launched in 1993. The past decade has seen an explosion of interest in the subject of female sexuality, and Black Lace has always been at the forefront of debate around this issue. Editorial policy is constantly evolving to keep the writing up-to-date and fresh, and now the books have undergone a design makeover that completes the transformation, taking the series into a new era of prominence and popularity. *The Best of Black Lace 2* will include extracts of the sexiest, most sizzling titles from the past three years.

Coming in September

SATAN'S ANGEL
Melissa MacNeal
ISBN 0 352 33726 5

Feisty young Miss Rosie is lured north during the first wave of the Klondike gold rush. Ending up in a town called Satan, she auditions for the position of the town's most illustrious madam. Her creative ways with chocolate win her a place as the mysterious Devlin's mistress. As his favourite, she becomes the queen of a town where the wildest fantasies become everyday life, but where her devious rival, Venus, rules an underworld of sexual slavery. Caught in this dark vixen's web of deceit, Rosie is then kidnapped by the pistol-packing all-female gang, the KlonDykes and ultimately played as a pawn in a dangerous game of revenge. **Another whip-cracking historical adventure from Ms MacNeal.**

I KNOW YOU, JOANNA
Ruth Fox
ISBN 0 352 33727 3

Joanna writes stories for a top-shelf magazine. When her dominant and attractive boss Adam wants her to meet and 'play' with the readers she finds out just how many strange sexual deviations there are. However many kinky playmates she encounters, nothing prepares her for what Adam has in mind. Complicating her progress, also, are the insistent anonymous invitations from someone who professes to know her innermost fantasies. **Based on the real experiences of scene players, this is shockingly adult material!**

Black Lace Booklist

Information is correct at time of printing. To avoid disappointment check availability before ordering. Go to www.blacklace-books.co.uk. All books are priced £6.99 unless another price is given.

BLACK LACE BOOKS WITH A CONTEMPORARY SETTING

☐ THE TOP OF HER GAME Emma Holly	ISBN 0 352 33337 5	£5.99
☐ IN THE FLESH Emma Holly	ISBN 0 352 33498 3	£5.99
☐ A PRIVATE VIEW Crystalle Valentino	ISBN 0 352 33308 1	£5.99
☐ SHAMELESS Stella Black	ISBN 0 352 33485 1	£5.99
☐ INTENSE BLUE Lyn Wood	ISBN 0 352 33496 7	£5.99
☐ THE NAKED TRUTH Natasha Rostova	ISBN 0 352 33497 5	£5.99
☐ ANIMAL PASSIONS Martine Marquand	ISBN 0 352 33499 1	£5.99
☐ A SPORTING CHANCE Susie Raymond	ISBN 0 352 33501 7	£5.99
☐ TAKING LIBERTIES Susie Raymond	ISBN 0 352 33357 X	£5.99
☐ A SCANDALOUS AFFAIR Holly Graham	ISBN 0 352 33523 8	£5.99
☐ THE NAKED FLAME Crystalle Valentino	ISBN 0 352 33528 9	£5.99
☐ CRASH COURSE Juliet Hastings	ISBN 0 352 33018 X	£5.99
☐ ON THE EDGE Laura Hamilton	ISBN 0 352 33534 3	£5.99
☐ LURED BY LUST Tania Picarda	ISBN 0 352 33533 5	£5.99
☐ THE HOTTEST PLACE Tabitha Flyte	ISBN 0 352 33536 X	£5.99
☐ THE NINETY DAYS OF GENEVIEVE Lucinda Carrington	ISBN 0 352 33070 8	£5.99
☐ EARTHY DELIGHTS Tesni Morgan	ISBN 0 352 33548 3	£5.99
☐ MAN HUNT Cathleen Ross	ISBN 0 352 33583 1	
☐ MÉNAGE Emma Holly	ISBN 0 352 33231 X	
☐ DREAMING SPIRES Juliet Hastings	ISBN 0 352 33584 X	
☐ THE TRANSFORMATION Natasha Rostova	ISBN 0 352 33311 1	
☐ STELLA DOES HOLLYWOOD Stella Black	ISBN 0 352 33588 2	
☐ SIN.NET Helena Ravenscroft	ISBN 0 352 33598 X	
☐ HOTBED Portia Da Costa	ISBN 0 352 33614 5	
☐ TWO WEEKS IN TANGIER Annabel Lee	ISBN 0 352 33599 8	
☐ HIGHLAND FLING Jane Justine	ISBN 0 352 33616 1	

☐ PLAYING HARD Tina Troy	ISBN O 352 33617 X
☐ SYMPHONY X Jasmine Stone	ISBN O 352 33629 3
☐ STRICTLY CONFIDENTIAL Alison Tyler	ISBN O 352 33624 2
☐ SUMMER FEVER Anna Ricci	ISBN O 352 33625 0
☐ CONTINUUM Portia Da Costa	ISBN O 352 33120 8
☐ OPENING ACTS Suki Cunningham	ISBN O 352 33630 7
☐ FULL STEAM AHEAD Tabitha Flyte	ISBN O 352 33637 4
☐ A SECRET PLACE Ella Broussard	ISBN O 352 33307 3
☐ GAME FOR ANYTHING Lyn Wood	ISBN O 352 33639 0
☐ FORBIDDEN FRUIT Susie Raymond	ISBN O 352 33306 5
☐ CHEAP TRICK Astrid Fox	ISBN O 352 33640 4
☐ THE ORDER Dee Kelly	ISBN O 352 33652 8
☐ ALL THE TRIMMINGS Tesni Morgan	ISBN O 352 33641 3
☐ PLAYING WITH STARS Jan Hunter	ISBN O 352 33653 6
☐ THE GIFT OF SHAME Sara Hope-Walker	ISBN O 352 32935 1
☐ COMING UP ROSES Crystalle Valentino	ISBN O 352 33658 7
☐ GOING TOO FAR Laura Hamilton	ISBN O 352 33657 9
☐ THE STALLION Georgina Brown	ISBN O 352 33005 8
☐ DOWN UNDER Juliet Hastings	ISBN O 352 33663 3
☐ THE BITCH AND THE BASTARD Wendy Harris	ISBN O 352 33664 1
☐ ODALISQUE Fleur Reynolds	ISBN O 352 32887 8
☐ GONE WILD Maria Eppie	ISBN O 352 33670 6
☐ SWEET THING Alison Tyler	ISBN O 352 33682 X
☐ TIGER LILY Kimberley Dean	ISBN O 352 33685 4
☐ COOKING UP A STORM Emma Holly	ISBN O 352 33686 2
☐ RELEASE ME Suki Cunningham	ISBN O 352 33671 4
☐ KING'S PAWN Ruth Fox	ISBN O 352 33684 6
☐ FULL EXPOSURE Robyn Russell	ISBN O 352 33688 9
☐ SLAVE TO SUCCESS Kimberley Raines	ISBN O 352 33687 0
☐ STRIPPED TO THE BONE Jasmine Stone	ISBN O 352 33463 0
☐ HARD CORPS Claire Thompson	ISBN O 352 33491 6
☐ CABIN FEVER Emma Donaldson	ISBN O 352 33692 7

BLACK LACE BOOKS WITH AN HISTORICAL SETTING

☐ PRIMAL SKIN Leona Benkt Rhys	ISBN O 352 33500 9 £5.99
☐ DEVIL'S FIRE Melissa MacNeal	ISBN O 352 33527 0 £5.99

☐ WILD KINGDOM Deanna Ashford	ISBN 0 352 33549 1	£5.99
☐ DARKER THAN LOVE Kristina Lloyd	ISBN 0 352 33279 4	
☐ STAND AND DELIVER Helena Ravenscroft	ISBN 0 352 33340 5	£5.99
☐ THE CAPTIVATION Natasha Rostova	ISBN 0 352 33234 4	
☐ CIRCO EROTICA Mercedes Kelley	ISBN 0 352 32257 3	
☐ MINX Megan Blythe	ISBN 0 352 33638 2	
☐ PLEASURE'S DAUGHTER Sedalia Johnson	ISBN 0 352 32237 9	
☐ JULIET RISING Cleo Cordell	ISBN 0 352 32938 6	
☐ DEMON'S DARE Melissa MacNeal	ISBN 0 352 33683 8	
☐ ELENA'S CONQUEST Lisette Allen	ISBN 0 352 32950 5	
☐ DIVINE TORMENT Janine Ashbless	ISBN 0 352 33719 2	
☐ THE CAPTIVE FLESH Cleo Cordell	ISBN 0 352 32872 X	

BLACK LACE ANTHOLOGIES

☐ CRUEL ENCHANTMENT Erotic Fairy Stories Janine Ashbless	ISBN 0 352 33483 5	£5.99
☐ MORE WICKED WORDS Various	ISBN 0 352 33487 8	£5.99
☐ WICKED WORDS 4 Various	ISBN 0 352 33603 X	
☐ WICKED WORDS 5 Various	ISBN 0 352 33642 0	
☐ WICKED WORDS 6 Various	ISBN 0 352 33590 0	
☐ THE BEST OF BLACK LACE 2 Various	ISBN 0 352 33718 4	

BLACK LACE NON-FICTION

☐ THE BLACK LACE BOOK OF WOMEN'S SEXUAL FANTASIES Ed. Kerri Sharp	ISBN 0 352 33346 4	£5.99

To find out the latest information about Black Lace titles, check out the website: www.blacklace-books.co.uk or send for a booklist with complete synopses by writing to:

Black Lace Booklist, Virgin Books Ltd
Thames Wharf Studios
Rainville Road
London W6 9HA

Please include an SAE of decent size. Please note only British stamps are valid.

Our privacy policy
We will not disclose information you supply us to any other parties. We will not disclose any information which identifies you personally to any person without your express consent.

From time to time we may send out information about Black Lace books and special offers. Please tick here if you do <u>not</u> wish to receive Black Lace information. ❏

Please send me the books I have ticked above.

Name ....

Address ....

....

....

....

Post Code ....

Send to: Cash Sales, Black Lace Books, Thames Wharf Studios, Rainville Road, London W6 9HA.

US customers: for prices and details of how to order books for delivery by mail, call 1-800-343-4499.

Please enclose a cheque or postal order, made payable to Virgin Books Ltd, to the value of the books you have ordered plus postage and packing costs as follows:

UK and BFPO – £1.00 for the first book, 50p for each subsequent book.

Overseas (including Republic of Ireland) – £2.00 for the first book, £1.00 for each subsequent book.

If you would prefer to pay by VISA, ACCESS/MASTERCARD, DINERS CLUB, AMEX or SWITCH, please write your card number and expiry date here:

....

Signature ....

Please allow up to 28 days for delivery.